# In Satan's Shadow

by

John Anthony Miller

# In Satan's Shadow

ISBN: 978-1-943789-21-4

TAYLOR AND SEALE PUBLISHING, LLC

Cover layout by WhiteRabbitgraphix.com

DEDICATION:

For my father, C. Raymond Miller, telling jokes to the angels.

# ACKNOWLEDGMENTS

Special thanks to my family: Cindy, Chris, Danielle, Steffany and Mark, Marlene, and Penny, my agents - Donna Eastman and Gloria Koehler at Parkeast Literary, my publisher - Mary Custureri and editor, Veronica Helen Hart, at Taylor and Seale, and all the advanced readers who helped make the manuscript the best that it could be.

# PROLOGUE
London, England
November 26, 1946

London was alive with optimism after the war ended: ruins in renovation, the hurt healing, the separated reunited, and the dead honored and mourned. The future offered so much more promise than the past, when two global conflicts in a generation left tens of millions dead, and many living who wished they were not. But hundreds, if not thousands, of Nazi leaders responsible for the recent cataclysm had vanished, eluding the net cast by the Americans, Russians, British, and French. It was feared they assembled in an unknown country and continent, birthing the Fourth Reich on the ashes of the Third.

Michael York stood in the Victorian Treasures book store, gazing at a display of recent releases. His face was solemn, his eyes showing a muted pain, as he looked at the week's bestseller. It was a book of photographs, Berlin in the last decade, as night fell and darkness draped the world.

From the store front window he could see Tower Bridge, the Thames winding underneath it. A double-decker bus stopped, blocking his view, and two Canadian soldiers got off, followed by some schoolchildren. The bus drove away, revealing an American soldier in a red telephone booth, probably calling his British girlfriend. London was inundated with military personnel savoring a last look at the greatest city in the world before they returned home. Most were American, buoyant and brash but friendly, while others represented the British Empire: Canadians, South Africans, Australians, and some from the Caribbean. They wandered the streets, the world theirs for the taking, savoring every pleasure the global metropolis had to offer.

He opened the book, turning to the dust jacket, and studied the author's picture. It was a good photograph, capturing the twinkle that lived in her eye, a smile that came so easily to her face, and wavy black hair that cascaded upon her shoulders. Amanda Hamilton, born to Scottish royalty, had married a German, a leader in the Nazi party. Leaving her homeland behind, she spent ten years in Berlin, absorbing a new culture, starting a new life. Her photographs documented a world collapsing around her, civilization at its ebb, humanity at its worst. Now they were shared with mankind.

Michael York turned the pages, her pictures bringing the past to life, memories returning. Germany's evil geniuses were caught in poses the world had never before seen. Berlin's finest buildings: Kaiser Wilhelm Church, the Reichstag, the Berlin Cathedral, and the Brandenburg Gate were shown in their original splendor, before Allied bombs destroyed them. And birds, not knowing they had trespassed on a calamity, posed innocently but proudly.

Fate had placed her on the enemy's doorstep, friend to some of the most hated men on earth during the most tumultuous days in human history. A favorite of Hitler, admired by Goebbels and Göring, her photographs documented life in the upper echelons of the Nazi party, a world that none on earth ever dreamed existed. It was there that Amanda Hamilton, never the author of an evil thought, walked in Satan's shadow.

# CHAPTER 1

Ferrette, France - near the Swiss border
September 30, 1942

The bullet had done much damage. Piercing his chest and tearing the muscles of his shoulder, it left a large, gaping hole in his back as it exited his body. Blood flowed freely, staining his shirt and dripping lazily on the dirt below.

Michael York lay beneath a rocky outcrop, his body wracked with pain. He stared vacantly at the half moon, listening intently. A hundred meters behind him, spread along the trees that rimmed the hill, twenty German soldiers approached.

"Leave me," he whispered. "Save yourselves while you still can. I may not be able to make it."

"We cannot," Jacques insisted. He was young and short and muscular, a farmer no one suspected of aiding the British.

"You're too important, my friend," said Michelle, the farmer's wife. "That's why the Germans are so persistent." Tall and slender to compliment her stocky husband, they had been rescuing downed airmen for months. York was their first spy.

"How bad is it?" York asked.

Michelle pressed a kerchief against his chest. "We have to stop the bleeding. And then just two more kilometers and you'll be safe in Switzerland."

York ignored the pain. He heard the Germans calling out to each other, looking for him, fanning out on the hillside, searching. Some moved farther away. Others came closer.

He tried to move, his muscles weak. He shivered, even though the night was pleasant, the weather warm.

"Quiet!" Jacques hissed. "They are coming."

Two Germans walked towards them, sticking bayonets in shrubs. They were talking, pausing to study the hillside, watching the rocks, looking for movement. One soldier approached, the other observed, vigilant, his rifle ready.

York, Jacques, and Michelle crouched under the ledge. They could hear the German's boot slipping in the soil, dirt and pebbles sliding past them. Then he stood just above them.

Jacques withdrew his knife. He moved against the rock, crouching, prepared to attack.

A black boot descended, less than a meter away, and then gray trousers. The German faced away from them, tentatively maneuvering down the hill. Soon both legs were visible, and then his torso.

When his entire body emerged, Jacques crept forward, his knife drawn. Using one hand to cover the surprised soldier's mouth, he drove the knife in his back, near the kidney. Pulling the German towards him, he withdrew the blade and slit his throat.

Jacques pulled the soldier under the overhang. He lay there gasping, dying, blood seeping from his body and blotting the soil.

Seconds passed silently. Jacques crouched near the edge, hidden from view. York and Michelle lay in the cleft, huddled together, barely breathing.

"Hans?" the second German called. "Hans?"

Jacques waited, knife in hand.

They heard the second German approach. When the barrel of his rifle peeked past them, Jacques grabbed it and pulled. The German tumbled over the edge, landing on his back. Jacques pounced on him, thrusting the knife in his chest. He pulled the body under the overhang.

"We have to keep moving," he said coldly, his

face pale.

Michelle and York climbed out of the alcove and started down the hill, struggling with the incline, their shoes slipping in the soil.

Jacques looked over his shoulder. "Quickly," he said. "The others will be looking for them."

As York continued on, hunched and humbled, slipping and sliding, he felt his strength waning. Jacques and Michelle stayed beside him, propping him up, moving him forward, trying to stem the flow of blood.

"At the base of the hill, we'll cross the dirt lane and enter the woods," Michelle said. "There's a clearing past the trees; the Swiss border is just beyond it."

They moved down the hill, stumbling, trampling wildflowers that sprinkled the landscape, leaving an easy path for the enemy to follow. But it didn't matter. They only had to beat them to the border.

York was amazed at Michelle's strength. She held him upright, supporting him, enabling him to walk as quickly as she did. Jacques stood behind them, guarding, watching over his shoulder.

They slid the rest of the way down the slope to the road, finding a narrow gully beside it. They looked over their shoulders, up the hillside. The soldiers had reached the overhang above them, finding their dead companions.

"Hurry," Jacques said. "Into the woods before they see us."

They were interrupted by a vehicle in the distance, gears shifting. Headlights cast a soft glow on the lane, then off into the woods as it negotiated a bend, and back to the road.

Jacques held up his hand. "Wait until the lights aren't shining on us."

The vehicle came closer. The road wound, the headlights moved, but instead of pointing into the trees, they twisted at an odd angle, briefly shining on York, Michelle and Jacques before turning away.

The Germans saw them and scrambled down the hillside, shouting. A shot was fired, the bullet creating a plume of dirt less than a meter away.

"Stay low," Jacques said, guiding them forward.

They crossed the road, hunched over, moving swiftly, knowing they were now most vulnerable. More shots were fired, bullets peppering the road, pinging off rocks, imbedding in trees.

The vehicle sped forward, closing the distance, as they made their way into the woods. They angled to the right rather than forward, staying parallel to the road just a few feet into the woods, avoiding the shortest route to the border to confuse their pursuers.

The vehicle, a German panel truck, the Nazi symbol on the sides, stopped where they had entered the woods. Two soldiers got out and stood in the road, watching, waiting for those coming down the hill.

The soldiers reached the road in groups of two and three, talking frantically to the driver and his companion. Some pointed to the woods; others faced the hill, describing the pursuit. A few minutes later the rear doors of the truck opened. Dogs started barking.

"There's a stream just ahead," Michelle hissed as they shared alarmed glances. "The dogs will lose the scent in the water."

They kept moving, struggling in the dark but still making progress. They had the advantage of knowing the terrain. The enemy didn't.

The dogs barked loudly, the noise constant. But as minutes passed, the sound grew dimmer.

"The Germans are forcing the dogs forward," Jacques said. "They don't believe we're near the road.

They think we're trying to reach the border."

Michelle frowned. "But that won't last long. So we must hurry."

They continued onward, pushing through the underbrush. At times it was dense, and they had to cut through it, and often it was sparse, more like a clearing. After three or four minutes passed, they noticed a change in the dogs' barking. It was getting louder, coming towards them.

"We're almost at the stream," Michelle said. "How are you doing, York?"

"I'll make it," he said, his teeth clenched. But he wasn't so sure.

Fifteen meters more and they reached the stream. It was knee-deep, ten meters wide, and twisted away from the road. They stepped in, walking with the current, making rapid progress.

The dogs were moving quickly, having picked up the scent, and were coming closer. They could hear soldiers shouting to each other as they fanned across the forest, slowly starting to encircle them.

"The stream has a fork just ahead," Michelle said. "Left goes to the border. Right moves parallel with the road. We'll go right for a half kilometer and then east, crossing the farm fields into Switzerland."

The German voices were louder, but the sound of barking dogs grew fainter. They had divided their forces. Some crossed the stream with the dogs, moving east, assuming the shortest route to the border was taken. The others, those whose voices could be heard, were coming closer, moving south, trying to flank them.

Michelle's plan was succeeding. Using the stream and alternate paths, they were eluding the Germans. But they were no closer to the border.

York was gasping for air, the loss of blood

making him weaker. His legs felt like lead, but he plodded forward, knowing each step took him closer to safety.

They sloshed through water until they could no longer hear soldiers or dogs, then they left the stream, moved through more forest, and reached a clearing. It was a farmer's field, the edges marked by hedges. Rows of thigh-high wheat stretched before them.

"There's a road at the edge of the field, where that far hedge is," Michelle said, pointing. "It's bordered by a stone wall, not impassable, a meter high at most. The fence marks the border."

York stared ahead and summoned his remaining strength. He reached to his breast pocket and felt the faded photograph he always carried with him, next to his heart. He could make it. He was sure of it.

"How far after that?" he asked.

"There's a safe house a kilometer up the road," Jacques said. "We'll take you there."

"And we'll get a doctor," Michelle added.

They left the trees, knowing they were exposed, and started through the field. They crouched low, maintaining the smallest possible profile, moving quickly. Michelle and Jacques flanked York, propping him up, sometimes dragging him.

There were no dogs, no Germans; they seemed safe. They walked across the field, each step taken bringing safety and security. They had almost reached the hedges, only twenty meters more, when York glanced over his shoulder.

He saw the tiny light far in the distance. It was orange, an ember, not even a flame. Like someone inhaling a cigarette.

Using all the strength he had remaining, he shoved Jacques and Michelle to the ground. The sharp report of a machine gun sounded a second later.

York felt the biting sting of a bullet in his left thigh. It was followed by another, and then another, as the gunner raked his leg with bullets.

# CHAPTER 2

Basel, Switzerland
March 26, 1943

Frost clung stubbornly to the windowpane, the sun's rays struggling to break its tenacious hold. The last of winter snows powdered cobblestone streets, white and pure and reluctant to succumb to the change of season. Along the eaves of the fourth and final floor of the quaint hotel, a jagged icicle dangled precariously, waiting patiently for the warmth to release its tender hold so it could plunge to the innocent earth below.

Michael York stared pensively through the window at the ancient city of Basel and briefly marveled at the durability of its buildings. They stood proud and defiant, daring both man and nature to destroy them as days became weeks and seasons became centuries. And as these monoliths of wood and stone passively guarded generations of inhabitants, the world revolved around them in a timeless kaleidoscope of catastrophes.

He glanced at his watch, mindful of the time, grabbed his coat and left. Two blocks away, near the river, sat a quiet tavern, frequented by a devoted clientele that knew not to ask questions when visitors arrived. York paused at the door, glanced up and down the street, and entered.

A man sat in a darkened corner with a half-empty beer stein, his back against a wainscoted wall. He had blond hair feathered with gray and blue eyes, the perfect Aryan image of the German master race. Except he was British.

For reasons unknown, he was estranged from a wealthy family. Educated at Oxford, he studied European history and was captain of the cricket team.

As president of the Philosophical Society he developed an affinity for Nietzsche, which is why he understood the enemy so well. Fluent in French, German, and Italian, desirable skills during global conflicts, he joined British Intelligence during the Great War. He had been stationed in exotic cities around the globe ever since, always accepting the most dangerous assignments, comfortable mingling with the enemy. His real name was Covington Blair. His codename was Max.

His face was barely visible, masked by shadows. "Sorry I haven't seen you since your escape from France, old boy," he said as York sat down. "I've been busy with new networks in Germany."

"All part of the business," York said with a faint smile, glad to see a familiar face.

"How did you ever get out alive?"

York sighed, the memory still painful. "The Resistance. After I was shot, a young couple dragged me to the Swiss border. We hid there most of the night. When the Germans looked elsewhere, we went to a nearby safe house."

"That was close. I didn't think you would make it."

"Neither did I," York said, knowing his life had been changed forever. "I still don't know who betrayed me."

"It's too late to worry about that now. How's your recovery?"

York sipped his beer, pensive. "My shoulder is fine, but my leg might never be the same. It's stronger, but still stiff."

"I saw the limp when you came in. It's quite pronounced."

York shrugged. "I manage." He paused, studying Max, knowing he controlled his fate. "I want to come back."

Max's face showed satisfaction. It seemed to be what he wanted. Maybe the mission ahead was too difficult for anyone else. "How's your German?" he asked.

"*Einwandfreie*," York said. "Flawless."

"That's good," Max said, rubbing his chin, studying one of his best agents. "Because you're going to Berlin."

York wasn't expecting the destination. He assumed he would return to France, maybe Paris instead of Lyon. Berlin would be different, more challenging.

"And my mission?"

"Your predecessor, Maxwell Kent, was offered valuable information from a musician in a Berlin string quartet."

"Do you know who it was?

"I don't know for sure," he said. "But it may have been a former British citizen named Amanda Hamilton. She's been married to an influential German for nine or ten years. Hitler adores her. She moves in the right social circles, has access to the Nazi elite. More importantly, they trust her."

"Then why would she betray them?"

"She caught her husband with another woman about six months ago. There was some sort of public display – a hysterical argument. It was even in the papers, which is unusual given the current political climate. Of course, he denied it. But as I recall, she almost had a breakdown. I think she was even hospitalized. Outside the city, of course, in a country retreat."

"You think Kent may have approached her because of that?" York asked.

Max shrugged. "I don't know. But she's a good

possibility. I'm sure she was bitter and hurt. And she knows there's nothing she can do about it. It's not like she can walk out of Berlin and go back to Scotland."

"So she's either very vulnerable, or she forgave him."

"It's the latter," Max said. "They've since reconciled, and now she's pregnant. They give every indication that they're happily married."

York was quiet, assessing the unknowns, determining the dangers. It would be easy to make the wrong assumptions. Maybe that's what Kent did.

Max put an envelope on the table. "I have pictures of the four musicians, with some background information and addresses."

York opened the envelope and withdrew a photograph of a woman with wavy dark hair.

"That's Amanda Hamilton," Max said. "Born in Edinburgh, Scotland, she's the first violinist for the Berlin String Quartet, although she's also a renowned amateur photographer. Her husband is Manfred Richter, highly placed in the Nazi party, official role unknown. Consider him extremely dangerous."

York studied her photograph. "Maybe we can turn her, even if she wasn't the original contact. Especially given the infidelity. Does she have any loyalties to Britain?"

He shrugged. "I have no idea. And neither does anyone else."

York imagined himself in her situation. Would he stay loyal to his country of birth? It depended on the strength of the marriage − she had just reconciled with her husband − and her relationship with her Scottish relatives, if she even had any.

"That leaves three others that may have made contact," Max continued, withdrawing the remaining photographs. He pointed to a picture of a handsome man, dark hair, a patch over his left eye. "This is Gerhard Faber, the viola player. He's a bit flamboyant, arrogant. The patch over his left eye is from a childhood accident. He works for the Ministry of Armaments when he's not performing."

"He would have access to military information," York said. "Although we don't know what his motivation might be."

Max moved to the next photograph. "The cello player, Albert Kaiser, will be easy to remember. He has a shock of white hair, is a bit portly, and constantly smiles. He owns several properties that provide financial support. The string quartet seems more of a hobby. His brother is a general, a potential source of information, and his wife's brother is a government official."

"So far, he seems the least likely," York said. "I can't imagine a motive."

"Agreed," Max said. "The second violinist is Erika Jaeger. She's blond, slender and attractive, a pleasant personality. She works in the logistics division at the War Ministry and does odd jobs, but always seems in need of money. She's a widow. Her husband was killed on the Russian Front."

"She has access and motive," York said. "And might be bitter about losing her husband. The need for money is curious."

"It's an interesting puzzle," Max said, eyeing a buxom waitress that brought them more beer.

York waited until she left before speaking. "How did they communicate?"

"Through a drop at the Friedhof Heerstrasse Cemetery in the Charlottenburg section of Berlin, just below Olympiastadion. There's a map in the envelope. Enter from Trakehnerallee, not the main entrance, the smaller one, and go to the third row on the right. The twelfth grave on the right has an ornate iron railing. Notes are placed in a pineapple-shaped cap on the corner post closet to the entrance. Drops are made on Wednesday or Saturday, but only when needed. So every Sunday and Thursday the drop should be checked."

"Isn't that too public?" York asked with skepticism.

"Kent liked it. There's a lot of trees and foliage, some benches tucked among shrubs."

"But it's still a cemetery. And a cemetery has visitors. Especially now."

Max shrugged. "Kent thought it effective to hide in plain sight."

York considered the alternatives. There weren't many. "Are you familiar with their addresses?" he asked. "I should try to stay in a central location."

"Three of the four live in Charlottenburg, east of the cemetery. Kaiser is close to there, near Pottsdamer Platz in Tiergarten. You'll be surprised by Berlin. The war is just starting to impact the city, as absurd as that sounds. The Germans have plundered the occupied countries to keep their citizens satisfied. They have ration cards but ample supplies of everything except coffee, which has a chicory substitute like France. There's been little Allied bombing, although that can certainly change, especially with the tide starting to turn."

York was pensive for a moment. "It's a dangerous mission, but an interesting one."

"Agreed," Max said. "There's just one problem."

"What is that?"

"Although we knew Kent made contact with one of the quartet, we've since learned he may have approached all four."

15

"And what happened to him?"

"He was killed by the Gestapo. One of the four betrayed him." He looked up from his mug, a sly smile on his face. "You just need to figure out which one."

York sighed and sipped his beer. It would be difficult enough to survive in Berlin. Solving a mystery that might cost him his life only added to the danger. For someone who had been a history teacher only a few years before, the risk was unfathomable. But he was strong, cunning, and determined, and he didn't intend to fail.

"Here are your papers," Max said, handing another packet to York. "You're a disabled veteran, decorated in the Polish campaign, wounded in North Africa, no longer on active duty. Your recent injuries, especially to your leg and the noticeable limp it produces, will be part of your cover."

York studied the documents, looking for errors sometimes so apparent in forgeries. The stamp was correct, an eagle over a swastika, as were the paper texture and content. He wasn't sure about the unit.

"The quality is good," he said. "But how do I know the information is accurate."

"Because it's real. We got them from a German captured in North Africa, Michael Becker. His family immigrated to Argentina a few years ago. That makes it hard for authorities to verify details."

"How easily can I move about Berlin?"

"Normally you couldn't," Max said gravely. "It's difficult enough to get into Germany, let alone Berlin. And if you do get in, you can't get out. Once there, every resident of the city will be watching you. It's almost impossible to survive."

York smiled. Max was always very dramatic. But in this case, it might be warranted. "So how do I survive?"

"We built an excellent cover for you, which your limp plays into nicely. Michael Becker is a Wehrmacht sergeant on convalescent leave, seriously wounded in North Africa. I'll deliver a uniform to your hotel room tomorrow. You can wear it occasionally, which will lend credibility to your cover."

"Wouldn't I be assigned to some staff position?

"Yes, I've already made the arrangements. The real Michael Becker is fluent in English, which has been verified both through interrogations at his POW camp and via his military records. Given that ability, which isn't as common in Germany as you might think, you will report a few days a week to a nondescript building where you will translate the personal ads in the *London Times* from English to German."

York was skeptical. "That doesn't seem too credible."

"The Nazis know newspapers are used to relay messages. Several others on convalescent leave will be there also, masters of other languages. It's a good cover. It's not too taxing, you'll only work a few hours each week, and it gives you the ability to move about Berlin. Your papers are impeccable. You should be safe."

"What If I'm reassigned to active duty?" York asked, assessing the possibilities. He couldn't run, and could barely walk, but he could drive an ambulance, or cook for men on the front lines, or do a dozen other tasks if the Wehrmacht wanted him to.

"You won't be," Max said with a confident grin. "Your commanding officer is a double agent. German captain, British spy. He'll make sure you stay as an interpreter."

York was impressed. Max had penetrated far deeper into Germany than he would have imagined, a task that was almost impossible. "How long will I be in

Berlin?"

"It depends on the information you get. It could be months; it could be years."

York touched the photograph he always kept in his pocket, caressing it, missing the person it depicted. He didn't want to be in Berlin for years. But he knew that he had a duty to perform, a role in ending the war, and the future of mankind was more important than his happiness.

Max sensed his apprehension. "I'll be in Berlin, too. I have other agents besides you, larger networks. I don't intend to abandon you."

"When are you arriving?"

"I'll meet you six weeks from today at 10 a.m. at Olivaer Platz in Charlottenburg. I'll be on a bench on the north side of the park. Sit next to me, but not too close. You can also contact me in an emergency. Do you know what method to use?"

York nodded. "Personal ad. Same as we used in Lyon."

"Yes, use *Die Welt* newspaper. The day after the ad appears, we'll meet at the Kaiser Wilhelm Memorial Church at noon."

York nodded, envisioning the road ahead. He would have to immerse himself in the culture, become German, and speak the language as perfectly as his Austrian mother had.

"How do I get across the border?"

"The Swiss have an agreement with the Germans," Max explained. "Trains to and from Germany and Italy can pass through Switzerland without interference as long as the cars are sealed."

"How do I gain access?"

"A train from Genoa to Freiburg will stop a kilometer northeast of the Basel terminal two weeks from today at midnight."

"I thought trains passed through, but didn't stop," York said.

"That's correct. But a herd of cattle crossing the tracks will force the train to stop. It will take exactly seven minutes for the cows to be moved."

"So I have seven minutes to board the train?"

"Exactly seven minutes," Max emphasized. "The last car of the train has a trap door in the floor, mid-length. The cargo area above has been packed with a space large enough for you to sit in, a small cave in a sea of crates."

"I get off the train in Freiburg?"

"Yes, adopting the role of Michael Becker, wearing your sergeant's uniform, boarding a passenger train to Berlin. The real Michael Becker has an aunt and uncle who own a farm twenty kilometers outside of the city. You've been convalescing there for six months. That's how long Michael Becker has been in captivity."

York arched his eyebrows. "I'm impressed, Max. You've thought of everything."

"You better hope I did, old boy. If I didn't, you're a dead man."

# CHAPTER 3

April 15, 1943
Amsterdam, Holland

No one saw them remove the rail from the track that led to Berlin. Four men, sweating in the spring chill, took the long iron bars and went to the next section. They put the flat end just under the spike and, with the opposite end now elevated, they all leaned downward, prying the spike from the timber a centimeter at a time. Forty kilometers from Amsterdam, they had chosen a rural location, and a sloping curve, to sabotage the train.

They were surprised when they heard voices, more light laughter than words, the sound coming closer as seconds passed. They grabbed their iron bars, scampered down a small embankment, and hid in the edge of the trees.

The men looked at each other anxiously. Their work was not complete; they needed more time. And anyone could see that the tracks had been tampered with.

The voices became clearer, a man and a woman, not yet visible.

The leader looked at his watch. It was 5:05 p.m.

A few minutes later they came into view, a German soldier and a young Dutch girl, smiling and holding hands as they strolled down the tracks, young lovers hiding from a world that wouldn't approve.

The men waited, watching anxiously. The pair blocked their escape path. If they saw the missing rail, they would tell the authorities. Then the Nazis would find them.

"The train will still crash with only one rail missing," a man whispered. "We should find a different way out."

The leader again glanced at his watch. "Just to be sure, we should remove two," he said patiently. He considered their predicament and the risk they faced. What if there were others following the young couple? "We'll wait ten minutes. No more."

"What if they see the rail missing?"

The leader paused, watching the couple as they came closer. He was determined not to fail. "Then we have to kill them."

The German, no more than twenty, stopped abruptly. He turned to the girl and kissed her. She responded, wrapping her arms around his neck, her eyes closed.

The leader frowned. "We have to make them leave or they could be here all night." He thought for a moment, deciding what to do. "Come, follow my lead."

He strutted from the trees as if he hadn't seen them, the others following, not knowing what to expect. They went to the track and looked in the distance, away from the couple.

"I'm sure the stream is just across the tracks," he said loudly. "And I swear to you, it's the best fishing around. I will show you."

They walked down the embankment, talking loudly, scanning the trees on the other side, searching for a stream that didn't exist.

The soldier and girl pulled away from each other, shocked at the intrusion, their privacy compromised. They turned, embarrassed, and started walking down the tracks in the opposite direction. They didn't look back.

The saboteurs continued searching noisily for the stream, watching warily as the couple faded from sight. They waited ten minutes more, ensuring they didn't return. After scanning the area and finding no one else, they retrieved their tools.

It took thirty minutes to remove the next section, grunting, leveraging the long iron bars. Once the rail was pried from the ties, they pushed it off the track, down a small embankment and onto the soggy soil. Now twenty meters of rail was missing. The train was doomed.

They disappeared into a wooded area, emerging a kilometer away. A panel truck with the name of a grocer stenciled on the side was parked at the edge of the forest. The men climbed in and slowly drove away, careful not to arouse suspicion. It was 5:45 p.m.

The members of the Berlin String Quartet walked towards the Amsterdam railroad station, their military liaison, Captain Klein, leading them forward. A veteran of the Great War, now near sixty, he was slight and wiry, secretive and reserved, and always acted as if he managed massive responsibilities. He kept a constant eye on the group, greeting his role with enthusiasm, but treating them like children. Just not like his own children.

A porter rolled a cart behind them, five suitcases resting upon it, along with the curved case that contained the cello. The violinists and the viola player carried their instruments, too protective to let anyone else handle them. They approached the station entrance, a sprawling building marked by two towers and three arched windows, and took one last glance back at the city, interlaced with canals, its architecture unique, its residents warm and friendly.

Amanda Hamilton, almost five months pregnant, had a camera hanging from a strap around her neck. She stopped in front of the station, put her violin case on the ground, and raised the camera to her eye. She took a series of photographs in rapid succession:

the terminal entrance and the people passing through it, an elegant arch bridge that crossed a canal, the ornate ironwork looking like lace, a bicyclist with a poodle parked on the handlebars, and a five-story townhouse, an iron beam sticking from the highest window, a bureau hanging from it by rope as it was raised to the third floor.

The station was sprinkled with civilians, most traveling on business, but was dominated by German soldiers. Transferred by railroad, some troops from the west were going on leave before reassignment to the Eastern Front. They were replaced by new recruits from Germany's conquered territories, usually Poland or the Ukraine. To the residents it didn't make much difference. They didn't care where they came from. It was still an occupation force.

The musicians paused, an isle in an ocean of uniforms, and studied the hectic terminal. Large boards hung from the walls, identifying arrivals and departures to and from major cities: Paris, Brussels, Copenhagen, and Berlin. Germans swarmed into the station and around the trains, stopping at kiosks to buy newspapers and coffee.

"Our train doesn't depart until 7:40," Captain Klein said. He glanced at the tickets, and then his watch. It was 5:55.

"You're early," the porter said. "There's a train at 6:25. You should try to make that."

The string quartet, two women violinists, an elderly cello player, and a dashing viola player, waited for Klein to exchange their tickets. They were tired, having given six performances in two days at the Concertgebouw Orchestra. They wanted to go home, the sooner, the better.

Amanda Hamilton stood beside Erika Jaeger. She absentmindedly rubbed her belly and then jumped with a start.

"What's the matter?" Erika asked, concerned.

"It's the baby," she said. "I felt her move."

Erika smiled. "Her? Are we certain?"

Amanda laughed "It feels like a girl. And I will spoil her for the rest of my life." She paused, looking a little guilty. "But I'll do the same for a boy."

"Have you settled on names?"

"If we have a boy, Manfred insists we name the baby after him. He's still upset he named my stepson Kurt."

"And if it's a girl?"

She rolled her eyes. "He prefers Wilfrieda, after his grandmother."

Erika cringed. "And what does the mother-to-be prefer?"

"I like Elisabeth."

"A beautiful name. It sings like a bird. Appropriate for a third generation violinist."

Amanda thought of her father, a violinist for the London Symphony Orchestra. She wished he were still alive; they had left so many things unsaid. Although she knew he tried, he really wasn't a very good parent, even to his only child. He was cold and distant, a brooding loner, more of a shadow than a man. But he might have done better with a grandchild.

Captain Klein approached. "I was able to change our tickets, but we must hurry. Come with me. Quickly."

They rushed through the terminal and stepped on the train. Amanda and Erika moved to the front of the car, sitting just past the door. The three men turned in the opposite direction, moving towards the rear, near the baggage rack. Kaiser and Klein sat together while Gerhard Faber, newest member of the group, sat in front of them.

They were barely seated when the doors closed. The train began to pull away from the station, moving very slowly, the engine struggling to pull the cars behind it. But the speed gradually increased from a crawl to a run, and soon the buildings of Amsterdam moved past in a swirling sea of colors, the narrow townhouses wrapped in beige, mauve, amber, and crimson, separated from interlaced canals and narrow bridges that spanned them by cobblestone lanes.

Amanda looked out the window as the train gained momentum, watching the city of Amsterdam glide by. She put her camera to her eye and snapped a series of photos, capturing the houseboats that lined a canal and six bicycles stacked against a lamp post, secured with a single lock and chain.

"I'm glad we got the earlier train," Erika said. "I can get to the War Ministry on time in the morning."

Amanda lowered the camera and turned to her friend. "I wish you didn't have to work so hard."

Erika shrugged. "I don't have much choice. I need the money. You know how sick my mother is. And I have other relatives I care for, too."

"I would be glad to help you," Amanda said.

Erika smiled. "I know you would. But I can't let you. It's my family, and my responsibility. The work keeps me busy. I don't think about Wilhelm as much."

Amanda covered Erika's hand with hers and gently squeezed it. Wilhelm was Erika's husband, killed in Russia the year before. He was an artist, a woodworker who made beautiful cabinets, a craftsman with talents few could mimic. A uniform never fit him, mentally or physically; he looked out of place. A man with a big heart, a ready smile and a gentle soul, he was better suited for heaven than the Third Reich.

"Maybe I can help with your mother," Amanda suggested. "I could spend some time with her while

25

you're working."

Erika considered the offer. "I wouldn't want to impose," she said reluctantly.

"You're not imposing. Ask your mother. She might like having some company."

Erika motioned to the camera hanging from Amanda's neck. "But then you wouldn't have time for photographs. Or your violin."

"I can spare a few hours. It'll be nice to get out of the house. Manfred is rarely home, the war keeps him so busy. Kurt is growing up. He's always with his friends."

The train increased its speed as the last of the townhouses yielded to scattered homes and then forest and fields. The steady motion, and rhythmic sound of the train's engines, lulled Erika to sleep, her head resting on Amanda's shoulder. Amanda's eyes closed a few minutes later.

They awakened with a start, the train screeching along the rails, the wheels screaming in protest, brakes fully applied. The sheer weight of the cars prevented an abrupt stop, momentum pushing the train forward.

Amanda gasped and grabbed Erika's arm. Cars hurtled down the tracks, their speed barely impacted by the squealing brakes, the offensive shriek sending shivers through their bodies.

They were flung forward, bodies slamming into the seat in front of them, their eyes wide, faces pale. They screamed and braced themselves, grasping the arm rests, their feet planted firmly on the floor.

The car leaned to the side, pulling away from those behind it. With an ear-shattering screech, it skimmed off the rail, tilting heavily. It hurtled into space, branches brushing the windows, as it sped down the embankment, sliding through dirt and stones.

Amanda flew over the seat in front of her,

banging her head on the ceiling. As the car twisted she was flung to the side, slamming into the doorway, and then hurtled backwards as it fought to right itself.

With a final lunge the car careened off a tree, its wheels grinding into the ground. But as it slid to a stop it leaned precariously and then toppled over, trampling trees and shrubs beneath it.

Amanda flipped and slid, beaten by luggage hurtling through the car. As she rolled and turned, fighting and falling, her mind was overcome with a jumble of images: her mother's smile, Edinburgh in the rain, her first violin, her favorite photographs, and the child in her womb.

The violin was her life. It always had been. She was a child protégé who went to the most famous music schools in England and, from there, to the grand stages of Europe. She could make the violin sing, the bow massaging the strings as her fingers caressed the neck. The instrument was an extension of her being; it could feel, connect, and communicate. She made the listener laugh or cry, mourn or rejoice. Or she clenched their hearts and pulled, coaxing emotions so deep that they didn't know they existed. She made every cell yearn to hear more, anxious, anticipating, uplifted in appreciation.

But even though the violin was her life, the camera was her love. Seldom seen without it, she took pictures of people and places, buildings and birds, having an innate ability to catch living things in natural states, or people posing without knowing they were observed. She captured the ordinary, but expressed the extraordinary.

Rarely was one so gifted in two artistic pursuits.

"Doctor, her eyes are opening," said a voice, dwarfed and distant.

Amanda saw the light above her, a halo wrapped around it. She closed her eyes a moment, and then reopened them, her vision focused on two faces that looked at her curiously. There was a sterile smell, like alcohol, and the walls and ceiling were white. She tried to rise but couldn't, her body wracked with pain.

"Keep still," a man whispered soothingly. "You're in the hospital. You were in a train accident."

She realized he was the doctor, and that the woman beside him was a nurse. She was exhausted, and struggled to keep her eyes open. When she tried to speak, to ask a question, she couldn't. Her mouth was too dry. She turned her head to the adjacent bed and saw Erika, sleeping, a purple bruise spreading from cheek to temple. Then her eyes fluttered closed and, as much as she wanted to open them, she couldn't.

The doctor turned to the nurse. "Try to contact her husband again. She may not live through the night."

# CHAPTER 4

Manfred Richter was a handsome man, black hair graying at the temples, a bright smile, and a charming personality, which he usually leveraged to get his way. If unsuccessful, and his patience waned, a quick temper produced an evil, sadistic man who took pleasure in others' pain. Given that combination, he almost always got what he wanted.

Guided by a Prussian father who was disciplined and domineering, critical and condemning, Manfred was an early devotee of Hitler. A persuasive speaker, he ensured the Fuehrer's interests were always protected, his ideas developed, his visions created – no matter how demented they seemed. His devotion had not gone unnoticed, and his responsibilities within the Nazi Party had grown as the years passed. He was now one of Hitler's most trusted disciples.

His suite at Hotel Abendstern was tasteful, but not elegant. The floral wallpaper was defined by crisp white crown molding, the parlor functional with a pleated leather couch and an oak coffee table, the feet made of hand-carved lion's paws. A bottle of wine and two half-empty glasses, the first marred by lipstick, sat on the table beside a vase of roses, one of which was wilting.

He had only been there thirty minutes when the telephone rang. He ignored it.

Now he wondered if he should have taken it. Few people knew where he was: one of his aides, a friend who served as his alibi for the evening, and the hotel clerk, who was always discreet. But he was paid to be discreet.

The call could have been important. Maybe there was an emergency that needed his attention. He had tremendous responsibilities, and he shouldn't ignore them. Why should he risk angering the Fuehrer or those around him, just for a few hours of pleasure?

A briefcase leaned against the table leg, and he opened it, withdrawing a typewritten paper from a manila folder. Three columns, neatly spaced, provided dates, names and telephone numbers. It was a list of the aides in his office and who was on duty. He looked at the date and corresponding name. The man listed had earned his respect. If he was the caller, the message was important. Manfred considered calling him, but then decided not to.

He shrugged, and put the paper away. If it was that important, they would call again. He would answer the next time. His mind wandered to other issues, for a moment drifting to maps of the world with unusual routes and locations, the path that money takes in international transactions.

A nagging doubt prevented him from returning the briefcase to the floor. He withdrew one of the maps and unfolded it, muttering to himself. He grabbed a pencil and scribbled a note in the margin, capturing his thought.

He was blessed with a fabulous memory, and easily remembered rivers and routes, cities and sanctuaries, battles and ballistics. He never forgot names or faces; he catalogued strengths and weakness, and he could exploit any adversary, making them do what he wanted with minimal persuasion. He remembered all of his enemies, knowing there was little likelihood they would ever be friends.

"Is everything all right, darling?" asked Anna Schneider, a local cabaret singer. Blond with a hint of darker roots and lavishly made up, most would consider her attractive, even if a bit too salacious for Berlin, especially given the current environment.

"Yes," he muttered, putting the map back in his briefcase and returning it to the floor. "I just wanted to make some notes."

"Can't you forget about that for a few hours?" she asked, miffed that she didn't have his attention.

"I'm sorry," he said, casting her a smile. "How could I possibly think about maps with such a beautiful woman sitting beside me?"

"What was the map of?" she asked, curious.

"South America."

She looked at him strangely. "All of Berlin is talking about the Russian Front, but you're making notes on a map of South America."

"It's a military issue," he said tersely. "I'm sure the details would bore you." He smiled again, his eyes twinkling, his hand moving to stroke her hair.

She gave him a quick kiss, unable to resist his charm, then sipped her wine. "Who do you think was calling?"

"I'm not sure," he said tentatively. "But I probably should have answered. Not many people know I'm here. Now I wonder who it was. I keep thinking about it."

"I can distract you," she said with an alluring pout. "It won't take much effort."

He smiled, kissed her lightly on the cheek and then moved his lips to the lobe of her right ear, gently taking it into his mouth. He traveled to her neck, planting tiny kisses, drinking the scent of her perfume. His fingers caressed her shoulder, trailed to her breast, and lightly teased her nipple though the fabric of her dress. He was interrupted by the phone ringing.

"Don't answer it," she said.

He hesitated. "I had better. That's the second time."

"It can't be that important. I'm sure the world

31

isn't ending."

"It could be something for the Fuehrer. I have to answer."

She sighed and rolled her eyes. "Manfred, it's just as hard for me to get away as it is for you. Let's not waste the evening on the telephone." To punctuate her statement, she brushed her fingernails across his chest, down his torso, and lightly across his thigh.

He sighed and leaned back on the couch just as the ringing stopped. "You're right," he said. "Why waste an opportunity?"

He turned to face her, his lips finding hers. He kissed her, lightly at first and then hungrily, his hand roaming her body, caressing her tenderly before finding a home on her thigh, just below the hem of her dress.

The telephone rang again.

Anna pulled away from him, frowned, and glanced at her watch. "You may as well answer it. It won't stop ringing until you do."

"It must be important," he said firmly.

He rose from the couch and walked to an octagonal table against the wall. He picked up the phone, looking out the window at Stuttgarter Platz, cobblestone streets, the trees lining the road, tiny buds on branches hinting of spring. Taxis and sedans passed below, merging with busses, a dozen bicycles, and a streetcar, while a handful of pedestrians strolled along the pavement, some pausing to look in shop windows.

"Yes," Richter asked, the receiver in his ear.

He listened, not speaking, his face firming, the muscles of his cheeks tightening. "Yes, yes of course. I'll get there as soon as I can."

He put the phone in the cradle and turned to Anna Schneider. "I'm sorry, darling. I have to go. It's an emergency."

# CHAPTER 5

Basel sat on the Swiss border, the Rhine separating both the city and its neighbors: France and Germany. Michael York wandered through the city streets after winter turned to spring, walking to Marktplatz where he enjoyed the Swiss architecture: brick and stone arches, French doors that led to baroque balconies, and an onion-shaped dome hinting of Russia in the shadow of the Alps. It was a beautiful city and, with the weather warming, the square was alive with people enjoying the sun, regardless of how weak it might be. They stopped at vendors' carts for books and pastries and vegetables, or stared in shop windows at clothing, housewares, and cuckoo clocks.

He stopped at an antique shop and looked in the window, studying a cane that leaned against a roll-top desk. It was oak, the hand-carved stem depicting a vine that traveled the length. Topped with a gnarled, tee-shaped handle, one side longer than the other, it was designed for a hand to comfortably hold.

Although he could manage without a crutch or cane, limping severely and leaning to his right, he was intrigued. The cane was unusual. And it was something he could use, something he needed. More interesting, he had never seen anything like it before.

He walked into the store, finding an elderly man with a broom-bristle moustache sitting behind the counter, his head bowed, focused on a woodcarving that sat before him. York walked in, waited politely until he looked up, and then nodded.

"Excuse me," he said, the soft German accent influenced by his Austrian mother. "I'm interested in the cane in the window. Is it really a weapon?"

The man rose, briefly stretching a back that

33

ached from stooping and rubbing eyes strained from tedious work. "Yes, it is. It's unique. A pistol and a knife. It's English, actually. Decades old."

As they walked to the display, he first noticed York's limp. "And it's functional," he added. "Oak. Very strong."

He took the cane from the window display. "It's ingenious. The barrel is the longer side of the tee. Underneath the handle, you'll find a metal lever, the trigger, and a tiny brass latch, the safety. Move the latch, point the handle, pull the lever, and the shot is fired. It only holds one bullet at a time. The new round is loaded from the other end."

"Do you have ammunition?"

"Only one package of twelve bullets."

"Can I see it fire?"

"Are you interested in buying it, or are you just curious?"

"If it works properly, and fires like any other gun, I will buy it."

"Then come to the back. I will show you."

The shopkeeper led him to the rear of the store, a storage room cluttered with shelves and boxes. There was an archery target lying on the floor, composed of dense hay. He leaned it against the wall and moved about three meters away. He showed York the mechanisms, and fired.

York was surprised by the power. It was loud; there was no disguising that a gun had discharged. The acrid stench of sulfur tinged the nostrils; a puff of gray smoke drifted from the barrel. The bullet pierced the target and imbedded in the stone wall.

"Perfect," York said, awed by the design. "I'll take it."

"Wait," the man said. "There's more. If you move this catch and twist, the top handle comes off."

The man showed him, sliding the catch to one side. The stem fell to the floor, revealing a thin stiletto. The shopkeeper smiled wryly. "If the shot misses, you can surely do some damage with this."

A week later, well after dark, York walked towards the Basel rail terminal, two stone towers with an arched dome connecting them, neo-baroque, graceful and balanced, marble statues adorning the roofline. He passed the building and remained in the shadows, studying the surroundings, and then furtively started down the track towards the German border.

He carried one large suitcase, all his belongings packed into it, the linings filled with Reichsmarks. Several one-carat diamonds were sewn into his clothes' pockets, should he need more cash. He hobbled forward on his cane, carrying a leather satchel with more money tucked in the bottom, covered by books and personal effects.

His documentation was in order, the finest forgeries available, his German perfect, although hinting of an Austrian accent, and his limp genuine but mitigated by the cane, proving his cover as a veteran no longer able to serve. The photograph he always carried was in his shirt pocket, close to his heart. Just where it belonged.

Although most of the city was sleeping, he still had to hide from occasional beams cast by headlamps of approaching cars or trucks. He left the city center, the houses growing sparser, and continued along the tracks until he reached a large linden tree standing sentinel over carefully cultivated farm fields. This was the landmark Max had provided; it was where he would catch the train.

He waited in the darkness, eyeing his watch. It was close to midnight when he heard cowbells, and then the rustling of animals through the fields. A few seconds later a lantern lit the darkness, and two men were seen at the railroad, waving the light back and forth in the night.

The track begun to rumble, a light piercing the darkness, and a train whistle sounded from behind him. Seconds later the train appeared, its brakes squealing in protest, the massive line of cars gradually slowing.

The train halted feet before the cattle crossing. As York moved to the last car in the lengthy train, he could hear the conductor and engineer shouting at the farmer, telling him to get off the tracks. He slid underneath, removed a small flashlight from his pocket, and saw the door handle. He undid the catch, opened the door downward, and pointed the light into the car.

It was just as Max had described: a void among crates and cartons, two meters high and one meter square. He shoved his suitcase and satchel into the car, and then climbed in.

Seven minutes after it had halted, the train began to belch steam and slowly chug forward. Minutes later it was back to full speed, crossing the border into Germany and moving towards Freiburg.

York opened his suitcase and removed the German uniform. He changed clothes, the small flashlight clenched in his teeth, and then settled in for the journey. While he waited, he mulled over the information Max had offered on the Berlin String Quartet, provided by Kent, his predecessor. He had to find a spy among four potentials, one of whom was actually a Gestapo informant.

Amanda Hamilton was the most interesting. A British citizen anchored in Germany, her loyalties could lie anywhere, especially after her husband's infidelity. Although it seemed their marriage had been saved, their relationship reconciled with a child on the way, York wondered if that was really the case. Was Amanda Hamilton trapped in Berlin, with no past or future? Could she be vulnerable, open to approach, especially if the hint of freedom was attached to it? He didn't know. But he had to very carefully find out.

Erika Jaeger was also intriguing, primarily due to her need for money, always a strong motivator. She could be either a supplier of information or a Gestapo informant. Both paid well. He wondered what her political beliefs were, especially after losing her husband on the Russian Front.

Gerhard Faber, the patch on his left eye, was an enigma. A note on the back of his photograph claimed he needed money also, just like Erika Jaeger. What drove the need for money? Was it family? Or an addiction: gambling, alcohol, sex. Both Gerhard and Erika had to be approached with caution.

Albert Kaiser, the elderly cello player seemed least likely to betray his country or inform on those who might. He lived within his means, surviving on rental income and his salary as a musician, happily married with grown children. York decided to observe him carefully, but considered him the least dangerous.

Once he evaluated each candidate, he rated Erika Jaeger and Gerhard Faber the most dangerous, Amanda Hamilton the biggest mystery, and Albert Kaiser the one who required the least of his attention.

Two hours later, the train slowed, and then gradually stopped. York quickly slipped out, gathered his luggage, and closed the trap door. He slid out from underneath the train, surveyed the area as he brushed himself off and, after finding no one nearby, scrambled onto the loading dock.

As he walked into the terminal, he passed an elderly janitor pushing a broom across the floor. The man glanced at his German uniform and continued sweeping. York saw a policeman standing against the wall, sipping a cup of coffee, observing the few dozen people that wandered the terminal. York watched their reactions closely, but neither showed any suspicion.

He purchased a ticket for Berlin, via Stuttgart, sat in the terminal waiting room, and tried to relax. His train departed at five a.m., almost three hours away. His first test would come shortly: his identity papers must be flawless, and he must speak German with no accent.

Shortly after four a.m., he boarded the train with a handful of others. He chose a seat at the end of a car, with no one nearby. He put his luggage in the rack, keeping his satchel beside him.

He sat patiently, waiting with the other passengers. Five minutes later, the car doors opened and a Gestapo officer entered, his black uniform accented with a Nazi band on the left bicep. He moved down the aisle, inspecting passengers' documentation, spending seconds with some, minutes with others.

The closer he came, the more anxious York felt. His mouth was dry, his heart beat faster, his stomach felt queasy. He took a deep breath, annoyed. How would he ever function in Berlin, the Nazi capital, if he couldn't maintain his composure talking to a Gestapo agent that had no reason to suspect him of anything?

He forced himself to relax, looking out the window at the suburban landscape. A stone wall flanked the rail, with houses scattered beyond. A field lay on the opposite side, rising to a hill on the horizon, its peak purple against the rising sun. For a moment he was lost in thought, watching a black grouse, a red patch just above his eyes, sitting on the wall, studying the train.

"Papers, please," the Gestapo officer said.

# CHAPTER 6

York handed his papers to the officer, ensuring he made eye contact, and offered a polite nod.

The officer ignored the greeting, took the documents, and studied York for a moment, no expression on his face. He looked at the papers, squinted, and removed his spectacles, polishing them with a handkerchief. He then took the documents between his thumb and index finger, rubbing them tenderly, checking the texture and ensuring the minutest details were correct.

"Why were you in Freiburg?" he asked.

"I was visiting family, sir," York replied cautiously.

If he found York's accent unusual, or his pronunciation strained, he didn't show it. He continued to review the documentation, now checking the seal. He brushed his finger across it, lifted it to his nose to smell it, and then lowered it, seeming satisfied.

"What family?"

"An aunt and uncle."

"On your mother's or father's side?"

York hesitated. He wasn't prepared for the question. "Mother's," he said haltingly.

The officer's eyes left the papers and zeroed in on his. "What was your mother's maiden name?"

"Dietrich," York said, trying to think quickly, giving the first name that came to his mind.

"Just like the movie star," the man said sarcastically. "How convenient."

York felt beads of cold sweat on the back of his neck. How could he be so stupid? He couldn't invent a better name than that?

The officer's gaze was intense. His eyes

wandered, searching for anything suspicious.

York maintained a puzzled look, as if surprised he was being questioned.

"You were stationed in Africa?" the officer continued.

"Yes, sir."

"Are you returning to duty?"

"Not at this time."

"Why not? Any good soldier wants to return to duty."

"And I do, also, sir," he replied, pointing to the cane. "But I was badly wounded."

"Where are you traveling to?"

"Berlin."

The officer looked at York's clothing, the buttons primarily, to ensure they were cross-stitched, which was different than the English and American style. He studied the bag in the overhead compartment, York's shoes, and even the crease in his trousers. When satisfied all were German, he returned the papers and started down the aisle.

York exhaled slowly. It had been harder than he thought, the officer smarter than expected. He sat rigid, cautious and alert, while the officer checked the remaining passengers. A few moments later he walked briskly down the aisle and left.

It was another five minutes before the doors closed and the train began to pull away from the station. York relaxed and read a newspaper, idly passing the time while occasionally gazing out the window at the rural landscape.

He changed trains when he reached Stuttgart, using the same tactics, blending in and keeping a modest profile. No one sat beside him, which he preferred. He didn't want to be bothered with conversation. He opened a book, Hermann Hesse's

*Steppenwolf*, and started reading.

When the train was thirty minutes from Berlin, a German colonel came down the aisle, returning from the dining area. Strutting through the car, his posture ramrod-straight, he arrogantly eyed each passenger, as if they shouldn't occupy the same space that he did. He stopped in front of York.

"What are you reading?" he asked sternly.

York tensed, sensing danger. He held the book up, showing the cover, and cast an innocent glace at the colonel.

"Did you know that author's books are banned?"

"No, sir, I didn't," York said uneasily. He didn't need trouble. But now he didn't know how to avoid it.

"His wife is a Jew," the colonel said with disgust, as if the mere pronunciation of the word was distasteful. "The Reich has a new policy. Even Jewish vermin married to good Germans have been identified for resettlement. Greater Germany will finally be free of all Jews, regardless of who they're related to."

"I'm sorry, sir. I wasn't aware. I bought the book in Freiburg while visiting family."

There was an awkward silence as York observed him. He didn't seem to care where the book was purchased. Trying to appeal to his sympathies, York added, "After recovering from my war wounds."

The colonel's expression changed. "Where were you wounded?" he asked, his tone softening.

"North Africa, sir."

"And you're fully recovered and ready to serve the Fatherland?"

York sighed, showing disappointment. He raised and lowered his right arm. "Bullet to the shoulder, but fully recovered." He extended his left leg, pain mirrored on his face. "Machine gun. The bullets ran right up my leg. It will never be the same."

The colonel grimaced, watching the limited movement of the limb. "See a good doctor in Berlin. They may be able to help. And give me that book. Before the wrong person sees it."

York caught a taxi at the Berlin terminal, sickened by the Nazi flags draped from buildings, hanging from streetlamps, and affixed to the bumpers of government vehicles. He went to Charlottenburg, to the west of the city center, and found a family-owned hotel in an old building on the Kurfürstendamm. Known locally as the Ku'damm, it was a broad avenue, fifty meters wide, lined with towering plane trees, some as high as forty meters; it was Berlin's Champs-Élysées.

The architecture was distinctive, blocks of five- or six- story buildings with ornate cornice and fascia, decorative brick and stone facings adorned with cherubs and gargoyles, balconies and overhanging bay windows and walls. Flower boxes hung from upper story windows, blotting the buildings with splashes of color – lavender, gold, crimson and blue. The ground floors contained cafes, antique shops, boutiques, and restaurants, ensuring the pavements were filled with pedestrians, regardless of the time of day. The boulevard, which ran for over three kilometers, was crowned by the Kaiser Wilhelm Memorial Church, a towering structure of Romanesque Revival design, with a steeple that stretched almost to heaven.

York registered, planning for an indefinite stay, and brought his bags to the room. It was sparsely furnished, a bed and nightstands, an oval table with chairs under a window, and a worn couch beside a bureau against the far wall. The drapes were dated, the plaster on the wall chipped near the crown molding, but it was functional and would easily meet his needs. He unpacked, leaving the money hidden in the baggage lining, and then went to a café around the corner and had some soup and sauerbraten.

The following morning, he took a taxi to the cemetery. It was in a beautiful location, thick with trees, and sprawled around the Sausuhlensee, a small lake named for wild boar. It sat in the shadow of the site used for the 1936 Summer Olympics, on the western edge of the city. York followed the directions given by Max and was soon standing before the tomb assigned as the drop. He studied the landscape, looking for places where someone might be hiding, watching. When satisfied it was safe he studied the lane and those that crossed it, but saw no one visiting tombs. He waited for an older woman, walking from a grave, to pass from sight, and then removed the cap from the newel, as directed. He reached into the cavity. Empty.

He retraced his steps and made sure he was in the right place. He was. Disappointed, he returned to the hotel, purchased a newspaper, and went to the same café to order lunch. He opened the paper and read the headline: *Berlin String Quartet Injured in Train Wreck.*

# CHAPTER 7

The mood in the hospital room was somber and sad, the gloom not impacted by bright arrangements of carnations and chrysanthemums. Baskets and vases lined the ledge along the window; displays on metal stands were scattered around the room. A huge array containing a hundred roses stood on an ornate pedestal that looked like lace, the placard boldly stating: *My thoughts are with you and your speedy recovery, Adolph Hitler.*

Amanda Hamilton lay in bed, pillows propped under her head, staring listlessly at the white ceilings and walls. She saw no future, could envision no time when a smile would ever appear on her face, and only focused on what could have been, the life she might have had.

A curtain was drawn beside her, providing separation and privacy from the neighboring bed, which was sandwiched into a slender area by the door. Amanda had far more space, which had grown by the hour as more floral arrangements arrived. But it seemed dismal, the drapes partially drawn, even though a twelve-pane window allowed sunlight to bathe the room.

Behind the curtain, Erika Jaeger sat up in bed, her nose in a book of poetry. Although bruised and battered, she was recovering. Musical scores were scattered about, along with two books sitting on her nightstand. A vase of flowers was perched beside the books, sent by her mother, while a large arrangement stood next to the bed. It was from the Richters – Amanda, Manfred and Kurt. There were no other flowers, just as there were no visitors.

Erika wasn't offended by the privacy curtain;

she knew it wasn't personal. Nothing had been more important to Amanda than having a child. It would have been the fulfillment of a lifelong dream, the family intimacy that she had never known, a new beginning with Manfred. And now, because of a sadistic saboteur, and being on the wrong train at the wrong time, she had lost her baby.

She knew Amanda needed time alone, just as Erika had when her husband Wilhelm died. And even though her friend's sobs broke her heart, she didn't interfere, only offering kind words to comfort her. She knew the time would come when Amanda needed her. It just wasn't now.

The door opened and a handsome man entered, black hair graying at the temples. A boy was with him, sixteen years of age, resembling the father but tall and lanky, like a faltering colt.

"Manfred, how are you? And Kurt," Erika said, her eyes showing deep compassion. "I'm so sorry about the baby."

Manfred moved to the bed and gave her a hug. "Thank you," he said. "It's hard to accept, especially after months of elation. And then it's shattered, gone in an instant."

"I'll do anything I can to help," Erika said.

"Thank you, I appreciate that. You're a good friend." He smiled weakly, showing his appreciation. "And how are you? Not hurt too badly, I hope. You look well, for the most part."

"A bit bruised and sore, but otherwise all right. Very fortunate, I suppose." She glanced at the drawn curtain. "Amanda was awake a few minutes ago. I think she's been waiting for you."

"I was in secret meetings," Manfred said. "That's why no one could reach me. I left strict orders not to be disturbed."

Erika didn't believe him. She knew what Manfred was like. He had even made advances towards her, which were swiftly refused. Manfred had laughed, pretending it was a joke. She never told Amanda; she knew it would break her heart.

"It took almost two days to find you," she whispered, her tone accusing. "And for a while the doctors were afraid she wouldn't make it."

Manfred nodded politely; he owed Erika no explanations. "Get some rest," he said, as he and Kurt moved past the curtain.

They found Amanda lying in bed, a purple blemish on her jaw, her right eye blackened and swollen shut. As soon as she saw them, her lip quivered and she started crying.

Manfred moved to her side, hugging her. "It's all right," he said softly.

"No, it isn't," she said between sobs. "Where were you? No one could find you."

"I was with the Fuehrer," he said. "It couldn't be helped. But I'm here now. And you are all right. That's what's most important."

The tears trickled down her cheeks. "But I lost the baby."

"I know," he said softly. "It's horrible. It really is. But in time the pain will ease. There will be other babies."

They cried together, and then Kurt, a boy trying so hard to be a man, joined them.

Captain Klein and the men of the Berlin String Quartet fared better than the women. Seated in the rear of the rail car, against the wall that formed the baggage compartment, they suffered only minor bruises and sprains. Albert Kaiser had a laceration on his scalp, the blood staining his white hair, but it was easily mended with a few stitches. Captain Klein sprained an ankle, which caused him to lean on a cane for a few weeks, and Gerhard Faber had a swollen lip and bruised ribs. They were very fortunate, and returned to Berlin the next day.

Erika Jaeger and Amanda Hamilton remained in the hospital for two more days, along with a hundred soldiers wounded in the train wreck. The train's conductor, engineer, and coal handler were killed, along with seven soldiers in the front of the car. In retaliation for the sabotage, the Nazis executed fifty people from the closest village – men, women and children.

It was three weeks later when the quartet performed again. Most of the physical wounds had healed, bruises faded, sprains recovering. The mental anguish and emotional scars that Amanda suffered still lingered, like any nightmare would.

Those in the audience, including the Fuehrer, would never notice they were not quite at their best. When Amanda Hamilton stood, playing her first solo, the notes were moving and emotional, leaping from the strings and gripping the listener's heart, holding it and caressing it. She played with her soul; the others played with their fingers.

As for Michael York, a British spy, music lover, and amateur pianist who sat in the last row of the upper balcony, her performance brought tears to his eyes. He knew which member of the string quartet he wanted to approach first.

# CHAPTER 8

Two days each week, York was assigned to a nondescript building three blocks from the Ku'damm, closer to the Kaiser Wilhelm Memorial Church than his hotel. He wore his sergeant's uniform on his initial visit, ensuring all the insignia were correct, and was greeted by a bored lieutenant who led him to a cramped room with four tables and chairs. Three other men, two in civilian clothes, the other in a Luftwaffe uniform, sat at the tables. There were newspapers in front of them. None appeared to be recovering from war wounds.

The officer led York to a seat by the window that faced an alley littered with rubbish cans. Two cats rummaged through them, looking for food. A housewife from a nearby apartment, wearing an apron stained with cooking ingredients, emptied some trash and the cats scampered away.

The Sunday edition of the *London Times* was lying on the table. There was a headline about an RAF bombing in northern Germany. It made York wonder when they would start bombing Berlin. A blank tablet and a pen lay next to the paper.

"Read the personal ads," the officer instructed. "On the pad, write the date and name of the paper, and translate any ads that seem suspicious."

York looked at the newspaper. "This is last week's edition, sir."

The officer shrugged. "I do as I'm told. You should, too."

"Yes, sir."

"Come at least two days a week."

"Yes, sir. Will you be here?"

"Not likely."

He turned and left, leaving York with the other

men. He studied them briefly, and realized that each intended to mind their own business, perform their task, and leave as soon as possible. He squinted, trying to see the nationality of the newspapers they reviewed. One was French, another Russian, the third looked Italian, but he wasn't sure.

York unfolded the paper and scanned the front page, hungry for news from the United Kingdom. A glance at his comrades showed they did the same. As they leafed through the pages, read some articles and ignored others, he followed their lead. After fifteen minutes of casual reading, he arrived at the personals.

There were more ads than he had expected. He considered his direction to document anything that looked suspicious. It was a vague order. He glanced at his comrades again. They documented nothing. They were reading the paper.

York suddenly felt uneasy. He scanned the room, looking for surveillance devices, but a casual glance showed none. But something was wrong. It didn't make sense.

Why would he review a newspaper that was over a week old, searching for pertinent information? The Germans must have spies in London. Wouldn't they be better equipped to do what he was doing? And didn't the same situation apply to the others in the room? What was their real purpose?

Maybe the whole operation was staged, developed solely to protect Max's network. Or maybe he was in danger, being watched and evaluated.

Max's reach probably wasn't as wide as he thought. The officer and the translators were playing roles assigned to them. York was being tested. If he failed, he was dead.

He had already shown one weakness. He had actually read the newspaper. Someone assigned to review the personal ads for coded messages would not be reading the news; they wouldn't care. Maybe his comrades were baiting him, watching to see how interested he was in the articles. They knew he wasn't following instructions. But they weren't, either.

On the top line of the tablet he wrote his name and the date, followed by the order given, to review the *Sunday London Times* from one week earlier. Next, he listed the first task: read all news articles for potential hidden messages, and found none. He hoped that eliminated any suspicion.

He started reviewing the personals, and finally decided to translate several of them. He knew that even innocent ads like, *Charles – mother misses you*, could identify a missed drop, an interrupted meeting, or mean nothing at all. After each translation, he scribbled a potential meaning, relevant to the war effort but solely conjecture.

It took him two hours to get through the ads. During that time, none of his companions left the room, and their eyes never left their newspapers. But they didn't pick up their pens, either, not even once.

They were there for one purpose. They were watching York.

# CHAPTER 9

Charlottenburg, which was formerly an independent city, sat on the western edge of Berlin. It was upscale, architecturally distinct, and contained an eclectic mix of theaters, cabarets, shops, restaurants, residential areas and businesses. York found it alive and exciting, inhabited by artists and intellectuals, entrepreneurs and party officials. It was also the neighborhood where three of the Berlin String Quartet resided, the exception being Albert Kaiser, who lived in Tiergarten.

York was disappointed that the drop at the cemetery had not been used since his arrival, which he attributed to the train accident and subsequent recovery of those involved. He contemplated his next move, wondering if he should cautiously approach each member, try to gain trust, and determine if any of them had information to offer. It seemed to be the only alternative. He had already decided to start with Amanda Hamilton. He didn't know if she was Kent's contact, but he did know she was vulnerable.

Her home was ten blocks from his hotel, on a street off the Ku'damm. It was a large nineteenth century building, the entrance elevated above the street, reached by winding stone steps with a small garden beside them. The decorative iron railing had a Nazi flag draped from the handrail, as did a window on the upper floor. The building was ornate, almost castle-like in construction, with cylindrical turrets jutting from each corner on the second floor and extending upward the length of the four-story building. It was constructed of a reddish-brown stone, as were neighboring properties on the block.

York spent a few days watching the property as

Amanda Hamilton came and went. She was close to the Ku'damm, and walked to the main boulevard almost daily. When he observed her stopping at a nearby café on two different occasions, he noted the time and decided that was his best opportunity.

His first chance came three days later. He went to the café, six blocks from his hotel but in the midst of the many shops that lined the boulevard. It was a warm day in the end of May, and he sat at an outdoor table, enjoying a pint of beer after finishing his meal. He took the photograph from his pocket that he always carried with him and looked at it lovingly, his heart sinking with sadness. He smiled grimly, thinking of a time that no longer existed, and returned it.

When a petite brunette wearing a plain green dress and carrying two shopping bags approached, he studied her closely. Her face was solemn, as if the weight of the world was carried on her shoulders. She sat at a table near the iron railing that defined the café's perimeter, putting the bags on the cobblestone near her chair. York watched as she ordered her lunch and then sifted through her purchases while she waited for her meal. It was Amanda Hamilton.

She ate lightly, a salad and croissant, sipping some water. She scanned a folded newspaper, only the headline story attracting her attention. Once her plate was empty, she ordered a coffee, or the war-time substitute, and watched the passing pedestrians.

York picked up his mug of beer and walked across the café, sitting at an empty table beside her. "I enjoyed your performance the other night, Miss Hamilton," he said with a slight nod of respect. "It was a moving Mozart rendition."

She turned to face him, startled he recognized her, and he had such an appreciation of classical music. "Thank you, I'm glad you liked it."

"Very much so," he said. "I'm especially fond of the Haydn quartets, number nineteen in particular, and you played it superbly."

Her face showed surprise. "I'm honored someone as knowledgeable as you enjoyed it so much, Mister…"

"Becker," he said, using his alias.

"Are you a critic, Mr. Becker?"

He chuckled. "No, not a critic. Just an amateur who appreciates greatness."

She looked at him with interest, and he could tell she was starting to enjoy the conversation. She probably had no one to discuss music with, other than those in the string quartet. He suspected her husband showed no interest at all. He probably looked at her absentmindedly, his eyes vacant, politely nodding his head and thinking of something else while she talked. And her stepson was at the age where nothing his parents did interested him very much. He was glad he had prepared, having spent hours studying string quartets.

"Do you play the violin, Mr. Becker?"

"Please, call me Michael," he said. "No, not the violin. But I do play the piano. Strictly as an amateur. I can read music and make my fingers play the notes. In the end it sounds respectable. But there's no emotion. Not like you. Your heart and soul take control, drenching each note in passion." He smiled shyly. "I was moved to tears by your performance."

She was flattered, just as he wanted her to be. "That is so kind. Thank you very much." Then she smiled. "Are you telling the truth about your own abilities?"

York nodded. "Yes, I'm being quite honest. If you heard me play, you would certainly believe me."

She laughed, and then eyed him curiously for a

moment. "Have you seen many of my performances?"

"No, last night was the first," he admitted. "I've just returned to Berlin." He paused, reflective. "I've been convalescing from war wounds."

"I'm so sorry," she said, her face showing compassion. "I wish you a complete recovery."

"Thank you, that's very kind, although it's not likely. But I am grateful to be alive."

The sadness returned to her face, reflecting perhaps, on her own loss. She looked at her watch and managed a weak smile. "I suppose I should be going."

"So soon? I was enjoying our chat. And there's so much more to talk about."

"Yes, it was nice. I enjoyed it, also."

"Maybe we can continue another time."

"Perhaps," she said, just being polite. She rose from the table and got her bags. "It was nice to meet you."

"It was nice to meet you, also. Hopefully our paths will cross again."

She shrugged. "Anything's possible."

As she started to go, he rose from his table. "I think I'll leave, too. Suddenly the café is not nearly as interesting as it was."

She blushed and smiled uneasily. Then she saw his limp and the cane, and looked at his leg for a moment before her eyes returned to his face. "Take care," she said, her voice sincere.

He watched her walk away, the next phase of his plan beginning to focus.

# CHAPTER 10

Amanda walked from the café, a shopping bag in each hand, thinking about Michael Becker. He was interesting to talk to, and his story seemed true. There didn't appear to be any agenda. And there was the limp. She had sympathy for him. She could only imagine the horrors he faced. But then, she had faced horrors, too.

She had fully recovered from the train accident, at least physically. But the loss of the baby was more than she could bear, and she found herself suddenly crying when she least expected it, mired in depression for days at a time, unable to eat or sleep, pacing the floors at 3 a.m.

There was really no one she could talk to except Erika. But she wasn't quite ready to do that, although she knew the time would come when she was. Manfred didn't want to discuss it; he acted like it never happened. Maybe it was his way of dealing with it. Or maybe it was his way of avoiding any discussion that might lead to his former mistress. And she couldn't talk to Kurt, regardless of how close they were. He was at that awkward age when it's difficult to discuss emotions. He kept his hidden away because he thought that's what men were supposed to do. So Amanda felt truly alone – a woman with no country, isolated in her own household.

Nothing was more important to her than family. An only child, she was raised by parents who were too busy for her. Even though she lived in Edinburgh, her father spent most of his time in London, playing with the orchestra. She rarely saw him. Her mother was involved in a variety of volunteer and charity organizations, an admirable quality but one that left little time for her daughter. Amanda had grown up in a series of boarding schools, shuffled around the United Kingdom, classmates serving as the family she never really had.

She had wanted the baby so badly. It had taken ten years to get pregnant, and it seemed like a miracle when it finally happened. What better way for her and Manfred to strengthen their relationship after his affair. As soon as she thought about it, her stomach wrenched. She had caught him, but she had forgiven him, even though she would always wonder if there were others. What else could she have done? It wasn't like she could go back to Scotland. But she still could have left him. And left Berlin. But she didn't.

She wondered where he was after the train accident. It was three days before he arrived at the hospital, and it had taken two days for authorities to reach him. She had been worried the whole time if he was with another woman. Although she had promised him all was forgotten, she doubted she could ever trust him again.

That's why the baby had been so important. It was a fresh start, a new beginning. Now she doubted she would ever get pregnant again. But if she did, she would give up everything: the violin, the crowds, the admirers, the lifestyle, she would even give up her camera, her most prized possession in the world. There was just one problem. She couldn't bring herself to be intimate with Manfred. And she didn't know why.

She walked into her apartment, setting her bags down by the door. She had purchased two dresses, a conservative charcoal one with white buttons, the other emerald green. White gloves, a smart gray hat accented by a lighter gray band, and a pair of black high heels completed her new ensemble. Clothing was becoming scarce with the war; she bought it as soon as she saw something she liked. Authorities did well supplying other basic necessities. Most foods were easily obtainable, although amounts were dictated by ration cards, but coffee was not. Anything was available via a thriving black market. And it was amazing how many people used it.

Kurt was in his bedroom when she walked past. He was bent over his desk, immersed in whatever lay before him, not even aware she was there.

Amada watched him, a smile curling her lips. She loved Kurt. She may not have her own children, but she was blessed to have him in her life. Six years old when she married Manfred, he had always been quiet and sensitive, somewhat of a loner, although he did have a few friends. He idolized his father, who was often too busy to spend time with him, and was often too critical when he did.

She knocked lightly on the door frame. "What has you so intensely occupied?"

Kurt turned and smiled. "I almost have it. Come see."

Amanda walked into the room and looked over his shoulder. On top of the desk was a decorative bottle with the logo of an old pharmaceutical company. It was lying on its side, the interior filled with a miniature ship, a replica of a seventeenth century Spanish galleon. The sails had just been raised to a vertical position via a string held in Kurt's hand.

"Kurt, that looks fantastic," she said, surprised by the results. "I know how long you've been working on it. Congratulations. Now you've mastered it."

"It did take a long time," he said, beaming, pleased that she recognized how difficult it was. "But I think the next one will be much easier."

She leaned forward, wrapped her arms around his shoulders, and kissed the top of his head. "Good for you. I'm proud of you. You never gave up."

"Thank you," he said, smiling. "I can't wait to show father."

Manfred Richter did not come home for dinner, his aide calling to say he had prior obligations. He was rarely home evenings; his Nazi party responsibilities demanded commitments beyond the normal work day: meetings, conferences, entertaining clients at theaters or cabarets. And Manfred Richter thrived in social environments.

They lived in a luxurious house with live-in domestic help, a young woman named Hannah. Olive-complexioned with black hair, she was married to a German soldier stationed in Norway.

As Hannah served dinner, Amanda asked Kurt about school, his friends, and lent a sympathetic ear to the trials he experienced as a teenager in Berlin. They were close. Amanda listened to what he had to say; she paid attention to him. He appreciated it.

After dinner he left to see his friends, as he normally did. They were all classmates, most of whom lived within a few blocks. Amanda liked them; they were polite and well-behaved.

Amanda had a last cup of coffee as Hannah cleaned up from dinner. She talked about her husband, the last letter she had gotten, the winter he endured in Norway, and how much she missed him. Amanda listened, but didn't say much. She didn't think she had to. Hannah just needed to talk, and Amanda understood that.

When Hannah retired to her room, Amanda was alone. She treasured these hours, which she spent not practicing the violin, but tucked away in a private study for her use only. The room housed her camera, a dark room to develop the film, large folios of photographs, from nature to architecture to pictures of the Nazi elite, including Hitler and Goebbels and Göring and Hess, all meticulously filed. The walls were crammed with framed examples of her work, her favorite a large picture of the Fuehrer that hung above the fireplace. Photography was Amanda's true passion, the hobby she loved above all else, even playing the violin.

She removed some negatives from her camera, and went into the dark room to process them. She studied the photographs as the images developed, slowly coming into focus, vague and hazy at first, and then becoming crisp and clear. There were three different rolls, all taken in the last few weeks. She sorted through them as she hung them to dry, pictures of birds on one side, buildings on another, people in the center.

Suddenly, with a start, she looked at one photo, shocked by what the camera had captured.

# CHAPTER 11

By the time he left the café, York was obsessed with Amanda Hamilton. She was fragile, like a cracked porcelain vase, yet an inner strength filtered through each flaw, hinting of a depth that was easy to underestimate. An aura of sadness surrounded her, like a clouded halo, her eyes dull, mirroring pain, all understandable given the loss of her baby, especially since the tragedy was published in the Berlin newspapers. Another private matter, her unfaithful husband, had also been made public.

She seemed modest and unassuming, her intellect impressive, but wrapped in a quiet, calm demeanor that showed no need to impress, no desire to brag, comfortable with who she was and what she had become. He found her interesting but mysterious, and he couldn't determine why. At least not yet.

Nothing from their brief discussion hinted that she offered information to Kent, his predecessor. Just as there was no indication she betrayed him. He realized he didn't know enough to form conclusions. But he did know what café she frequented. And for now, or at least until there was a message in the drop, he would continue to arrange chance meetings. Then he could get to know her better. But he had to be careful. Just because he thought she was vulnerable didn't mean that she actually was.

He got a taxi, waiting for almost ten minutes to find one, and went to the cemetery to check the drop. It was a beautiful area of the city, blanketed with trees, the residences and apartment buildings around it evenly spaced, hidden with foliage and fences and walls. The lake in the middle of the graveyard offered serenity, a quiet solitude not available in sections of the city more densely populated. It was a nice place to spend eternity.

He entered the cemetery, cautiously studying those who walked by, looking for graves not recently visited, or moving to tombs they had seen many times before. There was a respectful silence, and it seemed only whispers were used to not offend the dead.

York walked through the lanes near the drop and, when satisfied that no one was watching, he went to the tomb and removed the finial from the wrought iron fence. It was empty. He quickly replaced it, glancing in all directions, noticing nothing suspicious. He then stood there for a moment, pretending to mourn a loved one.

He was beginning to wonder if there really was a spy. Or an informant, for that matter. Maybe Kent, his predecessor, had hoped to enlist one of the quartet, most likely Amanda Hamilton, but had been caught by the Gestapo before he could. The members of the string quartet may have had nothing to do with it, especially with a drop in such a public location.

He waited a moment more, contemplating, before walking away. He turned the corner, moving towards the exit, when he saw a woman a few meters ahead of him, blonde, slender and attractive, looking familiar. It was Erika Jaeger.

York was startled, not expecting to see her. His mind raced, recalling the faces he had seen near the tomb where the drop was located. Could she have been there without him noticing? She might have checked the drop just before he got there. Maybe that's why there weren't any messages. She was waiting for him to leave one.

He considered calling out to her, but knew it was too risky. He had judged Erika Jaeger and Gerhard Faber as the most dangerous of the quartet. The Gestapo informant might also know about the drop, and maybe that was her. He decided not to approach her, but to follow her instead.

He stayed a discreet distance behind, minimizing his limp but still leaning on his cane, following her to the exit. He passed an elderly couple, the woman's hand wrapped in her husband's arm, an empty, saddened glaze on their faces. York thought they might be visiting their son's grave, probably a soldier. He wondered how many other parents and wives and children made similar visits with the same pained expression and hollow hearts.

He watched Jaeger subtly, maintaining a safe distance, nonchalantly walking to the exit like any other mourner would. She never turned or seemed worried she was being followed. He continued walking behind her, occasionally pausing at a tombstone, or stopping to study a bird that sat on a branch, singing. When she left the cemetery, he too moved to the exit, glancing at his watch as if he were waiting for someone. She walked ten or fifteen meters down the pavement and stopped at a bicycle that was chained and locked to the iron fence.

It wouldn't be easy to follow her. The cemetery was on the western edge of the city; Erika Jaeger's house was not nearby. She lived close to Amanda Hamilton, which was four or five kilometers away. But what better way to travel than by bicycle. It was the most popular mode of transportation in the city, if not the entire continent.

He watched her pedal away, knowing the route, ensuring she didn't divert from it. If she stopped to meet a contact, or even talked briefly to someone, it could be the Gestapo. She could be reporting her progress, or receiving instruction.

She turned down Sensburger Allee, disappearing from sight. York knew it led to Heerstrasse, which was the main road towards the city proper and her home. The route was correct. He just needed to make sure she didn't deviate along the way.

The taxi was waiting for him. He told the driver he wanted to follow the woman on the bicycle, but without her knowing it. The man listened closely, a sly smile creeping across his face. He probably thought York was a secret admirer.

They let her have a few minutes start and then followed at a distance, maintaining enough space to avoid suspicion. Traffic increased with each kilometer they traveled, making it easier to avoid detection, merge with other vehicles, or pull off to the side of the road and wait if they got too close. Eventually they reached the Ku'damm, passing York's hotel and the street that led to Amanda Hamilton's house.

Jaeger turned off the boulevard and onto a residential street several blocks from where she lived. York knew her address, even though he had yet to visit it. The homes were respectable, but not luxurious, more working class than Amanda Hamilton's neighborhood.

She continued pedaling, traveling the street parallel to hers. The homes were intersected with alleys, each with a few carriage houses designed for wagons but now housing automobiles. Eventually she turned down a dirt lane, stopping behind a paneled truck, the green paint fading, with no lettering on it.

"Go past the alley and park," York told the driver. "Wait for me. I won't be long."

He got out of the car and moved quickly to the alley entrance. The street was alive with people. Some sat on their steps, neighbors talking, a man walked his dog, and two small girls passed on bicycles. No one paid attention to a man with a cane. He peered around the corner.

The truck was parked fifty meters away from the street, perched in the dirt lane next to a small carriage house. The driver stood in the rear of the vehicle, doors open. York could see shelves in the interior, stacked against the sides, boxes and open crates perched on them, but he couldn't see what was in them.

Erika Jaeger removed two cloth bags that were clamped in the storage rack on the rear of her bicycle. She reached in the pocket of her skirt and withdrew money, handing it to the man. He took the cloth bags and started to fill them with packages wrapped in paper, round items that he handled delicately, then larger pouches. After he filled the bags he handed them back to her. She put them over her handlebars and gave him two more. He filled those as well, but now with produce: lettuce and carrots and peppers and onions.

York hurried back to the driver and gave him the name of his hotel. When Erika Jaeger pedaled out of the alley and turned towards the taxi, he ducked down while she moved past. After she was thirty or forty meters in front of them, the taxi pulled away from the curb and turned at the next cross street. She never noticed them.

York wondered why she had purchased four bags of food from an unmarked van. Many Berliners bought food on the black market, especially items with limited availability. But Erika Jaeger lived with her mother. There were only two people in their household.

Why did she need so much food?

# CHAPTER 12

York went to his translator assignment every Monday and Wednesday. Since the availability of British newspapers was sporadic and sometimes non-existent, he sometimes went on Friday, also. Even then, he rarely had much to do.

The scenario was always the same. He walked in the room with four tables, a single chair at each. A pad of paper, a pen and, occasionally, a newspaper that needed translation was waiting for him. But sometimes when he arrived the table was bare. He would wait awhile, in case someone arrived with a newspaper, but no one ever did.

He never saw the lieutenant who had given him the assignment, but each time he went, one of the four men who was there during his indoctrination waited, reading their newspaper rather than translating it, but always watching York very carefully. He now knew they were Gestapo, but he acted as innocent as possible, leaning heavily on his cane, exaggerating his limp, favoring his right arm and occasionally massaging his healed bullet wound, perfectly playing the role of a front line soldier on convalescent leave.

"Is there anything interesting in the Moscow newspaper?" York asked that Wednesday, directing his comment to the other occupant in the room.

The man looked at him sullenly, as if he didn't want to be bothered. He didn't voice a reply, frowned, and shook his head. He raised the paper a bit higher, so York couldn't see his face.

York got the message, although he had enjoyed irritating the man. He returned to his paper, translating the personals, and finished as quickly as he could.

An hour later he walked out of the office. The

65

man with the Russian newspaper was still in there; no one else had come or gone. He exited into the alley, walking past the rubbish cans, and went down the side street and up to the Ku'damm.

It was a beautiful day, with thick, cottony clouds sprinkled across the sky. Pedestrians passed, shopping or hurrying to work. Cars and bicycles moved down the road, competing with taxis and trolleys. York paused, enjoying the weather and watching the bustling city. For a minute, he almost felt like he was in London. And then the Nazi flags draped from the buildings reminded him that he wasn't.

He gazed across the street, studying a crowded café, and noticed an attractive brunette, her wavy hair almost to her shoulder, standing on the pavement. It was Amanda Hamilton.

He wondered whether to shout and wave, or to hurry across the boulevard to greet her. For some reason, his instinct told him not to. He remained where he was, moved behind the stout trunk of a tree and pretended to wait for the tram. But his eyes never left her.

She stood still, her hand at her mouth, her attention riveted to a black Mercedes parked a half block down the road. A German soldier sat in the driver's seat, his eyes directed forward.

A few minutes later the rear door opened, and a man dressed in a grey suit got out. He reached in the car for another passenger, and a feminine hand became visible, followed by a shapely leg. A slender brunette emerged, smiling, dressed smartly.

The man was Manfred Richter. He hugged the woman tightly, holding her for a moment, and then he kissed her, lingering on her lips. She pulled away, smiling, and started walking down the street. Richter turned and watched her, staring for a moment, and then climbed in the car, a smile on his face.

Amanda Hamilton stood motionless, her eyes wide, her face pale.

# CHAPTER 13

Amanda was nauseous, her heart breaking, as she watched Manfred embrace another woman. Her eyes misted, tears slowly dripping down her cheeks, and then she closed them, wishing the image would go away. But she knew it wouldn't. Just like it didn't six months before. Only then it was a different woman, a redhead.

She opened her eyes and watched as the Mercedes pulled away from the curb. The woman walked towards her, almost to the café, but turned into a gray granite building housing the Berlin Bank. She was older, probably early forties, dressed in an expensive charcoal skirt and blue silk blouse. She seemed happy, with a bounce to her step and a smile on her face, as if her life had changed for the better.

Without even knowing why, Amanda followed her into the bank. She was numb, stunned and shocked, feeling like a fool for forgiving a man who didn't deserve it. But what would she do now? She couldn't confront the woman. But she still wanted to know more about her. She kept at a distance, staying near a handful of customers that filled out deposit slips.

The woman went to an office located just past the tellers. It was plush, two leather chairs sat in front of a mahogany desk. She walked to a window, pushed the drapes open a bit farther to capture both the sunlight and a view of the side street, and scanned some papers on the desk. She then looked up, as if she realized she was being watched.

Amanda didn't move. She stared at the woman, her expression pained, her eyes misty. Even though she wanted to, she couldn't seem to avert her gaze.

The woman looked at her curiously and, when

Amanda's stare continued unabated, she walked to her office door and closed it. The sign, now visible, read: Gretchen Baumgartner, Bank Manager.

Amanda left the bank, dazed, and climbed into a taxi, mumbling her destination to the driver. As he pulled away she stared out the window, seeing nothing. She didn't know whether to cry or scream, but she knew that sooner or later, she would figure out which.

When she arrived home she fled to the sanctity of her music room, but didn't play her violin. She stared at the walls, a vacant look in her eyes, an occasional tear dripping down her cheeks. She felt like a fool. Manfred had convinced her he had only strayed once, that he was sorry, that he was a good husband, and it would never happen again. But in reality, it had been happening all along, and with more than one woman. She had devoted ten years of her life to someone who couldn't care less. She had given up everything for him, and now she was a British island in a German sea.

Her sadness eventually turned to anger and, if Manfred was there, she probably would have hit him. But instead she only fumed at her predicament, annoyed for not having seen it, mourning the years she squandered. She didn't want to waste another minute with a man she didn't trust, regardless of how much she loved him, if it was even possible to love him knowing what he was.

She was even angrier at herself. She was stranded, stuck, no escape possible, and there was no one else to blame. She understood the risks when she married him and moved to Germany, but she had somehow managed to minimize them. Now, even if she could flee Berlin, Manfred would find her. And she could never get back to the United Kingdom. She didn't have many options.

Two days passed before he finally came home.

He had sent no message, never called, offered no explanation why he was gone. He just appeared, as if he had left only minutes before, expecting to be welcomed by his loving wife.

She confronted him as soon as he walked in the door. "I saw you with the bank manager the other day," she said, amazingly calm given the situation.

He looked at her like she was crazy. "I don't know what you're talking about."

"The Berlin Bank, Gretchen Baumgartner. I know all about her." She shook her head with disgust, fighting tears. "And I was stupid enough to think you were going to change."

His expression altered, knowing he was caught and that a confrontation couldn't be avoided. He shrugged. "So I'm guilty of a mild indiscretion. Do you know how hard it is for a man as powerful as me to resist these temptations?"

Her face grew taut. "I think it would be easy if you loved your wife."

"Amanda, don't be ridiculous. This has nothing to do with love. It's sport, a game, no different than football. No different than enjoying a good cigar."

"You are so disgusting," she said, her voice trembling. "I don't even know you. I only thought I did."

He laughed. "You're always so dramatic. What are you going to do about it? Tell me, because I can't wait to hear."

She didn't answer, hatred in her eyes. Without warning, she swung her arm in a wide arc, trying to slap his face.

He caught her hand and pushed it away. His face reddened, his anger brewing. "I'll tell you what you're going to do," he said, pointing a finger in her face. "Absolutely nothing. You're going to pretend you don't even know. Like a good German wife."

"I will not," Amanda said defiantly, her lips trembling. "I have no interest in a fake marriage, wasting my life with someone I don't love."

"Really?" he asked with feigned disbelief, sarcastic and condescending. "You're not going to leave me and go back to Scotland, are you?"

"If I could figure out how, I would."

He grabbed her as she fought to push him away, hugging her tightly, kissing her forehead, trying to annoy her.

"Get away from me!" she demanded.

He released her, amused. "Amanda, darling, we make a perfect couple. Let's not forget that."

"Not anymore," she said. "I'm leaving you. I'll move out and go to a hotel."

His face hardened. "I'm afraid that's not possible," he said, struggling to control himself. "Because if you leave, I will find you. And then I will have you put in an insane asylum. The headlines will read: *Violinist has nervous breakdown after losing baby in train wreck.*"

She glared at him. "I despise you."

"You'll learn to overcome that," he said, mocking her. "And you'll stay in Berlin, in this house, and be the dutiful wife, making sure your husband's needs are met. Because there's nothing else you can do."

# CHAPTER 14

York went to Olivaer Platz at 10 a.m. on Friday. A park intersected with cobblestone walkways, lined with trees, accented with flowers, and sprinkled with benches, it offered an oasis of serenity in a sea of streets and boulevards. He was meeting Max, six weeks after their initial contact in Basel, just as they had planned.

York had worked with him in France. He was brilliant, always one step ahead of everyone else, seemed to know what the enemy would do before they did it, and he had the uncanny ability to answer a question before it was asked. York respected him; he learned from him and he admired him.

But Max could also be demanding, expecting results when they might not be achievable. He probably assumed York had the riddle solved, and already knew which string quartet member was the Gestapo informant and which was willing to cooperate. But York knew nothing. He assumed Erika Jaeger was somehow involved, and he had a chance meeting with Amanda Hamilton that had yet to yield results. But he still hadn't surveilled Gerhard Faber or Albert Kaiser.

He walked through the park, a cobblestone path winding around the trees. It was more crowded than he expected. He passed a woman with a baby stroller, an older man with a young boy who was probably his grandson, and a group of foreign workers walking briskly down the lane, either passing from one city block to another or enjoying a pleasant morning.

Max was waiting on a bench on the north side, tucked off the path and somewhat secluded. He wore very thick spectacles and held a cane, posing as someone visually impaired. It was a good disguise, explained why he wasn't in uniform, and proved how cunning he could be.

York sat beside him, but on the opposite end. When satisfied no one watched them, they moved closer and began to talk, whispering in English. They switched to German when anyone came near, and talked louder, as if they had nothing to hide.

"How's your cover?" Max asked.

"When I first reported, there were four men there," York explained. "Now I go a few times a week and, even though one of those four is always there, they rarely speak. And they never engage in any causal conversations. I feel like they're watching me."

Max glanced at an older couple passing on a nearby walkway. "They are watching you. All of Berlin is watching you. You can't trust anyone. A child can turn you in to the Gestapo as easily as a grandmother. The minute you forget that, you're dead."

York was pensive, reevaluating the danger. "I suppose I should wear my uniform a bit more, especially when wandering around the city."

"It reduces the risk," Max said. "You're in tremendous danger, don't underestimate that. The minute you do, the second you start to feel comfortable, you're done."

"I'll remember that," York said softly. Max had a penchant for drama but, in this instance, he provided an accurate depiction of life in Berlin. York valued his advice. He always had. He just had to make sure he followed it.

"Tell me what's happened since your arrival."

York described the train crash, and the encounters with Hamilton and Jaeger. He also admitted that he hadn't discovered much. He didn't know who had offered information, why Kent had been betrayed, or who had betrayed him. He also mentioned that he had no interaction with Faber or Kaiser.

"You've made some progress with the women, but it isn't enough," Max said, disappointment evident in his voice. "We're running out of time. We need access to whatever information Kent was offered, even if we risk our lives getting it. It could be critical, something that changes the outcome of the war."

York was quiet, pensive. "I don't know why the drop hasn't been used," he said. "Could Kent have had another communications method?"

Max shrugged. "I don't know. I suppose he could have. But I think he would have mentioned it if he did." He paused and looked away for a minute, studying a policeman hurrying through the park. When he was no longer visible, his eyes returned to York. "Let's try something different. We'll change tactics."

"And do what?"

"Leave a message at the drop. Keep it simple; just say you're waiting for contact. Let Jaeger respond, assuming it is Jaeger."

"Unless she's the Gestapo informant," York said. "She might be watching the drop, just like we are."

"Perhaps," Max said. "But either way, you'll flush her out. And then we'll see what she's all about."

"Should I avoid Hamilton to concentrate on Jaeger?"

"No, of course not. Increase contact with her; find out what she knows and what she's willing to share. Even if she isn't the one we're after, you may be able to convince her to work with us. She is British. Just like you and me."

"Being British isn't enough," York said. "If it was, she would have left Germany long ago. But I was watching her the other day, and she saw her husband with another woman."

"Again?" Max asked, shocked.

York was surprised. He rarely discovered anything that Max didn't already know. "Yes, a local bank manager. I don't know if that's the same woman she caught him with before. But that might persuade her to cooperate."

"Or it might not," Max said. "There's no way to know for sure. It could even be a trap. Did she see you?"

York hadn't thought of a trap. But it didn't seem likely, especially given her reaction. "No, I don't think so."

Max was quiet for a moment, considering options. "I don't know what she has access to, but she's worth the effort. Her husband is highly placed, definitely in Hitler's inner circle. He works in shadows; we don't even know what he's doing. But I guarantee it's vital to their war effort, and worse than we can imagine."

"What about Kaiser and Faber?" York asked.

"I'll try to check on Kaiser," he said, referring to the elderly cello player. "Assuming I have time. But I do have other networks to run. I was actually counting on you to handle this."

"If we're fairly certain Jaeger is the one offering information," York said. "We only have to rule Kaiser out as the informant."

"That's true. And I do doubt that it's him. The informant is likely Hamilton, believe or not. Not many people realize it, but the majority of informants are women. Usually because of the men in their life."

York weighed the statistics against the woman he had met in the café. It was possible. It might even be probable. She was married to a German, even if the marriage was disintegrating.

"I'll watch Faber," York said, referring to the one-eyed viola player. "He lives in Charlottenburg, at the western end."

Max looked at a couple holding hands, the man in a German officer's uniform. They approached slowly and then turned towards the street. "Let's meet a week from today, same time. But not here, there are too many people. There's a café on Kantstrasse, near Savignyplatz. Sit outside. Be careful. I need you, old boy."

He rose abruptly and walked away.

York waited ten minutes more, watching birds on the branches above, the people bustling by on the boulevard beyond. When satisfied no one had noticed them, he got up and walked in the opposite direction. He paused when he reached the main walkway and looked each way, ensuring he wasn't followed. He then continued through the park.

He moved down the curved walkway, limping, leaning on his cane. He nodded to a mother with a small child as she passed, smiling politely. When he turned a corner, headed towards the street, he walked abruptly into Amanda Hamilton.

She was standing on the path, camera glued to her eye, taking photographs of a bird perched on a branch, primping and posing for the lens.

"Mr. Becker," she said crossly, lowering the camera. She folded her arms across her chest, studying him with a stern look.

York stopped, surprised to see her, not knowing why she was so angry. He decided to charm her.

"Miss Hamilton," he said, smiling. "What a pleasant surprise."

"Are you following me?"

He was stunned. "No, I'm not. I was just walking. I had no idea you were here, although I'm certainly glad to see you. Why would you think I'm following you?"

"First I see you at the café, and now the park."

He tried logic. "We met at the café and had a very pleasant conversation. I had no way of knowing you would be here."

"Is there something else you want to tell me?" she asked, glaring at him, her face taut.

York was guarded. She obviously knew something that he didn't. "I'm sorry," he said. "I don't know how I offended you. I enjoyed your company the other day, and I would very much like to continue our friendship. I think we have a lot in common."

She sighed, looking away. For a moment she studied the bird she had photographed, watching him as he watched her. Then she turned to York, a bit calmer.

"I like to take photographs," she said, finally explaining herself. "Birds are one of my favorite subjects. A few days ago, I took a picture of a bird from the terrace of my home. I accidentally captured a man in that photograph. He was standing near some shrubs, hidden in the shadows, watching my house."

She paused dramatically, her eyes trained on his. The silence was awkward, but she seemed to enjoy it. After a moment had passed, she continued. "That man was you, Mr. Becker. Would you like to explain yourself?"

York shrugged, trying to appear harmless, but annoyed he risked the operation with his carelessness. "I read a magazine article about you. The story listed your address, and your home is not far from my hotel. I was out walking and came across it. I wasn't watching you. There was no ulterior motive. It was simply a coincidence."

She shook her head slowly, her expression not changing. "Nice try. But you haven't seen the photograph. You were hiding. But not quite good enough. And you were watching. What did you hope to see?"

"Miss Hamilton, I already told you what happened. If I offended you, I apologize. I can't help but admire you. But you already know that."

"I want an explanation. And I want it now. If I don't get it, I will report you to the authorities."

York was getting worried. "There's no need to be upset. I told you what happened."

"And I told you I don't believe you. Now, do I call a policeman or do you tell me the truth?"

"I did tell you the truth."

She wasn't budging, defiant and determined. "Why are you watching me?"

He could tell she suspected something, but she wasn't sure what it was. He decided to gamble, expose who he was and what he was. She had just caught her husband being unfaithful for the second time in six months. Maybe she was vulnerable, desperate, trapped. Maybe she was anxious to escape.

"As I said…" he began, but then paused.

She waited, her arms still folded, anxious for an explanation.

He switched from German, and spoke English: "We have much in common."

# CHAPTER 15

Erika Jaeger bicycled to her house two days each week with four satchels of food dangling from the handlebars, returning from where she met the man who sold goods on the black market. Her apartment occupied the upper two floors of a hundred-year-old building that sat three dwellings from the corner, the neighborhood pleasant, the people friendly, a good place to raise a family. Although some of the houses on the tree-lined street were a bit tired and in need of repair, renovations would have to wait with most of the men away at war.

The apartments were accessed via a common vestibule, a grand staircase to the right, the first floor apartment entered from the left. The area above the vestibule was open for four stories, the stairs winding around it, stretching all the way to a plaster ceiling sculpted with floral designs. Erika lived in the fourth floor apartment with her mother Millie.

Internal to her apartment was a smaller staircase that led to an abbreviated fifth floor. On the fourth: kitchen, parlor, bath and Millie's bedroom, which was just off the living room. On the fifth, two rooms: Erika's bedroom and her music room. She spent most of her time on the fifth floor, practicing at least three hours each day and more on weekends, even while working at the War Ministry and any other odd jobs she could find to earn money. She always needed money.

She used her bicycle often; it was the most economical way to travel in a large metropolis like Berlin. When not in use, she chained and locked it to the iron fence that defined the courtyard at the rear of the property. Other residents did the same. The courtyard was secluded, backing to an alley, and hidden by a neighbor's carriage house that stood beside it. Their bicycles were safe there. Not that anyone in Charlottenburg would take them, anyway.

Erika arrived home on Monday, carrying four satchels of groceries up four flights of stairs. Her mother was in the parlor, listening to a radio program while scanning the front page of the newspaper. Not yet sixty, Millie was sickly, thin and frail. She tired easily and had dark circles around her eyes. And she seemed to get a little weaker with each day that passed.

Erika greeted her with a hug. "How was your day?"

Millie smiled. "It was no different than yesterday, and tomorrow will be no different than today. But any day is nice, especially in summer."

"Did you take all your medicine?"

Millie rolled her eyes. "Yes, I took all my medicine," she droned.

"Good," Erika said, the child playing parent. "What do you want for dinner?"

"It doesn't matter," she said. "Whatever is easiest for you."

"How about bratwurst and kartoffelsalat? I have some beer and bread."

Erika grabbed the bags of groceries and took them in the kitchen, putting them away in the cabinets and small refrigerator. She put some beer and chopped onions in a pan on the stove, heated the mixture, then added the bratwurst, far more than she and her mother could ever eat. She took a large container out of the cabinet and started to make the kartoffelsalat, peeling potatoes, adding a bit of bacon and salt and vinegar, making enough to fill the bowl.

Millie set the table while the bratwurst cooked, and Erika got some sheet music from the parlor, a work by Haydn, and studied the part for the second violin, imagining her fingers dancing along the neck.

She continued her mental exercise, practicing the piece two times, musical movements intertwined with frying bratwurst. When she was finished preparing the food, she sat at the kitchen table with Millie and they began to enjoy their meal.

"What was on the radio?" Erika asked.

"Mostly news about the war," she said. "The Fuehrer announced a summer offensive on the Eastern Front. He said Russia will be defeated by the end of the year."

Erika knew better, from the information she had access to at the War Ministry. Not only were the Russians also preparing an offensive, but they were slowly pushing the Germans westward across a broad front. But the average citizen didn't know that. And the government didn't want them to.

"Why did they say the war in Russia would end?" Erika asked, curious. She was always interested in the difference between public announcements and what she knew as fact.

Millie shrugged. "I wasn't really listening. I'm tired of war."

Since losing the Battle of Stalingrad in February, there had been few Nazi successes on the Eastern Front. Erika hoped the summer offensive, centered near the city of Kursk, did bring the war to an end, but she tended to doubt it, even though she was busy providing the logistics needed for its success: supplies, routes, spare parts, ammunition.

"Anything else of interest?" Erika asked.

Millie thought for a moment, sipping a glass of water. "There's going to be a parade on Saturday. It's for some regiments from France. They are moving eastward for the Russian offensive. They're marching right down Ku'damm."

81

Erika knew exactly which regiments they were. She had arranged their transport by train from Paris to Berlin, and then to a rail station near Kursk. But she didn't know about the parade.

"That might be nice to watch," she said. "Although I should really practice for the concert Saturday night. We're doing a new piece by Haydn."

"I'm sure you'll play superbly, whether you practice or not. You always do. Watch the parade. You deserve some fun."

Erika smiled. Her mother had been her greatest inspiration. A classical music lover and amateur violinist, she had taught Erika how to play. She never tired of telling Erika how proud she was of her accomplishments. It meant a lot. Erika was fortunate to have family so supportive. She only wished her father was still alive to see her success.

They finished their meal and cleaned up, still chatting about the parade and gossiping about the neighbors. Millie then returned to the parlor with her newspaper, while Erika went to the fifth floor, carrying the Haydn music.

She also carried several pots and containers. They were filled with bratwurst, rolls, and kartoffelsalat.

# CHAPTER 16

Manfred Richter sat in a conference room at the Reichstag, flanked by a group of leading industrialists. They represented the largest companies in Germany, all major contributors to the war effort and a large part of the nation's economy. They were focused on two topics, labor and foreign investment, at a time and place dictated by the Nazi Party, represented by Manfred Richter.

The initial presentation, given by a representative from Friedrich Krupp AG, made a request for additional labor needed to meet increasing product demands. Richter listened intently, always courteous and polite, usually the first to offer a joke, but always aware of the extreme power he held, the resources he controlled. He could tell the industrialists were acting as a united front, a bargaining position of strength, but he didn't really care. They would do what he told them to. He could be congenial, if he wanted to, or he could be demanding and dictatorial. It really didn't matter. Ultimately, he would get what he wanted.

"How mobile are your production capabilities?" he asked, catching them off guard.

The answers varied, the businessmen wary and cautious. They knew Richter was cagey, and none wanted to over-commit and risk disappointing him or the Fuehrer.

"There are opportunities on the Russian border, the Ukraine, Latvia, Estonia, and Lithuania. Build your factories, and you will have workers. The concentration camps, and the labor they provide, are also a possibility. Tell me how far from Germany you can economically manufacture and how soon you will be ready. And I will ensure you succeed."

Several of the men exchanged wary glances. After Germany's defeat at Stalingrad, the Russian theater was not as secure as it once was. A factory built in Latvia or the Ukraine could soon be under Russian control, especially if Germany didn't start reversing recent losses.

"We think closer to the Fatherland, or slightly east, is most feasible," one of the businessmen said delicately, wary of Russian advances.

If Richter understood the veiled meaning, he didn't show it. He stood and paced the room as the discussion continued, his hands clasped behind his back. He liked to be in control.

"We also have to be safe from Allied bombings," the executive from Friedrich Krupp AG reminded him.

"Then I suggest building new factories at concentration camps and prisoner of war facilities, or expand what you already have there. The labor is free and the Allies will never bomb them."

The industrialists seemed relieved, a potential success path provided. They whispered among themselves before another self-appointed spokesman, an executive with the chemical giant IG Farben, offered a solution.

"Give us one week," he said. "And we'll provide desired locations."

Richter turned and studied the man's face, reflecting on the offer. "One week," he said. "That's fair. Now for the next issue on the agenda."

He pointed to a map of the world that dominated one wall of the conference room. "Is everyone clear on where investments will be made overseas?"

Those in the room nodded. They knew nothing ranked higher on Richter's priorities than this. They also knew that complete cooperation was expected.

Richter pointed to several countries around the globe, many in South America, others in the Middle East. "There must be funding centers from Germany to these locations. Each corporation will deliver their plans for expansion to me in one month. I expect them to be very detailed."

He left the conference, got into his chauffeured sedan, and directed his driver to the home of the German State Radio. He entered the building, found the office of the program director, but was stopped by a receptionist.

"I'm sorry, sir. You need an appointment."

Richter smiled, nodding politely. He would use his charm. If that wasn't effective, he would use his temper. "I'm sure that's normally the case. But as a personal envoy of the Fuehrer, I don't think it applies to me." He handed her a business card.

She read the card and paled. "Yes, of course. Excuse me for just one moment." She poked her head in the office door, spoke softly for a few minutes and then motioned him forward.

Richter entered the office to find an owl-like man behind a large desk cluttered with papers and records.

"Mr. Richter, what a pleasant surprise," the man said. "I am Hermann Gunther, program director. How can I be of assistance?"

Richter muttered a greeting and handed the man a record. "Play this song, often and with enthusiasm. I expect many people to buy it once it airs."

Gunther glanced at the label. The artist was Anna Schneider. He had never heard of her. "I'm not familiar with the singer," he said hesitantly.

Richter smiled in the arrogant, superior way that power allows. "And what does it matter if you are familiar with the singer or not? I told you to play it.

Nothing else should concern you."

Gunther's eyes widened, stunned by Richter's attitude. He paused a moment, trying to carefully phrase his answer. "Between newscasts and music dictated by the state, we have little air time for popular music. Given that, I only accept the best."

Richter's face hardened. He leaned across the desk. "Maybe you misunderstood me. I told you to play this record, and to play it often."

Gunther felt beads of perspiration forming on his forehead. "It's not that simple," he said delicately. "A panel of station experts must approve the record. We get many requests each week. From those submittals, we choose what will be played."

Richter noticed a framed photograph on Gunther's desk. It appeared to be his family, a lovely wife, two daughters, maybe teenagers, and a young son. He stared at Gunther with a meaningless smile, reached across the desk, and picked up the photograph. "Is this your family?" he asked.

Gunther paled, understanding the implications, the veiled threat that Richter appeared to be making. "Yes," he said softly. "It is."

"Very handsome," Richter said, studying the picture. "I assume they're serving the Fatherland?"

"Yes, of course," Gunther said, stuttering. "My wife works in an armaments factory, my children are in school."

Richter nodded, his smile fading. "That doesn't seem to be enough," he said casually. He put the picture back on the desk. "I think they could be doing more. How old are the children?"

Gunther paled and moved the photograph closer, as if by doing so he could protect them. He looked at Richter, his eyes wide. "I will do everything I can to accommodate you."

"Mr. Gunther, it's very important that you listen to me closely." Richter paused, watching, letting his words weigh on the listener. "I told you when I came in, that this record will be played on your station, and with enthusiasm. I think you understand that perfectly, don't you?"

Gunther was not a brilliant man, but he was smart enough to know when a battle was lost. "Of course, Mr. Richter," he said, shocked and stunned. "I would be happy to honor your request. We can't wait to play Miss Schneider's record. I'm sure it will be very popular."

Richter stood to leave. He shook Gunther's hand, his polite smile returning, even though it wasn't genuine. "I knew it would be a pleasure to do business with you, Mr. Gunther. Miss Schneider is a rising star. And that's exactly how you will treat her."

# CHAPTER 17

Amanda Hamilton looked at York, her eyes wide, her mouth moving but producing no sounds. She glanced quickly in all directions, scanning the park to ensure no one was watching them, before her eyes returned to his. Another moment passed before she finally spoke.

"Are you trying to get yourself killed, Mr. Becker?" she asked, in German.

"No, I'm not," he replied. "I'm trying to keep a lot of other people from getting killed."

"And what do you want from me?"

He paused, trying to think of how to ease the tension. He didn't want to end up like Kent. He smiled slightly, trying to disarm her.

"Continued conversations like we had at the café?" he asked, his eyebrows arched innocently.

"Somehow I think your interest goes beyond music."

He sighed, studying her cautiously. "It does. Although I thoroughly enjoyed every word of our conversation."

She tensed, her eyes fiery. "Why have you approached me like this? Who do you think you are?"

"As I said before, we have much in common."

"You don't even know me," she argued. "Why are you putting me in such a precarious position?"

"It wasn't my intent," York said. And he meant it. He didn't want her harmed. Even if she was at risk.

"Then what is your intent?" she demanded.

He decided to be honest. "Information," he said simply.

"What makes you think I have any? And if I did, what makes you think I would share it with you?"

"You have a wealth of information," he said. "You just don't realize it."

"I don't know why you think so. I'm a musician and a photographer. I have access to no state secrets. If you think I'm privy to what my husband does, you're mistaken."

"It's much simpler," he explained. "Information can be the people you know, the parties you attend, conversations you overhear. All of that can be summed, glued together like the pieces of a puzzle. Thousands of lives could be saved as a result."

"I am a German citizen. Why would I do that?"

"Because your heart and soul are Scottish."

"I would never betray my husband."

York wondered if she meant it, especially after the latest infidelity. But he decided not to challenge her. "You can set your own boundaries. Tell me as much or as little as you want."

She studied him closely for a moment, calculating, assessing his offer. "I don't need any complications in my life," she said, a saddened glaze consuming her eyes. "I'm vulnerable right now, very fragile. You don't understand."

"Yes, I do. I understand perfectly." He paused, wanting to continue but not knowing if he should. He decided to reveal some of what he knew, but not to mention her husband. He touched her arm lightly. "I'm so sorry about the baby."

Her face showed shock, wondering how he knew. But then she remembered. The newspapers described the accident and the extent of her injuries. She searched his eyes for sincerity, as if she wanted desperately to be understood and appreciated, to feel the sympathy of another human being.

"Thank you," she said softly.

He saw a green uniform approach through the

trees, walking slowly down the cobblestone lane. It was the Ordnungspolizei, or Orpo, the Berlin police. His eyes widened, knowing the danger, and shifted towards Amanda.

She saw his expression and turned, just as the policeman rounded the corner and came towards them. She studied him a moment, watching as he approached, and turned to York.

He looked at her, pleading, as her eyes met his. He knew how easy it would be. All she had to do was stop the policeman. She could tell him anything, fact or fiction. And York would be as good as dead. He knew that. So did she.

The policeman walked slowly, strolling, whistling softly, studying the leaves on the trees and flowers in their beds, birds that sang, and butterflies that fluttered across his path. He nodded to an elderly lady carrying a bag with fresh bread peeking from the top, chatted a moment, then continued towards them.

York watched Amanda eyeing him sternly, and realized she controlled his destiny. He was helpless. He waited, his eyes trained on hers, the seconds passing with agonizing slowness.

"Good morning," the policeman said when he reached them. "What a beautiful day. I love this weather."

Amanda kept her eyes locked on York's. "I do, too," she said. "Especially after the winter we had."

"Summer is already here," the policeman said, slowly moving away from them. "In a few more weeks, we won't even remember winter."

Amanda continued staring at York. When the policeman was out of earshot, she whispered: "See how easy it would be to destroy you. That's what you need to think about."

He knew she was right. But she didn't betray

him. Her actions, or lack thereof, spoke volumes. "Thank you," he said.

She nodded. "A favor to a fellow musician. Don't expect any more."

He took a deep breath, knowing not to press her. She needed time to think. But while she did, he was totally exposed. Max might be right. She could be the Gestapo informant, even if she did let the policeman pass without saying anything. And if she wasn't, she could still become one, as she just hinted.

"Why don't you think about it for a few days? Meet me at the café on Monday. We can talk then."

"And what if I choose not to? Is my life in danger?"

"No, of course not," he said with disbelief. "Don't be ridiculous. If you choose not to, we can still be friends. We just limit our conversations to music."

She laughed lightly, blushing. "I'm not sure my husband would like that."

"Then maybe we shouldn't invite him," York said, feigning indignation.

She shook her head slowly, a faint twinkle in her eye. "You are persistent," she said, surrendering just a bit. "I will grant you that. I'm flattered. I really am. But I don't think a friendship would be a very good idea."

He ignored her, his mind wandering. "Are you really a good photographer?"

She shrugged, not expecting the question. "Some people think so. Above average, I suppose. I absolutely love it."

He fingered the faded photograph in his pocket, reminiscing. "I have a favor to ask you. It's about photography."

Her interest was piqued. "What is it?"

He grinned. "I'll tell you on Monday. That will

give you some incentive to come."

She watched him closely, fighting the urge to let her lips curl into a smile. "And what if I don't come?"

"You'll wonder for the rest of your life if we have the same interest in photography that we have in music."

He turned and abruptly walked away, beads of sweat on the back of his neck.

# CHAPTER 18

Amanda Hamilton was still shaken when she left the park, stunned that she had been approached, irritated at being compromised, anxious and afraid. She had suspected the Allies would contact her, since she was born in Scotland and married to a very influential German. But somehow she thought she could elude them, hiding in a cocoon of violin concertos and photographs of buildings and birds. Now she knew that was impossible.

As she walked home, she evaluated how exposed she was. Her mind raced, flooded with a million different thoughts, some jumbled, some clear. She realized that if she denied Michael's request, he would only make it again. She would deny him again, and eventually he would go away. But a replacement would come and the process would start all over. But if she agreed to cooperate she risked her life, as well as Kurt's and Manfred's, even though she didn't care about him. Even Hannah, her domestic, was in danger. It didn't seem worth it. It wasn't her fight. Or was it?

She also realized that, if the British were smart enough to contact her, the Germans were shrewd enough to realize they would. They might start following her, if they weren't already, or feed her with false information, something easily validated if the Allies acted upon it. It seemed no matter what she did, her life was about to drastically change.

She wondered if she should tell Manfred. It seemed the safest course. But now she despised him, and would rather not talk to him at all. If she did tell him, it meant the loss of any freedom she still had. German agents would watch her constantly, or escort her, like Klein did when they gave concerts outside of Berlin. And it meant Michael's arrest and probable death; that was certain. She wasn't sure she wanted to be responsible for that.

She had to admit she liked him. Mr. Becker, the wounded German soldier, classical music aficionado, amateur piano player who was really an Englishman with a photographic riddle to share. How much did he tell her that was untrue, other than his nationality? Somehow, and for no reason at all, she didn't think he had lied about much else, including his attraction to her. She hated to admit it, but he showed more interest in her music during their ten-minute conversation at the café than her husband had in ten years.

Manfred had proven how despicable he was. Amanda wondered how long he had been unfaithful. How many women were there? Was it only the bank manager, and the red-haired woman she caught him with the past winter? Or were there many – multiple affairs juggled concurrently. He even had the audacity to tell her it would continue, and there was nothing she could do about it. What made it all worse, almost surreal, was that he was probably right.

Fortunately she rarely saw him; their paths never crossed except on Sunday. On the few days he was home, he left the house early in the morning, before she awakened, and returned late at night, well after she was asleep. Usually he didn't come home at all, when some crisis caused him to stay in his office. That had become much more frequent, which was fine with her. She didn't care if she ever saw him again.

She had a thought, fleeting, but alive long enough to plant a seed. Maybe Michael Becker the Englishman could help her. But what would he want in return, if he did? She had information she wouldn't hesitate to provide, who influential Party members were, or the horrible treatment of Jews. She could disclose what she knew without compromising her family. Maybe there was a solution, maybe there was a way out.

When she returned home, she went to her music room, frantic and overwhelmed. She needed to practice; she needed to find refuge in the sweeping movements of the masters. It gave her solace.

The parade was that Saturday, highlighted by the German troops from France on leave before reassignment. The citizens of Berlin turned out in earnest, lining the Ku'damm and saluting or waving small hand-held Nazi flags. The troops goose-stepped past, their faces stern, their loyalty unwavering, keeping an appointment with destiny on the barren steppes of the Russian Front.

Amanda stood on the pavement, her camera raised to her eye whenever something caught her attention. In rapid succession she took photographs of a small boy saluting, a teenage girl who ran into the street to kiss a passing soldier, a stern policeman with a handle-bar moustache, and a yellow bird on the limb of a sycamore tree, squawking at the commotion.

Her stepson Kurt stood beside her, his face flush with enthusiasm, his right hand raised in salute. He belonged to the Hitler Youth, membership in the organization compulsory for boys and girls over the age of ten. His uniform, a long-sleeved tan shirt and dark tie, short pants above the knee, and long socks that rode high on the calf, mimicked dozens of other youths in the crowd. He studied the troops with fascination and envy, perhaps seeing his own future, dreaming of the day when he too marched to battle.

A thousand boots clicked in unison, the cadence even and ominous, thunderous and throbbing, echoing through the street and capturing onlookers in dream-like trances. People packed the pavement, waving, watching a nation that had emerged from ashes, beaten and humbled, now proud and strong and defiant.

Nazi flags were draped from the windows of public buildings, hung from flagpoles on streetlamps, and sprouting from the bumpers of public vehicles. The city was overcome with nationalistic fervor, caught in a kaleidoscope of victory and conquest with world domination as the ultimate end. But since losing the Battle of Stalingrad, cracks had begun to show in the nation's armor. And those that watched wondered what waited on the horizon, if the Third Reich was destined to fade like the setting sun.

Amanda Hamilton Richter watched the frenzy with ambivalence, her life intertwined with the Nazis, her past linked to the enemy. For the first time in her ten years as a Berlin resident, she felt like she didn't belong. She was a misfit, out of place, and whether that realization was prompted by Manfred or Michael, the seed of discontent had been planted and was starting to nurture and grow.

Amanda and Kurt watched the parade for almost two hours, the crowds remaining, dwindling when the tail of the column became visible on the horizon. It was only when the last soldier passed, and the cars and taxis and buses and bicycles that normally filled the Ku'damm appeared, that the crowd dispersed, disappearing into homes and cafes and stores, and walking down the smaller streets that intersected the boulevard.

Amanda knew Kurt enjoyed the parade far more than she did. He was still talking about it when they sat down for an early dinner, since she had a Saturday night performance. Hannah served them steaming bowls of eintopf, a stew with cubes of meat, potatoes and vegetables in simmering gravy.

She watched him, devouring the meal like any

teenage boy. She saw his Hitler Youth uniform with new eyes, tainted by the triumphant march of the troops, and an awareness provided by Michael Becker, or whatever his real name was.

"What are you doing in your Youth organization?" she asked, more curious than normal.

"We march, like the soldiers we saw today," he said. "And we learn to read maps and how to survive in the forest. It's good training for when we join the military."

Amanda was starting to lose her appetite. "Let's hope the war ends before you're old enough. I thought you wanted to be a doctor. You do well in school, why give that up for the life of a soldier?"

"Father said I will be an officer. Maybe someday I'll be a general."

Amanda smiled at his enthusiasm. "Concentrate on your studies. You're only sixteen. You'll make a fabulous doctor."

"I'll be seventeen soon. And father said the age for service might be lowered. In a few months I could be in the army."

Amanda feigned a smile, fighting the nausea that was creeping over her. Suddenly the impact of war was very close to her heart. "Surely you learn other things. Topics that help you further your education. There won't always be a war."

"We study history and politics," he said. "And we learn about the Jews. The government pledged that Berlin will be free of Jews this year, even the few stragglers that remain, spouses of good German citizens. What a marvelous day that will be, when all the vermin are gone."

Amanda excused herself from the table and went to her room. She didn't want Kurt to see the tears streaming down her face.

# CHAPTER 19

Manfred Richter watched the troops march down the Ku'damm from the fifth-floor window of an Art Deco hotel near the Kaiser Wilhelm Memorial Church. He studied the crowds, waving and cheering, watching from windows and rooftops, the soldiers strutting down the boulevard with legs lifted in unison as Nazi flags flapped in the breeze. He looked away, glancing at his watch. He didn't want to waste time watching a parade.

The bathroom door opened, the room steamy from the hot shower, and Anna Schneider emerged, her naked body still damp, wrapped in a towel strategically positioned to prevent Richter from seeing everything he wanted.

"I'm sorry I kept you waiting," she said seductively. "I wanted a quick bath."

"It was worth it. But I would wait for eternity, if you wanted me to."

She smiled. "You're such a sweetheart."

She walked towards him, letting the towel slip just a bit, briefly exposing her breasts. It was only for an instant, just enough to torment him, before she covered again.

"I have something for you," he said, enjoying the glimpse of her nakedness.

"What is it?" she asked, coming closer, toying with the towel.

He held his right hand behind his back, smiling. "You have to guess."

"Manfred, I can't," she pouted. "Tell me what it is. Is it a present?"

"Just a trinket," he said. He pulled her close and

kissed her.

She playfully moved away. "Darling, stop teasing. Tell me what it is."

He took his hand out from behind his back and handed her a necklace, the diamond pendant sparkling in the dim light of the hotel room.

"Manfred!" she exclaimed, holding it around her neck and turning to look in a mirror. "It's gorgeous. Look how it sparkles. What did I ever do to deserve this?"

She kissed him, tentatively at first, and then more hungrily, letting the towel fall to the floor.

An hour later, Anna climbed out of bed and Richter heard the shower running. He looked at the necklace lying on the bureau and smiled, recalling how he got it.

A few years before, he had gone to the home of a wealthy Jewess with two Gestapo officers, demanding to see her papers. She was at first indignant, thinking money and pedigree entitled her to specific rights, privacy among them. She didn't realize that she had no rights.

Her papers were reviewed and the house searched, with no reason given. Richter took most of her jewelry, some of her clothes and rare books, porcelain china, and two rare vases. The woman grew irate, claiming he was nothing but a common thief, but Richter only laughed. And then, just so she understood her place in society, he ordered her to scrub the cobblestone street for one hour, using her silk lingerie and fur coat as rags. To ensure she complied, he remained to observe, stubbing cigarettes out on the street and then making her clean them up.

He had done the same thing to dozens of other Jews. Now, next to his office, he had an entire room filled with what he had stolen: gold, silver, jewelry, clothing, books, and paintings. He only wished he had stolen more.

He was in a generous mood, so he decided to give the diamond necklace to Anna. He even got a fox wrap for Amanda, a potential peace offering, and a leather-bound volume of *Faust* for Kurt. He would give Hannah, his housekeeper, an opal bracelet.

"I have to go," Anna said. "I'm taking the children to see their grandparents. They've been visiting friends, but they're probably home by now." She had two children, a boy and a girl.

"You're leaving so soon?"

"Yes, I'm sorry. I promise to make it up to you." She kissed him and started for the door.

"I heard your song on the radio today."

She stopped, spinning around to face him. "My song?" she asked with disbelief.

"Yes, the record you made."

"It was on the radio?"

"Yes, it was."

"You're joking, aren't you?"

"No, it's true. Listen to the radio. You'll hear it. I'm sure it'll be on again."

She walked back and gave him a last kiss. Then she skipped out the door, a broad smile pasted on her face.

Richter took a quick shower and left the hotel. He didn't feel like going home, he rarely did, so he browsed in some shop windows and then went to a restaurant for a late lunch. When his meal was finished he had a few drinks, lingering until he knew Amanda would be gone for the concert.

When he arrived home he went to Kurt's room, glancing for a moment at the bottle that contained the miniature ship. The room was empty, clothes stacked neatly on the bottom of the bed, waiting to be put in the bureau. A pair of leather boots sat beside the desk, dirty socks stuffed inside them. He put the leather volume of *Faust* on his bed, attaching a brief note: *a small gift for you, love, Father.*

Richter went to the lower level of the house, down a set of stairs to an area that contained a bathroom, a small parlor, and a bedroom. He waited at the door, listening for a moment, before he lightly tapped on it.

A moment later it opened, and Hannah stood before him.

"I brought you something," he said softly.

She glanced nervously up the stairs.

"It's all right," he said. "No one is home."

"What is it?"

"I have two things, actually." He took his right hand from behind his back to reveal a bottle of wine. Then he removed his left, handing her the opal bracelet.

"Oh, Manfred, it's beautiful!" she said.

"I thought you would like it," he said smugly. He walked in to her suite, closing the door behind him. "Let's open that bottle of wine."

Amanda didn't like the fox stole, even though she pretended to. Manfred gave it to her just after dinner on Sunday, with Kurt watching. She didn't want her stepson to know that she despised his father. But she also hoped Manfred didn't think a trinket would make her forget his latest affair.

He made a big fuss about it, how he had carefully selected it, going from one store to another, not satisfied until he found just what he wanted. Then, after rambling about the precious gift he had purchased for his devoted wife, he left to smoke a cigar with the man down the street.

It gave her an eerie feeling, reminding her of a

helpless animal's death. After she looked at it for a moment, and searched her memory, she realized there was another reason why she didn't like it.

It was very distinctive, the crimson color, the white spots, and it seemed familiar to her. After thinking about it for a moment, she recalled where she had seen it. It was on the shoulder of Gertrude Rothman, a prominent Jew and benefactor of the Berlin String Quartet. Amanda could have been mistaken, and her fur could simply resemble another, or Manfred could have stolen it.

She wondered what had happened to Gertrude Rothman. She had vanished, with all the other Jews, supposedly resettled outside the German borders. But somehow Amanda doubted anyone had been resettled. She suspected something horrible had happened to them; she just didn't know what it was.

She was asleep when Manfred returned, but he made so much noise he woke her. When he crawled into bed she kept her eyes closed, pretending, but he snuggled next to her anyway and started caressing her back.

"Are you awake?"

She smelled schnapps on his breath. Apparently he had done more than smoke cigars. "I am now," she said softly.

He continued to caress her, his hands traveling down her back and across her buttocks. His lips trailed along her neck, nibbling on her ears, the stench of alcohol stinging her nostrils.

"Please, Manfred," she said softly. "I don't want you to touch me. Not now and not ever."

"You're being silly," he scoffed, and returned to kissing her neck. "It was just a lapse in judgment. Nothing you should be concerned with. I don't care about her. I only care about you."

"I mean it," she said firmly. "Don't touch me."

"Everything will be all right," he said, his words slurring. "You'll see. The first time will be the hardest. Then it will be just like it was before."

He rolled her on her back and kissed her on the mouth.

"Manfred, no," she pleaded, trying to push him away. "I mean it."

He pinned her hands over her head, holding them tightly with his left hand. As his right hand roamed across her torso, he kissed her again, forcefully. Then he climbed on top of her.

# CHAPTER 20

York knew he was risking his life. Amanda Hamilton could be dangerous, ally or enemy, a spy or Gestapo informant. The policeman was his only clue as to where her loyalties might lie. She could have turned him in, but she didn't.

He didn't think she was the one who provided information to Kent, but he didn't discount it. He had surprised her, caught her unaware, and she may not have trusted him. Maybe she thought he was Gestapo, especially after her issues with her husband, and they were testing her, plotting and planning like they normally did. But since she couldn't be sure, she did nothing.

But she could also be the informant, as Max suspected, the musician who cost Kent his life. If that was true, she didn't have him arrested for a reason. She would pretend to cooperate, baiting him, so she could arrest everyone he interfaced with, like Max, and then those in his networks. She might have even told her husband or some Gestapo agent the story of their meeting. But that didn't seem like the woman he had chatted with at the cafe.

Although not certain about Amanda, he did suspect that Erika Jaeger was providing information to Kent. But that was based on seeing her at the cemetery and not actually at the drop site. Somehow he had to prove it was her, especially before he approached her. And he had to solve the riddles in her life, like why she needed so much food.

He decided to spend Saturday watching her. If he was right, she would go to the cemetery and he could watch her at the drop. Then when positive it was her, and after exchanging a few messages and observing her behavior, he could arrange a meet. But he had to be careful. She might know about the drop from Kent, when he was betrayed. And she could just as easily be the informant, watching the drop, as he was. It was confusing, and the wrong assumption could be deadly.

He left his hotel Saturday morning and went to the neighborhood where Erika Jaeger lived. Arriving near 10 a.m., he found a location just down the road where he could see both her house and the alley that led to the rear of her apartment building. To avoid suspicion he moved about the street, wandering up and down but still observing, and at times sitting on the bench for a bus stop, reading a newspaper. He took Max's advice. He was suspicious of everyone he saw, assuming they were just as suspicious of him.

He watched and waited, walked a bit, and chatted with an older man walking his dog about the curious loyalties canines have to their masters. Then he watched three boys kicking a football about the street, even offering a tip on improving their game. When over ninety minutes passed with no activity, he wondered if he was wasting his time. But then near noon, the door to the building opened and Erika Jaeger came out.

She went down the steps, nodded to a woman sweeping the pavement with a straw broom, and turned towards the Ku'damm. She strolled down the street, stopping to pluck a tulip from a flower bed, holding it to her nose and then putting it in the buttonhole of her blouse.

York was relieved she was walking. At least he didn't have the bicycle to contend with. He followed her, staying a discreet distance behind, hobbling on his cane.

The closer they got to the Ku'damm, the busier the street became. People were leaving their houses and apartments, businesses were emptying, and everyone walked towards the boulevard. Then York remembered the parade, having seen a poster at his hotel. That's where everyone was going, including Erika Jaeger.

He followed her into the crowd, feeling hidden among hordes of people, but struck by the obvious absence of men. There were old men, and teenagers, and small boys, but the vast majority of people were women and children of all ages. Since most men were in the armed forces, he wondered how strange he looked to the casual observer. He should have worn his uniform, but he thought it would be noticeable while he observed Jaeger's house. Now he regretted that he didn't.

When he reached the Ku'damm, he found a place on the pavement, just past a jewelry store, where he could see Jaeger clearly. He kept looking down the boulevard, along with everyone else, waiting anxiously for the troops to come, but keeping his eyes on Jaeger. He watched every move she made, and made a mental note of everything she looked at or the people she talked to. He wanted to know everything about her. And watching her was a good way to learn.

He had been studying her for about ten minutes when someone tapped him on the shoulder. He turned to see the green uniform of a policeman.

"You seem more interested in the crowd than the parade," the policeman said sternly. He was older, past military age, with white curly hair and round spectacles. He no doubt wondered why an apparently healthy man was not on the battlefield.

York smiled innocently. "Sometimes the crowd is more interesting."

The policeman wasn't convinced. "May I see your papers?"

York was alarmed, wondering what he did to arouse suspicion, but recovered quickly. He knew it was better to avoid scrutiny, and any potential confrontation, so he used a technique he perfected in France: distraction.

"I'm sorry, sir," he said, leaning heavily on his cane. "I was told General Rommel was here and would mingle with the crowd. I served under him in North Africa. I'm on convalescent leave and decided to come to the parade, hoping to see him. But it's just a rumor, I suppose."

York watched the policeman's posture relax, the tension starting to dissipate. "I know of no such rumor, although the General is in Berlin. Where did you hear it?"

York shrugged dumbly. "A man at the café told me. He served under the General in France a few years ago. But you're right, I suppose. How would he know?" He fingered his pocket. "Did you need my papers?"

The policeman studied him for a moment, looking at the cane, the way he leaned on it for support, the stiffness of his leg. He looked at York's clothes, the fit, the cut, the stitches, and then at his eyes, searching for a hint of fear or apprehension.

"No," he said with a wave of his hand. "Not necessary. Enjoy the parade."

As the policeman turned and walked away, York breathed a sigh of relief. Even though he was sure his papers were in order, he took pleasure in averting the risk. Policemen were unpredictable. Too old or sickly for military duty, they often took what little power they had to extremes. Sometimes it had catastrophic results.

Once the policeman had wandered away, York turned to Erika Jaeger, but she was gone. He spun his head in all directions, looking for her, but couldn't find her. He frowned, fearing he had lost her and wasted the entire day. He had wanted to see if she went to the cemetery. Now he lost his chance.

He pushed his way through throngs of people until he reached the curb. The troops were nearby, barely a block away, coming quickly. He heard their footsteps, pounding the pavement, the echo reverberating down the street as they approached. All eyes were upon them, arms raised, cheering.

The policeman he had avoided was a few meters away, controlling the crowd. York stepped back behind a heavy woman, turning his head away, hoping to avoid him and any additional unwanted questions, but the man saw him. He nodded, casting a curious glance, but took no action.

York decided to stay away from him. He ducked into the crowd, out of the policeman's sight, and moved back from the curb. He went to the entrance of a café, pausing to study the window display of kreppels, eyeing the donuts hungrily, and stood on the step, elevated above the pavement. From there he studied the people, keeping a wary eye for the suspicious policeman.

After scanning the crowd for a few minutes, occasionally distracted by the parade, he saw Jaeger standing about ten meters away. She had moved to where the crowd was sparser, and got a better vantage point.

He made his way to her, moving through the people, until he stood only a meter away. Cautiously, he stepped closer, standing behind her, the scent of her perfume lingering, her blonde hair cascading towards her shoulder, waving in the breeze. He watched the parade, Jaeger not even noticing him, her attention drawn to the troops goose-stepping down the boulevard, interrupted by groups of children in Hitler Youth uniforms and members of the Nazi party, lower-level city officials. As Jaeger watched the parade, York watched Jaeger.

She stayed for the entire procession, remaining until the crowds slowly dispersed. Then she entered the café, brushing against York as she walked past, and emerged a few minutes later with two packages, fresh kreppels peeking from the wrappings. She walked briskly to her house, York following at a distance, hobbling on his cane.

He returned to his vantage point, watching both the alley and the entrance to her apartment building. Mimicking his behavior from the morning, he occasionally walked away, traveled around the block, gambling he would miss her but hoping to avoid suspicion. She remained at home until early evening, when a taxi arrived at her residence. She left the building, carrying her violin case, and climbed into the car.

On Sunday morning, York took a taxi to the cemetery. The weather was beautiful, a bright June morning alive with chirping crickets, singing birds, and blooming flowers. There were few visitors at the cemetery, Sunday a day of rest for most. He made his way to the drop, cautiously observing the adjacent lanes and making sure no one saw him. When he was comfortable it was safe, her removed the finial and looked for the note he had left there.

Someone had retrieved it.

But it wasn't Erika Jaeger.

# CHAPTER 21

York arrived at the café early on Monday, but stood across the street and watched, searching for anything suspicious. He realized Amanda Hamilton was unpredictable; she had the entire weekend to consider his proposal. She might not do anything, never show, choose not to be involved in any way. Or it could be the other extreme. The Gestapo could be watching, waiting to swoop in and arrest him. He was taking a chance, but he knew that if successful, her information could prove invaluable to the Allies. But Max's warning also echoed in his ears: everyone was watching him.

Ten minutes later, he saw her walking down a side street towards the Ku'damm, still a block away, her body swaying in a light mauve summer dress. Her camera was absent, not dangling from her neck like it usually was, but a large pocketbook was slung over her shoulder. Maybe the camera was inside it.

It was a pleasant afternoon, and half the outdoor tables at the café were occupied. York eyed the patrons closely, trying to determine who, if any, was dangerous. There were two couples: an older pair sitting against the wall, and another closer to the street, much younger, maybe a soldier on leave with his wife. Two middle-aged women sat at a center table, talking continuously, their arms moving to emphasize their statements. A German policeman sat in a corner, by the pavement. He was a large man, threatening to burst the buttons on his shirt, hurriedly eating a leg of turkey, occasionally glancing at his watch. None seemed suspicious.

He looked at the pedestrians, mostly shoppers, wandering up and down the street, all intent on going somewhere. None seemed interested in what happened at the café. They looked in shop windows, chatted among themselves, and moved down the boulevard, faces changing as seconds passed to create a collage of humanity.

Amanda Hamilton reached the café, briefly looked around at those already seated, and chose a table at the very edge, against the railing that bordered the pavement. The adjacent tables were empty, the policeman sitting closest. She looked relaxed.

York watched a moment more. At least she had come; she wasn't going to ignore him. Even if she chose not to get involved, she would tell him in person. He respected that. Or she might be willing to cooperate. He scanned the surrounding area, and when convinced he wasn't in danger, crossed the street and went to her table.

"Good afternoon, Miss Hamilton," he said with a slight bow of respect. "May I join you?"

"Yes, of course," she said with a faint smile.

"You look radiant today," he said as he sat down, choosing a chair where he could see the street.

She wasn't expecting a compliment. She blushed.

"Are you ordering lunch?" he asked.

"Maybe some soup," she replied. "Nothing else."

He summoned a waiter and ordered two soups and two coffees.

"How were the concerts this weekend?" he asked, offering pleasantries while he ensured they weren't being observed. "I'm sorry I wasn't able to attend."

"They went well," she said. "Although we were a bit off on a Haydn piece. It will come in time, though."

He watched her closely. She didn't seem nervous, as he would expect if the Gestapo was about to

111

barge in. And she didn't seem angry. But she did seem incredibly attractive. That in itself could be dangerous. At least for him.

York leaned closer. "Have you thought about my request?"

Her expression changed, from buoyant to serious. "I did," she said. She paused for a moment, looking at the other patrons, and then to the pedestrians passing by. "If pressed for an answer when you approached me, I definitely would have said no."

The waiter arrived with their soup and coffee, and she put her hands in her lap, waiting for him to leave.

She tasted a spoonful of soup before she spoke. "I spent the weekend being observant. I studied this city I have grown to love, remembering that Nazi flags were draped from every building. I watched the troops at the parade on Saturday, and I discussed the Hitler Youth and what they teach our young with my stepson. I thought about all the Jews who were treated so horribly and now seem to be missing, their destinations unknown. When I looked closely, I didn't like what I saw. Then I very painfully realized that somewhere, somehow, and right before my very eyes, my husband had become a different person. Someone I don't really know, or care for, anymore."

He listened respectfully, letting her talk, sensing an inner turmoil she was struggling to control. She didn't know he was aware of her deteriorating relationship, and he decided not to tell her. He would listen if she wanted to speak, if she needed a caring ear, or he would pretend he didn't know anything, whichever made her feel more comfortable.

"Ultimately I decided that, not only am I not happy with my personal life, but I'm not happy with the world. I don't like what Germany is, and I don't like what we've become."

"So you've decided to help me?"

She frowned slightly and shrugged. "You're overestimating what I can do. If you think I can get information from my husband, you're mistaken. Quite frankly, I'm embarrassed to admit that I have no idea what he actually does. I know he often sees the Fuehrer, but I don't know what for. And even if I asked, I don't think he would tell me."

"You don't realize what you have access to," York said. "Not many people socialize with Adolph Hitler. But you do. For now, just share any conversations that might be valuable to the Allies."

She thought for a moment. "I'm not sure that will work. Those conversations occur behind closed doors, even at parties or social events."

"But you are willing to try?"

He watched as she studied him, assessing and evaluating. He wondered what she was thinking, what conclusions she would draw. But he knew as well as she did, that she was at a crossroads; she was about to make a decision that would forever change her life.

"Yes," she said softly. "I am willing to help. But to save my family, primarily my stepson, not betray them. I thought about the best way to do that, how to assist the Allies but still be true to myself."

He could see her struggle. She wanted to do what she thought was right. But she didn't want to hurt anyone. It was an honorable approach, but one that was rarely successful. He suspected that, in the end, she would be the one that got hurt.

She reached into her pocketbook. "I think I found the answer. I brought some photographs for you. These are just a small sample, but look through them and tell me if they're useful."

The pictures were of Hitler, Göring, Goebbels,

Himmler, and a few generals: Jodl, Keitel, von Manstein. And Eva Braun, Hitler's mistress. The backdrop was breathtaking mountain scenery, majestic peaks with shimmering lakes thousands of meters below.

"Where is this?" he asked.

"It's Hitler's retreat at Berchtesgaden. It's on a mountain on the German-Austrian border. I performed there at his birthday celebration last year."

York studied the photos. He was interested. The location could be identified, and potentially bombed. Hopefully when Hitler was there. He continued looking through the packet.

"The rest are from social events in Berlin, and show many generals and high-ranking officials. I wrote their names and dates in pencil on the back."

"This is excellent," York said, amazed at the cache of information.

A black sedan, the standard Mercedes used by the Gestapo, pulled up to the front of the café, slowly coming to a stop. A few seconds passed but no one got out. The vehicle just sat there, motionless.

York eyed it cautiously, trying to see those inside. There were many black Mercedes in the city, mixed among the Volkswagens. But there were also many Gestapo that drove them. He wondered what this sedan was doing at the café. A survey of the street showed several places to park, so why there?

He tensed, and looked behind him. Another black sedan was parked a block away, but he couldn't see inside. And across the street, a hundred meters down the road, was another Mercedes. Something wasn't right. He suspected a trap.

"What's wrong?" Amanda asked, noting his expression.

"The sedans," he said, glancing at each. "They

are all black Mercedes."

The front door opened and a soldier got out. He stood erect, at attention, and opened the rear door. An officer stepped from the back seat, tall and slender with a gaunt face and gray eyes, cold and observing. His uniform was black, a red arm band with a swastika on it. He paused, talking to the soldier that opened the door, as if giving direction, while the driver joined them.

Then the officer abruptly strutted towards York and Amanda, the two soldiers close behind him.

# CHAPTER 22

The Gestapo officer walked through the decorative iron railing that wrapped the outdoor tables, while the two soldiers stood and flanked the entrance. York watched warily as he came towards them and paused for a moment, as if considering a nearby table. York put down the photographs, relieved he wasn't there for them. Even the Gestapo ate lunch.

"Stay calm and change the subject to music," he whispered. He looked at the sedans parked behind him and across the street. He didn't see any occupants. They must be harmless. But he was annoyed that he hadn't noticed them before.

Amanda thought his behavior odd, but she still complied. She was used to seeing German officers; she didn't recognize the threat. But she did sense danger.

"The concert was sold out," she said as the officer approached. "That's one thing about Berliners. The world can be at war but they love concerts, the theater, cabarets. They want to be entertained."

The officer, a captain, stopped in front of their table, nodding politely, an interested expression on his face. "Photographs?" he asked, extending a hand.

York's heart began to race. He didn't want the Gestapo looking at the pictures. They didn't need the attention.

Amanda intervened. "Would you like to see them?" she asked, snatching them from York. "I'm an amateur photographer. I took them of the Fuehrer."

The captain took the pictures and started to leaf through them, shock registering on his face. He got to the fourth photograph and his eyes narrowed, his suspicion showing.

"You took these photographs?" he asked.

116

"Yes," Amanda replied. "At the Fuehrer's birthday party last year."

"Really?" the officer asked, not believing her, an amused smile erasing the skepticism. "And what were you doing at the Fuehrer's birthday party?"

"Performing," she said. "I'm a violinist. Amanda Richter."

The officer's eyes widened, his mouth opened. Once he recognized the name, his behavior changed quickly. He bowed, snapping the heels of his boots together. "Mrs. Richter, I'm honored. I'm sorry I didn't recognize you."

She smiled. "I like not being recognized," she said, waving away his apology. "Look at the rest of the photographs. The party was fabulous."

"I'm sure your husband is very proud," he said. He returned the pictures to the table, embarrassed to look, not wanting to offend Manfred Richter's wife.

He turned to York, looking at him curiously, an arrogant sneer returning to his face. "I'm sorry, sir. And you are?"

"Michael Becker," Amanda said, answering for him. "A music critic."

"Sergeant Michael Becker, sir," York said, saluting. "I'm on convalescent leave from wounds in North Africa." He motioned to the cane.

"Are you anxious to get back to the front, Sergeant?"

"Yes, sir," he said. He managed a weak smile. "I'm tiring of my staff position. It's not quite the same. If it weren't for my appreciation of classical music, and the ability to attend concerts and critique the performances, I'm afraid Berlin wouldn't suit me."

"Yes, sometimes I feel the same," the officer said, his eyes trained on York, still wondering what he was doing with Amanda.

"I'm hoping the Berlin doctors clear me for duty soon."

"As what?" the captain asked.

York shrugged. "As an ambulance driver, if nothing else. At least I could serve the Fatherland."

"Sergeant," the officer nodded. "Enjoy your lunch." He smiled at Amanda. "It was a pleasure, Mrs. Richter."

The captain walked to the café door, his guards remaining on the pavement. He went inside, grabbed a newspaper, and sat at a table near the window. When a waiter approached, he ordered lunch, paying no more attention to them.

"Amanda, you were marvelous," York said softly, expressing his admiration. "That could have been a nasty situation."

She grinned. "I told no lies."

"The music critic was a stretch."

"Not really," she said innocently. "Anyone can be a critic. He assumed you were a professional. But I never said you were."

While keeping a wary eye on the Gestapo, York glanced through the photographs again. There were about thirty in total. After a quick survey, he put them in his pocket.

"What do you have on your calendar for the next few weeks?" he asked, returning to their original topic.

She thought for a moment. "I think there's a party at the Goebbels. I'm not sure exactly when. I don't know if the Fuehrer will be there, but other leaders will."

"I'll coach you on what to listen for," he said. "It's primarily anything related to the military: weapons, troop movements, strategies. Anything."

"I'm not sure how effective I'll be," she said.

"I'm much better with photographs."

He looked at the soldiers standing guard. They were watching pedestrians, not interested in the patrons. Then he glanced in the café. The Gestapo officer was reading his newspaper, sipping a cup of coffee. A half-eaten piece of schnitzel and some noodles remained on his plate. With his eyes on the paper, he moved his fork into the noodles and took a mouthful.

York turned to Amanda. "There are about thirty pictures here. Do you have more?"

She smiled, her eyes lighting with laughter. "My hobby is photography. Do you think I have more than thirty pictures? I have thirty boxes."

"More like these?"

"Yes."

"What else?"

"Mostly birds, but I know you're not interested in them. And buildings, especially those that are architecturally significant. Some history and natural landscapes. I tried to document the ten years I've been here." She paused and her face hardened. "I have one box that is very important. I must get it to you as soon as possible, and you must send it to London."

"What's in it?"

"I'll bring the photos the next time we meet," she said evasively. "Only that box is unique. The rest are buildings and birds, and Berlin during the last ten years."

He was intrigued. "I want to know what's in that box."

"You will," she said, shifting uncomfortably.

He watched her a moment and decided not to press the issue. "Actually, I would love to see them all. But not for what you think. When the world isn't at war, I'm a history teacher. History and languages, German and French."

"Really?" she asked, surprised. "I never would have guessed."

He shrugged. "My livelihood, I suppose."

"I would love to show you more, if you think you're interested."

He looked at her, the smile brightening her face, her dark eyes twinkling. She was enjoying this. He suspected no one ever showed any interest in her, not even her husband.

"I would like to see the buildings, too. I love architecture. I guess you could say it's my hobby. But you'll have to teach me about the birds."

"We'll have to take a walk some time," she said. "There are many beautiful buildings right in this area."

The Gestapo officer rose, preparing to leave, reminding York of the potential danger.

"Do you have more pictures like those that you gave me?"

"Yes, probably a few boxes."

"Can we meet tomorrow? You can bring the photos from the box you told me about, and we can look at some more like these."

"I suppose," she said, a flicker of anxiety crossing her face. She looked up and down the street. "But this is not a good place. I know too many people in this area. I don't want to be seen with you repeatedly. It looks suspicious." She added softly: "Like we were lovers."

Their eyes met and for a brief instant he wondered if they had found something more than an interest in ending the war. Their gaze was interrupted by the Gestapo officer opening the door.

He paused at their table, bowed courteously and then motioned to the soldiers. They walked to a streetlamp on the edge of the pavement and taped a small poster on it so that anyone passing would see it.

When satisfied it wouldn't blow away in the breeze, a soldier opened the rear door and the officer climbed in. The soldiers got in the front, the engine started and the car pulled away from the curb.

York excused himself and went to the streetlamp to look at the placard, shocked at what he saw. He could see a face on it, and the warning: *Wanted by the Gestapo.*

He glanced at the other patrons, and then the passersby. No one had been watching the officer; they didn't see what he had posted. After making sure he wasn't being observed, he took the notice down and returned to the table.

"What's the matter?" Amanda asked, sensing something was wrong.

He showed her the poster. "I know this man. Have you ever seen him?"

She looked at it and shrugged. "No, not that I remember."

"We had better go," he said, glancing around. "I'll meet you tomorrow at nine a.m."

She rose from the table, reluctantly. "Can we make it ten? I have to practice."

"Ten a.m. How about at Olivaer Platz, where we met Friday?"

"Yes, that's fine. But wait, don't go yet."

"Why, what's the matter?"

"You said you have a favor to ask me?"

He had forgotten. But he didn't have time. Not now. He had to go. "I do. And it's very important to me. Can we talk about it tomorrow?"

"I suppose."

"The park is more isolated. We can spend more time together there."

"Until tomorrow," she said, smiling.

He paused. There was something he wanted to

121

say, even though he knew he shouldn't. But he said it anyway.

"You're a very special person."

He turned and walked away, his limp noticeable, a look of surprise draped across her face. He wanted to stay, but couldn't. It was too dangerous. He had to contact the man whose face was on the wanted poster.

It was Max.

# CHAPTER 23

Amanda left the café and walked back to her house, wondering if she was doing the right thing. She kept thinking about Michael, evaluating the risk but unable to see the reward. Maybe she could help shorten the war, a major contribution to mankind, but she didn't understand how some old photographs would do that.

Right or wrong, it took courage and soul-searching to do what she was doing. But she knew she couldn't turn back, even if she did change her mind. It had already gone too far. She was guilty in the eyes of the Gestapo and, if apprehended, it would cost her life. So whatever danger Michael confronted, she faced, also.

She knew the Gestapo poster was an unexpected danger, but she wasn't sure why. Her impression of Michael was that he was careful, methodical, with a calmness that came with being prepared. He wasn't prepared for the poster.

She had to make sure she never did anything to hurt him, even if protecting herself. That might mean only a few more meetings, just a handful of photographs, or revealing a dozen whispered words she might overhear. Maybe it meant a few more days, or weeks, but not more. But somehow she didn't think so.

When she looked at him she saw honesty and sincerity, compassion and commitment. He was handsome, with piercing brown eyes muted by an inner sadness just like hers, a vulnerability that was hidden and sheltered, with a mental wall built around his heart for protection. She knew he was much more than a British agent; he was a teacher, historian, musician, and someone with interests similar to hers.

He seemed to genuinely care about who she was

and what she did. And she couldn't remember anyone else in her life that ever did. Not her mother or father. Not Manfred or Kurt. And for reasons she couldn't explain, she knew her life was about to change dramatically. But she didn't know if it would be good or bad, happy or sad. She only knew it was because of him. And that she couldn't control it.

Neither Kurt nor Manfred were home when she got there. Not that Manfred would be. And not that she cared. She went to her photography studio and started going through files, choosing snapshots she thought Michael could use. She was sensitive to military information: generals, troops with insignia visible, locations, major contributors to strategy, and she weighted the selections to the more recent, using a scattered few to offer a timeline of Berlin. When she finished, she had chosen about forty photos to represent her collection, knowing she had many more if needed. She put them with the special box of photographs she had told Michael about, a box she always kept hidden.

She was about to put everything away when she remembered their conversation. He was interested in architecture, and even asked about birds. She went through her files again and picked a handful of Berlin buildings: the University of Berlin, the Pergamon Museum, the Brandenburg Gate, the Kaiser Wilhelm Memorial Church, and three bridges, the Castle Bridge, Frederick's Bridge, and the Kaiser Wilhelm Bridge. Then she scanned her collection of bird photographs, selecting six more.

She spent the remainder of the afternoon with her violin, drifting into the mystical world that music always took her. Her eyes closed as her fingers caressed the neck, the bow moving gracefully across the strings. She was always amazed at how much time passed while she played, immersed in a trance-like cocoon.

When she left the music room and went downstairs, she was surprised to see Manfred and Kurt in the parlor, immersed in discussion, a fatherly dissertation on the world and those who lived within it. Manfred frequently lectured Kurt, usually correcting some trivial shortcoming that was barely worth mentioning. He was extremely critical, which he had learned from his Prussian father, who probably treated him the same way. He had a drink in his hand, as he usually did before dinner, and already seemed a bit drunk.

"Manfred, I'm surprised to see you," she said sternly, the memory of their last encounter not a pleasant one. She found the mere sight of him revolting. "Are you having dinner with us?"

He knew she was uncomfortable, and he seemed to enjoy it. "Yes, I am," he said. "I can't resist Hannah's home-cooked meals."

Amanda sensed something wrong. Manfred was never home during the week. She searched his face for a reason, something that may have made him suspicious, but she found nothing. Did he know about her meeting with Michael? What made today different?

"I was just showing Kurt this poster," he said, dropping it on the table.

Amanda looked at it, struggling to hide her emotions, fighting to control herself. It was the same picture the Gestapo posted at the café; it was the man that Michael knew.

"Can you imagine that?" Manfred was saying to Kurt. "A British spy foolish enough to come to Berlin? Did he think no one would notice?" He started laughing, as if the enemy were all idiots, and sipped his drink.

Amanda felt beads of perspiration dotting her forehead. She sat down on the chair next to the sofa, and pretended to be interested. This was one of the opportunities that Michael had described. Listen, try to ask harmless questions, and remember all that was said.

"The Hitler Youth can find him," Manfred said, his words slurring just a bit. "Why waste the Gestapo's time? You'll enjoy it, Kurt. It's more fun than marching and map reading."

"How can you tell he's a British spy?" Amanda asked. "He looks innocent enough. He can easily pass for German."

"An informant told us," Manfred said. "He'll get caught, though. I give him two or three days at most."

Amanda looked at her stepson, memorizing the picture.

"Isn't this too dangerous for Kurt?" she asked, looking to her husband with concern.

"Of course not," Manfred scoffed. "If he sees the man, he tells the authorities. There's no danger in that."

"And I want to do it," Kurt told her. "It's like being a soldier."

"But this man is the enemy," Amanda said. "You need to be careful. I don't want you to get hurt."

Kurt ignored her and turned to Manfred. "What happens after he's caught? Does he go to prison?"

"Only if he's lucky," Manfred chuckled. "And smart enough to betray his friends. That's the problem; we think there's more than one."

# CHAPTER 24

York hurried from the café and took a taxi to the *Die Welt* newspaper office, arriving just after two p.m. He wanted to warn Max with a personal ad, the emergency contact method they established in Switzerland. Although Max was now in Berlin, and the ad was intended as an interim measure until he got there, York didn't know how else to communicate. It was a long shot, but he had to do something. He only hoped Max would see it.

He walked up to a window labeled *advertisements,* finding a bored clerk on the other side. The man was young, with the left side of his face horribly scarred, the eye missing and sewn shut, the cheek disfigured, skin pulled taut.

"Good afternoon," York said politely, pretending not to notice the man's mutilated face. "I want to place a personal advertisement in this evening's edition."

The clerk looked at a clock on the wall with his good eye. "You're too late. It has to be in by two p.m."

York was annoyed by his abruptness. "But the office is still open. And I'm only ten minutes late."

He shrugged. "Sorry, it's policy."

"But it's very important," York said.

"Can't be helped," the clerk replied. As if to emphasize his apathy, he picked up a newspaper and scanned the front page.

York hid his frustration, knowing the battle was lost. "All right, fine. I need to place a personal advertisement for tomorrow's edition."

The man put down the paper and again eyed the clock. "I hope it makes it," he said sarcastically. "I may have to push it through."

127

"And why is that?" York asked tersely, wondering if he had to bribe the man. "What's the problem?"

The clerk yawned. "No problem," he said, tiring of the game. He pushed a slip across the counter. "Fill this out."

York scribbled the message he and Max had agreed on in Switzerland: *Max, mother is looking for you.* He handed it to the clerk.

He read the note and stamped a date and time on the form.

"Are you sure that will be in tomorrow's paper?"

"I said it would, didn't I?" the clerk asked. He put the advertisement in a slot behind him, where several openings, all labeled, lined the wall. Then he sat down with his newspaper.

York remembered the agreement he and Max made in Switzerland. The ad would be in Tuesday's edition, which meant York would meet him at the Kaiser Wilhelm Memorial Church on Wednesday at noon. That's assuming Max saw it. If he didn't, York couldn't warn him until their scheduled meeting on Friday. And that might be too late.

York's mind was racing as he left the *Die Welt* office, still searching for answers. How was Max betrayed? He had just seen him on Friday. The Gestapo issued the wanted poster on Monday. Sometime over the weekend he had either been seen by someone who knew him, or betrayed by the quartet informant. And the only one he intended to observe, and possibly contact, was Albert Kaiser, the cello player.

York got another taxi and returned to his hotel. He was starting to feel caged and cornered. He mulled over what he knew, what he had determined was fact, trying to use logic to form conclusions.

Amanda Hamilton probably did not betray Kent or Max. If she did, York would already be in Gestapo custody, unless the Gestapo was watching him, trying to find Max. But he always ensured he wasn't being followed, so that seemed like a remote possibility.

He was sure Amanda did not offer information to Kent. She had been too shocked when York approached her, and too naïve when they met at the café. But she had shown she could be useful. Her photographs proved that.

Even though Erika Jaeger was at the cemetery, she didn't retrieve the note York left. Somebody else did. But she did have a secret, frequent food purchases on the black market and a constant need for money. As far as he knew, she had no contact with Max, at least not on Saturday because he watched her all day, but he didn't know about Friday night or Sunday. So she could be the informant, selling information to the Gestapo. And she could have betrayed Max.

The last member of the quartet was Gerhard Faber, the one-eyed viola player. York had barely thought about him. He planned to follow him on Tuesday, even though he would be at the Ministry of Armaments, his primary source of income. But he could still learn something about him, especially when he left work. York didn't know if he ever offered Kent information, could be the Gestapo informant, or if he knew who Max was. He remained a mystery, at least for the present.

And then there was one last possibility. Maybe Kent had betrayed Max before the Gestapo killed him. He could have been tortured, talked under duress, or tried to bargain for his own life. There was no way for York to know. But it was a plausible explanation.

He opened a bottle of whiskey and took a swig. He was confused and overwhelmed. There were too many possibilities, and too many people involved. He suddenly had tremendous respect for Kent, his predecessor. He had gotten farther than York did. At least he obtained information from one of the four.

He took another sip of whiskey. Nothing made sense. But he wasn't sure why.

# CHAPTER 25

York walked down the alley off the Ku'damm on his way to the interpreter's office, and saw a man across the street watching him. The man wore civilian clothes, but was young enough to serve in the military. He leaned against the brick wall of a tailor shop, smoking a cigarette. He might be waiting for clothes to be altered, or he may be waiting for a bus or a tram. Or he could be watching the alley that led to the tiny room where York and a few others translated documents for German Intelligence.

York entered the room, the décor unchanged: four tables with chairs, newspapers sitting on each. He sat in the same chair every time he went, as did the others. But this time when he entered the room, it was empty. For the first time since his arrival in Berlin, he sat in the room alone.

He pretended nothing was amiss, in case he was still being watched somehow. He got the notepad and pencil, and started to read the newspaper. It was the *London Times*, just a few days old, and a bit thinner than normal.

He scanned the paper, pausing to read some of the articles, most of which focused on the war. But as he read advertisements displaying clothes and food, upcoming sales at Harrods and Marks and Spencer, he was suddenly homesick, feeling very much alone. He put the paper down and rubbed his eyes, realizing how weary he was, sick of war, tired of pretending to be something he wasn't, and he only wished he could stand before his history class and tell heroic tales of the British Empire in days gone by.

After a few minutes of reminiscing, and daring to dream, he returned to the newspaper. The sooner he translated the personal ads, the sooner he could leave. There weren't many, and it took less than an hour. When he left the office and walked down the alley back to the Ku'damm, he saw the same man in civilian clothes, still leaning on the brick wall of the tailor's shop, smoking another cigarette, still watching the alley. It was only then that York realized that he was being watched. Only this time, it was from outside the room rather than from within. He caught the tram, and headed down the Ku'damm towards his hotel.

He met Amanda at Olivaer Platz at 10 a.m. She had her camera in hand as she anxiously led him to a bench tucked behind some shrubs at the far end of a walkway. Once they sat down, and ensured no one was nearby, she told him about Richter and the poster, sparing no details, recalling the conversation verbatim.

He was thoughtful for a moment, lines of worry creasing his forehead. "He used the word informant?"

She looked around nervously, recalling the conversation. She wanted to be certain. "Yes, he did."

"He didn't use a person's name?"

"No," she said. "I'm positive."

"If the informant was someone you knew, would he tell you?"

"Yes," she said with no hesitation. "Especially with Kurt listening. He would use the informant as an example of what good Germans do."

"Did he say anything about me, or did he just say there was more than one?"

She shifted on the bench. "He said, we think there's more than one."

York watched her for a moment. She was uncomfortable, afraid, probably questioning her decision to get involved. "Are you all right?"

She shrugged, an apologetic look on her face. "I don't know. I'm risking everything. Even sitting here is dangerous. What if someone I know sees us?"

He knew she was right. She was a famous violinist. And her husband was well known, highly placed in the Nazi party. They couldn't keep meeting in public places. Maybe once or twice, but it was too risky to do it continually. It was only a matter of time before they were discovered.

"My hotel isn't far," he said. "There's a back entrance, from the alley. You can enter and leave without being seen. We would be safe there."

She eyed him cautiously, wondering if he had an ulterior motive. "Not very proper. Especially for a married woman."

He rolled his eyes. "Amanda, you have to trust me."

She was quiet for a moment, contemplating the risks. "I do have some very important photographs to show you. And I even brought some of buildings and birds."

"I'm going to the hotel. Just follow me."

He didn't give her a chance to respond. He rose quickly and started walking, leaning on his cane. As he moved down the Ku'damm, he stopped to look in shop windows or nod to passing pedestrians, ensuring they weren't followed. He turned occasionally, keeping a wary eye on Amanda.

She followed twenty meters behind him, varying the distance. She paused at each block, taking photographs of birds, a large Nazi flag that the breeze blew over the face of a von Hindenburg statue, and a horse-drawn wagon loaded with produce, frozen in time, like it belonged to a different century.

York left the Ku'damm and used the street adjacent to the hotel, which was less traveled, and stood at the alley entrance until Amanda rounded the corner. He went down the lane to the rear of the hotel and waited for her, looking at the adjacent buildings to make sure no one was watching.

They walked up the rear stairs to the third floor. York's room overlooked the side street, not as exposed to the noise from the Ku'damm. He turned the key in the lock and opened the door, guiding her in.

The bed was on one side of the room, underneath a framed picture of the River Spree. It was mussed, partially made, making it obvious he wasn't expecting visitors. It lent credibility to his claim there was no agenda. Across the room was a window, faded burgundy drapes on either side. It was cracked open and the sounds of Berlin could be heard: delivery trucks, pedestrians, taxis, an occasional horn. An oval table with two chairs sat under it.

"This is nice," she said, although she really didn't mean it. She stood against the wall, her arms folded across her chest. Her face was stern, her body rigid.

York went to the table and pulled the chair away for her to sit down. "I want you to be comfortable."

She hesitated. "I've never been in a strange man's hotel room before."

He laughed. "I'm not a strange man. We're countrymen, remember? Come sit down and show me your pictures."

She smiled, seemed to relax a little, and sat in the chair he offered. Then, as she removed a package from her satchel, a serious look draped her face. "These photos are very important. I only have a limited number. I was prevented from taking more."

York's eyebrows arched as she laid the packet on the table. He looked at her.

She was upset, pale. "I don't think people realize what horrible things have been happening in Germany. For years."

He opened the packet. There were about fifty photographs. The first dozen showed Jewish shops, clearly marked, vandalized, their owners being shoved through the streets.

He looked up. "How old are these?"

"It started soon after Manfred and I were married, but treatment of the Jews got progressively worse. It became extremely harsh six or seven years ago. Then in 1938, it got violent."

"The Allied nations know," York said. "Which doesn't make it right, but many Jews immigrated to other nations."

"And where are those that remained?"

"I don't know," York said. "I know in France they were collected and sent east. Is there a settlement somewhere? Maybe in Poland?"

"Look at the rest of the photographs," she said. "They show the Jews being put in rail cars, crammed in like cattle, for an unknown destination. They were told they were being resettled."

"How do we know they weren't?"

"Look at the last fifteen or twenty photographs. They are camps where the Jews are kept. I saw them while returning from concerts. Most of the pictures I took were confiscated. These are all I have."

York was sickened by the photographs. They depicted emaciated people with vacant, hollow eyes, imprisoned behind barbed wire. "Do the German people know about this?"

She shook her head. "I don't think so. Everyone knows there are labor camps. But the rest isn't common knowledge."

York squinted, studying the photos more closely. "These people are being worked to death. Or worse, if that's possible. How can they not know?"

Amanda shrugged. "Maybe they don't want to

know. I haven't been able to live with myself since I saw this."

York put the photographs back in the packet, nauseous. The world knew how horribly the Jews had been treated since Hitler came to power. But they didn't know everything. He had to do something.

He got up and walked to a small stove with a single burner that was between a bureau and the bathroom door and made some coffee. "I'll get these photographs to London," he said. "The world has to know what's happening."

Amanda looked out the window, studying the people passing, looking relieved. It was as if the photographs were poison, and the sooner she handed them off, the easier it was to clear her conscience, the easier it was to accept that she had done her best, even if it wasn't enough.

York sat back down and gave her a cup of coffee. "Let's look at the rest of the photographs."

Amanda took the remaining packets from her purse. "I separated them. This stack is what you're looking for. And these are birds and buildings that I thought you might like to see."

York watched her. With the information about the Jews provided, she now seemed excited to share something she was proud of, something private and personal. He suspected no one took the time to look at her photographs, at least not as closely as he did.

"Let's look at these first," he said, grabbing the military photos. "Then we can have some fun."

He started going through the pictures. She had meticulously written the dates and any known information on the backs, just as she had for the previous ones. He was impressed. She had taken her role seriously and put a lot of effort into it.

"Are they worthwhile?" she asked as he

examined them.

He was shocked by the information offered. The photographs identified Nazi officials and their roles, leading military personnel and their assignments, troop locations and movements, and factories, including their purpose and address.

"They're fabulous," he said, mesmerized by the details. "Do you have more?"

"Oh, yes," she said. "I have boxes. But it takes time to identify everyone and record the information."

"They're very valuable." He was looking at the photographs of factories. They were in Berlin, with enough detail provided to target an air strike.

"I'll bring more next time," she said. "And the Goebbels party is next weekend. So I will listen closely and try to overhear something."

"I can't thank you enough," he said. "Actually, the Allies can't thank you enough." His face hardened. "Especially for the information about the Jews."

She looked away, not feeling very proud. "I'm doing this to help end the war before more horrible things happen to good people. And to prevent my stepson from being part of it. I couldn't bear to lose him. He's a child, quickly losing his innocence."

He was moved that she risked her life to save his. And he noted that she never mentioned her husband. "That's an admirable motive," he said quietly.

She wanted the topic changed and grabbed the other photographs. "Let's look at these. I can't wait to show you."

He was amused by her childish enthusiasm. She was excited, and couldn't wait to show him, anxious to share things she normally enjoyed alone.

"We'll look at the birds first," she said. "I've brought some of my favorites. The first is a Girlitz, with beautiful yellow feathers and black and white highlights. I like this one because he's a bit pudgy and looks so serious. It's almost like he knows I'm taking his picture and wants to show how important he is."

York laughed, finding her narrative amusing. He didn't know much about birds. But he suddenly wanted to learn.

"This one is a Neuntöter, white with brown wings. Look at the black around his eyes. It looks like a mask. He reminds me of a raccoon."

As York studied the photographs, he realized how much they meant to her, maybe more than music or the violin. And definitely more than her husband.

"Two more," she said. "This is a Gartenrotschwanz, with orange feathers and a black face. He looks angry when his picture is taken. And this is a Grünfink, which has a beautiful lime green coat."

She was finished, looking at him with apprehension, as if seeking approval.

"They're fabulous," he said, sincerely meaning it. "I'm interested in seeing more. You're extremely talented."

She blushed and turned away, but not before revealing a smile. "I wasn't sure if you would like the birds."

"I did," he said. "I meant it when I said I want to learn more about them."

"I can teach you," she said eagerly. "I love birds. Sometimes I watch them for hours."

"I would enjoy that," he said, noticing how her hair fell over her forehead.

"These are architectural," she said, displaying more photos. "You like buildings, don't you?"

"I do," he said. "I like to draw them."

She was surprised. "Really? I would like to see that sometime."

"I'm sure someday you will," he said, flirting,

but not sure why.

She smiled subtly and thumbed through the photographs. "I brought a selection. The University of Berlin, with its ornate window trim and Corinthian columns, the Pergamon Museum, which is very Greco-Roman, and the Kaiser Wilhelm Memorial Church, just at the end of the Ku'damm, with its signature steeple that stretches all the way to heaven."

York looked at the church and thought of Max. He wondered if he received the newspaper message. Would he be at the church rendezvous? If not, would he be at their Friday meeting? Or was he already in the hands of the Gestapo?

"I also brought some photographs of the Brandenburg Gate, which is a Berlin icon. It's neoclassical, composed of twelve Doric columns, and the sculpture on the top is called the Quadriga. It's a chariot pulled by four horses driven by Victoria, the Roman goddess of victory."

York studied the picture, intrigued by the image and the explanation. He imagined using it in one of his history classes. If he ever got back to London.

"And then I brought some pictures of bridges. They're my favorite, especially arch bridges. So I have the Castle Bridge, Frederick's Bridge, and the Kaiser Wilhelm Bridge, all beautiful, low profile arch bridges that rival those in Paris."

York studied the structures, simple but elegant, functional but beautiful. He could look at her photographs forever. She truly was an artist, the birds almost posing, the light captured perfectly, the angle used for the buildings and bridges displaying their graceful design and elegant construction.

He looked at her, smiling. "I really enjoy your photographs. You're gifted in many different ways."

She was pleased. "You're too kind. And very

flattering. But now it's your turn."

"What do you mean?"

"The favor you need. Tell me about it."

He hesitated, unable to scale the wall he'd built around his heart. He looked at his watch. "You had better not stay too long, at least not the first time you're here."

She studied him curiously. "A few more minutes won't matter."

He wasn't ready to share something so personal. Even though he wanted to.

There was an awkward silence, and Amanda realized the favor was very painful, difficult for him to discuss. She waited a moment more and, when he still seemed reluctant, she smiled and rose from the chair.

"When you're ready," she said. "I will listen. And I will do everything I can to help you."

He took a deep breath, not realizing how hard it would be. "Thank you," he said. "It was more difficult than I thought."

"No problem," she said, gently touched his arm. "When do we meet again? I'll bring more pictures."

He was seeing her with different eyes, even though he knew he shouldn't. He considered a risk that might not be worth taking, but he couldn't help it. "Let's meet at a secluded restaurant for dinner."

# CHAPTER 26

Gerhard Faber looked in the mirror and adjusted the patch over his left eye. He ran the comb through his hair for the third time, taming a rebellious strand that had strayed from the remainder and dangled over his forehead. Then he adjusted his necktie and left the bathroom, returning to his desk at the Ministry of Armaments, where row after row of drafting tables stood in a large, rambling hallway. Each was identical, elevated at a slight incline, with trays of rulers and squares. It was here that dozens of draftsmen turned engineers' sketches into blueprints used to build weapons in factories.

He sat on his stool, sighed with boredom, and returned to work. Sometimes he got interesting designs to draw, cannons or submarines or tanks. But for the last four days he had nothing but bolts: long bolts, short bolts, thick bolts, cotter pins and nuts. It was hard to stay awake, it was so monotonous. But he knew it wouldn't be long before something exciting crossed his desk, and that would make it all worthwhile.

Just before the end of his shift, with the blueprint of his last bolt completed, Faber's supervisor approached, carrying a handful of papers.

"Start on these next," he said. "It's for an artillery shell that pierces tank armor. And when you're done with that, we should have a new rocket design ready. It's a revolutionary weapon that could change the course of the war."

Faber leafed through eight sketches that made up the shell design. It wasn't an innovative weapon, but it would make a difference, especially on the Eastern Front. He started drawing, meticulously producing the fine lines and labeled dimensions that would support production. An hour later his shift ended.

He left work and rushed home, greeting his wife and three small children in their modest townhouse in the western section of Charlottenburg. After spending a few minutes with his family, discussing what the children did during the day, he went to his study and removed his treasured viola from the case. He sat before the music stand, looked at the Haydn piece that sat on it, and started to practice. He needed to improve. His last performance wasn't as crisp as it needed to be.

Three hours later he emerged, confident in his ability to play the piece to perfection. He had also mastered a Mozart work that challenged him, refining an annoying string of sixteenth notes that he had always found difficult.

He showered and dressed in a charcoal suit with matching tie, ensuring no wrinkles existed. Then he kissed his wife, promised not to be home too late, and hugged each child before hurrying out the door and down the steps.

He quickly traveled three blocks to the U-bahn, the underground transit, and took the train to the city center. He walked a few blocks, enjoying the July evening, and arrived at Hoffman's Restaurant just prior to 8 p.m. It was one of the most exclusive eateries the city had to offer, and he saw several Party officials mingling around the bar as he entered. He gave some money to the head waiter and was given a secluded table, hidden by broad-leafed potted plants, beside a window that overlooked the River Spree.

Astrid Braun, a Berlin socialite, arrived ten minutes later. Tall and slender, her black hair was cut close to the scalp, a large curl hanging over tropical blue eyes that studied all with a hint of amusement. Her indigo evening gown clung tightly to her frame, accenting her cleavage with a low neckline.

The head waiter, a pompous man with plastered hair parted in the middle, led her to the table. Faber rose to seat her, and she kissed him lightly on the lips before she sat down.

"I'm sorry I'm late," she said. "Have you been here long?"

"No, just a few minutes," he said, taking her hand in his. "I ordered a bottle of wine. I hope you don't mind."

"Oh, Gerhard, you spoil me."

The Brauns were an influential family prior to the turn of the century, but as the years passed their power had waned, as had their fortune, even though their name was still recognized by most. They lived in a large home, majestic in its day, but a little tired and in need of repair. Once home to servants as well as family, it was now inhabited only by Astrid and her mother.

Astrid's mother urged her to find a wealthy man to wed, someone who could restore the family fortune. Gerhard Faber seemed like the perfect match. But Astrid and her mother didn't know he was already married, or that he had three children. They didn't know he toiled each day as a draftsman at the Ministry of Armaments. They did know he played the viola for the Berlin String Quartet, but thought it was only a hobby. For Faber had told them he was a war hero who lost his eye on the Eastern Front, and that he ran the family business, continuing where a long line of wealthy industrialists had left off.

"How was your day today?" Astrid asked after the wine had arrived.

"Stressful, as always," Faber said, eyeing the entrée prices on the menu.

"Oh, my poor darling," she cooed. "What happened?"

Faber had a vivid imagination. It was one of his

gifts. "The Fuehrer called me this morning about a new artillery shell. He wants it delivered to the Eastern Front for the summer offensive."

"I don't know how you do it," she said, her eyes wide with fascination. "Daily calls from the Fuehrer, or from Göring or Dönitz. Isn't there anyone else they can turn to?"

He sighed and shrugged. "I suppose not, at least not for a critical issue. But then, I have proven myself over and over again. And they know that."

"But you work so hard," she said. Her hand dropped to his thigh, lightly caressing him.

He looked at his watch, conscious of the promise he made to his wife. He didn't want to get home too late.

"Is everything all right?" she asked. "That's the second time you checked the time."

"Yes, of course," he said. "But I have to go back to the office after we finish dinner. And I'll probably work through the night. It's exhausting. I'm never home anymore. I can't be. But I have to support the war effort."

"Gerhard," Astrid pouted. "Mother was hoping you could come to the house after dinner. She wanted to ask you something about some renovations."

"What renovations?" he asked, a sinking feeling in his stomach. He suspected the conversation would lead to money. And he didn't have any money.

"I'm not sure," she said, innocently batting her eyelashes. She leaned forward, her dress slipping away from her torso, letting his eyes drink the view. "It's such a beautiful house. Of course, it does need some work, we both realize that."

They each ordered fish, and another bottle of wine, and then coffee and Black Forest cake for dessert. Faber mentally added the bill as they were eating. It would take all the money he had, with little left over. But he had the rest of the week to get through. How could he ever afford to have Astrid Braun as a mistress?

He needed money badly. But there had to be a solution, a way to have both the worlds he wanted. His mind drifted to the new artillery shell.

# CHAPTER 27

York spent another morning translating personal ads, this time from the *Edinburgh Sentinel*. The room was occupied; the man who interpreted French newspapers was there for a few minutes before he rose and left. And then, after a moment or two, the door opened and the Russian interpreter entered, yawning, carrying a cup of coffee.

York found it amusing. He knew he was being watched, either from those within or from someone outside, but he wasn't sure why. There was no deviation to his office visits; he did nothing to arouse suspicion. He shrugged, reminded himself of Max's warning that everyone watched him, from kindergartners to octogenarians, and behaved accordingly.

He left the office, had a cup of coffee and a kreppel at a café down the street, and arrived at the Kaiser Wilhelm Memorial Church fifteen minutes before noon, dressed in his German sergeant's uniform, gazing at the Gothic spires that stretched so majestically to the clouds. He remembered the photographs Amanda had taken, and he could imagine her walking the grounds, trying to find the proper angle, staring through the lens until the light was just right so she could capture the perfect image.

He walked around the block three times but saw no one suspicious, no one lurking about waiting for him or Max. It was just a typical week day in Berlin. Women shopped at the grocer, older men and foreign workers went to factories or banks or shops, a few younger men in uniform enjoyed their leave. Policeman walked their beat and children played. An old man with spectacles sat on a bench and scanned a newspaper.

And wives waited for husbands to return from the war.

York entered the church to find the interior awe-inspiring, portraying humility, serenity, and love for God. It was quiet, only a handful of people scattered among the pews, all praying silently, while a few wandered the corridors. He stood still for a moment, his head bowed, respectful, and said his own prayers, private and pensive.

None of the churchgoers noticed him, all immersed in worship. He looked at each in turn, ensuring Max was not among them, and that none were watching him. They offered an interesting cross-section of the city's residents, skewed toward the elderly, seeing their second world war, hearts broken from lost loved ones.

He watched them a few minutes more, the image captured for a future history class, assuming he was ever fortunate enough to teach again. He realized they probably prayed for sons or daughters or grandchildren, wishing for a world that had vanished, hoping desperately that it returned.

He stepped away quietly, walking through the church, watching the shadows and searching for faces that weren't really there. After finding no trace of Max, he sat on a bench where he could see the entrances. He waited forty-five minutes, but no familiar faces appeared. He even went outside and circled the exterior, scanning the adjacent streets.

Max had not come.

The restaurant Amanda chose was on a side street shaded by linden trees, away from the main boulevards, tiny but private. Each table was sheltered and somehow secluded, offering the perfect private dining experience. It was owned and operated by the family that lived in the house attached to it, the food fresh and well-prepared, the ambiance serene. It was just the place for those who didn't want to be seen, and was known for the owner's discretion as well as the good cuisine.

Amanda arrived looking very different. She wore more cosmetics than normal, a hint of rouge, some eyeliner and lipstick. Her hair was pinned high on her head, exposing a graceful neck and pearl earrings, with a delicate necklace that matched. A close-fitting green dress, accented with white lace, showed off a figure she normally hid.

"You look stunning," he said once they were seated.

She blushed. "I was trying to change my appearance so I wouldn't be recognized."

He could tell she appreciated the compliment. He wondered if she got any at home.

When the waiter arrived, he ordered wine and they scanned the menu, each choosing Sauerbraten. They chatted through dinner, discussing winter concerts planned in Vienna and Budapest, the spring concert in Amsterdam. They talked about Berlin, and compared it to London and Edinburgh. They chatted about music, focused on the masters: Beethoven and Bach, Mozart and Chopin. As dinner ended and Bundt cake arrived for dessert, they discussed their next meeting, selecting Friday afternoon at York's hotel so Amanda could prepare for Goebbels's party.

"I think now is a good time, don't you?" Amanda asked.

"A good time for what?" York wondered, puzzled.

"We've had a marvelous dinner, and we managed to discuss a variety of interesting topics, but we still haven't gotten to the favor you need. Or the story behind it."

York studied her face, sincere and compassionate, concerned and cooperative. She was more energetic and enthusiastic than when he first met her, less inclined to dwell in the past, more interested in the future. His as well as hers. And now she wanted to help him, even if it meant only listening.

He hesitated, not knowing how to share or what walls to tear down. "I don't know where to start," he said, fumbling for words.

She covered his hand with hers, lightly caressing. "The beginning is usually best."

He was distracted by how soft she was, the delicate fingers gently stroking the back of his hand, barely touching. A friendly gesture meant to reassure him, it could easily be confused with affection. At least by him.

He decided to trust her, forcing the words. "I married young," he said softly, collecting his thoughts. "We were childhood sweethearts, neighbors growing up. I think we knew each other from the time we were infants." He smiled, reminiscing. "We probably shared the same baby stroller."

Amanda laughed. She enjoyed the glimpse into his past. Her eyes encouraged him to continue.

"We were very happy in the beginning, enjoying our new life. I started teaching and she worked for the newspaper. We found a small flat in London, not far from Hyde Park. A little over a year later, we had a daughter. For me, it was a dream come true."

He hesitated, looking pained, conscious of the baby Amanda had lost. "A family was very important to me," he said softly. "I was an orphan, adopted while still a baby. I never knew my mother and father. But I am eternally grateful to the people that raised me, they truly are my parents. There's just always a bit of emptiness, sort of an incomplete feeling, because I don't know where I came from. So when my daughter was born, I wanted to make sure she never felt that void. I wanted her to be totally engulfed in her father's love."

Amanda listened closely, her gaze intense, her fingers still caressing his hand. Maybe she was reliving her own childhood, seeing similarities to his. Or maybe she remembered her elation when she learned she was expecting her own child. Only to have that happiness snatched away.

She smiled, hiding her pain. "It sounds idyllic," she said, urging him to continue.

"It was at first. But as so often happens with those that marry young, we grew apart as the years passed. It wasn't long before we didn't seem to fit as well as we once did."

"Did you realize it was happening at the time?" she asked. "Was it something you could have corrected?"

"I'm sure I recognized it and knew it wasn't right, but I didn't want to believe it was really happening. And then the war started. I enlisted right after the invasion of France. Since I speak French and German fluently, I ended up in clandestine operations. I went to France in July of 1940, dropped via parachute, and remained until last autumn. That's when I was wounded. I escaped to Switzerland, recovered from my injuries and was sent here."

"So you haven't seen your family in three years?"

"No, I haven't," he said sadly. He looked away, sighing. "But it's worse than that."

She cringed. "What happened?"

He paused, his eyes moist. "Shortly after I arrived in France I received a letter from my wife. It seems she no longer loved me. She hadn't for some time. She had taken up with my best mate, a childhood friend, and they had run off to start their life together."

She squeezed his hand. "I'm so sorry."

He nodded, silently expressing his thanks. "It was no surprise that I lost her. When I thought about it, it was a long time coming. But what is so painful, what I can't seem to cope with, is that she took my daughter. And she never told me where they went."

A tear dripped from his eye, his hand hurriedly moving to hide it. "And now this is all I have of her." He reached into his pocket and withdrew a faded photograph, wrinkled, a bit damaged. He handed it to Amanda. "I was hoping you could touch it up a bit."

She was moved by his story, her eyes moist, sharing his tears. "I'm sure I can fix it," she said, fingering the paper, testing the quality. "It won't be perfect, but it'll be better." She studied the photograph and smiled. "What a beautiful little girl. How old is she?"

"She's twelve years old now." Then he chuckled. "But she acts like she's thirty."

"What's her name?"

"Elizabeth."

# CHAPTER 28

York went to the cemetery on Thursday morning. As he walked in the entrance, he passed an elderly man wearing a medal from the Great War, probably visiting an old comrade's grave. York nodded with respect and then continued down the cobblestone lane, sheltered by trees, and greeted a woman with a baby carriage. There were a lot of baby carriages in Berlin, pushed by women whose husbands might not be coming home.

He was more alert than usual. The poster issued for Max made him wonder what else the Nazis knew. Maybe they were looking for him. Or they might know about the drop, or the quartet member who was selling information. Maybe they knew about Max's other spy networks, too. Or they might not know anything at all.

He strolled past the lane where the drop was, feigning grief and trying to look like he had reason to be there. He went two lanes farther before turning, passing a mother holding a little girl by the hand and then an older woman, sad and alone. Walking down a row of tombs, markers, and mausoleums, he saw no one that wasn't there to show their respect for the dead, people with sorrow etched in the wrinkles of their faces, loss and emptiness in their eyes. They made him think about Amanda. It must have been hard to lose a baby, especially after trying to conceive for ten years.

He rounded the last corner, a lane away from where the drop was. As he exited, turning towards the entrance, he saw Erika Jaeger on her way out, just as he had the week before. Maybe she did go to the drop on Saturday, but after her concert was over.

He stopped, wondering whether to follow her, ignore her, or approach her. Any of the options were dangerous, although in varying degrees. But he had learned through the years that doing nothing normally led to his greatest regrets.

"Miss Jaeger," he called boldly. "May I speak to you for a minute?"

She froze, her back to him, and then turned slowly. Her face showed no sign of recognition, only fright. "Excuse me?" she asked, her voice quivering.

He motioned to a bench that was shaded by trees, flanked by shrubs. It was private. "I need to speak to you. Please, let's sit down."

She stared at him, her eyes were wide, her face flush. She stood rigid, rooted to the ground, unable, or unwilling to move.

"Come," he said. "I won't hurt you."

She hesitated a moment more and then reluctantly came to the bench, sitting at the far end. "What do you want?"

"I have seen you in the cemetery before, Miss Jaeger. We may be here for the same reason."

She looked at him quizzically, no doubt wondering how he knew her. "I don't think that's possible."

"We are here the same day of the week."

She shrugged, still guarded. "That may be true. I come every Thursday."

"And Saturday, also?"

"Sometimes, although not often. But on Thursday, I work afternoons. So I come here in the morning."

"I still think we have a common interest."

"I'm not sure what it could be." She searched his face. "Were you in the army?"

York was confused. Maybe she wasn't there for the drop, or she was hiding that she was. "Yes, I was," he replied cautiously.

"Did you know my husband Wilhelm?"

He felt a sickening feeling in his stomach. He was wrong. And now he could jeopardize the entire operation. As well as his life. "No, I didn't know Wilhelm," he answered softly.

She looked at him strangely, wondering what he wanted. "My husband Wilhelm was killed in the war. I come here to visit his grave."

York turned away, thinking of a different path. It was too late to change direction. But he might be able to salvage something. Jaeger had access to valuable information, and he suspected she was doing something illegal, which is why she bought food on the black market. Maybe the threat of extortion would make her cooperate, assuming she wasn't the Gestapo informant. He had to be careful, phrase each sentence with hints and innuendos. It was the only thing he could do. He didn't have any facts.

"And you have my deepest sympathies," he said delicately. "My thoughts and prayers are with you."

"What do you need to talk to me about?"

"A business arrangement," he said.

Her eyes narrowed. She was less afraid, more suspicious. Then she gasped. "Are you the Gestapo?"

"No, I'm not," he said slowly, with just a hint of distaste. The fear in her eyes proved she wasn't the Gestapo, and he knew why she was afraid of them. He had to use that fear to his advantage.

She was frustrated, confused, the fear waning. "I don't see how we could have anything in common. Or any need to conduct business."

"But I assure you we do."

She was quiet for a moment, and then her eyes lit with alarm. "Are you an informant?"

"No, of course not."

She looked at him skeptically. "How do I know

you're telling the truth?"

He paused, letting the silence increase the tension. "Because I'm an Englishman."

Her eyes widened and she stood abruptly, sensing danger, and started walking away.

"Miss Jaeger," he called. "You know my secret. But I know your secret, too."

She stopped and stood still, her back to him.

After a few tense seconds, she turned and walked back to the bench, sitting closer to him. She surveyed the landscape, showing caution, ensuring no one was watching. When convinced they were alone, she spoke. "What do you want?"

"Information," he said softly. "Troop movements, supply shipments, weapons transfers. The logistics that fuel the war effort. In return, I will pay you handsomely."

She was quiet, considering his offer. "And if I say no?"

"I can't afford to take chances. I will either expose you or kill you. I'm not sure which."

She was cornered, like a caged animal. But she stayed calm, calculating. "What if I call the authorities?"

"You won't," he said firmly, even though he wasn't so sure.

She looked away, trying not to show her thoughts. "What if I don't need money?"

He knew she was bluffing. Money buys food. And she bought food on the black market because she had extra mouths to feed. She was hiding people in her home. They were probably Jews.

"I know that you do," he said. "So you can help the people you're hiding."

She gasped, and her eyes signaled surrender. She glanced at the neighboring walkways, making sure no one was coming. "Please, don't tell anyone. Good people will die if you do."

"I promise you I won't," he whispered, pleased he had guessed correctly. He paused, scanning the cemetery grounds, and then continued. "So it seems we have a business arrangement after all."

"I don't know what I can do. I can't steal documents. I would get caught."

"For now, remember what you hear and what you see, documents that cross your desk. I will find a way to use it."

York knew she was anxious and afraid; she understood the risk. But he suspected she hated the Nazis. And those hidden in her home proved it.

"Let's meet on this bench next Thursday at 10 a.m. That gives you some time to collect information."

"And you will pay me?"

"Yes," he said. "I will pay you well. In time I will do more."

Her interest was piqued. "And what is that?"

"I will try to help those you have hidden."

She didn't want to acknowledge he was right. But she was definitely interested. "What is your name?"

"Michael."

"Good day, Michael. I will see you next week."

She rose from the bench and started to walk away, headed for the bicycle that was locked by the iron fence that bordered the cemetery.

"Erika," he called as she walked away. He used her first name to show they were friends.

She stopped and turned, a questioning look on her face. "What is it?"

He studied her for a moment, slender and fragile yet brave enough to risk her life to save others. He admired her courage. And her talent. "I think you are a fabulous violin player. I absolutely adore your performances."

Her mouth opened in surprise, but then broke into a smile. "Thank you," she said, blushing, her appreciation evident. "Thank you very much."

# CHAPTER 29

York watched Erika Jaeger leave the cemetery, climb on her bicycle, and pedal down the boulevard. She talked to no one, even though there was a policeman and two older women standing near the entrance. He didn't know what she would do when he could no longer see her, but he was sure she wouldn't approach the authorities. She had as much to hide as he did.

He had assessed two of the string quartet, Amanda Hamilton and Erika Jaeger. Neither was the potential spy, although he had brought them into his network and would be obtaining information from both. He knew neither was the informant. That left Gerhard Faber and Albert Kaiser, one informant, one spy.

After a quick walk down the adjacent lanes, pausing to read a headstone or two and ensuring that no one was watching him, York went to the drop. He removed the finial on the iron post, surprised to find a piece of paper tucked inside, folded and creased into a small rectangle.

He looked around quickly, making sure he was alone, and shoved the message in his pocket. Shielding his movements with his body, he replaced the cap on the fence post. He then strolled to the bench he and Jaeger had shared, hidden among the trees and shrubs that defined the edge of the cemetery.

He sat down and waited for a moment, feigning interest in a bird that sat on a nearby branch. When no one approached, he furtively withdrew the paper from his pocket and unfolded it.

WHERE HAVE YOU BEEN? I HAVE DRAWINGS FOR ARTILLERY SHELL

THAT PIERCES TANK ARMOR. I WILL
DELIVER ON SATURDAY. LEAVE
MONEY.

York sat back smugly. The riddle was solved.
The spy was Gerhard Faber, the one-eyed viola player
who worked at the Ministry of Armaments. Assuming
he was correct about Amanda and Erika, and York was
certain he was, that left cello player Albert Kaiser as the
informant, the grandfatherly man with the shock of
white hair. The man Max went to observe just before
the Gestapo issued the wanted poster.

York had never been comfortable with the drop
at the cemetery, its location selected by Kent and a
potential contributor to his demise. How did he know it
wasn't a trap? He had prepared his own location, even
though it was temporary. He took a scrap of paper from
his pocket and scribbled the following:

PAYMENT IN ADVANCE TO SHOW
GOOD FAITH. DROP LOCATION
CHANGED. LEAVE PLANS IN REAR OF
BERLIN THEATER ON KANTSTRASSE.
FOURTH BLOCK ON GARDEN WALL IN
PARKING LOT, BEHIND LINDEN TREE.
LIFT CAP. BLOCK IS HOLLOW.

He returned to the drop, again made sure no one
was watching, and removed the finial from the
fencepost. He stuffed some Reichsmarks into the
opening and replaced the cap. Then he turned and
walked away, hurrying to the taxi he hoped was still
waiting for him.

Friday morning was cloudy, with a slight drizzle
that cleared just as York left his hotel. It was several

long blocks to the café on Kantstrasse, near
Savignyplatz, but he decided to walk. His leg was
getting stronger, he could feel it, but he still
exaggerated the limp to prove his cover.

He enjoyed the Berlin streets. The people were
interesting, a collage of young and old, immigrant and
resident, teacher and student. The outdoor cafes rivalled
those in Paris, with lace iron tables and chairs. And the
building designs were bold and dramatic, granite and
sandstone, balconies and buttresses, strong and defiant,
promising to last a thousand years even if the Third
Reich did not.

The walk took him over thirty minutes, but he
found it invigorating. Now he would find out if Max
was safe, having eluded the Gestapo or not even aware
that they were looking for him, or if he had vanished,
just like Kent, his predecessor.

The café occupied a century-old building with
an arched doorway. The windows displayed various
dishes, from kreppels to fruit to bread. A dozen
wrought iron tables were scattered about the pavement,
where a teenage waitress wearing a white apron was
wiping the last remnants of rain drops from those that
weren't occupied.

York glanced at the tables, saw no sign of Max,
and walked inside. The café only had a few customers.
An elderly couple near the entrance chatted with a
waiter, and a group of teenagers sat in the back.

He went outside and chose a table where he
could see the street and ordered a coffee and kreppels.
He waited, scanning a newspaper, keeping a wary eye
on the street, hoping to see Max's familiar face.

The outdoor tables were nearly empty. The
earlier rain, and the time of day, midway between
breakfast and lunch, left most patrons grabbing a coffee
or doughnut and continuing on their way. But a few still

enjoyed the morning, sipping coffee and snacking, engaged in casual conversation.

An older man and a young boy sat on the other side of the café, a workman on break near the street, and two women against the café wall. York wasn't concerned; they all seemed harmless.

He waited for fifteen minutes, pretending to read the paper but still baffled by who betrayed Max. He recalled their last discussion, remembering almost every word. Unless something drastically different had happened only Albert Kaiser, the man he now suspected of being the informant, could have turned him in. And York could not explain how.

A Berlin policeman peered in the café window, studying the pastries before walking inside. His green uniform was a bit baggy, his blond hair feathered with gray. Large black spectacles, looking out of place on his slender face, covered his blue eyes.

He emerged a few minutes later holding a plate with three or four Schmalzkuch and a cup of coffee. He paused, unable to decide whether to sit down or continue on his way. A moment later he walked up to York's table and pointed to the empty chair.

York looked at him, annoyed, and motioned to the empty tables. "I'm waiting for someone," he said.

The policeman glanced around, acted as if he were about to leave, then sat down abruptly. "How are you, Michael?"

York looked at him with surprise. "Max?"

"Yes," he said quietly. "It's one of my Berlin disguises. Don't you love it? I was actually directing traffic the other day."

"It's a good one. I didn't recognize you, and I've known you for years. Have you seen the posters?"

"Yes, I did, fortunately before it was too late. So I haven't ventured out unless wearing my policeman's uniform. I'm in a boarding house a few blocks away."

"I used the classifieds, but I guess you didn't see it."

He frowned. "No, I'm sorry, but I didn't even think to look."

"Did Kaiser betray you?"

He looked surprised. "No, he couldn't have. I watched his apartment for an afternoon, but he never left. He may have looked out his window and saw me. But why turn me in? He doesn't know who I am."

York was disappointed, his theory discounted. He searched for another explanation. "How about Kent? Maybe Kaiser saw you with him, and then saw you watching his apartment?"

Max thought for a moment. "I did meet Kent here in Berlin a few times. But it was always in a secluded location. I doubt Kaiser could have seen us. Maybe Kent betrayed me after he was captured?"

"But then how did they get your photograph?"

Max shrugged. "I have no idea."

"Could it be an informant from one of your other networks?"

"No, I don't think so. Most communication is through drops. I only meet two contacts in person. And I trust them both."

"Maybe you were followed."

"I could have been, last weekend, or maybe Friday. But by whom?"

York sighed. "I don't know. I'm just trying to make sense of it all."

"Maybe it was Kaiser," Max said. "Although I'm not sure how."

"So what do we do now?"

"I stay in disguise for a few weeks, maybe a month. By then the wanted posters will be gone and forgotten. If they aren't already."

York wasn't convinced. "Just be careful with your other networks. Especially if you don't think it was Kaiser."

Max was silent, watching pedestrians walking down the street, the sun peeking from behind the clouds to promise a brighter day. "What progress have you made, old boy?"

York summarized the week and its successes: Amanda and her photos, especially the information about the Jews, the drop and Faber's message, Jaeger's secret and possible cooperation.

"If you give me the photographs, I'll get them to Switzerland. I'm sure London will be interested in the Jews. Nasty business, isn't it? And don't bother sorting through them. Headquarters can do that. Get the negatives, too."

"What do you make of Faber and his offer?"

"I'm not sure," he said skeptically. "But be careful. I'm afraid if he doesn't get what he wants he'll switch from spy to informant. Maybe that's what happened to Kent. So I think it was a good idea changing the drop."

York was pensive. "That's something I hadn't thought of. The person offering information could also be the informant."

"And I do think Faber could be both. But so could Jaeger."

"I don't think so," York said. "She has too much to lose."

"But you don't know that. You assume it."

"I think the food she bought on the black market proves she's hiding someone."

"Probably Jews," Max said.

"Do you think we can get them out?"

"Yes, I think so. But it won't be easy, so don't make any offers yet. Just tell her you might be able to help."

"What about Kaiser? Should we rule him out as the informant?"

"I think Faber playing both roles is more likely. But why don't you approach Kaiser and see what you think? Just keep the conversation innocent; don't do anything to make him suspicious."

"I'll make contact tomorrow."

Max stood up and prepared to go. "We should meet more often. At least for the next few weeks. I'll come to your hotel Monday about 10 a.m. You can tell me what happens with Kaiser then."

# CHAPTER 30

Amanda came to York's hotel room around 1 p.m. She grinned as she strolled in, the sadness that had consumed her the last eight weeks slowly starting to dissipate. Her eyes were brighter, housing a glimmer that showed a love of life, and the corner of her lips had turned to form a permanent smile. A bounce showed in her walk, enthusiasm in her expression, and York was beginning to see the woman described in the information he received in Basel, just before the train accident.

"Hello," she said as she walked to the table. "I brought two coffees and some more photographs."

She was attractive on many different levels. Her characteristics were common: black hair, a bit wavy and not quite to the shoulder, dark eyes, a nose that made a slight upturn at the end, and a petite frame. Her cheekbones were high, her neck graceful, one ear just a tad higher than the other, just like her eyebrows; it was something no one would ever notice unless they studied her very closely, like York did. Although all very average, they somehow blended with her optimism and passion for life to make her incredibly attractive.

She brought pictures she had taken at the wedding of a Nazi official. Himmler was there, and Goebbels, but not Hitler. There was also a sprinkling of industry leaders, the heads of I.G. Farben and Friedrich Krupp AG, and a few other conglomerates. More interesting were the military leaders not normally in the public limelight, generals and field marshals.

"I showed your pictures to my contact," York said. "He was impressed, and would like all the photographs you have. He'll get them to Switzerland, and then to London, where they can be evaluated. He

165

was especially interested in the information about the Jews."

"Hopefully something can be done in time to help them," she said, a helpless sorrow crossing her face.

"At least the world will know."

"If they don't already," she said, wondering.

"Will you be able to give me all your photographs?"

She was hesitant and gave him a wary look. "I have thousands. Ten years' worth. Are you sure you want them all?"

"Yes, but don't take risks removing them from your house. Maybe whatever you can carry when you come to see me. Just like you have been doing."

She studied his face, a hint of uncertainty clouding her eyes. "Most of my pictures are of birds, with others of buildings and bridges or trees or cats or dogs. The vast majority aren't military or political. I don't think anyone would be interested in them except me." Then she smiled. "And maybe you."

He hadn't thought of that. She primarily took photos of nature. The Nazi elite were just mixed in. "Some of the bridges might be important, but not many of the buildings – other than government or military structures. And factories, like those you showed me last week, especially if you remember the locations. But not birds or trees or anything like that. Why don't we start with the military pictures, like those you brought today?"

"All right, but only the photographs. No negatives." She paused, her eyes trained on his, hoping he would understand. "I can't part with them. They're a part of me. Like the passion that goes into the violin."

"Of course," he said softly, feeling like he violated a trust. "I'm sorry. It was stupid of me to suggest it. The photographs are enough."

She leaned back in the chair and the smile faded from her face. He could see the load she carried, the stress she bore. She wasn't accustomed to danger and deceit. And now she was mired in it.

"I can see where this ends," she whispered.

"And where is that?"

She turned away, gazing out the window, studying a bird hiding in the leaves of a tree. "I will have to be smuggled out of Germany by you and your friends."

"We don't know that," he said, although he certainly knew it was possible. "Our goal is to end the war, and we're working towards that. It could happen soon, or come much later. We'll do the best we can."

She continued looking out the window, not facing him or making eye contact. "I wouldn't be opposed to that," she said. "If that's what it came to."

He suddenly realized how terribly lonely she was, trapped in a foreign country, married to a man who didn't love her. He felt sorry for her, imagining the turmoil erupting inside her. Do you betray your husband because he was unfaithful? What allegiance do you have to your adopted country, home for ten years? What would the ultimate outcome be? Was it worth the risk? There must be a thousand questions racing through her mind. Probably foremost among them was what would happen if she got caught.

"Let's talk about the party," he said, changing the topic. "Do you like to go to them?"

"Yes, normally I do. There's good food and entertainment. It's always fun. But I'm a little apprehensive this time."

"Don't do anything different. Act like you always do, socialize with who you normally would. Be attentive to what you overhear, and eavesdrop on conversations with military or political content. Anything that might be related to the war. But don't take any chances."

She nodded, her expression tentative. "That sounds easy enough. Although I told you, the important discussions are normally behind closed doors."

He shrugged. "If you don't hear anything valuable, it doesn't matter. It's just an opportunity. There will be others. Are you bringing your camera?"

"No, not this time. But I will have my violin. I'm performing. Just a few pieces. Maybe thirty minutes. There are other performers as well."

He looked at her, so talented, so impressive. She was like a diamond with a dozen different facets, altered each time the light changed. If it were another time or another place he would see her with different eyes. But he couldn't afford to do that now.

"I have something for you."

"And what is that?"

She handed him the photograph. "I did the best I could with it."

He looked at the image, his heart consumed with contrasting emotions, joy and sorrow. "Thank you. You did a fabulous job." He smiled through the sadness in his eyes. "I just love her so much."

Amanda hugged him. She held him tightly for a few minutes, longer than she probably should, and then released him slowly, almost as if she didn't want to. "I'll be back Monday afternoon. I want to hear all about Elizabeth."

# CHAPTER 31

York had nothing to do on Saturday so he took the U-bahn to Potzdamer Platz, which was close to the apartment of Albert Kaiser. He got off the underground, climbed the steps to the surface, and found a circular intersection busy with streetcars, taxis, bicycles and pedestrians, all merging, avoiding traffic, and then going in different directions. The circle was surrounded by buildings five or six stories high, the architecture grand and ornate and built in the last century. The ground floors housed shops, restaurants, and outdoor cafes; apartments occupied the upper elevations. Clogged with pedestrians, some hurrying down the boulevard intent on their destination, others casually looking in store windows, Potzdamer Platz formed the intersection of the many neighborhoods that defined Berlin.

On the southwest corner stood a majestic building constructed of brownstone, six stories high with turrets at the corners and decorated with patterned fascia and cherub cornices. A restaurant, a book store, a butcher, and a dress shop occupied the first floor, apartments the remainder. A building of similar design but smaller in scale sat beside it, like a little brother, and it was there that Albert Kaiser lived.

Facing Potzdamer Platz from the northeast, directly across from the apartment buildings, was a small café tucked into an angled corner of a building. A dozen tables sat outside on the pavement, half-filled with patrons, eating and drinking and reading newspapers. York took a table against the café wall, ordered a coffee and kreppels, and watched Kaiser's building entrance across the street, stealing glances at the pedestrians who passed: foreign factory workers, women with strollers, children, older couples, a few soldiers, and a policeman or two.

Forty minutes and two kreppels later, a man with a shock of white hair emerged from the building entrance, a leash in his hand, leading a black and gray dog, a small schnauzer. York exited the café, hurriedly crossed the street, and followed him.

The man walked down the street towards the Brandenburg Gate, leading the dog to a small park, the grassy area sprinkled with trees, shrubs, and benches. York hurried to catch him, walking passed him hurriedly and then stopping abruptly, a feigned look of surprise on his face.

"Are you Albert Kaiser?" he asked, his face lit with admiration. "The cellist?"

Kaiser was surprised; he had few admirers. He smiled. "Yes, I am."

"Mr. Kaiser, it is an honor to meet you, sir. I am Michael Becker, a man who can appreciate one of Europe's greatest musicians."

Kaiser was flattered. "Are you a critic, Mr. Becker?"

"No, not a critic. But I suppose you can say I'm an aficionado."

"A fellow cellist?"

"No, I'm afraid not," York said with a slight frown. "A pianist, actually. Although a rank amateur compared to you. But a lover of the classics, just the same." He winced, grasping his thigh. "Could we sit down a moment?" he asked, pointing to his leg. "War wound. It can be quite painful at times."

"Of course," Kaiser said, moving to a bench. "I have a few minutes. No concert this evening. Our first violin had a party to go to."

"I attended one of your performances last month and truly enjoyed it, "York said as he leaned over to pet the dog. "What's the dog's name? He's a friendly fellow, isn't he?"

"Yes, he is," Kaiser chuckled. "His name is Rudolph; he's my constant companion."

York fussed over the animal, who loved the attention. He rubbed his head and, when Rudolph rolled on to his back, he scratched his stomach.

"What did you like most about the concert?" Kaiser asked.

York leaned back on the bench, leaving Rudolph lying in the grass. "Probably the Beethoven piece in A minor. Number fifteen, I think. The start of the second movement is so powerful, when you play an octave below the others, but in unison."

Kaiser was surprised. "Mr. Becker, you really do know your music, don't you?"

"I think the entire quartet is fabulous," York continued. "But you are the true virtuoso. How long have you played together?"

Kaiser sighed, running the calendar through his mind. "I have been with the quartet about fifteen years. Amanda Hamilton joined soon after she settled in Berlin. She is absolutely amazing. What talent. And so young."

"I did find her solo exceptional."

"It moves me every time I hear it. I just feel so sorry for her, given her recent loss."

York appeared confused, but then showed recollection. "I do remember reading something in the newspaper. A train wreck, I think. She was badly injured."

"She lost the baby she was carrying. After nine or ten years trying to conceive. She was devastated." He slowly shook his head and sighed. "She's like a daughter to me. I try to protect her. But I couldn't shield her from that."

"It's amazing she still performs with such passion."

"She enters another plane of existence when she picks up the violin. I love her dearly and want only the best for her." He looked away, seeming a bit sad.

York realized that Kaiser liked to talk. He also realized he was a harmless old man. But he offered a fabulous opportunity. He had a wealth of information.

"I suppose it's been hard for her," York said. He then leaned closer, as if speaking confidentially. "I mean being Scottish. It must be hard to live in Berlin."

"I'm sure it is," Kaiser said. He glanced around and lowered his voice, now that they were being honest. "And her husband is no angel, I can tell you that. He wanders a bit, if you know what I mean. She caught him with another woman last winter. That was a nasty scene. She's tougher then you think. But they've since reconciled. Do you know her husband?"

"No, I don't. Isn't he highly placed in the Party?"

"Yes," Kaiser said. "Although no one knows quite what he does. I'm sure it's no good."

York was surprised Kaiser spoke so freely. He wasn't sure why. He wondered if he spoke that casually, and unguarded, with everyone. "He certainly has a fascinating wife, regardless of what his role in the Party is."

"Yes, he does."

"How about the others? Are their lives as interesting?"

"No, not really," Kaiser said, rubbing his chin, thoughtful for a moment. "Erika Jaeger works harder than anyone. Amanda helps her with technique. She's been with us about three years. She improves almost daily. A very nice lady. Somewhat shy. I don't know much about her personal life. I know she has financial issues. But she cares for an elderly mother. I assume that's it."

"How about the other gentleman, the viola player?"

"Gerhard Faber. He's our newest member, been with us for a year or so. He's also the weakest musician. He wouldn't be with us if the war wasn't going on, I'm sure of it. Erika might not be, either, given the many talented musicians who now serve our country."

"He seems conscientious enough."

"He is. He tries hard. I think he has three or four children. And rumor has it, a wealthy mistress. But I've met his wife and she's an absolute sweetheart."

"Who does Albert Kaiser, the great cellist, feel closest to?"

"Amanda, undoubtedly. And I'm also friends with our liaison, Captain Klein. He thinks he's our manager but he's more like a mother hen, very protective of his little chicks." He looked at his watch and then tugged on the dog's leash. "I had best be going. My wife will wonder what's kept me. It was nice to meet you, Mr. Becker. I enjoyed our chat."

# CHAPTER 32

Gerhard Faber went to the cemetery drop on Saturday afternoon. He was short of money and with no concert scheduled because of Goebbels' party, he had no prospects for getting any until his next paycheck. He was anxious to see what the British spy had left in exchange for the artillery shell diagrams. Hopefully, it was a lot. He needed it to satisfy Astrid Braun's expensive tastes.

He walked towards the tomb, anxiously looking behind him, studying the lane in front of him, and examining the trees and shrubs intermingled among the tombstones. When he reached the wrought iron fence he moved to the corner post and, after shielding it with his body, removed the finial. He found a roll of Reichsmarks and a note tied with a string. When he saw the thickness of the wad he got excited, expecting a large payout. But he was disappointed to find bills in small denominations, barely worth two weeks' expenses given his current spending rate.

Faber put the money and note in his pocket and replaced the finial. He moved to a nearby bench and read the message, which instructed him to leave the plans in a new drop location behind the Berlin Theater.

He brooded for a moment. He felt like he was being used. And he wasn't going to stand for it, especially given the risk he was taking. Now he had more information, something better. The new rocket design could change the war; the British would realize that. He decided to be firm, to tell him what he expected. And he would dictate the drop location, no one else. Then he was struck with a sudden realization and a broad grin crossed his face. He could also sell the same plans to the Russians.

He glanced at his watch. It was getting late. He barely had time to go to the new drop and make it to the Braun's house on time. He returned to the tomb, folded the first four pages of drawings, and placed them in the finial. Then he hurried to the taxi waiting at the cemetery entrance.

"The Berlin Theater on Kantstrasse," he said to the driver.

As the taxi pulled away from the curb, Faber withdrew a pen and piece of paper from his pocket and scribbled the note he would leave at the new drop location.

HALF OF DRAWINGS PROVIDED FOR PAYMENT RECEIVED. YOU NEED TO PAY MORE. ADVANCED ROCKET DESIGN NEXT, PRODUCTION STARTS SOON. LEAVE MONEY AT CEMETERY DROP, NOT AT THEATER. THAT'S WHERE THE PLANS ARE.

Fifteen minutes later, the taxi came to a stop in front of the Berlin Theater. Faber told the driver to wait while he walked behind the building. A bakery sat beside the theater, and he could smell the bread being baked in their ovens. As he rounded the corner he saw the lot was almost empty; only five cars were parked there.

A large linden tree abutted a garden wall that defined the edge of the lot. It was about a meter high, made of stone, and probably pre-dated the buildings around it. Faber strolled towards it, making sure all the vehicles were empty, and studied the windows of nearby buildings. He didn't see anyone watching, not that he looked that carefully.

He glanced anxiously at the entrance and exit,

and made his way to the wall behind the tree. He heard a door open, but ignored it. A woman was talking, but he couldn't tell where she was. But it didn't matter anyway. He was in a hurry; he had to get to Astrid's house.

There was little room between the tree trunk and the wall, but Faber squeezed between them and found the capstone that was loose, glanced around to make sure no one was watching, and lifted it. He put the note in the cavity, restored the cap, and walked briskly back to the taxi, quite satisfied. He would give the orders from now on, not take them.

Astrid Braun and her mother lived in a mid-nineteenth century mansion on Von-der-Heydt-Strasse, south of Tiergarten, on a broad avenue shaded by mature linden trees and accented with a rainbow of flowers. The properties were all distinctive: brick, granite, and sandstone with decorative cornices, balconies, sculptured gardens and wrought iron fences. Faber left the taxi a few blocks from Astrid's house and walked the rest of the way, past the Spanish embassy on Regenenstrasse and the embassy for Imperial China, both housed in residential mansions from a time now past.

As he approached the Braun three-story villa, he saw that the spacious gardens were a bit overgrown. The trees and shrubs had to be pruned, flower beds weeded, and walkways repaired. The paint on the shutters was chipped, a brick or two on the entrance steps was loose, the mortar crumbling, the ornate railing a bit rusted and wobbly. The property needed attention, unlike its neighbors.

Astrid's father had died of cancer a few years before. Her two brothers were soldiers, stationed in Italy and Greece. Faber suspected the family fortune was long gone, and the pay earned by the family fell far short of what was needed to maintain the property. Astrid and her mother both held clerical positions, earning enough income to sustain them but not much more.

He rang the doorbell, but no one answered. After standing there a few minutes, he realized it wasn't working. One more item for the list of needed repairs. He knocked on the door, admiring the carvings in the wooden panels as he waited.

Astrid answered a moment later wearing a stylish green dress, a pearl necklace, and a broad smile. "Gerhard, how nice to see you." She leaned forward and kissed him on the lips. "Please, come in."

He handed her the bottle of wine he had brought, along with a bouquet of flowers. "For you," he said, as he entered.

She smiled. "You're too kind. Let me get these in some water. Come into the parlor."

He walked in and sat on a Victorian couch, the upholstery a bit worn, and studied the room. The crown molding was as beautiful as the day it was installed, the wallpaper it defined starting to fade. The hardwood floors contained an intricate pattern of oak and mahogany that offered accents and contrasts, its original luster still present. The drapes were a bit dated, and the Persian rug on the parlor floor was worn at the edges, exposing threads and the base mat.

Astrid returned a moment later with her mother.

He stood when the women entered the room. "Mrs. Braun," Gerhard said with a slight bow. He retrieved a small box of chocolates from his pocket, handing them to her.

"Mr. Faber, you are too kind," she said, beaming.

The mother was slender, like the daughter, still

attractive, the wrinkles and graying hair offering an air of distinction and sophistication. Faber imagined that Astrid would look just like her in thirty years. It was not an unpleasing image.

They sat in the parlor, enjoying a glass of wine, while Astrid went back and forth to the kitchen, checking on dinner. Faber enjoyed the charade; the Brauns pretended to be wealthy and so did he. But neither was. He also pretended to be available. But he wasn't.

Mrs. Braun had issued the invitation, arranging for her daughter to have dinner at their home. The romance was progressing rapidly, a little too rapidly, and before her daughter took it too far, she wanted to make sure Gerhard Faber was what he claimed to be. She was a good judge of character, and she had contacts of her own. The family may have lost their wealth, but they hadn't lost their influence.

"What intriguing project are you working on now, Mr. Faber?" Mrs. Braun asked.

"Mother, please," Astrid urged. "I'm sure Gerhard doesn't want to discuss business. He came here to relax and enjoy a nice dinner."

"No, it's fine," Faber said. "I don't mind at all." He sighed, glanced around the room as if someone could be listening and, when convinced there was not, he continued. "I have just started manufacturing an advanced rocket. The Fuehrer thinks that once deployed it will force Britain to surrender. Then the Reich can focus on the war in the East and crush the Russians."

"That's certainly an important assignment," Astrid said, impressed.

"I should say so," Mrs. Braun agreed. Then she decided to pry. "Is such an endeavor lucrative?"

"By all means," he said. "Beyond your imagination."

"I had better check on dinner, "Astrid said. She would leave the questions to her mother.

"I think it's fascinating that you're so successful," Mrs. Braun said. Then she leaned forward, acting as if she didn't want Astrid to hear. "There was a time when the Brauns were also. Astrid has no idea, but the family finances have taken a turn for the worst. Much was lost during the global Depression. Even the house needs attention: the rugs are worn, the paint peeling, the garden, once the most beautiful on the street, is nothing but overgrown weeds. If only I could find the money somehow."

Faber could not resist the urge to impress. He had a fistful of money in his pocket and he would soon have more. He would sell the rest of the artillery shell plans and then the rocket design. Not only to the British, but probably to the Russians as well.

"Mrs. Braun," he said. "I would be honored if you allowed me to take care of the gardens. Just as a token of our friendship and how kind you and your daughter have been to me. I can have workmen here in three or four days. And if you prefer, Astrid need never know."

"Oh, Mr. Faber," said Mrs. Braun, her hand over her heart, her face a look of surprise. "How kind of you. I would be so appreciative."

When Astrid called them into dinner, Mrs. Braun could barely conceal her glee. Although she suspected he was a fake, she really didn't care who Gerhard Faber was or where he got his money. She realized that as long as she kept her daughter almost obtainable, but not quite, she could control Faber just as she had been able to control other men throughout her life. She smiled. She had conned the con artist.

179

# CHAPTER 33

The black Mercedes drove slowly down the street before stopping in front of the Richter townhouse, Nazi flags perched on its bumpers waving gently in the breeze. Manfred and Amanda left their residence a moment later, her violin case held protectively under her arm, sheltered from the evils of the world. Neighbors and passersby watched as he led her down the steps, his arm wrapped around her, looking immaculate in a dark suit and tie, a fedora covering his black hair. Amanda wore a lavender evening gown, her hair bobbed and close to her head, mimicking one of the latest styles. Everyone knew they were celebrities, the highly-placed Party official and the famous violinist, and they watched in awe as the driver held the door for them.`

Goebbels's mansion was eight kilometers to the southwest, on Schwanenwerder Island, in Berlin's most exclusive area. The property had a hundred meters of frontage on Wannsee Lake and was beautifully landscaped, dotted with tall oaks and pines mingled with shrubs and beds of flowers. Amanda thought it was one of the most peaceful places she had ever seen, and had once tried to convince Manfred to move there. Many Nazi elite lived in the area, some of the properties confiscated from Jewish owners. Hitler's architect, Albert Speer, and his personal doctor, Theodor Morell, had residences near the Goebbels, and the Fuehrer was supposedly considering moving there as well.

They drove through the city, Amanda not saying a word to Manfred, reaching the stone walls that defined the Goebbels' estate about twenty minutes later. An iron gate marked the entrance, the metal twisted into a floral pattern matching the flowers that grew beside it. It was opened by two soldiers, both fully armed, who checked their credentials before nodding them onward. The mansion appeared, sitting on the edge of the lake, as they traveled down a winding lane. A rambling three-story building hinting of both Greco-Roman and Aryan design, it was square, with diagonal window grills that lent a Bavarian influence, while columns and statues decorating the lawn and gardens seemed more Mediterranean.

A soldier opened the door, an older man, ramrod straight. He led them to a banquet hall, rectangular in shape, gilded wallpaper accented by white chair railing. Large windows overlooked the lake; paintings by the Impressionists dressed the walls. Bronze busts of Beethoven, Mozart, Bach, and Brahms sat on marble pedestals in each corner, and a signed portrait of Hitler dominated the far wall. Long narrow tables circled the room, draped in red cloth adorned with the Swastika, and covered with appetizers, entrees, pastries, and salads. Several rooms branched from the main, one of which opened to a small stage with a dance floor before it. A piano was perched in the center, where a man in a white suit jacket played softly, his fingers roaming the ivory to create soothing melodies.

Amanda put her violin case behind the stage and then studied the room. She knew most of the attendees, having seen them through the years at prior events. The Fuehrer stood at the far end flanked by Martin Bormann and Joseph Goebbels, the hulking frame of Hermann Göring in front of them. Göring's second wife Emmy stood beside him, while Gerda Bormann and Magda Goebbels stood to one side, talking to the architect Albert Speer. Several generals were grouped in one corner, Jodl and Keitel, as well as a few that Amanda recognized but whose names she couldn't remember.

181

The remaining guests were party officials and leaders of industry, the men that kept the appetite of the massive war machine sated.

"Mingle, darling," Manfred said after their wine glasses had been filled. "I have business to conduct."

She cast him an annoyed look, somehow finding she could hate him more as each day passed, and walked away. She felt uncomfortable, glancing around the room for a conversation to join, conscious of the commitment she had made to obtain information. Hitler and the group surrounding him had retired to a study off the dining hall, and she could see them through the glass doors, sitting on plush leather sofas engaged in an animated discussion.

She moved towards the generals, pretending to be interested in a nearby tray of apple sausage appetizers. As she grabbed a plate and utensils, she strained her ears, trying to capture tidbits of information, wondering if anything being said could be useful to the Allies.

"I was as surprised as you," said General Wilhelm Keitel, Hitler's War Minister. "Why would the Fuehrer halt the offensive at Kursk to redeploy troops to Italy? We could have sent reinforcements from the Balkans."

"He thinks the Allied landings in Italy are a diversion. And that the real offensive will be in the Balkans. There are …"

She walked away, her heart racing, knowing she had heard something important, but not wanting to get caught eavesdropping. It was an arena in which she had never performed, and she could feel her breath, short and shallow. The wine in her glass swayed dangerously in one hand, the plate with two sausages shook in the other. She took a deep breath and sipped more wine, gathering her courage, and went to the stage where she pretended to listen to the piano player.

He was very good, and she gradually relaxed as she watched his hands glide across the keys. Listening to the music made her think of Michael, and she wondered how well he played. She knew he liked classical music, but wondered what else. Had he studied music, or was he self-taught? Did he play daily when in London, or just occasionally? All were questions she wanted to ask, among others, but there had really been little time to learn about each other. Not that they should, given their current roles.

She had to admit that he was an interesting man. Logical but creative, and sensitive yet strong, he was a former teacher who loved architecture and music and many of the things that she did. It was a unique combination. Her heart had broken when he told her about his wife leaving with his daughter, Elizabeth.

Sorrow gradually consumed her as she relived their conversation. He had chosen the same name she had for her child, although not the Anglo spelling. Elisabeth was the German version. And she loved the name. It sounded like a song, rolling off the lips and tongue, the letters linked, syllables complimenting each other.

"Are you enjoying the party?"

Amanda was startled, lost in her own world. She turned to find Col. Klemp, a short, chubby man with round spectacles and a balding head. She didn't know him that well, only that he was the dean of a military school.

"Yes, I am," she said. "It's very nice."

"Will you be playing for us this evening?"

She nodded and glanced at her watch. "In a few minutes, actually. I'm waiting for the piano player to finish."

"I'm sure your performance will be exceptional,

as always."

She smiled. "Thank you. You're too kind."

"You must be so proud of Kurt," he continued.

She was confused. "Of course, I am. He's a wonderful child."

"Child?" Beck asked jokingly.

She laughed. "Yes, but I suppose he'll soon be a man."

"He'll do well at the academy," Beck continued. "Manfred insisted that he start officer training as soon as possible. Then he'll advance quickly when he joins the military."

Amanda felt her heart sink as a wave of nausea consumed her. Manfred was sending Kurt away and he hadn't even told her. She tried to maintain her composure. She didn't want Klemp to know how upset she was.

"Where exactly is the school located?" she asked, feigning forgetfulness. "I know Manfred told me. But I just can't remember."

"In Saxony-Anhalt. About 180 kilometers southwest of Berlin. The official name is the National Political Institutes of Education. We are thrilled to have Manfred's son attending."

"And we are excited to have Kurt trained by some of the brightest minds in Germany." She cast a smile she didn't feel. "If you'll excuse me, Colonel, I have to get ready to perform."

It was difficult to practice; she had trouble concentrating. She was close to Kurt and she couldn't bear to lose him, even though she knew she already had. His father and the Nazi Party were destroying him. Day by day he was changing, polluted by the Hitler Youth. Now he would become a trained killer.

And then she was on stage. Her mind entered a different world once her fingers traveled the violin's neck. Her melodies were so moving, so dynamic, that those attending the party stopped their mindless chatter and, within minutes, they all gathered to listen. The doors opened to the side office and Hitler emerged, moving to the stage. His eyes, alive with passion and evil and insanity, watched her intently, awestruck at the talent, overwhelmed by the emotion. When she completed her first selection, he immediately started clapping, and the rest followed, mimicking their master.

She played for forty minutes. Few in the audience took their eyes from her. Hitler stood, arms folded across his chest, totally mesmerized. When she finished her final piece and bowed, the room was consumed with applause, emphatically led by the Fuehrer. As she stepped from the stage he approached, acknowledging her with a nod of his head and an outstretched hand.

"True talent, Mrs. Richter," Hitler said loudly, nudging Bormann who stood beside him. "A magnificent performance. I have never been so moved."

She smiled and bowed gracefully, knowing all eyes were upon her. "I'm honored, mein Fuehrer."

The clapping gradually subsided and the audience broke into groups, sampling the wine and food and talking among themselves. The pianist returned to the stage, playing a tender melody that brought a few couples to the dance floor.

Amanda put her violin in the case. She was exhausted, as she was at the end of every concert. She used every ounce of strength, with each cell of her body contributing, to create the passion and muster the emotion that defined her performances. She sat on a chair behind the stage, recovering.

Ten minutes later she rejoined the party, accepting a glass of wine from the waiter. Still upset about Kurt, she decided to confront Manfred. She found him with a group of business leaders. As she approached, his back to her, she heard an intense discussion.

"With a separate route to each destination," he was saying. "We need banking and industrial presence in each location. South America will be the primary focus, with Buenos Aires as the hub. And then the Middle East, mainly Syria and Egypt, the operation run from Cairo. Spain will be the European center. All have governments sympathetic to our cause, and people who believe in us." He then paused dramatically, eyeing each man in turn, all of whom listened intently. "These locations will launch the Fourth Reich, should the situation demand it." He paused again, and then spoke quietly. "In the event the Third Reich does not survive."

Amanda slowly moved away, unnoticed. She had no idea what Manfred was talking about. And she doubted that Adolph Hitler did either.

# CHAPTER 34

"Captain Rufus Klein," Max said with disgust. "This is the second war I've fought against him. I'm surprised the old goat is still alive."

York had just described his encounter with Kaiser. Given Max's reaction, it seemed they may have identified the informant. Maybe it wasn't a member of the string quartet. It could be the man who was watching them.

"What happened in the Great War?" York asked.

"I was behind enemy lines, posing as a Belgian farmer. The local headquarters for German military intelligence was just down the road. I got a little too aggressive, if you know what I mean, and attracted Klein's attention."

"And he captured you?"

Max nodded. "Me and a few others, although he had no proof. Not that he needed any. Klein kept us chained in a barn for seven months. He was convinced we knew a lot more than we really did. But I don't think he ever got anything useful."

"Then what happened. Did you escape?"

"No, actually, the war ended."

York listened closely, never having heard the story before. He wondered why Klein would keep Max in a barn for seven months. Why not send him to a prisoner of war camp? He was about to ask, when Max continued.

"Kaiser and the others may think Klein is their liaison, or manager, or whatever they want to call him. But the Klein I know would never settle for a role like that. Although he is older now, probably past sixty, I'm sure he contributes to the war effort somehow. I can't

187

imagine him babysitting a group of spoiled musicians."

"Do you think he suspects one of them is selling information?"

"What do you think?" Max asked, his eyebrows arched in a question. "I'm sure he does. They travel to entertain the troops. They give concerts. They're exposed to the public. They're certainly accessible. And Klein knows that."

"Maybe Klein spotted you watching Kaiser's apartment," York said. "And he remembered you. He notified the Gestapo, and that's where the wanted posters came from."

Max shrugged. "I suppose it's possible, but not very likely. We haven't seen each other in twenty-five years. I wouldn't recognize him if I saw him today; I doubt he would recognize me, either."

"Then who do you think it is?"

"I don't know, maybe someone I bought information from."

York didn't find the explanation plausible. "Then it should be easy to find them."

Max shrugged. "I don't think we need to. The posters have vanished anyway. An informant told me the Gestapo arrested someone that resembles me; that probably explains why. Hopefully they let the poor bloke go after questioning."

York cringed. He didn't want to think about an innocent man suffering at the hands of the Gestapo, even if it did save Max. But the Gestapo would know fairly quickly that they had the wrong man, and then increase their efforts to find the right one.

"There's something missing," York said. "There has to be a reason for the posters, and there has to be someone behind it. Regardless of who was arrested, the person that betrayed you is still in Berlin. And they can betray you again."

"I agree," Max said, although he didn't seem to care. "But it could be anyone. It doesn't have to be Kaiser or Klein or someone who gave me information. It could be the remains of whatever mess Kent, your predecessor, got himself into."

York shrugged, confused and bewildered. They had nothing specific, just unanswered questions.

"I'm beginning to wonder about Kaiser, after what you told me," Max said. "He seems to know a lot about everyone."

"I wouldn't worry about him." York said. "He likes to gossip. He was only friendly because I complimented him and he thought I was a fellow musician."

"But didn't he say Klein was his neighbor? He must know he's Gestapo or some sort of military intelligence."

"Why would he care? I'm sure he has friends who are Gestapo, or policemen, or party officials."

Max glanced at his watch. "What else do you want to talk about? I only have a few more minutes."

"I'm meeting Amanda this afternoon to discuss whatever information she got at the party, and I meet with Erika Jaeger on Thursday."

"Are you sure she isn't the Gestapo informant?"

"Yes, I'm certain," York said with no hesitation. "She has too much to lose."

Max was quiet, pensive. "I suppose that alone would make her cooperate."

"I do think she has access to valuable information, so it'll be worthwhile. But she'll want to know if we can get her friends out of the country. Have you given that any more thought?"

"Some," Max replied. "As I said before, anything is possible. We need a safe route, which takes a little research. But it can be done. It'll be much harder than France, though. We can expect little or no help from the locals here. Too loyal to the Austrian painter, if you know what I mean."

York smiled at his reference to Hitler, but knew he was right. "I'll tell her we're working on it. That will give her some hope. Maybe she knows people, Germans that aren't loyal to the Nazis."

"Wait until you have her hooked before you offer too much," Max said, again glancing at his watch, and then starting for the door. "I have to go. I don't want to be late."

"What if Kaiser and Klein have something going on, the two of them?" York asked. "Something they're afraid we'll find?"

"What do you mean?"

"They see you watching them, and the wanted posters appear. Now you'll stay away from their apartment building. Suppose they notice me hanging around, and wonder what I'm up to. They send Kaiser down for a friendly chat so I'm convinced he's above suspicion and I won't bother him anymore."

"That theory assumes they know us and what we're here for."

"Exactly."

"It doesn't make sense," Max said. "They would just have us arrested."

"Unless we're pawns in their chess game, not ready to be taken."

# CHAPTER 35

Amanda arrived near noon, carrying an umbrella and a small box of photographs. She cast a weak smile as she entered, seemed a bit preoccupied, but sat at the table by the window, nervously glancing outside. When satisfied no one was lurking on the street, she sat back in the chair and looked at York.

"Why so glum?" he asked.

"A guest at the party is the commandant at a military school. He told me that Manfred enrolled Kurt. At first I didn't believe it, but it was true. Kurt left yesterday."

"Manfred never told you?"

She studied him for a moment, almost as if she was wondering how much she should tell him. "I don't speak to Manfred," she said. "Not ever."

He gave her a questioning look, although he suspected he knew the reason. "Do you want to talk about it?"

"It's long story."

He reached across the table and gently held her hand, tenderly caressing it. "I would be happy to listen. As a friend, of course."

She hesitated, and then spoke. "Not right now. I'm upset about a lot of things. Kurt is just the latest. I know he's not my child, but I've raised him for the last ten years. I love him and I already miss him."

"Are you lonely?" he asked, prying, even though he knew he shouldn't.

She hesitated, as if she had built a wall to protect herself and didn't want him to peek over it. "Kurt and I were together every day, even if just during dinner. We talked a lot. He confided in me, sharing everything from his first kiss to his dreams for the future. Now he's gone."

He noticed that she didn't mention Manfred, and instead kept the conversation confined to her stepson. "I'm sure he'll miss you, too."

She shook her head. "I don't think so. He won't have time to think about me, not with all his military training. And the dreams of glory his father put in his head."

"All the more reason for the war to end," York said.

She glanced out the window again. She seemed nervous, as if something wasn't right. A premonition, maybe.

"I did try to eavesdrop at the party," she said.

"Did you hear anything interesting?"

"I overheard two discussions, although I'm not sure I understand them. Hopefully, they're helpful."

York was encouraged. "Let's hear them."

"The first conversation was between some generals. Jodl and Keitel were there with a few others, just after they talked privately with Hitler."

York was intrigued by the access she had to Hitler and his inner circle. Jodl and Keitel were his chief military strategists.

"Hitler was at the party?" he asked.

"Yes, and others: Bormann, Goebbels, Göring, Albert Speer, some industry executives."

"I think we may spend the entire week talking about this," he said, trying to imagine the Nazi elite all gathered in the same room. "What did you hear the generals say?"

"They were talking about the Russian offensive at Kursk."

York was pensive, trying to visualize a map of Russia. "Kursk is a city on the front lines. What did they say, specifically?"

"They are halting the offensive and diverting troops to Italy because of the Allied invasion."

York rubbed his chin, thinking, a distant look in his eyes.

"What's wrong?" she asked. "You look confused."

"Why take troops from Russia to reinforce Italy? Why not take them from France or the Balkans?"

"Someone mentioned that," she said. "It's because Hitler thinks the Italy invasion is a diversion, and that the real Allied offensive will come in the Balkans."

York's eyes widened. Not only had the Russian offensive been halted, but the weakened front line could now be exploited. And since no troops would be taken from the Balkans, the Allies could feign an offensive so Germany maintained a large force there, starving other regions of resources.

"Was there more?" he asked.

"I'm sure there was, but that was the gist of it. I only listened for a minute. I didn't want to arouse suspicion."

"That's the type of information I was talking about," he said. "It seems like an innocent conversation, just an informal discussion on tactics. But if true, and the Allies can adjust and react, it can have a significant impact on the Eastern Front."

York watched her reaction. She seemed overwhelmed, tiptoeing into water that was much too deep. He was sure she felt as if the world was so immense, along with the problems in it, that photography and classical music seemed insignificant. He decided to be gentle, not to probe too forcefully. He didn't want to scare her away just when she was proving so valuable. "Can you think of anything else?"

"There is more. But it involves Manfred." She

hesitated, thought for a moment, and then continued. "I know that, when we met, I said I wouldn't betray him. I'm not sure that's the case anymore."

York's interest was piqued, but he tried not to show it. He realized the wealth of information she had access to. "Tell me as much, or as little, as you're comfortable with."

She paused. "This is a big step for me. Maybe if we talk about something else for a while. Then we can discuss Manfred." She looked around the room. It was bare, stark, giving no hint to its occupant. Then she remembered. "Tell me about Elizabeth."

The pain in his eyes was immediate, the sorrow on his face consuming. He knew she saw it, could feel it. And he could tell she identified with it. He cringed, tried to talk, but turned and looked out the window, watching a light rain bathe the cobblestone streets.

She leaned forward and touched his arm. "I know it's hard. I can feel your pain. If the child I lost in the train accident had been a girl, she would have been named Elisabeth."

He turned to look at her, his eyes searching, showing compassion. "I didn't know that," he said softly. "So we like the same name."

She smiled, trying to be strong, but feeling her eyes mist at the thought of the child she would never have. "Yes, we both like the name. Now tell me about her."

York couldn't keep a smile from crossing his face. "I'm not sure where to start."

"How would you describe her – in one word?"

York chuckled. "I'm not sure. Whirlwind, I suppose. She has an opinion on everything, and is convinced she knows more than any other twelve-year-old child on the planet. She likes cricket, a bit unusual for a young lady, and she's fascinated with the Royal family."

"King George VI?"

"No, not the King. She actually adores his daughter Elizabeth. She loves that they have the same name. She digests every word written about her in the press."

Amanda was amused. "She could have worse hobbies."

He laughed lightly. "I'm not complaining. I think it's cute. She reads biographies of Queen Victoria and Queen Elizabeth, or whatever else she can find about them." His face clouded, happy memories masked by sorrow. "But I don't know if I'll ever see her again."

Amanda moved to his side and hugged him. He didn't resist. He felt comforted, enveloped in her arms, drinking the scent of her perfume, feeling her compassion. Then all too quickly she moved away and returned to her seat.

"Time to change the subject," she said. "I'm ready to discuss Manfred now."

He took a second to collect himself and urged her on. "Go ahead."

She thought for a moment, wondering how to begin. She started slowly. "Manfred is a powerful man, and he's very dangerous. He is closely tied to Martin Bormann."

"Hitler's inner circle."

"Bormann is more than inner circle," she said. "He's Hitler's right hand."

York corrected her. "The Allies view Goebbels, Göring, and Himmler as those closest to Hitler."

She shook her head. "It's not true. Bormann has tremendous power, and extreme influence with the Fuehrer. Manfred used to talk about it a lot. He doesn't say much anymore. But then, I hardly see him."

"Do you have any photographs of Bormann?"

"No, he rarely allows his picture to be taken."

York studied her face, the upturned nose, her eyes sincere and intense. "I didn't know that. But I don't think many people do."

"I overheard Manfred talking to some industrial leaders at the party. They were discussing something he has been working on with Bormann. I know it's important."

York was in unknown territory, hanging on every word, drinking information like a man dying of thirst. It seemed too good to be true. And for a moment, he wondered if it was.

She described the planned escape routes from Germany, the importance of Buenos Aires and South America, secondary locations in Spain and the Middle East. She mentioned the money trail and industrial presence, and how they would be launched when the time was right.

He was amazed. "It's almost like they're planning for Germany's defeat. And the Nazi elite will flee and continue the struggle from abroad."

"I think that's exactly what it is," she said. "I heard them refer to it as the Fourth Reich."

For York, the whole concept was beyond belief, the creation of hell on earth. "That doesn't sound like something Hitler would sanction. It reeks of defeat."

"That's what's strange," Amanda said. "I don't think Hitler knows about it."

# CHAPTER 36

York went to the Berlin Theater on Kantstrasse, planning to meet Erika Jaeger at the cemetery afterwards. He furtively went to the parking lot behind the building, finding only a few parked cars, their owners enjoying the show inside. He wandered to the garden wall and sat beside the linden tree, near the loose capstone, watching the parking lot and adjacent buildings. When satisfied no one was looking, he lifted the stone and looked in the cavity below.

He found only a message, no plans, and his face hardened as he read Faber's note. York didn't like him, and he had yet to even meet him. It was important to follow instructions. When you didn't, you got killed. Maybe that's how Kent got caught, Faber controlling him, instead of Kent controlling Faber. And maybe Faber led him time after time to the cemetery drop, which may have been compromised. York had to be cautious. Faber was dangerous.

York took a taxi to the cemetery, eyed the few visitors he passed as he entered, and waited on the bench for Erika Jaeger. Ten minutes later she arrived, sat next to him, and studied the landscape, looking at the cobblestone lanes, the birds, the people that wandered past. When satisfied it was safe, she spoke, but she continued staring straight ahead and didn't look at York.

"I'm not a supporter of the Nazis," she said quietly. "And I never have been."

"Good," York said, easing the tension. "We have something in common."

"But I never considered betraying my country," she added.

He wasn't sure what direction she was taking.

Her statement had an ominous tone, almost a threat or warning. He gazed cautiously around the cemetery, looking for anyone suspicious: Gestapo, policeman, informants. After a minute had passed, and he was satisfied it was safe, he turned to face her.

She wasn't looking at him. She looked at the grass, and a few roses that bloomed at the edge of the shrubs. Then she looked towards the entrance.

Could she be stalling for time? Maybe they were under surveillance. Was the Gestapo about to rush forward and arrest him?

An awkward silence ensued. He watched her shuffling uncomfortably on the bench and decided to proceed. They seemed safe, alone and unnoticed. He would probe her weakness, his belief she was hiding someone in her home.

"You could help other people with the money I give you," he said, trying to convince her. He leaned towards her, as if sharing a secret. "If there was someone in trouble that you cared about."

She turned away, expressionless, and studied the lane. No one was coming. The bench was tucked away between shrubs, not somewhere you would go unless you knew it was there.

"The Nazis do terrible things," she said, her face twisting with hatred. "I've seen it. I've watched it for ten years."

He didn't reply, but let her think. He waited, watching her closely, compassion washing his face. A moment passed before she continued.

"I lost my husband in the war," she said quietly. "He was a gentle man, loving and considerate, my constant companion. A talented craftsman, an artist, he wasn't a fighter; he never should have carried a gun. Now my life will always be empty. A piece of my heart is missing that can't be replaced."

Her eyes misted and she looked away, sighing. She wiped them with a fingertip, dabbing at tears, before turning to face him, her expression determined. "If I can help, I will. But I want something in return."

He avoided asking, although he suspected he knew what it was. "What information do you have for me?"

She hesitated. He knew she was aware she couldn't retrace her steps once the walk was started. "I work in the logistics office of the War Ministry. Usually I route supplies, sometimes, weapons. It's normally routine, not very exciting, and somewhat predicable. At least until the last few weeks."

"What's changed?" York asked.

"There has been a redeployment of troops from the Russian city of Kursk. The summer offensive has been halted."

"Where are the troops being sent?"

"To Italy, to stem the Allied offensive."

York listened as she spoke, softly and sincerely, wanting to change the world but not knowing how. She had confirmed what Amanda overheard at the party. Now he had to get the information to Max.

He reached in his pocket and withdrew some Reichsmarks. It was more than she deserved, almost double what he had paid Faber. But he knew she needed it. She had an elderly mother to care for. And whoever else she was hiding.

Her eyes widened when she saw the money. It was more than she expected.

York could tell she felt guilty, profiting from the misery of others. She probably wondered how many men would die because of the information she provided. Just like her husband had. But she thought she was doing the right thing.

"Thank you," she said. "I need the money

badly." She put it in her purse, scanning the area as she did so.

"May I ask you a few questions about those in the quartet?"

She was confused, not seeing any connection, but shrugged and agreed anyway. "Of course."

"How would you describe Amanda Hamilton?"

Jaeger thought for a moment. "She's caring, a good person, a close friend, a fabulous violinist, and a great photographer." She looked up, her eyes on York. "And she's very lonely."

York studied her for a moment, hiding a smile. He would have used the same description. For a moment he wondered if he was becoming too attached to Amanda.

"How about Gerhard Faber?"

She crinkled her nose. "He can be arrogant. I don't know him that well, so I suppose I shouldn't say anything. He's just different. But I can't say why. I usually don't bother with him."

"Albert Kaiser?"

She smiled. "Father figure. He likes to talk. One story after another. Sometimes he reminds me of Father Christmas. He's very protective of Amanda. But they have known each other for many years."

"Captain Klein?"

She shrugged. "He spends most of his time with Albert. I think they're neighbors. They served together in the last war. But Klein can be annoying, very nosy, intrusive, watches everything and everyone. But I guess that's what he's supposed to do. He pretends to be our manager, making arrangements and ensuring we're on time. But his real role is to observe."

"Kaiser was in the war with Klein?" he asked, finding the information disturbing.

"Klein said something once and Kaiser got mad.

I never heard either mention it again." She looked up, smiling faintly. "Is that any help?"

"Yes, actually it is. It confirms information I already had, but offers a bit more."

"Do I get more money?"

He laughed. "No, not just yet. How about Manfred Richter?"

She frowned. "He can be charming and sincere, as if he would do anything for you. But he's really dangerous, sly, and selfish. He has a dark side, seems to always be scheming. But it's something you don't find out about until months later."

"Does he have a mistress?"

She hesitated. "I don't want to answer that. Out of respect for Amanda."

"You don't have to," he said, knowing she already had. "Is there something you want to ask me?"

She nodded, her eyes pleading for help, her lips afraid to mouth the words. "Can you get people out of Germany?"

He paused, pensive. "Possibly," he said cautiously, not wanting to give her false hopes. "Where to?"

"Somewhere safe. I suppose Switzerland is easiest."

"Or Sweden," he said. He wondered how serious Max was. Would he really offer assistance?

He studied her face. Sadness consumed her eyes; compassion lived in her heart. He couldn't refuse her. She was a good person, risking her life to protect others. It was probably a former neighbor or friend, probably a Jew.

"I'll do the best I can," he promised. "How many people are we trying to rescue?"

She looked away, uncomfortable. A moment passed before she found the courage to face him.

"Eight," she said quietly.

York's eyes widened with surprise. "Are you serious?" he asked. "You have eight people crammed in an apartment?"

She was silent, her arms folded across her chest. She shrugged defiantly. "Maybe."

He studied her closely, searching for clarification, seeking a hint of truth. "Eight people who may or may not be in your apartment," he said, trying to ease the tension.

She stood, preparing to go. "No more information. Not until you agree to help me."

"And get your friends out of Germany?"

"Yes," she said quietly. "Think about it."

He watched her walk to the exit, her demands now known. She didn't look back.

York was impressed. She was a remarkable woman. A war widow with an elderly mother, she was risking her life to hide eight people. And even though she might have help from others, it was still an unbelievable effort. What he found absolutely amazing, was that she did it while playing violin for the Berlin String Quartet, one of the most demanding endeavors on the planet.

# CHAPTER 37

Once Erika Jaeger had gone, York walked towards the drop to see what Gerhard Faber might have left him. An elderly couple passed, arm in arm, still in love after many years together. York watched them walk down the lane, suddenly feeling an emptiness in his heart. He wondered if they realized how fortunate they were to have found each other. After watching them a moment more, he realized that they probably did.

He carefully surveyed the landscape and, when sure no one was watching, he moved to the tomb where the drop was, leaned against the fence, and removed the cap from the corner post. He expected to find the rest of the artillery shell drawings, and promise of delivery for rocket diagrams, as originally agreed.

Instead he found another note from Faber and two pages of blueprints, not four as anticipated. He studied the cemetery, peering through bushes and shrubs, past tombs and mausoleums, and made sure no one was watching. Then he opened the note.

PRICE JUST DOUBLED. TWO OF FOUR DRAWINGS DELIVERED. LEAVE MONEY FOR MORE.

York frowned. He was tiring of Gerhard Faber. But he wanted the plans for the rocket even more than the artillery shell. He weighed whether the weapons were as valuable as information he had gotten from Erika or Amanda, or even the gossip obtained from Albert Kaiser. He knew that it was.

He sighed, faced with a dilemma. He had given Jaeger more money than planned because he felt sorry for her. Now he had just enough to meet Faber's original demand, which would only buy two more blueprints.

"Let's see how badly he needs money," York uttered aloud. He put the bills in the cavity formed by the hollow finial cap with a note.

REST OF MONEY AT OTHER DROP. LEAVE DRAWINGS THERE, WITH SAME FOR ROCKET.

He folded the drawings and put them in his pocket, made sure the cap was secure, and walked out of the cemetery.

York took a taxi to Max's boarding house, finding the Berlin traffic heavier than normal. He went to a rear entrance when he arrived, climbed the stairs, and tapped lightly on the door. After a few minutes, he tapped again. The door opened a crack, and Max peered out.

As soon as he saw York, he opened the door, glanced down the hallway in both directions, and led him inside. On a small table against the wall sat a few slices of pumpernickel bread, a block of sharp cheese and a knife. A bottle of red wine stood beside a half-filled glass. Max sat down and motioned for York to join him.

"Are you all right?" Max asked, surprised by the impromptu meeting.

"Yes, I'm sorry for the intrusion. But I had to talk to you right away."

"Is anything wrong?"

York shook his head. "No, but I have a lot to discuss. And it's important. I'll show you."

He took the drawings of the artillery shell from his pocket, showing Max the details, what else was expected, and about the potential rocket design. Then he described how Faber had acted.

Max frowned. "What disturbs me most is that he's probably selling the same thing to the Russians. And I bet he's making a nice living doing it."

"I think he needs to be taught a lesson," York said firmly.

Max shrugged. "Have some fun with him. Makes no difference to me."

"I think I will."

York gazed out the window, watching the traffic pass, a streetcar and bus, a few Volkswagens, bicycles moving along the curb. Pedestrians walked on the pavement past the trees that bordered the road, flowers in beds beside the curb. All were framed by Nazi flags hanging from street lamps and balconies.

"I also have valuable information for you," he said quietly.

Max had been slicing a piece of cheese from the block. He put down the knife and looked at York with interest. "What is it?"

York explained Hitler's decision to halt the offensive at Kursk so he could redeploy troops in Italy, and his belief that the Italian campaign was a diversion for the real assault, which would be in the Balkans. He gave Amanda's version and source, and then Jaeger's confirmation.

Max listened intently, his eyes trained on York. He rubbed his chin, thoughtful, then looked away. He motioned to York, offering bread, cheese, and wine, but still not speaking.

York broke the impasse. "Jaeger asked again if we can help get her friends out of Germany."

Max took another sip of wine. "I told you we could. Especially if she continues to cooperate."

"There's just one wrinkle, I'm afraid," York

said.

"What is it?"

"She's hiding eight people."

Max glanced at him, eyebrows arched, eyes wide. "A resourceful woman," he said. "I think we've been underestimating her. She must have them hidden around the city, maybe with friends or relatives."

"What should I tell her?"

"Keep promising. We'll get them out eventually. But up the ante a bit. Demand more information."

"Of course," York said, his heart sinking. He thought of Erika Jaeger's face, so hopeful, so trusting. She needed his help desperately. And she believed him when he said he could provide it.

Max wrapped the bread and cheese, put the cork back in the wine, and rose from his chair. "I have to find my radio operator and get a message to London," he said. "Do you have anything else?"

York explained the efforts of Manfred Richter, and possibly Martin Bormann, to develop centers and escape routes around the world for Nazis fleeing Europe, ultimately to form the Fourth Reich.

Max was stunned. "That means some in the Nazi party have accepted defeat. They're either planning their escape from Europe, bringing the war to new continents, or there is a growing opposition to Hitler and he'll be overthrown by a group already postured for world domination. Either way, they could be planning a war on a far grander scale."

"Which is unfathomable," York said gravely.

"I don't want to pass that along just yet," Max said. "We need to confirm it. But halting the offensive in Russia has to be relayed immediately. Good work, old boy."

York stood and started for the door.

"Did you get any information on Kaiser and Klein?"

York nodded. "A little. I haven't asked Amanda yet, but Jaeger confirmed what we already knew." He put his hand on the doorknob and paused, remembering. "Except for one thing," he added.

Max, in a hurry to get to his radio operator, was right behind him. "What is it?"

"Kaiser and Klein served in the last war together."

# CHAPTER 38

Workers toiled in the Braun family garden, tediously correcting years of neglect. They removed dead and dying foliage, trimmed and shaped overgrown shrubs, and pruned trees whose limbs stretched in unintended directions. Flower beds were weeded and renewed with scarlet roses accented by golden daisies, white chrysanthemums, and lavender hyacinths. Masons repaired a flagstone walkway, replacing the mortar between the joints, and fixed the flower bed retaining walls which had crumbled in several places. After a few days of intense activity, the gardens were starting to look like they once did, rivaling those of the neighbors.

"How does this dress look?" Astrid asked her mother. It was the third change of clothes she had modeled.

Mrs. Braun turned from the twelve-pane window that overlooked the garden. She cast a final glance at the mason, ensuring his work was performed to her satisfaction, and then studied her daughter's apparel, admiring how the dress hugged her frame. Gerhard Faber was coming for dinner that evening, and she wanted to keep the subtle seduction alive.

"I suppose it's all right," Mrs. Braun said, although her face showed she didn't think so. "But I like the light gray dress better, the one that's low cut. You have such a nice shape, Astrid. Why hide it?"

Astrid blushed. "It shows too much cleavage."

Mrs. Braun could imagine Gerhard Faber stealing peeks down his daughter's dress throughout dinner, imagining the prize obtained if he was patient. She smiled. Her goal was to never let him get there.

"Don't be silly," she said. "You're entertaining

a very interested suitor in the comfort of your own home. You should be comfortable. Go change. Put on the gray dress."

Astrid shrugged and headed for the steps. She never questioned her mother's judgment. Even though they both knew exactly what Gerhard Faber's motives were.

For the past week, Mrs. Braun had been checking on her daughter's latest love interest. She still had some influence in the government, although limited and primarily with minor officials. Given that, she really couldn't determine much. He did play viola for the Berlin String Quartet, which he claimed was only a hobby. That had been easy to verify. But she couldn't ascertain if he was the wealthy industrialist and Nazi Party insider he claimed to be. And she couldn't find his residence, which he said was on Schwanenwerder Island in Wannsee Lake. He even said Goebbels lived only a few houses away. But it really didn't matter who or what Faber was. She didn't think he would be a permanent fixture in Astrid's life.

Gerhard Faber cursed loudly and slammed the cap on the corner post of the iron fence. Remembering he was in a cemetery, he glanced around furtively to ensure no one had seen him. He stood there a moment with head bowed, appearing to pay his respects, before moving to a bench just across the lane.

The money left was much less than he expected, even after he had made his demands, and now he had to go to the Berlin Theater to get the rest. He sat there fuming, wondering what to do next. He waited a few minutes more, trying to calm himself, before deciding on a course of action.

He scribbled a note on a piece of paper and removed the last artillery shell drawing and one page of the rocket blueprint from his pocket, leaving the rest undisturbed. He went to the iron fence, looked in all directions for anything suspicious, and took the finial from the corner post.

He tucked the stern note he had written in the fencepost, along with the drawings. He would make his latest demand clear, no longer tolerating insolent behavior. And he meant it. There were other customers, Russians and Americans, who were more than willing to pay handsomely for what he had to offer.

On the way to the Braun's house he stopped at the Berlin Theater. He made his way to the parking lot, wiggled behind the tree and removed the capstone, and found some more money inside. But it was still not as much as he expected. He left no drawings, because he had no intention of coming back to Berlin Theater. And that's what the note in the cemetery had said.

The Brauns were expecting him for dinner. The workmen in the garden would be waiting for him. He had planned on using the money from the blueprints to pay them, funds he now didn't have. He would have to make up the difference from his rent money. But then he would put his family at financial risk. He thought of his wife and children and, for a moment, he wondered why he endangered them by not controlling his sexual urges. There had to be a solution.

He changed tactics and returned to the garden wall, inserting the three other rocket drawings he had with him, the balance of the first delivery and a quarter of the total. He removed his original note, carefully considered what to say, and jotted down a message with a softer tone.

FIRST INSTALLMENT DELIVERED. PAY ACCORDINGLY OR NO MORE INFORMATION. THERE'S MUCH MORE

AVAILABLE. CHECK CEMETERY FOR
OTHER DRAWINGS AND ALL FUTURE
COMMUNICATIONS.

When he returned to the cemetery on Sunday,
he should have enough money to pay the rent and get
his family's finances on track. He mentally noted how
many concerts the Berlin String Quartet had in the
upcoming month, and then added his salary from the
Armaments Department. He might make it, if they paid
him appropriately for the drawings.

The information wasn't as valuable as he
originally thought. Only the plans for the rocket casing
had crossed his desk. The internals and their intricate
guidance systems were somewhere else, with other
draftsmen. He could try to find them, but that was too
risky. He had to find something else to offer, something
the Allies had never seen before. Something that proved
so valuable he would be rewarded handsomely. And he
had to control Mrs. Braun. His wallet couldn't keep up
with her.

"Mr. Faber, I'm so delighted you've come for
dinner again," Mrs. Braun said as she opened the door.
"The gardens look lovely, the best they have in years."

"I'm glad you're pleased," he said as he entered.
"I talked to the workmen on my way in. They are just
finishing up."

"They did a marvelous job," Mrs. Braun said as
she led him into the parlor. "Although they did mention
some of the stone walkway on the other side of the
house needs to be replaced. I suppose even stone breaks
over time. The one workman said he could fix it all in a
few days, and repair the steps at the rear entrance at the
same time. I haven't showed you that yet, but if I were
you, I would get him to secure the railing, too. It's loose

right at the base. I think we would all feel terrible if someone grabbed that for support and fell and got hurt."

"Yes, of course," Faber said, the smile on his face hiding the queasiness in his stomach. "I know exactly what you mean."

Astrid made a dramatic entrance, coming down the sweeping staircase, her hair short and tight to her head, the gray dress clinging to her body seductively. The low cut at the bosom attracted Faber's immediate attention.

"Astrid, you look beautiful," he said, his eyes wide with wonder.

She smiled and hugged him, just tightly enough that her breasts pushed against his chest. She kissed him on the lips, briefly, innocently letting her lips part slightly to offer a sensual moistness.

"It looks like the workmen are getting ready to leave," Mrs. Braun said. "Did you want to speak to them, Gerhard?"

He was mesmerized by Astrid, but managed to break away. "Yes, yes of course," he stammered. "Excuse me, Astrid. I'll be right back."

# CHAPTER 39

Amanda entered York's hotel room late Friday morning, sat down at the table beside the window, and set another box of photographs on the table. Her face was drawn, the twinkle absent from her eye, the smile missing from her face.

York suspected what was wrong. "Have you heard from Kurt?"

"Yes, I have," she said, folding her arms across her chest. "He telephoned the other night. It's the first I've heard from him since he left."

"How's he doing?"

She shrugged. "He seems to be enjoying himself. He wasn't interested in any alternate plans I might have for him."

York studied her face, feeling the pain in her voice. His eyes were searching, compassionate and sincere. He wanted to help. But he didn't know how.

She looked at him, smiling weakly. It seemed she appreciated his unspoken concern.

He knew she was lonely, but for the first time he realized just how much. Years of neglect from her husband had taken its toll, and she had transferred her own hopes and dreams to her stepson. But he had dismissed them, never making them a part of him, as they were a part of her. And now her husband had abandoned her, finding other women to occupy his time. There was nothing for her in Berlin. She knew it, and so did York.

He watched her closely as she stared out the window, watching nothing in particular. She deserved more. He wasn't sure what it was, but he knew it wasn't what she had now.

He decided to shift her attention from Kurt.

"Can I ask you a few questions about the other members of the quartet?"

She shrugged. "Sure."

"Erika Jaeger."

"She's a close friend, although I don't see her much anymore except at concerts."

"Why is that? Did something happen?"

Amanda shook her head. "No, not at all. She just works so much. She has a government job at the War Ministry, but she also accepts any other work she can find. She cleans offices, works as a waitress, tutors children, whatever it takes to earn money."

"I wonder why," he prodded.

"Her mother is in poor health. Sometimes I spend a few hours with her, just so she has a companion while Erika is working. She's a nice lady. I like her."

York was quiet, thinking of the most manipulative way to ask the next question. "She must be very ill if her care is that expensive."

"I suppose," Amanda said, dismissing his statement. "I never thought about it. But Erika is a very caring person. Maybe she helps other family members, or her husband's family. Before all the chaos she taught school, small children, I think. I'm not sure why she gave it up."

"Why doesn't she do that now?"

"I don't know, maybe it doesn't pay enough."

York thought about the eight people Jaeger was hiding in her house. It had to take a considerable amount of money to support them, especially when buying food on the black market. No wonder she worked three or four jobs.

"She sounds like a truly remarkable person," he said. It was an easy statement to make; he honestly believed it.

"She is."

"How about Gerhard Faber?"

"I don't know him that well, but he makes me feel uncomfortable. I'm not sure why. He likes to flirt with Erika, but she doesn't respond. I don't think she likes him."

"Albert Kaiser?"

"He's a good man, almost like a father to me. He likes to tell stories."

"What type of stories?"

She smiled. "Albert has a story for everything. Just ask him."

"Military background?"

She thought for a moment. "No, not that I know of."

"Captain Klein?"

"A strange man. He pretends to be our manager, but I think his role is to observe us. He does have a military background. I believe he was stationed in France during the last war, and during the beginning of this one. But he's too old to fight, so he returned to Berlin. He's a friend of Albert's. They live in the same apartment building."

York had learned nothing new. The descriptions of all were consistent. And he shared them, even though he hadn't met Faber and Klein. But he knew that would change.

He wondered if there was a connection between Kaiser and Klein, other than neighbors. Maybe they had served in the military together as Jaeger had suggested. And maybe they were manipulating him and Max like puppets to support a secret scheme. But it didn't seem plausible, not for an ex-military intelligence officer and a real estate investor.

"Can we talk about Manfred?" York asked quietly.

"I suppose," she said tersely. "But I really have

215

no contact with him anymore."

"Do you know why he's establishing routes to other countries? And why doesn't Hitler know? Or does he?"

She looked out the window, watching the Nazi flags attached to the streetlamps blow in the summer breeze. She was embarrassed by how little she knew about her husband or what he actually did for the Nazi Party.

"I've been thinking about it for the last few days, and there are a lot of explanations. It could just be an effort to expand the Party's global influence. Countries in South America have always been sympathetic to Hitler. They share common ideologies."

"I suppose," York said, still troubled. "But why all the effort? Is it to escape?"

She shrugged. "Maybe it is."

"Is this something just Manfred and Bormann are involved in?"

She shook her head. "No, there are many others, from private industry and government. This isn't the only thing Manfred does. He's involved in everything from labor shortages to integration of occupied territories. That's why he's never home. He's so busy." She was quiet for a moment, reflecting. "He has other reasons for not being home," she added softly. "But we haven't talked about that yet."

York knew Amanda would discuss her personal life when she was ready. He also realized that Richter was a major force in the Nazi Party and no one in the Allied intelligence organization even knew who he was. That had to change. Richter should be his focus, or the focus of another agent. He was much more valuable than drawings of an artillery shell.

Amanda stood reluctantly, gazing at York. "I should go. I need to practice for the concert tonight."

She hesitated, and looked out the window. "Something isn't right, but I don't know what it is. Maybe we should meet somewhere else next time."

"Where do you suggest?"

"How about the park on Savignyplatz. At the entrance on Kantstrasse, near the southern side."

It was where he had met Max, right near his boarding house. "Sunday morning?"

"Yes," she said as she walked towards the door. "How about ten a.m.? I want to bring my camera. I can take pictures while we talk."

# CHAPTER 40

Amanda left York's room and walked into the hallway, closing the door behind her. She glanced in both directions, saw no one, and started for the back entrance. Just as she turned the corner, the door to a nearby room opened and a man stepped out. It was Manfred Richter.

She stopped short, leaning back against the wall. There was nowhere to hide. He was only six meters away.

He paused in the corridor, the door to the room still open, his back to Amanda. He didn't turn around.

"Are you coming, Anna?" he asked, focused on the room.

"Yes, darling, just give me a minute," a female voice called.

A slender blonde emerged, kissed him lightly on the lips, and then wrapped her arm in his. They strolled down the hallway, oblivious to Amanda Hamilton standing in the shadows behind them.

Amanda stood motionless, shocked and stunned. She stayed in the corridor, hiding in a darkened recess used for storage, struggling to cope with yet another of Manfred's mistresses. She stayed there for almost ten minutes, until she was sure they were gone.

She left the hotel, dazed and distraught, blind to traffic and pedestrians. As she crossed the street she was almost hit by a bicyclist, even though he shouted a warning. But she didn't care if he hit her or not. She ignored the Nazi flags that dominated every aspect of Berlin life, and kept walking, her eyes seeing nothing, her mind knowing the way. When she entered her front door, she barely remembered how she got there.

No one was home when she arrived, not even

Hannah. She went to her sanctuary, the music room and photography studio where she spent her private moments, and sat in a plush leather chair. Her violin sat untouched on a stand beside her while she stared vacantly at the wall. Minutes became hours as the last ten years of her life drifted through her mind, the days and weeks jumbled and confused, images distorted and disjointed. She wondered just how many other women were in his life. There was this blonde named Anna, the redhead during the winter, the bank manager, Greta Baumgartner. Who else? How many more?

Her life was a farce. She had convinced herself that she had a good marriage, even though she now realized she never did. She had thought her husband was a great man; she now knew he wasn't, and never was. She was sure he was in love with her; she now suspected he never was.

She had changed her whole life for him, surrendering who she was and all she had become. She had transformed into a German wife, living in a strange land, learning a new language, becoming everything he wanted her to be – and losing herself in the process.

Yet she had still excelled musically, even in a strange place, taking center stage and becoming the most popular violinist in Germany. It had been difficult. As a foreigner, she had always been viewed with suspicion and mistrust, although it waned with the passing years. But now she wondered what she might have become if she had stayed in Edinburgh or gone to London or New York instead of Berlin. She would never know.

She wondered how she could have been so foolish. When had Manfred turned into such a monster? Had it been gradual, so she hadn't noticed? Or had he always been that way? Was she the one who had changed, once blinded but now given the gift of sight?

If so, what had made her change? Was it actually seeing what she had always suspected, again and again?

Each flaw in their relationship seemed almost normal while Kurt was there. He had been the glue that held the household together, keeping the fantasy family alive. And only a few weeks after his departure, it had fallen apart.

As she reflected on the past, she realized Manfred had been home less and less as the years whirled by. Once the war started, he was barely home at all. But now that was better. She wouldn't have to look at him.

It had been six years since she had visited Scotland. She wondered what had changed, what was the same. Edinburgh was an ancient city; she couldn't imagine it looking much different. She could see herself back there, walking the winding city streets past the Craigleith sandstone buildings: the University of Edinburgh, the Royal Museum, St. Margaret's Chapel, Holyrood Palace, and St. Giles Cathedral. How would it feel to live with the Allies as opposed to the Nazis? There were so many things that she hadn't really thought about. But she did now.

There was no reason to remain in Germany. There was nothing left for her in her adopted home. But she had no idea how to get out, especially now with the world at war. She would ask Michael. He would help her. He was a good man, sensitive and sincere.

She contrasted him with Manfred. Michael was gentle, Manfred was rough. Michael was an introverted intellectual, thrust into a dangerous world because of unique abilities. He was comfortable alone, in his study by a fire, reading a book. Manfred was boisterous and extroverted, a man who enjoyed attention and loved crowds. Both were capable and talented. Both were handsome, Michael in a brooding sort of way, Manfred dashing and outgoing.

Manfred always sidestepped tragedy. He was constantly prepared, cunning and careful, never surprised. He was calculating, somehow able to predict the future and be ready for it. She thought of the escape routes and safe houses and finances he was staging to support the Fourth Reich. What did Manfred know that she didn't? Was Germany losing the war? Or was Manfred part of a plot to overthrow Hitler and rule in his place? Did Hitler know about the escape routes? Was he planning to flee, also? There were many unanswered questions.

She had never found politics very interesting. Now she struggled to remember her discussions with Manfred, or conversations she had overheard. What was he doing? She shivered while assessing him. He was planning, evaluating, and calculating, like he always did. But what was even more alarming, he was waiting patiently. But for what?

There was a time when she thought she understood him, although his motives were always a mystery. She wondered what role he had for her. Was the blonde in the hotel a diversion or her replacement? Was it lust or love? What about the bank manager? Who was his favorite, the bank manager or the blonde, or someone else? Manfred seemed like a stranger, and she felt like she studied him from afar, even if under a microscope.

Michael was different, so calm and supportive and reassuring. She smiled, remembering how interested he was in her photographs. And she winced, remembering the painful moments they had shared. He was so sad that he had lost contact with his daughter. Maybe someday Amanda could help him find her. She smiled. Wouldn't that be nice?

Suddenly she realized just how much she

enjoyed the stolen moments in Michael's hotel room. It felt good to be with someone who admired her, shared her interests, and enjoyed her company. When she really thought about it, she realized that they met much more frequently than her stolen bits of information really required. The photographs delivered were rarely reviewed anymore; they just talked instead. Michael gave them to someone who got them to London. But she didn't know who.

She was fortunate to have him in her life, especially now. He would get her out of Germany and she would return to Scotland, or maybe to London, and start her life again. She was getting excited. Instead of being what Manfred wanted her to be, she could be what she wanted to be. She was happy and sad at the same time: even though she could be whatever she wanted to be, she had no idea what that was.

She looked in the mirror that hung on the wall. She saw a good person, kind and compassionate. Not much effort was made to improve her looks, but she could be attractive if she wanted to. Maybe change her hair style, or use more cosmetics. She wasn't unattractive, just a bit ordinary. But she had a good heart. And she had a good head. She may have been weak for the past ten years, but she could be strong. She had to take one day at a time, plan carefully, maintain the charade until her escape could be meticulously arranged and executed. Then she would find a freedom she had never known in the last ten years: new adventures, new horizons, and a new life.

She picked up the violin, holding it under her chin, her fingers caressing the neck, coaxing the strings, the bow massaging and manipulating, and she escaped, drifting into a world of dreams to avoid a life of nightmares.

# CHAPTER 41

York planned to arrive at Savignyplatz thirty minutes before Amanda did. He wanted to walk the park's perimeter before she got there, making sure nothing looked suspicious. He was anxious and uneasy; there were too many loose ends, too many unanswered questions.

He couldn't understand why the wanted posters for Max appeared for a day or two and then vanished, the intense manhunt evaporating. Supposedly the Gestapo apprehended someone that looked similar, or maybe Max resembled the man that the Gestapo was seeking, York wasn't sure which. He just thought it odd that the British spy and any potential accomplices were never mentioned again.

He also wondered if Kaiser and Klein were more than musician and manager, especially if they had served together in the last war. If so, what could it be, what roles could they be playing? Maybe Klein observed the string quartet constantly, not just during trips. Maybe Kaiser did, too, posing as a father figure while watching every move the others made. York knew there were countless possibilities and endless scenarios, each more dangerous than the last.

He walked towards Savignyplatz, approaching Kantstrasse. Max's rooming house was a few blocks away, to the east, on Fasanenstrasse. On the far corner was a café, blue umbrellas open on the outdoor tables, shading patrons from the summer sun. Trees lined the curb, sheltering the sidewalks, beds of scarlet chrysanthemums at their trunk.

As York crossed Kantstrasse he gazed at the café, searching the faces at the tables. There were a few foreign workers, probably French, and a German soldier sitting with an attractive lady, maybe a wife or girlfriend. A group of middle-aged women shared another table. In the far corner, away from the street, he saw a familiar face.

Max was sipping a cup of coffee, facing Kantstrasse. A man was at the table with him, his back to York. He was older, white wisps of hair crowning his head, but York couldn't see his face or venture a guess at who he was. But he really didn't want to.

He quickened his pace, hobbling on his cane. Max ran other networks; he had contacts throughout the city. His companion was probably providing information. York didn't want to jeopardize the operation. He hurried from view, continuing down Savignyplatz, moving north and then west.

Once he had traveled the entire perimeter, he walked through the park. He saw nothing unusual, only pensioners enjoying the summer day, or mothers with their children. He stopped to watch two boys kicking a football, and a mother pushing a stroller, the infant sleeping soundly. He made his way to the bench where he was to meet Amanda, strolling casually down the walkway.

She arrived fifteen minutes later, her camera around her neck. She had a smile on her face, but it didn't consume her or light her eyes like her smile normally did. Her walk wasn't as buoyant, her face not as bright. She paused a few feet away to take a photograph of a bird on the limb above. Then she sat down, not leaving any space on the bench between them.

"How did the concert go?" he asked.

She shrugged. "As well as can be expected."

His eyebrows knitted with concern. "Is everything all right?"

She turned, her eyes on his, and then blurted

everything that had happened. She told him she had found Manfred in the arms of another woman at the hotel, and how she had hidden in the hallway, shocked and stunned. She told him about Manfred's affair during the winter, the reconciliation, and the bank manager she also caught him with. She described the hours of soul searching, mourning the missing years of her life, and all that she sacrificed, including her identity, until she didn't even know who she was. Minutes passed as she talked, sometimes not even making sense, her thoughts colliding in a rush to be expressed. It was like a catharsis, and the more she said, the more she needed to say.

York only listened, not interrupting, his face showing compassion, his heart feeling her pain. He knew what it was like to be betrayed, and he fingered the photograph in his pocket, remembering the daughter he couldn't find. When tears dripped from Amanda's eyes, starting as a mist and then rolling uncontrollably down her cheeks, he wiped them away.

When she finished talking, he hugged her. Although it was meant to show compassion and support, she held him closely, clinging, not letting go, her head buried in his shoulder. He could hear soft sobs, feel her body jerk slightly. Minutes passed with neither moving, safe in each other's arms.

"I feel like a fool," she said. "I gave him the best years of my life."

York gently pulled away, his eyes trained on hers. "I would argue that the best is yet to come."

She forced a smile she didn't feel. "Thank you, you're very sweet. But I can't stop thinking about what a horrible mistake I made."

"You're being too hard on yourself," he said. "We all make mistakes, but we learn from them and do better. We become stronger. That's life. That's what makes us who we are, determines how we cope and combat, defines what choices we make or don't make. What if you never found out about Manfred? You would have wasted your entire life with a man that doesn't care about you. At least now you can move forward."

He could tell she was afraid. Her face was pale, her eyes wide. It was hard, facing the unknown.

"I have to start all over again," she said.

"Think how exciting that will be. You'll be walking a path that has never been traveled before."

She shrugged. "I suppose you're right."

He put his hand over hers. "I will help you," he said softly.

She smiled, her eyes brighter. "I knew you would."

"Have you thought about what you want to do?"

She paused, for the first time voicing the plan she had spent the whole weekend developing. "I want to leave Germany. There's nothing left for me here."

"And go back to Scotland?"

"Or London. Even Switzerland, if that's as far as I can get."

He sighed, thoughtful, knowing he could get her out. It wouldn't be easy, but he could do it. And maybe he could help Erika Jaeger, too.

"We have to plan this very carefully," he said, drawing the escape route in his mind. "It'll be dangerous and difficult. You'll have to convince Manfred that nothing is wrong."

"That should be easy. I never see him."

"Start thinking about what you want to take with you. It can't be too much. We don't want to arouse suspicion."

"I already know what I'm taking," she said. "My violin, my camera, and all the negatives from my photographs."

"How much space will you need?"

"I can fit it all in a large canvas bag."

He was pensive, envisioning what was needed. He looked around the park. The same innocent faces milled about, no one seemed suspicious. But he didn't want to take any chances. "We should probably go," he said reluctantly.

She hesitated, shades of disappointment crossing her face. As they stood to leave she hugged him tightly. "Thank you for everything."

He smiled gamely, knowing the way forward would be challenging. "You would do the same for me."

She gave him a quick kiss on the lips. "You're right. I would."

# CHAPTER 42

York went to the parking lot of the Berlin Theater, cautiously surveyed the area, then slid behind the tree and removed the top stone on the garden wall. He found Faber's note, insisting that communication be conducted at the cemetery.

He frowned, annoyed at Faber's behavior. The cemetery wasn't safe. Did Faber realize that, or was it a trap? Were they both being observed, baited, controlled by the Gestapo until enough information had changed hands to ensure their deaths?

He had to find a new drop, somewhere information could be exchanged without fear of discovery. His predecessor's description of the cemetery drop, relayed through Max, did have some validity. There was something to be said for hiding in plain sight. No one suspected anyone would be brazen enough to do it. But that wouldn't last forever. It was only a matter of time before they were found out. He had to find another location, whether Faber liked it or not.

York got a taxi and went to the cemetery to put the money at the drop. The morning newspaper was lying on the back seat, and he read it with interest. The Kursk offensive, Operation Citadel, was more than a month old. The northern portion of the German advance, initially successful, had withdrawn to its starting point. The southern offensive still met with some success, but he wondered for how long, especially now that the Germans were taking troops and sending them to Italy.

The headlines portrayed the battle as a reorganization of the front lines to strengthen the German position. The Fuehrer, a military genius, was preparing for the next phase of Eastern Front offensives, tricking the Russians into the web he weaved. York wondered if the information provided by Amanda and Erika had reached the Russians. And if it did, was it a factor in the current stalemate?

More ominous for the Germans were the Allied advances in Italy. Starting in Sicily and advancing across the island, they invaded the mainland and started moving northward. York suspected an Allied invasion of France or Greece would follow, but he didn't know when.

Given the global conflict, and the many fronts that Germany would have to defend, York realized how vital Manfred Richter's initiative really was. The Nazis had no intention of surrendering. They were regrouping, changing the theater of war, retreating to fight another day. Suddenly he was nauseous. What if the war wasn't ending, but only beginning?

The taxi pulled to a halt at the cemetery entrance. York asked the driver to wait, telling him he would only be a few minutes. He exited the vehicle, studied the surroundings, and when satisfied he wasn't being observed, he walked down the lane that was lined with graves.

He didn't like the cemetery on Sundays. There were too many people paying respects to lost loved ones; it was too emotional. As he walked towards the drop, he studied those that passed him. There was a young lady with two small children, her face a mask of sadness, and then another woman with a teenage boy who looked lost and alone. York suspected they were the families of men killed in the war, lucky enough to be buried where they once lived. Maybe they had returned from the front to local hospitals, but then never recovered.

He went to the drop, walking fast but leaning on

his cane, and quickly studied the surroundings. When satisfied no one observed, he removed the finial, took the drawings, and stuffed some money inside. He walked to the edge of the lane. Just as he turned, he saw a man approach from the opposite end, hurried, frantic.

York left, waited a moment, and then walked back in the lane. The man was leaning protectively over the iron fence, his body hiding his movement. York was about to retrace his steps and try to exit unseen, when the man turned to face him.

As soon as he saw York, the man moved away from the fence. He tried to appear casual, staring at the tomb and pretending to pay his respects. A patch over the left eye identified Gerhard Faber.

York didn't want to arouse suspicion, but he also didn't want Faber to see his limp, a characteristic that made him easily recognizable. He turned to the nearest grave and bowed his head in silent prayer.

He could see Faber occasionally turn, watching him. He pretended not to notice, keeping his head low, his gaze focused on the headstone before him. After a respectable amount of time, he edged towards the end of the lane, waiting to exit when he wouldn't be seen.

An elderly couple entered from the opposite end. As Faber turned to observe them, York hurried around the corner, walking as straight as he could. He rushed back to his taxi, climbed in the back and waited. When Faber left, he would follow him and check the drop later.

Ten minutes passed, and then he saw the familiar figure of Gerhard Faber, slender and attractive, his hair meticulously combed, the patch placed strategically over his left eye. He stood at the entrance, studied people coming and going, then climbed into a taxi parked by the gate.

York ducked down in the seat, and instructed

his driver to follow them. The taxis moved towards the center of the road, on to the boulevard, weaving in and out of weekend traffic, battling a sea of bicycles.

As they continued driving eastward, York grew curious. He knew Faber lived in Charlottenburg, not too far from the cemetery, and he found the route they were taking intriguing. Where was Faber going? They continued across the western sector of the city to Tiergarten, where Faber's taxi turned on Von-der-Heydt-Strasse.

It was an exclusive neighborhood, beautiful homes, foreign embassies, breathtaking gardens. It wasn't an area he would expect Faber to frequent. His taxi stopped in front of a majestic house, a bit tired, the paint on the shutters faded, where a group of workmen were replacing the stone walkway in the garden.

York told his driver to stop halfway down the block, far enough away to not seem suspicious but where he still had a clear view. Faber exited the cab and greeted one of the workmen. The man showed him the walkway, pointed at some stone borders to the flower beds, and waited expectantly. Faber put his hand in his pocket, withdrew some money, and handed it to him.

York smirked, knowing Faber had just taken the money from the drop at the cemetery. Now he needed to find out what his connection to the property was. Could it be a friend or relative he provided financial support to, similar to Erika Jaeger and her mother?

As if his thoughts had been read, the front door opened and two women, one young, the other older, but closely resembling each other, came down the steps. The youngest walked up to Faber and hugged him, planting a quick kiss on his lips. The older, probably the mother, motioned to the garden, and pointed to some brickwork at the base of the steps.

York shook his head. So Faber was leading a

231

double life, supporting both a family and a rich mistress. Or maybe it was a one-time rich mistress. But it didn't really matter what Faber's motive was, as long as he provided information.

York directed the confused driver to take him back to the cemetery. After casually strolling around the area to ensure he wasn't being watched, he made his way to the drop. He removed the top of the corner post, finding only a note, no drawings. He looked around, made sure it was safe, and replaced the finial. Then he sat on the bench and read the note.

NO DRAWINGS UNTIL I GET MORE MONEY. MUCH MORE. DON'T DISAPPOINT ME.

York frowned. He had had enough of Gerhard Faber. He took a pen and scribbled on the bottom of the note:

WRONG MOVE

He had the perfect plan to improve Faber's attitude.

# CHAPTER 43

By the end of August, the Russians had beaten back German advances at Kursk, re-taking all ground lost during the initial offense. Their success was due in part to British Intelligence's knowledge of German plans in advance, with continued validations as the attack commenced. Many sources contributed to the Allied efforts, so the impact of information provided by Amanda and Erika would never be known. But the subsequent Russian victory gave further evidence of the weakening Third Reich, who had lost North Africa, retreated in Russia, and now had another front in Italy to defend.

York continued to get information from Erika and Amanda, delivering photographs and any gathered intelligence to Max for transmittal to London or Switzerland. Erika's logistics information was related primarily to German transfer of troops and supplies to the Italian and Russian fronts, but the movement of men and commodities provided an effective snapshot of the Nazi war machine.

He still reported to the intelligence office three mornings a week, sometimes for an hour, sometimes for two or three. The same men were always there, alone or in combination, also translating, or pretending to. He was sure they watched him, but he ignored them, diligently performed his assignments, and left, nodding to whatever occupant might be in the room.

York had decided to let Gerhard Faber think about his message for a few weeks before he put his plan into action. He knew how badly the viola player needed money, and he suspected he would do anything to continue the charade with his once-wealthy girlfriend.

Amanda and York met on a regular basis as she delivered photographs. Initially it had been twice each week, then three, and eventually four. And then without even realizing it, they met almost daily, although sometimes for only a few minutes. As time passed, there were fewer photographs with military merit and more of birds and buildings, which often prompted hours of discussion littered with laughter and occasional flirting.

The tap on the door was timid and tentative, totally unexpected. York looked at his watch. It was almost 8 p.m. He sat at the table by the window, Amanda's latest photographs spread out before him. He grabbed a pistol and tucked it in the back of his pants, took his cane and unlatched the safety on the hidden barrel.

The knock came again, a little more insistent. He put his hand on the knob and prepared to crack open the door.

He glanced back at the table, the photographs spread upon it, and rushed back to collect them. He shoved them in a large envelope and put them under the mattress, returning to the door as another knock was delivered.

"Yes?" he asked.

"It's Amanda."

He opened the door, smiled, and quickly glanced down the hallway. It was empty.

"Come in," he said. "This is a pleasant surprise."

"Manfred never came home for dinner," she said. "The maid said he left a message, claiming to be out of town on business." She smiled bashfully. "I know it wasn't planned, but I thought I would take a chance and see if you were here. I was hoping you might have time to talk."

He was glad she came. He touched her arm, gently caressing her without even realizing it. "Of course I have time. And even if I didn't, I would make time."

She laughed lightly, her eyes twinkling, and held up a package. "I brought a bottle of wine and some cheese."

"Great," he said, grinning. "We can have a party. Come sit down." He retrieved the envelope from under the mattress. "I was just going through some of your photographs. They're wonderful."

"Thank you," she said, having heard his compliments many times but still appreciating them. "I do love it. But the violin leaves little room for much else."

York made sure the curtain was closed and they sat at the table. Amanda poured two glasses of wine and cut up the cheese.

He put a slice in his mouth and washed it down with a sip of wine. "This is very good."

"I'm glad you like it. German cheese is so underrated. The Swiss get all the credit."

He smiled. "I'm glad you came," he said softly. "But isn't it risky, especially with your maid at home?"

She shook her head. "I don't think so. She stays in her room after dinner, and I stay in mine. Manfred is usually gone for days, sometimes the entire week, which is fine with me. Even when he does come home, I'm asleep when he gets there. I was very careful coming here. No one saw me."

He relaxed a little. She was petite and soft-spoken and had an innocent, child-like quality. But she was also strong and intelligent and aware. It was easy to underestimate her. She wouldn't make any mistakes.

"How long will it take to plan the escape?" she

235

asked. "It's already been a few weeks."

York frowned. He wondered what was taking so long, too. "I'm not sure. There are a lot of details to address, the route we take, our final destination. I have to discuss it with my contact, who communicates with London."

She looked anxious, and a flicker of fear crossed her face. "It's hard to act like everything is normal. Even with the string quartet. When will you talk to your contact again?"

"In a few days. I've discussed an escape route with him several times, but in regard to another issue. He's been working on it. We should be leaving shortly."

His answer seemed to satisfy her, and her thoughts drifted. "I found a canvas travel bag today," she said. "It's about this big." She held her hands apart. "It can easily be carried, and it will fit my negatives, violin, and some clothes."

"The less you take, the better," he said.

"I understand." She sipped her wine, pausing, hesitant. Then she looked at him. "I can't thank you enough for all you're doing for me."

"I'm honored," he said. "You've provided a wealth of information to the Allies and made a major contribution to the war effort."

She watched him coyly, and although he avoided her gaze, she was insistent, and eventually their eyes met. Her eyes were searching, inquisitive, looking for an answer.

"But that isn't your only reason, is it?" she asked softly.

He looked at her, vulnerable, unable to hide what he felt. After a minute had passed, he answered. "No, that isn't the only reason."

She moved closer, her hand on his, her face

near, their eyes locked. "What is the other reason?"

He wasn't sure what to say, hesitating before mouthing the words slowly. "You've made me see things I would never have seen, feel what I couldn't feel. Each day I see you, my life feels more complete."

"I'm touched," she said softly, her eyes not leaving his. "You've enriched my life, too. In more ways than you know."

He was uncomfortable, nervous, caught in emotions he couldn't control. "You're fascinating, probably the most intelligent person I ever met. But you would never flaunt it or use it against someone less brilliant. You're talent is amazing. You bring tears to my eyes when you play the violin. I look at your photographs in awe, fascinated how you somehow bring people or birds to life, capturing the light so perfectly, or the expression on someone's face."

She smiled subtly, already knowing what he had yet to realize.

He paused, his heart beating a bit faster, struggling to say what had to be said. "I find you incredibly attractive on so many levels, the way your eyes twinkle, your smile, the bubbly enthusiasm that surrounds you. Each day with you is cherished, never to be forgotten."

He stopped when he realized he was rambling. He looked away, embarrassed. "I'm sorry," he said. "I'm probably not making much sense."

"So there's more than just the need for military information?" she asked, hiding a smile.

He took a deep breath. "I have to admit...," he stuttered. "I care... I mean, you..."

He didn't complete the sentence. Her mouth found his, softly and gently, her lips brushing his lightly, then forceful and insistent, her tongue searching his mouth. They embraced hungrily as she pulled him closer, savoring the sweetness.

They parted, breathless, and he planted tiny kisses on her face, her cheeks, and then back to her mouth, lingering, and then moving to her ears and neck, his hands roaming her body, brushing her breasts. Their breathing became labored, hurried and frantic, a tingling warmth traveling through their bodies and into their loins.

York nudged her to stand, and led her to the bed.

# CHAPTER 44

The morning was overcast, chilled by an autumn breeze, a weak sun peeking through gray clouds to prove that summer was gone. Berlin bustled as always, buses, taxis, streetcars, and sedans moving down the boulevards, bicycles spinning beside them. Pedestrians walked to work and school, shopped or strolled, some intent on their destination, others in no hurry at all.

York walked among them, leaning on his cane, on his way to Max's boarding house. They hadn't met in a few weeks. Max had been called to Switzerland to meet with British Intelligence, and had just returned.

As he moved through the city streets, studying each face he passed and limping along with his cane, he couldn't stop thinking about Amanda, lying in her arms, looking in her eyes. Their souls were melded, their hearts entwined, and parts of him had awakened that he thought had died long ago.

He didn't think he would ever care about anyone after losing his wife and daughter. Not with the walls he built around his heart, thick and high and protective. But Amanda had scaled them, and now he realized he could love again. His feelings for her, so subtle and slow to develop, had crept upon him until, without even realizing it, she had grasped his heart, holding it tightly and refusing to let go. Now they were one, and they always would be.

He was overwhelmed by how much they had in common: music, buildings and bridges and birds, Britain, and beauty in all forms. She was an amazing person, and he knew his life would always be richer because she had walked into it. Now he couldn't wait to greet each day or anticipate tomorrow, and he laughed, wished, hoped and dreamed, all of which he never would have done only weeks before. It was because of her.

As he approached Max's boarding house, he quickly glanced behind him. No one was following him. He checked all directions, looked at passing bicycles and cars, and saw nothing suspicious.

He walked up the steps, carrying two cups of coffee and a bag of kreppels, when he noticed an old man sitting on the porch, reading a newspaper. The man glanced up, squinted at him over his half glasses, and put the paper in his lap. It seemed to be his business to know who came and went.

York tensed, immediately alert. The man had never been there before. Maybe he was a new guest. Or maybe he was there to see what visitors the guests had. As Max had told him before, you can just as easily be betrayed by a child as his grandmother. No one was above suspicion.

"Good morning," York said, exaggerating his limp. "How are you today?"

"War wound?"

York nodded. "North Africa."

"Shouldn't you be doing something for the Fatherland?"

York glanced around, pretending to observe all directions before leaning over and whispering to the man. "I've been helping Military Intelligence," he said, again looking for listeners. "I translate messages from English to German. We're trying to catch British spies."

The man's eyes opened wide, the amazement showing on his face. "Do you need help?" he asked. "I wouldn't mind lending a hand?"

Again York glanced around and, when satisfied no one was near, he whispered his reply. "I'll tell my superiors. They're always looking for good men."

He left the man sitting on the porch, his face

masked with surprise, and went to Max's room. He knocked on the door four times, evenly spaced, a signal they had previously arranged, and a voice from within directed him to enter. As he walked in, he noticed the wallpaper peeling away from the white crown molding in the corner, and a pile of dirty clothes on the floor beneath it.

Max sat at the table, looking at a map with a magnifying glass. He nodded as York entered, his eyes looking huge through the glass. After a moment, he raised his head and motioned York to the chair beside him.

York glanced at the map and saw southern Germany and the Swiss border. He put down the coffee and kreppels, grabbed one of each and left the remainder for Max. He sipped the coffee, took a bite of his donut, and studied the map.

"What are you examining so intently?" he asked.

"One of my informants gave me information on the Nazi escape routes to South America, which confirmed what Amanda overheard at the party. He provided some detail, although sketchy in places. He only mentioned some roads and mountain passes. Nothing substantial. I'm trying to locate some of the landmarks."

York watched him a moment and took another sip of coffee. "I think Richter is a major force in the Nazi party. He's more than you and I can handle. British Intelligence should dedicate an agent just to him. And it may take more than one."

Max frowned. "You're right, of course. I presented that case while in Switzerland. But even though I suggested that, they offered a far different approach."

York's interest was piqued. "What is that?"

"I've been assigned to Richter and his Fourth Reich initiative. London is particularly interested in the routes to South America. With the tide of battle turning in the Allies' favor, no one wants influential Nazis escaping, especially to the Western Hemisphere. If they have an established network and plan to continue fighting, the global conflict would destroy another continent."

"I can certainly understand the concern."

"I can, too. I just didn't expect to be the one dealing with it."

"If you're dedicated to Richter, who will I give my information to?" York asked. "I don't have a transmitter or a way to get photos out of Germany."

"I already thought about that," Max said. "You'll continue to work through me. But the rest of my network has been assigned to someone else, a man I've known for twenty-five years. I was just talking to him before I left for Switzerland."

"At the café on Kantstrasse?" York asked. He then felt uncomfortable, as if he had been spying. "I'm sorry. I happened to walk by on my way to meet Amanda."

"Yes, I saw you, strolling through the city, hobbling on your cane. Not very inconspicuous, but a good cover. But you're right. He's my replacement."

"I pretended not to notice. I didn't want to jeopardize anything."

"Wise move. The less you know, the better. And the same for him. But the network will be in good hands. He's very competent."

Max bit into a kreppel, the map momentarily forgotten. He held up a finger as he chewed, holding a thought until he finished. "What's going on with the quartet?"

York described Amanda seeing Richter and his

mistress at the hotel, but he omitted the feelings they had for each other. It was something Max didn't need to know. Relationships were one of his weaknesses. He had had many, all of which seemed to end in disaster. Maybe it was because he was never in the same place very long. Or maybe it wasn't.

Max shrugged. "It was only a matter of time before she realized he'd never change. What's that, three times that she's caught him? Three times that we know of, anyway. You and I know what he's like. And so does everyone else. Amanda was the only one that didn't. But she'll accept it, and eventually she'll get over it. Her husband is an important man. I'm sure many women are interested in him. She has to realize that."

York didn't say anything. Max wouldn't understand anyway. He avoided being protective of Amanda. He wanted Max to help her, but without knowing he was doing it. That was the key to getting Max's cooperation. Make him think that whatever you wanted was really his idea.

"How involved are you with Richter?"

"I'm consumed with the man," he said. "On London's orders. I even know what he has for breakfast every day."

"Then you know where he is at all times?"

York cringed as soon as he asked the question. There was no reason why he needed the information. His motive was selfish. He didn't want Richter near Amanda. Not that he ever was. Fortunately Max was too interested in his kreppel to notice.

"I know every detail of his schedule from a contact I have in his office. That's the informant I was talking about. And I have others in my new network that I use to watch him. But the man works eighteen hours a day. He's never home, eats in restaurants, and even sleeps in his office. When he doesn't, he's in a hotel room with one of his women."

"Do you need me to do anything?" he asked, hoping to get involved in tracking Richter's movements.

Max shook his head. "Just keep getting me information."

York nodded, reflective. "Are you still wearing the police disguise?

"Now and then, just for credibility. But I haven't seen any more posters. The Gestapo must have been satisfied with the man they arrested. Or maybe I only resembled the man they were looking for. Who knows? I'm sure someone paid the price. There was an extensive manhunt. Even the Hitler Youth units were involved."

York wondered who it was, now sitting in a Gestapo jail. It was most likely an innocent man caught in the web woven by war, unable to extricate himself.

"What else are you working on?" Max asked.

York thought of Erika Jaeger, and the eight people she was hiding, friends, neighbors, Jews, he didn't know for sure. He reminded Max again of their prior conversation and the promise he had made to Jaeger.

He listened, passing no judgment, asking no questions. "It will be difficult to get eight people out of Germany. We already discussed that. I told London, but they still haven't given approval. You know how slow bureaucracy is."

"When will you know for sure?" York asked. "I can't keep dangling freedom in front of them. We're starting to lose credibility."

"Just keep getting information," he said. "And promise whatever you have to."

"Erika has risked her life for months," York said

tersely. "We owe her more than that."

"We'll have an answer from London in a few days," Max said. "Then we should be able to help her. The problem is, I don't know a good route." He paused, and glanced at the map, his eyes wide, taken with a sudden revelation. "But I think I have a great idea."

"What's that?"

"Let me get one of the Nazis escape routes," he said slyly, proud of himself. "We'll use that. If it's good enough for the Nazis, it should be good enough for us. Don't you think so, old boy?"

# CHAPTER 45

Manfred Richter lay on the hotel bed and yawned. He stared at the picture hanging on the far wall, a photograph of Berlin around the turn of the century, horse-drawn carriages competing with streetcars for the boulevard, a throng of pedestrians mingled on the pavements, all wearing scarfs and heavy coats. There was snow on the ground. He decided it was Christmas.

"I was shocked my song was on the radio to begin with," Anna Schneider was saying. She lay naked beside him, fully exposed, her right leg crossing his. "Now I hear it constantly. My family and friends can't believe it, but I always told them I would be famous someday."

Manfred looked out the window. There was a linden tree blocking part of the view, and for a moment he studied the leaves, perfectly shaped, turning colors with autumn, a few drifting to the ground. The building beyond, just across the street, had an interesting cornice, an ornate stone trim around the windows. He wondered how many hours it took a man to do such detailed workmanship.

"I've already made arrangements to make another recording," Anna was saying. "I'll use some of the money you gave me. The man at the studio is so excited, especially since I already have a record on the radio. He's hoping he'll get more customers because I make my records there."

Manfred cringed, the sound of her voice annoying, the content even more so. He was beginning to regret making her song so popular. Maybe he would keep the next one from getting any air play, just so he wouldn't have to hear about it.

His thoughts drifted to his biggest project, his greatest responsibility. If the war went badly, and the tide had already turned, most of the Party leadership would be tried as war criminals. He couldn't let that happen. They wanted to change the world. And they still could. South America offered the greatest opportunity, an entire continent sympathetic, or at the least, apathetic, to the Nazi cause. And a continent could form the springboard for world domination. Their aims would still be achieved, only launched from a different direction.

He was working on several escape routes, through Austria and into Italy, leaving from Genoa or another Italian port. Or they could go to northern Germany and across the Baltic Sea into Sweden, or into France and then to Spain. Or they could always use select border crossings into Switzerland, and then smuggle personnel to different destinations.

Along each route he was establishing safe houses, places where those fleeing could get assistance. Some were men of similar beliefs, some were monasteries sympathetic to the cause, and others would be manned by former Nazis. At each step along the way, sufficient funds would be staged, available to assist the escapees. It was a tremendous effort. But he was almost ready. He only needed six more months.

His thoughts were abruptly interrupted when Anna poked him in the ribs.

"Darling, tell me," she was saying. "Which one of my songs should I record? I can do an upbeat number, like *One More Dance,* or a sensual love song like *Every Hour in Your Arms*. I wrote both of them in the same weekend. Isn't that amazing? Sometimes I'm overwhelmed by creative streaks, and I can't think of anything else until I have every note written down."

Richter wasn't listening, and he really didn't

care. He was thinking of Buenos Aires. The Argentinian city would be the focus of the fleeing Nazis, maybe the capital of the Fourth Reich. The Middle East faction would be centered in Cairo, a satellite capital. And for those wanting to disappear and leave their past behind, Canada and the United States offered fabulous opportunities. He had to arrange every detail, plan for every contingency.

"Manfred, which do you think?"

He hid a frown. "Why not do both of them?"

She was pensive for a moment. "I hadn't thought of that. I wonder how much more it would cost. What if I had three songs on the radio at the same time? Wouldn't that be fantastic?"

Richter was honored that the Fuehrer and Bormann, and leaders in the party elite, had placed such confidence in him. He knew others were involved, but development of the escape route rested with him. It was a monumental task.

He had never been to Cairo. He had never been to South America. It was hard for him to imagine leaving Germany, or the Nazi regime collapsing. But he had to be prepared. He briefly thought about Amanda and wondered if he should take her with him. He knew she wouldn't want to go. But it didn't matter what she wanted. It never had. All that mattered was what he wanted. And some prestige came with having a famous violinist as a wife.

He had barely seen her in the last few months. But even if intentional, it wasn't his fault. She hadn't been the same since she lost the baby. And then she found him with Greta Baumgartner. She couldn't get past either, couldn't move forward. Anything physical was repulsive to her. When she did consent, he got no enjoyment from it. Not unless he forced her. But he found that exciting.

He had no intention of taking Anna, or Greta, or Hannah with him. They were diversions, nothing more. And they would never be anything more. He knew there would always be women to satisfy him, regardless of where he fled. Women were attracted to power. And he was a powerful man. He thought for a moment about how exotic women of different cultures could be. He would enjoy that.

Maybe he would let Kurt choose their final destination. He was looking forward to starting a new life, enjoying his son as he entered manhood. How exciting it would be to create the splendor and glory of the Third Reich on another continent, involved from conception, avoiding the mistakes that had been made in Europe.

Anna was still talking continually. "I probably couldn't," she was saying. "It takes a lot of time to record one song let alone two. I should choose one, maybe the love song. People always like love songs."

Richter was bored with Anna Schneider. He had been for the past few weeks. He still had Hannah, his housekeeper, and Greta Baumgartner, the bank manager. And the woman who owned the café near his office had suddenly become very interesting. She seemed open to his advances. He decided to approach her. His chances were good. If he was wrong, she would just avoid him, although he could persuade her to cooperate if he really wanted to. He had so many tools at his disposal.

Anna Schneider was still talking when he rose from bed and started to get dressed. "Manfred, darling," she said with surprise. "You're not leaving already, are you? We just got here."

"I know," he shrugged. "I'm as disappointed as you. But the Fuehrer relies on me. He continues to assign me more responsibilities, and now I'm working on a special project at his direction. He demands results, with frequent updates. I have so much to do that I can't find time to finish it all. I really should go."

"We can't waste an opportunity to be together," she whined. "It's so hard to find the time. Every hour we have is so precious."

"I don't like it any more than you do," he said, faking a frown. "But duty calls."

She sighed, and then pouted. "I suppose you can make it up to me." Her face lit up. "Maybe another necklace?"

"We'll see," he said, smiling. "But I will make it up to you. I always do."

He finished dressing and leaned over, kissing her on the forehead. Then he left the room, leaving Anna Schneider lying naked in the bed.

# CHAPTER 46

York walked down the Ku'damm, leaning on his cane, watching the people as they moved past him. It always amazed him how, for the most part, people were the same wherever you went in the world. They loved their families, they worked to earn a living, they enjoyed the simple things in life. Only now the world was at war, and they were killing each other.

His thoughts drifted to Amanda, as they normally did, and he wondered how and when he had fallen in love with her. Had it really been gradual or had he just ignored it? Regardless of how it happened, Amanda had certainly recognized it. And when she did, she acted. Then his life changed drastically, caught in a collage of intense emotion. But even Amanda couldn't erase the pain that held a piece of his heart captive. He fingered the photograph of Elizabeth in his pocket. Amanda had offered to help him find her. Wouldn't that be nice if she did?

Even though he was incredibly happy, and anxious to greet each day, he still had a war to fight, and it was a conflict that could last for years. He wasn't sure how it all fit together, or if it ever would. If he got Amanda out of Germany, would he remain in Berlin, or return to London for a different assignment, maybe at headquarters, plotting strategies, planning victory. Maybe he would go to Buenos Aires, waiting for fugitive Nazis, and when they arrived, capture them for trial.

He kept walking, his leg cramping, until he reached the telegram office. It was located on the first floor of a stone building with no architectural merit, a nondescript structure squeezed between two majestic neighbors. Through the large window that marked its

251

façade, York could see a counter with two clerks behind it, and a few tall narrow tables, designed for one to stand at while composing telegrams. York entered, nodding to an elderly woman who passed him to exit.

He looked at the customers, ensuring it was safe. There was a blonde woman, a bit plump, who stood at a table in the corner, busily scribbling a message, perhaps to a husband on the front lines. An elderly man with wire-rimmed spectacles stood near her, carefully wording the telegram he planned to send.

York nodded to the man, got a blank piece of paper, and leaned on a counter beside the wall. He thought for a moment, smiling, and then started writing. When he finished, he slipped the telegram in the envelope and walked to the counter, handing it to the clerk, hiding a smile. He needed to calibrate Gerhard Faber. This should work perfectly. The telegram read:

GERHARD: MOTHER AND I WOULD LOVE TO ATTEND YOUR PARTY SATURDAY EVENING, OCTOBER 16, AT THIS ADDRESS. SIGNED: ASTRID

He gave the clerk directions, sending the telegram to Faber's residence, the one he shared with his wife and three children. He chuckled, imagining Faber's eyes growing wider as he read it. Of course there was no party, and the Braun's had no idea where Faber lived, but it would show Faber what York could do if he wanted. York was sure Faber would be much more cooperative after he realized that.

York had other plans for the day and, when he finished at the telegram office, he walked to the U-bahn station and caught the train to Potzdamer Platz. He still had nagging doubts about Kaiser and Klein, but he didn't know why. He planned to wander around their neighborhood, stay out of sight, and try to learn something. It was a pleasant day for autumn and the walk would do him good. And if he wanted, he could sit at the outdoor café and have a beer or a coffee.

He considered the occupations of the men he planned to observe. It was easy to accept Kaiser as a musician and real estate owner. And even Klein could be explained as the quartet caretaker, charged with ensuring they didn't get into trouble, watching those that came near them. It fit the mold of an older man, still trying to make a contribution to the Party, even with his physical limitations.

But something still bothered him. Someone had identified Max as a British spy, after he had been near the apartment building where Klein and Kaiser lived. Was it just a coincidence? It could be. But this was Max's second war. He had been a spy for both of them. Anyone from his past or present may have caught a glimpse of him and turned him in to the authorities. The most likely candidate was Klein. Max admitted he knew him.

York walked towards the apartment building, staying on the same side of the street, keeping close to the adjacent buildings. He walked around the block, studied the people, the vehicles, the windows of Kaiser's building. He walked through the shops and cafes that occupied the first floor. It was a large building. If Kaiser owned it, York could only imagine the rents he collected. No wonder the man always had a smile on his face.

He wasted another hour before realizing the involvement of either was unlikely. He eliminated Kaiser as an informant or a potential spy. The man was probably too busy with his cello and apartment buildings. And he couldn't concern himself with Klein, even though he realized the man could be a nuisance.

253

Even after removing them from the equation, he realized he had been very successful. Three members of the Berlin String Quartet had provided him with valuable information. And even though the fourth did not, he was harmless, impacting no one. But their military liaison was probably dangerous and should be avoided, which should be easy enough. He had no idea what the man looked like anyway.

He walked back to Potzdamer Platz to catch the U-bahn back to his hotel. As he approached an outdoor café, he stopped short. Max was at a table against the wall, a mug of beer in front of him. Across from him sat the man he had been with at Savignyplatz, who had come from London to run his network. He was much older, a slight man with white hair.

York turned away, and walked briskly across the street and around the corner. He didn't want Max or his new operative to see him. He really had no business being there. But then, he thought, neither did they.

# CHAPTER 47

Amanda Hamilton lay naked in bed, the crumpled sheet covering only her left calf, her head resting on York's chest. The fingers of her left hand traced the jagged scar near his shoulder socket, the flesh raised and purple, skin stretched taut. She studied it carefully, amazed a bullet could do that much damage.

"How long did it take for this to heal?"

York sighed, remembering but not wanting to. "Many months. It was a lot of work to regain my strength and mobility. A very stern Swiss nurse led my recovery. She never smiled, loved inflicting pain, and thought of nothing but work. Sometimes I despised her. Now I thank her every day."

"And your leg?"

"Same nurse, but recovery not as promising, although I could barely walk when I left Switzerland, so it is getting stronger. I think the limp will always be there, but hopefully I won't need the cane forever."

"Maybe when we get back to London, the doctors will be able to help you."

He didn't answer. It was an innocent statement with monumental implications. They would escape Germany, return to London, and then be together. Without the war, without the hatred, without the danger. A history teacher and a violinist that dabbled in photography, living peaceably, loving life. It sounded nice, too good to be true.

"What do you think of London?" he asked tentatively, wondering how much she had thought about their future.

She lifted her head and kissed him on the cheek. "I love London. I could be happy there. I don't have to live in Scotland. Although summers there might be nice, especially if you're teaching."

He smiled, content. "That doesn't seem consistent with a performing schedule. Aren't there concerts all year?"

She leaned up on one elbow, her face lit with excitement. "I've actually been giving that a lot of thought lately. I have a marvelous idea. I'm going to focus on photography, taking pictures of all the things I love: birds and buildings, people and politicians. It would be absolute heaven. I can do an occasional concert if I want to. Or I can teach." She kissed him again. "Just like you do."

He turned and faced her, kissing her lips softly and sensually, his tongue finding hers. He pulled her closer, holding her tightly. His lips moved to her neck, teasing her with tender kisses, pausing at the lobe of her ear, nibbling, while his hands traced the curves of her body, his fingers stroking, gently caressing.

An hour later they lay in bed, basking in love, wanting nothing more than to spend every minute in each other's arms. Their eyes drifted closed with small sighs of contentment.

"I have a marvelous idea," York said thirty minutes later, his fingers caressing her thigh.

She raised her head, her face close to his. "And what is that?"

"I found an isolated restaurant a few blocks away. I think it's where people go when they don't want to be seen."

She was thoughtful a moment, weighing the risks. "And you would like to go there for dinner?"

"I thought it might be nice."

They yielded to emotion, rather than logic, and decided to go. Reluctantly climbing from bed, they dressed. York watched in fascination as Amanda applied a bit of rouge and eyeliner, pinning her hair high on her head to alter her appearance. Then they quietly left.

It was risky to be seen on the street, but for some reason they felt invulnerable, shielded by love. They strolled through Charlottenburg, enjoying the tree-lined streets, the leaves fluttering to the ground, their colors a fiery auburn. Beds of flowers that bordered the cobblestoned streets were wilting, turning brown, yielding to the change of season.

The restaurant was located on Pfalzburger Strasse in the center of the block, tucked between a bakery and a tobacco store. It was close to the boulevard, but not too close, quiet and sheltered. They entered and saw that each table was hidden from the rest, with plants and borders tucked into small alcoves. York had described it perfectly; it was where people went when they didn't want to be seen.

Once they were seated, he studied the eatery. He heard murmurs from the tables on each side of them, but he couldn't hear the conversation or see the patrons. The aisle that led to their table was hidden by a potted plant, broad green leaves screening their table so it wasn't visible from the aisle. The nearest exit was through the kitchen, barely four or five meters away, while the entrance was at the far end of the restaurant. They were safe.

He ordered a bottle of wine and they relaxed, enjoying a rare visit in public. They chatted leisurely, focused on a fabulous future, ignoring the present, forgetting the past. After scanning the menu they ordered the same meal: potato vegetable cream soup, beef stroganoff with spaetzle and salad, and bee sting cake.

"When do you think we'll leave Germany?" Amanda asked. "I'm so anxious to go."

He frowned. He wanted to go, too. "I'm not

sure. I'm still waiting for permission from London. My contact is working on a safe route, determining what preparations are needed. Assuming London agrees, it might take a few more weeks."

He could see her disappointment. She wanted to leave immediately, at that very moment if possible. A month had passed since she decided to go. He didn't blame her.

"What if London doesn't agree?" she asked.

York shrugged. "I haven't really thought about it. I don't think they'll object."

She was quiet, pouting and pensive. "I've been invited to Berchtesgaden, the Fuehrer's private retreat, next month," she said. "I think it's the end of November. I really don't want to spend a weekend with Manfred. Will we be ready before then?"

He didn't want her to spend a weekend with Manfred, either. "Let's make a pact. I promise we'll leave before then, whether London agrees or not."

She seemed relieved. "That would be wonderful. I can't continue this charade much longer."

"How often do you go to Berchtesgaden?" he asked. "I remember the photographs you gave me from Hitler's birthday. Is that the only time you were there?"

"No, I used to go often, but not so much since the war started."

"Do you know where it's located?"

"Not exactly," she said, thinking. "But it's on the German-Austrian border. Just north of Salzburg, maybe twenty kilometers."

"How far from Switzerland?"

"About three hundred kilometers. Why, what are you thinking?"

"I don't know," he said. "I thought it might be easier for you to flee from there, but maybe not. Who will be there?"

"Hitler and his advisors, most likely."

"The rest of the quartet?"

"No, I'm performing alone."

"It might be something to think about. You'll be closer to Switzerland."

"Impossible," she said. "There are guards everywhere."

He frowned, knowing she was right. "We'll be gone by then anyway," he said. He wondered what was taking London so long. For the first time, he thought about leaving without them knowing.

Amanda looked at her watch. "Do you think we should go? Not that I want to, but it might be risky to linger."

He smiled. She was starting to think like him. "Yes, I suppose you're right."

They stood to leave, walking towards the exit, maneuvering their way around the many potted plants, and avoiding eye contact with any other customers. They were almost to the front door when it opened and a couple entered.

The woman had black wavy hair. The man was Manfred Richter.

# CHAPTER 48

York sat on the bench in the Friedhof Heerstrasse Cemetery, waiting for Erika Jaeger. He had already decided that they couldn't meet there anymore; it was too risky. He looked at the tree across the lane, the leaves disappearing, and remembered the first time he had seen it, the leaves sprouting. It seemed like much more time had passed, given the world stage and all that had danced upon it.

His mind drifted to Amanda, and he realized they took an unnecessary risk having dinner in public, even though he never expected Richter to be there. Fortunately, it had been easy to avoid him. They simply walked away, hiding in a different part of the restaurant, sheltered by plants, until he was seated. Then they hurried out the door.

It had been traumatic for Amanda. Not only was she shocked to see him, but he was with a different woman, not the one she had caught him with at the hotel, not the bank manager she had seen him with, and not the woman he had been with in the winter. Now she despised him even more. But she was also afraid of him. She had wanted to leave Berlin immediately, but York knew he couldn't arrange it that quickly. He felt sorry for her; he wanted to leave, too. Each day she remained was harder, riskier, more dangerous. And he realized that.

Erika Jaeger arrived a few minutes later. She looked haggard, worn and weary, her eyes accented by dark circles, as if she hadn't been sleeping. It seemed like there wasn't enough time to do what she needed to. In most cases, there wasn't.

She had probably just come from her husband's grave. It must be difficult. The grief was enough, living life alone when it was designed and envisioned for two. But she bore another burden, something much harder to carry. She was solely responsible for the safety and welfare of eight other people. It must be overwhelming and never ending.

She sat on the bench and cast a weak smile. "Hello, Michael."

"Erika, how are you?"

"I'm well. I have some information for you." She paused, collecting her thoughts. "You have to remember that I am only a clerk. I am doing the best I can to get valid troop and supply movements, but there's always the chance I can be incorrect."

"Just do the best you can," he urged.

She sat back, collecting her thoughts. "They are still moving troops into Italy, as you probably expected given the early Allied successes. I think they may be planning a counterattack."

"Do you know where?"

She shrugged. "I don't. Both troops and supplies are routed into central Italy."

York listened, knowing where the troops came from was also important. "Are they being withdrawn from the Eastern Front?"

"Mostly," she nodded. "But some come from France and the Netherlands. The Nazis also continue to reinforce the Balkans. They are convinced the next assault will be there."

York absorbed every word. "Do you know which section on the Eastern Front has been weakened to send troops to Italy?"

"I don't know that. I'm sorry. Maybe I will have more next week."

"Don't be sorry," he said. "You've done enough. Do you have anything else?"

"Production will soon start on the V-2 rocket,"

she said. "It's supposed to be a very advanced weapon. I don't know where the facilities are. At least not yet."

His interest was piqued. "You must tell me as soon as you find out. It's important."

"I understand," she said. "I'll know from material shipments." She paused, her eyes trained on his. "It's a very dangerous weapon."

York glanced towards the drop. He should have plans for the V-2 rocket shortly, assuming Gerhard Faber cooperated.

He reached into his pocket and withdrew some money and handed it to her. It was much more than she deserved. The information she provided wasn't a secret. He knew it before she told him, and so did the Allied command. But he felt sorry for her.

"Thank you so much. I hope you understand the money goes to a good cause."

"I know it does," he said. He paused, looking at her, waiting until she raised her eyes to meet his. Then he said, "You're a remarkable woman."

She shook her head, smiling shyly. "No, not really. Anyone would do what I do."

He wasn't so sure. "I admire you, your strength. And your loyalty."

She blushed. "No need to." She turned away, studying two women who passed, one with a small boy. "Have you thought about how to get my friends out of Germany?"

He found her choice of words interesting. He suspected she was being evasive, so she didn't reveal personal information, didn't place them in danger.

"Yes, I have. It takes time to prepare, I told you that. And I need London to approve. But an escape route is being developed."

She nodded, her face taut. "It seems to be taking a long time."

York didn't know what to say. She was right. "We're trying to prepare the safest route," he explained. "And we want to take all your friends at the same time."

Her eyes widened in alarm. "They must stay as a group. There can be no other way."

He wondered why she was so distressed. Why did it matter that they stay together? Was there something he hadn't considered? He realized then that he had to meet them. He had to assess their strengths and weaknesses. It was important to know them, and what they could contribute, if they hoped to be successful.

"There is something we have to do," he said. "At least before we go much further. But I'm afraid you might object to the next step."

She looked at him curiously. "What is it?"

"I need to meet them."

Her face showed a flicker of fear, although she tried to contain it. "Is that absolutely necessary?"

He put his hand on her arm to reassure her. "Yes, it is. The sooner the better."

She was quiet for a moment, considering the risks. "I must protect them," she said softly. "They rely on me. They have no one else."

York nodded, his face showing compassion. "I know. I won't betray that trust. But I need to finalize our plan. Meeting those involved is instrumental in doing that."

"You will keep my secret?"

"Yes, I will. I promise."

She sighed, knowing no further steps could be taken until she agreed. "All right," she said, surrendering. "If it must be done."

"It must. And we can no longer meet here. It's too dangerous."

She stood, preparing to leave. "Come to my home at four p.m. on Monday." She turned abruptly and walked away, her hands tucked in her coat pocket.

After she left, York walked down the neighboring lane to the drop. There were few people in the cemetery, as was usually the case on Thursdays, and he saw no one suspicious. He had taken less interest in Gerhard Faber, other than the prank he had just played on him. But he did have valuable information, plans to the V-2 rocket.

He went to the drop, waited a moment for an elderly couple to walk away, and then removed the finial from the fence corner post. The cavity was filled with papers, more than any other time.

He quickly replaced the cap, glanced around to make sure no one was watching, and went to the bench. There were several pages of drawings, completing the set to the initial offering. York saw the full rocket casing design. But he knew the internals were more important. Faber had left a note.

YOU WIN. I WILL COOPERATE, BUT NO MORE TRICKS. THIS IS THE V2 ROCKET. MORE DRAWINGS NEXT WEEK. PAY WHAT YOU WILL. USE THEATER FOR MONEY. DRAWINGS WILL BE HERE.

York took a taxi to Berlin Theater and slowly wandered back to the parking lot. It was normally deserted during the day, most movie-goers attended in the evening or on weekends, very few went to the matinee.

There were only three cars, but a dozen bicycles were parked in the rack, some locked, others owned by trusting individuals. York walked back to the garden wall, squeezed between the tree and a parked car, and removed the loose capstone. He took a generous amount of money from his pocket and stuffed it in the opening.

He returned to his hotel and sat at the table, sipping a cup of coffee. He glanced through the drawings, and when he realized how detailed they were, he studied them more closely. He had underestimated Faber and the information he could provide. He had to get the blueprints to Max. They could change the war's outcome.

# CHAPTER 49

York walked into the boarding house and climbed three flights of stairs to Max's room. He liked the architecture, the detail that went into older buildings that seemed absent in modern construction, but the property was a bit tired, the paint faded, treads on the steps worn from all the shoes that had traveled across them. But it was neat and clean and the residents seemed comfortable. He went to Max's room and tapped on the door, studying the pattern in the hardwood floor as he waited. He heard rustling from within and someone came to the entrance.

"It's me," York whispered.

The door opened and Max led him inside. He was wearing his policeman's uniform.

"Is everything all right?" York asked, alarmed. He hadn't seen the disguise since the wanted posters were distributed.

"Yes, everything's fine," Max said. "I'm on my way to observe Richter with some Party leaders. I thought the uniform would make me less suspicious."

"You had me worried for a minute," York said. "But I won't hold you up. I just brought some drawings."

Max glanced at his watch. "I have time," he said. "Sit down, I'll make some coffee."

York put a box of Amanda's photographs on the table and described his meeting with Erika Jaeger. Once the coffee was done, they sat down and reviewed the blueprints Faber provided.

"It's a secret weapon," York said. "It has a greater range and far more power than the V-1 rocket. I thought you would want to send the drawings as quickly as possible. He's getting the internals, including the guidance system, probably next week or the week after. According to Jaeger, production is about to begin. She doesn't know where yet, but she'll find out."

Max was studying the blueprints. "If all that is true, and the notes on these drawings are accurate, it could change the war. I don't think the Allies have anything like this. How does Faber have access to it, especially, if it's top secret?"

York shrugged. "I have no idea. He must be a draftsman, or works in a department that has access to blueprints. He just pretends to be much more."

He told Max about Astrid Braun, and Faber's need for money, including the stately mansion in need of repair. Then he described the fake message he sent, pretending it came from Braun.

Max started laughing. "That's brilliant, old boy. I wish I could have seen his face when he read the telegram."

York smiled. "I think he'll cooperate now. He's been humbled a bit."

"He's still a risk," Max said, glancing at the drawings. "Maybe that's what happened to Kent. Faber didn't get enough money selling information, so he betrayed Kent to get more. You had best be careful."

York had considered Faber playing both Gestapo informant and Allied spy and discounted it. But if Max thought it was possible, it was worth revisiting. "I suppose it's feasible. It wouldn't be the first time we dealt with a double agent."

"It makes more sense than Klein being the informant. He has all he can handle babysitting the string quartet. He can't manage much more."

York was thoughtful for a moment. "I don't even know what he looks like."

Max shrugged. "If you saw him, you wouldn't forget him. He's older, white hair. And he's as wide as

267

he is tall. Not a threat at all."

York dismissed any suspicions of Klein and gazed out the window, studying pedestrians passing on the street. Everyone seemed to have someplace to go, hurrying along, carrying shopping bags or briefcases or schoolbooks.

Max was watching him curiously. "Anything else?"

York repeated the question he asked at each of their meetings. "What about the escape route?"

Max shrugged. "I should have something in a week or two. Assuming London approves. Although they prefer that you wait until after the new year."

York frowned. "I've already waited eight weeks. I can't wait eight more. People's lives are in danger."

"But London values the information you get."

York knew Max was grateful for all he had done, especially coming to Berlin after being so badly wounded in France. But he had made promises to Amanda and Erika. They were risking their lives. It was time to reward them. "Someone else can handle Faber," he said softly.

"I suppose," Max said, not disagreeing. "Do you know who these people are?"

"I'm meeting them in a few days."

"It won't be easy getting eight people out of Germany."

York hesitated. "There's actually nine."

"Who else?"

"Amanda Hamilton."

Max was quiet, offering no reaction. If he did have an opinion, he didn't offer it. An eerie silence prevailed, with neither speaking.

York watched him, unable to read his expression. He had seen it before, the contemplation.

Max had many faults, but he was always fair, evaluating everything with equal scrutiny.

"London won't like that," Max said softly after a moment had passed. "It adds to the risk. She's married to Richter. The Nazis will launch an exhaustive search. You'll be putting the others in serious danger."

"You're assuming he'll even know she's gone," York countered. "You've been watching him. He goes a week or more without even seeing her. We only need a day or two to get to Switzerland."

Max sipped his coffee, offering no argument. "Yes, I suppose that's true. But don't they have a domestic? Richter must have her watching Amanda."

York hadn't thought of that; he made a mental note to warn Amanda. Max always thought of everything. He was just a bit quicker than everyone else, and he always had been.

"I'll run it by London," Max said. "After all, she is Scottish. If they understand the danger she faces, they'll help her get out."

"She's desperate," York said, trying not to sound emotional. "She wants to leave immediately, but I said we had to wait until London agreed." He paused, thoughtful. "She also has a trip to Berchtesgaden scheduled. That might be an opportunity."

"If we do help Amanda escape, it would be best if she went with the others. The security around Berchtesgaden is significant; it's Hitler's mountain headquarters. There's risk to two escapes, and there's greater risk to stealing her from underneath Hitler's nose. There has to be another way."

York was silent, considering what Max said. He was forced to agree with him. But he wanted the escape to happen sooner. "Why do you want to use one of Richter's escape routes? Isn't there an alternative?"

"I'm sure there is, but Richter's plan offers the

greatest chance for success. If the Nazis have an established route, I'm sure they assumed the entire countryside would be crawling with Allied troops when they use it."

"But will the route include Germany?"

"Given their penchant for planning, they have contingencies for every conceivable scenario. I'm confident I can get a path from Berlin to a crossing somewhere into Switzerland. The big problem is how are we going to transport nine people?"

York sat back in the chair with a smug smile. "I think I have an idea."

# CHAPTER 50

On Sunday morning, just after 8 a.m., there was a loud rap on York's door, evenly spaced, urgent and insistent. When he opened it a crack, he saw Amanda standing impatiently in the hallway. He glanced up and down the corridor and, after finding it empty, he led her in.

"Is everything all right?" he asked anxiously, surprised to see her.

"No, it's not," she said as she entered, her eyes wide. "I would have called, but I don't trust the housekeeper, especially after what you told me. I can't stay long; Manfred came home late last night, but already left for a morning meeting. I'm not sure if he's coming back or not."

"What happened?" York asked, a sinking feeling in the pit of his stomach.

"The Gestapo came to our concert last night. They arrested Gerhard Faber."

York slowly sat on the bed, a thousand thoughts running through his mind. If they had been watching Faber, they were probably watching him. He may have led them to Amanda without even knowing it.

His mind raced, trying to explain what had happened, trying to prevent what might occur. He had to tell Max. London was waiting for the rocket drawings, but he couldn't go back to the cemetery to get them. It was too dangerous.

"What was he arrested for?" York asked, developing a defense, forming a course of action.

She sat on the bed beside him, her hair a bit mussed, her eyes glazed. She probably hadn't slept all night. "I have no idea, but I bet Klein is responsible. When we were in Amsterdam he watched everything

271

we did. It wouldn't surprise me if he did the same in Berlin."

York was quiet for a moment. He wanted to tell Amanda that Faber was selling secrets, to somehow reassure her. But he wanted to protect her; it was safer if she didn't know.

"The Gestapo might question others in the quartet," he said, his tone calm and collected so he didn't frighten her any more than she already was. "You have no connection with Faber, so you have nothing to be afraid of."

Her eyes grew wide, her body animated, her hands clutching his. "What if they've been watching me, too? They might know about us."

He knew she was right; he was wrestling with the same realization. If the Gestapo had watched the drop, his arrest was next. If the trail led to him, it also led to her. And to Erika Jaeger.

He was quiet for a moment, reliving each time he was at the cemetery, recalling every face, every taxi, and every bicycle. There had been nothing suspicious; he didn't think the drop had been compromised. Unless it happened while Kent was in Berlin. But if it wasn't the drop, then who had betrayed Faber?

"Are you sure no one saw you come here?" he asked. His first concern was ensuring she was safe, that nothing had implicated her.

"Yes, I'm certain."

"How about the other times?"

"I don't think so. I always use the back entrance, in the alley. No one can see me."

York nodded, but he knew differently. Someone could have watched from windows in neighboring buildings, and anyone following her could easily determine which building she had entered.

"We should probably find another place to

meet," he said softly, his thoughts focused on protecting her.

She hugged him, burying her face in his shoulder. "But I need to see you. We should be safe here. It's only for a few more weeks."

He knew at some point he had to tell her that eight other people would be with them. But the less she knew the better. Especially with Faber captured.

"What happens to the string quartet now?" he asked, gauging the Gestapo's next move.

"Our concerts have been cancelled for the next three weeks. Tomorrow Erika, Albert, and I start to audition replacements."

York was thinking, calculating, barely listening. If the other members of the quartet were holding auditions, they must be beyond suspicion. But they still had to escape; there was too much risk.

He decided to give her some information, but not too much. "We may have others with us when we go," he said delicately. "At least until we cross the border."

"I didn't know that," she said. Her shoulders tensed, her eyes grew guarded.

"I'm not keeping secrets," he said, seeing she was hurt. "Really, I'm not. Sometimes the less you know the better."

"I understand," she said, although it didn't seem that she did.

"There's less danger that way," he said, still trying to explain.

She chewed on a fingernail, thinking. "Can we leave soon? I'm frightened. This is the world you live in, you can manage it. I can't."

"We may have to," he said. "But I'm not sure when. Definitely before Berchtesgaden, I already promised you that. It takes some organization.

Switzerland is eight hundred kilometers away."

"Can we take the trains?"

"We could," he said. "But they're the most dangerous. The Gestapo always watches the trains."

"Should we fly? We could go to a small airport."

He shrugged. "We could, but then there's the pilot, one more person we have to trust. We can't take that risk. I think a vehicle would be the best alternative. But we don't have petrol."

She sat up straight, her face lit with enthusiasm. "All we need is petrol?"

He looked at her curiously, confused. "Yes, but it's a lot. Even if the vehicle has a full tank, we'll still need about seventy more liters to reach the border."

She kissed him on the lips and then on the face, each cheek, his forehead, and then his neck.

He started laughing. "What is wrong with you?"

"Why didn't you tell me all you needed was petrol?"

"What difference does it make?"

"Because I can get all the petrol we need."

# CHAPTER 51

Erika Jaeger opened the door to her apartment and led York to the parlor. It was a stylish building, a century or so old, with ornate moldings that wrapped the windows and doors and defined the floors. The paint was crisp, only a few years old, and the floral print on the wallpaper was bright, recently updated. The hardwood floors were still beautiful even though they had lost their luster, the pattern indicative of a craftsmanship that was vanishing with passing years. Although the furniture was older, it fit well with the apartment, which was clean and tidy and comfortable.

Erika pointed to a closed six-panel door. "My mother is in her bedroom. She won't disturb us."

He glanced around the apartment, past the parlor and into a dining room. It was well lit, the curtains pulled back from the window, and occupied by a rectangular table, high-backed chairs, and a hutch displaying china that was probably never used. The furniture was handsomely crafted, appeared to be antique by design, but upon closer inspection York realized it was a modern reproduction. A framed photograph hung on the wall, Erika and a man, smiling, their arms around each other.

Beyond the dining room was a kitchen, simple but functional, plants on the window sill. There was a bathroom adjacent to the mother's bedroom, the door slightly ajar, exposing a pedestal sink. The stairs were beside it.

"There's no one else here," Erika said, watching his eyes wander the apartment.

York nodded, seemed satisfied, and turned to face her. "Were you there when Faber was arrested?"

"Yes, we all were. It was frightening."

"Do you have any connection with him at all? If you do, you'll be questioned."

Her face was pale, but her eyes showed strength. "No, I barely know him. Only through our music."

He watched her, anxious and afraid. She had probably been a model citizen before she hid eight people. And although she was a very brave woman, he knew she could never survive if caught. They would hurt her.

"I think you should escape with the others," he said firmly, studying her closely.

"No, I can't," she said, motioning to the closed door. "I have my mother. She's ill, and she'll never leave Berlin."

"Can anyone else care for her, a relative or friend?"

Erika paused, running the faces of those she trusted through her mind. "Perhaps. I will think about it."

"The danger has increased significantly with Faber arrested. The Gestapo could have been watching all of you, not just him."

"When is the escape?"

"In three weeks, or maybe sooner. But I have to see who is coming. They will need their documents forged, depending on who they are."

"I hadn't thought of details like that," Erika said softly, defeat and desperation flickering across her face.

"There will be one other adult coming with us," he said.

She was hesitant, not comfortable with the latest revelation. "Can they be trusted?"

"Implicitly. Your only concern is ensuring your friends are ready. They can't take much, just a small bag."

"I understand," she said, still pale. The full

realization of what was happening seemed to overwhelm her.

"May I meet your friends?" he asked.

She nodded, still reflective. "Yes, come with me."

Erika led him up the stairway and into a short hallway on the second floor. There was a room to the left, small and sparsely furnished, bright with sunlight from a bay wall. He saw a music stand, her violin, and two chairs. There was a desk in the corner. To the right was a larger room, the bed was against the far wall, wooden night tables beside it.

She led him into the bedroom. Matching wardrobes flanked the door, set towards the corners. They were massive pieces of furniture, mahogany, beautifully designed, delicately carved. A matching dresser sat on one wall, with a chair and table opposite it.

She saw him studying the wardrobes, admiring the craftsmanship. "My husband made them," she said quietly. "Before the war. The dining room furniture, too."

He saw the sadness in her eyes, and could only imagine the ache in her heart. "They're beautiful," he said. "Is that him in the dining room photograph?"

"Yes," she nodded. "He was such a good man, so very talented." She sighed and looked away, wiping a tear. "I miss him terribly. But he belongs in heaven. Now that Earth has become hell."

She led him to the far wardrobe and opened the doors. She removed boxes filled with shoes and hats, and then took out a panel, less than a meter square. It was a secret doorway, providing access back into the corridor at the top of the stairs. The hallway was longer than it seemed. It had been walled off, appearing to end when viewed from the steps. No one would suspect

277

there was more to the apartment. It was nicely done.

He climbed through the opening. Erika followed and restored the boxes and the wardrobe panel. They entered the corridor, just past the false wall. A bathroom was on one side, adjacent to the music room. There was a second room, larger, across the hall and next to the bedroom. She led him into it.

As he entered, he expected to find eight Jews of varying ages, primarily adults. But he couldn't have been more wrong.

Instead he saw a teenage girl, maybe sixteen years old, and seven children. But they were different than most children. One boy had a brace on his leg, a girl wore very thick glasses. They were all challenged mentally, gazing at York with an innocent fascination that only those who don't know evil can muster. They were very quiet, sitting around the room on pillows, probably doing exactly what they had been told. They all smiled. Their souls were pure.

York was speechless, his eyes misting. It certainly wasn't what he expected. The aura of the room was one he had never known, filled with innocence and love and trust and happiness. He looked at Erika, seeing the bravest and most compassionate person he had ever known.

She smiled weakly and shrugged. "This is Inga," she said, introducing the teenager. "She helps me."

She moved around the room, introducing each of the youngsters in turn. They all smiled and giggled, pleased that a stranger had come to see them.

York nodded and said hello. A small boy walked up to him with a book, showing him cartoons about animals. York sat on the floor and the boy leafed through the pages, patiently explaining the image on each one. With the slightest encouragement, the remainder joined him, and he was soon surrounded by children who introduced him to dolls and trucks, books and balls, all talking at once, vying for his attention and growing louder as each minute passed. Inga and Erika struggled to calm them, smiling as they did so.

"They're so pleasant," he said, surrounded by children and looking up at Erika.

She smiled. "I know. They'll never have our mental capabilities, but we can learn so much from them. They're so docile and trusting."

He stood up, looking directly into Erika's eyes. "You are an amazing person."

She nodded her thanks. "The Nazis exterminate them. They're inferior, weak, and not welcome in a society dominated by the master race."

"They exterminate them?" he whispered, worried the children might understand.

Erika led him back towards the door, a few feet from the children who played under Inga's protective eye. "It was called the T4 Program. I learned about it when I was teaching school. I had a handicapped boy in the class and one day he disappeared. His mother told me the Germans enrolled him in a special school, one that attended to his needs."

York shrugged. "That seems harmless enough."

"She was notified three weeks later that her son had died of appendicitis."

"That's terrible," York said, seeing the pain in Erika's face as she told the story.

"It is," she said. "Especially since the boy already had his appendix removed."

York winced, cringing. "I don't even want to imagine."

"Don't. It's as horrible as it seems."

"How did you come to rescue these children?"

Erika glanced at Inga. She attended to the

children, but was still listening to their conversation. "Not now," Erika whispered.

York nodded, knowing she would eventually tell him. "I admire you in more ways than I can ever express," he said softly.

"Thank you," she said as she turned to face him. "But I hope this doesn't change anything. Can you still get them to Switzerland?"

"Absolutely," he said with no hesitation. "I just have to change our approach."

# CHAPTER 52

For the first time since his arrival in Berlin, York was alone in the intelligence office where he did his translating, with no one perched outside, watching the building. He was immediately suspicious, alert because of Faber's arrest, and uncomfortable he was in a situation that was different than ever before.

He tended to his newspaper, the *Liverpudlian*, and started working his way through the personal ads. He had translated for almost thirty minutes, hurrying through the paper, when the door opened and a lieutenant entered, a man he had never before seen.

York rose and saluted.

"Sit down," the officer said. "Continue with your work."

"Thank you, sir."

"When were you wounded?" the officer asked.

"A year ago, sir. In North Africa."

"Really?" the officer asked. "With the Afrika Corps?"

York felt the hairs rise on the back of his neck. The officer's demeanor was stern, questioning. It was an interrogation. "Yes, sir."

"Who was your commander?"

"Colonel Dorfmann," York said, not knowing if a man by that name even existed.

The officer thought for a moment, rubbing his chin. "No, I don't know him. I was there in '41. But I suppose many men have come and gone. How were you wounded?"

"A rifle shot to the shoulder. Machine gun to the left leg." He pointed to the cane. "I'm still convalescing."

"Really?" the officer said with disbelief. "After

281

a year?"

"Yes, sir."

"I would think there was something you could do at the front. Can you cook?"

"Yes, sir."

"And you can drive, I assume?"

"Yes, sir."

The officer eyed him closely, studying him. "You are Sergeant Michael Becker?"

"Yes, sir."

The officer wrote his name on a piece of paper. "Carry on, soldier," he said, starting for the door. He then turned, an arrogant sneer on his face. "I think you can carry a gun, or at least drive an ambulance, or maybe cook for our glorious soldiers on the Russian Front. I'll make sure you get that opportunity."

Even though it was a chilly day, York walked to a planned meeting with Max. He wore a heavy coat and scarf he had purchased from a local clothing store when the weather got colder, but still shivered a bit when the breeze blew. The damp air caused his leg to stiffen, masking prior improvements, and he found himself leaning more heavily on his cane.

There were fewer pedestrians on the pavements now that winter approached. Those on the street had a reason for being there, no one strolled aimlessly or paused to study merchandise in shop windows. It was too cold. The birds were fewer, slowly disappearing as they journeyed south, and Amanda's camera now captured inanimate objects: buildings and bridges, bare trees, and dying flowers.

York was a few blocks from the hotel when he glanced over his shoulder, making sure he wasn't being followed. A man attracted his attention, moving at the same pace, barely a block behind. He was short and stocky, wore a black coat and hat, and had a round face with circular glasses. He seemed innocent enough. But something about him piqued York's interest.

He wasn't sure how long he had been there, but he did notice that the man was more focused on him than his immediate surroundings. He didn't look at other pedestrians, ignored passing traffic, and sped by shop windows with barely a glance.

York searched his memory, wondering if he had seen the face before, near his hotel or at the cemetery, or even at any of his meeting places with Max or Amanda. He couldn't recall, not that he would have remembered. There were a lot of short, stocky men with glasses in Berlin.

York was worried, wondering what he might have missed. He had to determine if the man was a threat. He paused mid-block to cross the street, waiting until the traffic subsided. When a streetcar approached, he hurried in front of it, knowing it would delay the man behind him.

Once he was halfway down the block, he saw that the man had crossed the street when he had, ahead of the streetcar and half a block sooner. He was still in pursuit, the distance equal, the pace constant. His face maintained the same impassive stare, seeing nothing to the right, nothing to the left, only continuing onward, intent on pursuing his prey.

York was alarmed, knowing there was little likelihood of coincidence, little chance they were destined for the same location or had left from the same starting point, moving at the same pace. He paused, stopping to look in the window of a pastry shop, pretending to study the sweets displayed. When he turned slightly, he could see the man in his peripheral vision. He had also stopped, and was looking in the window of a jewelry store.

York knew he had to elude him. At the next cross street, he turned right. He was still in route to meet Max, but straying from his original path. After a few minutes passed, he again looked over his shoulder. The man was no longer there. York quickened his pace, leaning heavily on his cane, pushing forward. Twenty meters down the street, he turned again. The man appeared, hurrying around the corner.

Now there was no question; York was certain he was being followed. But it didn't make sense. The man was too obvious, not very good at what he was doing. It almost seemed like he wanted York to know he was there.

York continued in the general direction of his meeting with Max, but wandered a bit. He made a left at the next cross street, and then a right. The man was still there. York varied his pace, walking slower, as if his leg was bothering him, and then speeding up, as if it wasn't. The man was undeterred.

At mid-block York turned abruptly and ducked into a café. He dawdled, studying the cakes and kreppels, letting an attractive woman go in front of him in line, chatting with the cashier.

He bought a cup of coffee, lingered a moment more looking at a chocolate cake. He glanced at the back of the café, searching for a rear exit, but didn't see one. He looked at his watch and, after wasting five or six more minutes, he came out of the building.

York casually looked up and down the street, but saw no sign of the man. He looked at nearby shops, peered in the windows of those he could see, and saw nothing suspicious. That didn't mean the man wasn't in one of them, hiding, watching from afar, but there was nothing he could do about that. He walked to the nearest cross street, looking in shop windows more closely, studying those that passed, wary of an accomplice that might pick up his trail, but noticed nothing unusual.

He stood on the corner, sipping his coffee, perplexed. It could have been a coincidence. The man was far too incompetent to have really been following him. But York didn't believe in coincidences.

He continued to his meeting with Max at the café on Kantstrasse, near his boarding house, constantly looking over his shoulder, warily watching those he passed. He arrived ten minutes late, ensuring he wasn't followed the rest of the way. Max was waiting for him, standing on the pavement, talking to a grandmother pushing a baby stroller. That was just like him; he could chat with anyone like he had known them his entire life.

They chose to eat inside. The day had grown overcast, hinting of snow. They found a table near the front window and ordered lunch, potato salad and sausage with beer, watching pedestrians pass on the street, wary of anyone that posed a threat.

"I think I was followed on my way here," York said softly once their waiter left and they could speak freely. "And a different officer came to the intelligence office today. He asked a lot of questions, took my name, and said he would reassign me to a post on the front."

Max raised his eyebrows. "Gestapo?"

York shook his head. "I'm not sure about the officer at the intelligence office, but not the man following me. He was too inept to be Gestapo."

"Don't be so sure," Max warned. "Maybe the one following you wanted you to know he was there. Just to rattle you, force you to make a mistake. And I think it's interesting that an unknown officer shows up at military intelligence and challenges you, then someone follows you a few hours later."

"I don't know," York said. "Maybe it's all a

coincidence."

"Not likely," Max said warily. "Best keep an eye out. We don't want any mishaps."

"We already have one."

"Why? What happened?"

"Gerhard Faber was arrested Saturday night, although neither Amanda nor Erika knew why. I don't know if he slipped up, or if the entire quartet is under surveillance."

"That makes the man that followed you even more disturbing," Max said with annoyance. "Add the officer at military intelligence into the mix, and I think the Krauts are on to you."

"Agreed," York said grimly.

"We'll probably never know what happened to Faber. He did need money badly, the way the mistress was draining him. And he may have been selling information to the Russians, too."

"I should have paid what he wanted," York said with remorse.

"I'm not sure about that," Max said. "Whatever you paid, it wouldn't have been enough. He was trying to impress the woman. I've been in the same situation myself."

York smiled, thinking of Max's past. "I haven't gone back to the drop yet. It's probably being watched. I'm sure the Gestapo tortured Faber to get the location."

Max was quiet for a moment, thinking. "If they weren't watching it already. Maybe that's how he was caught. But plans for the rocket internals are very valuable."

"I'm worried that if Faber was being watched, the Gestapo might be looking for me."

"It's possible, especially given your visitor this morning. But I think it's more likely that Faber sold information to someone else, a double agent or informant. That's still not a reason to risk going back to the cemetery, but it is something to consider."

York didn't want to take the chance, but he knew how important the rocket diagrams were. Maybe he'd go to the cemetery and see if the drop was under surveillance. If it wasn't, he'd get the plans.

"Did you meet Erika's Jews?" Max asked abruptly.

"There weren't any Jews," York said, still moved by what he had found in Erika Jaeger's house. "Only handicapped children, mentally challenged."

Max yawned, far less interested. For some reason the Jews intrigued him, mentally challenged children did not. "Do you still intend to get them out of Germany? Seems a waste, only being children and all."

"Yes," York said, puzzled by his apathy. "They're people, too."

He shrugged. "It's up to you. I am finalizing a route through my informant. It's one of the escape paths the Nazis will take if the war goes badly for them. It'll be a lot of back roads. Then all you need is a vehicle and petrol."

"I solved the petrol problem. Amanda said she can get whatever I need."

Max was perplexed. "Where does a violinist get petrol?"

York shrugged. "She really didn't say. But I'll find out once we're ready to go."

"You still need a vehicle, and you need a plan."

York smiled smugly. "Actually, I think I have both."

# CHAPTER 53

Manfred Richter sat in his office at the Reich Chancellery, maps and financial reports scattered across his desk. He had established a series of safe houses to support routes through France and into Spain, others to Switzerland, and more through Austria and into northern Italy. Alternate routes were developed northward, across the Baltic Sea and into Sweden and Norway, and he was working on a new route that wound through Greece and then across the Mediterranean to Syria and Egypt.

He sighed, reflecting. It had been difficult getting Bormann to approve his plans. There was a constant demand for revisions and alternatives, secret routes known only to a handful, but eventually he had been satisfied. Then they had delicately briefed the Fuehrer, presenting the option not as a retreat, but as a counterattack, an expansion of the global conflict to other continents, strengthening the Reich. He had even gone to Hitler's headquarters in East Prussia, remaining there for two weeks while the final details were settled, ensuring each trivial comment was addressed, guaranteeing perfection.

The escape routes hinged on the ports: Genoa, Barcelona, Stockholm, potentially Athens. Once a port was reached, transportation could be arranged on freighters or, in some cases for the more elite, through a secret rendezvous with Nazi submarines. Escapees could reach the satellite locations identified as hubs for the new Fourth Reich: Buenos Aires, Cairo, Asunción, and Damascus. He had worked with industrial leaders and Party officials, ensuring those that made the Third Reich great had a presence in each location, and the desire and ability to make the Fourth Reich even greater. Now with the development of the network in its final stages, he needed to consider his own future.

He knew his journey depended on the state of war at the time he evacuated. But he also knew that the future of the Third Reich was becoming increasingly more precarious. With the Russian army advancing daily from the east, and Allied armies entrenched in Italy and threatening invasions on multiple fronts, he must be nimble enough to choose a safe route with very short notice. In his favor, as creator of the process, was familiarity with all of them. And he had front line privileges.

His final destination was more unsettled. He was not as familiar to the Allies as the Nazi elite, those that visibly ran the Third Reich, from military strategies to governing conquered territories, from slave labor to extermination camps. But he knew he was just as culpable as they were, and he would likely receive the same treatment if captured: death by military tribunal. So if that meant leaving Germany a little earlier, when defeat was still in doubt, that's what he planned to do. And he knew that the degree of anonymity he enjoyed would let him go anywhere, even to the United States or Canada, if he chose. The entire globe was his for the taking. He knew the routes, had the contacts and, most importantly, he knew where the money was and how to access it. He was a survivor; he always had been, and he always would be.

For emergencies, he already had Argentinian passports for himself and Kurt and Amanda. But now he had second thoughts about taking Amanda. He had already decided not to take Anna Schneider or Greta Baumgartner, or the brunette from the café he had just started seeing, or Hannah, or any one of the women in his life that served as an occasional diversion. He would probably only take Kurt. They could start new lives in an exotic location. South America and the Middle East both appealed to him; either could satisfy his needs and lifestyle. He just needed to make sure he accessed appropriate funds.

He knew Amanda's public life as a violinist wasn't compatible with a fleeing Nazi whose life depended on secrecy. His new world would be clandestine, quietly enjoying his successes without anyone knowing who or what he was. But that would never be acceptable to her; she lived to perform, to stand on a stage and entertain. So he had to decide what to do with her. He couldn't take her, but he also couldn't leave her.

He smiled, comfortable, because he was always in control. He left nothing to chance. There weren't too many things that Amanda did that he didn't know about. He had let her roam, on the leash he provided, but he could yank it back whenever he chose, even snapping her neck if he wanted to. Or he could let her walk away, thinking she was clever, thinking she had somehow escaped, when in actuality, he had let her go like a pet released to the wild. He found the whole scenario amusing.

Thinking about Amanda made him realize how little he had seen her. Maybe he would have dinner at home that evening; it might be nice to visit. And if Amanda still hadn't accepted what their relationship had become and rebuffed him, he knew Hannah wouldn't. He found the idea interesting. It would be entertaining to see how uncomfortable he could make Amanda.

He had been so busy finalizing the escape routes, finding the funding, validating their chance of success, involving leaders of industry, and gaining the approval of the Party, that he hadn't had time for much else in his life. Now he intended to savor his success.

Hannah was the perfect choice for his celebration. Or maybe Amanda, with some mild persuasion.

Manfred moved most of the papers to the edge of his desk, but took one map and marked a route from memory, using a black pen to identify back roads and small thoroughfares that led from Berlin to Switzerland. He made a detailed note where the border crossing was, using neat, deliberate printing to annotate his comments. Then he put the map on the edge of his desk, unfolded, and left the office, heading for home. He knew how happy Amanda would be to see him.

# CHAPTER 54

Amanda had just finished practicing when Manfred walked into the house, setting his suitcase on the parlor floor. She cringed and closed her eyes, wondering if she could ever survive the evening. She had somehow convinced herself she could flee Germany before she ever saw him again. Now she knew that wasn't possible. But it had been weeks since she had seen him. Why did he come home now?

She put down her violin and took a few minutes to compose herself, sponging her face with a damp cloth. She came downstairs, even though she didn't want to, listening as Hannah fussed over him.

He was sitting in the parlor like he had never left, drinking schnapps. The newspaper was spread out before him, and he was talking to Hannah as she prepared dinner, not visible and almost out of earshot, but occasionally voicing a reply. Manfred's behavior was predictable; it seemed he had had several drinks before he got home.

Amanda realized how important it was to act normally, even though Manfred knew she despised him. But she could at least be civil, even though it would be the acting performance of a lifetime. She took a deep breath, struggled to slow a racing heart, and walked into the parlor.

"To what do we owe this honor?" she asked, unable to avoid being caustic.

He put the paper down and wrapped his arms around her, even though she resisted. It seemed to please him that she did. "It's good to be home. And I know how glad you are to see me."

"Has the Fuehrer given you a day of rest?"

"Hardly," he said, frowning, and then sipping

his schnapps. "There is no time for rest. I was in East Prussia for the last few weeks. It's been frantic since the Allied invasion of Italy, especially with the problems on the Eastern Front. When I looked at my calendar, I saw that tonight was the only chance I had to come home before we go to Berchtesgaden next weekend."

Amanda tensed with alarm, but fought desperately not to show it. "I thought it was two weeks from Friday?"

He slowly shook his head. "No, I'm not sure why you thought that. We leave Friday morning. The Fuehrer was talking about it yesterday. He's anxious to hear you perform."

She shrugged, as if it didn't matter, even though it did. "That's fine. I've been looking forward to it."

"I'd rather stay in Berlin," he grumbled, his eyes returning to the paper.

She waited a few moments, watching him, and then delicately spoke, searching for information. "I suppose you heard about Gerhard Faber," she said softly.

His face showed disgust. "Vermin. I'm told he was selling secrets to the Russians. He should suffer a slow and painful death."

Amanda's face paled, even though she was relieved by his disclosure. Maybe she and Michael were beyond suspicion. "Manfred, he has three children."

"He should have thought about that before he betrayed his country. The Gestapo is..." He paused, searching for the right word. "The Gestapo is extracting information from him now. As soon as they're done, he'll be executed."

Amanda felt a wave of nausea, but fought to keep an interested look on her face. She mustn't show weakness, or sympathy, or compassion. She pretended to agree.

"I suppose he should get what he deserves," she said.

"And his punishment will discourage others."

Hannah called them for dinner, and they moved to the dining room. The table was set with schnitzel and sauerkraut, served with a bottle of wine. Freshly baked rolls sat in a basket, still warm.

Amanda watched Manfred as he ate, and she realized just how much she hated him. He ignored her, reading the paper, looking up to flirt with Hannah when she came into the room. Any attempt Amanda made at conversation was met with grunts, an occasional word or two and, when he felt like it, a faint smile and vacant expression. But that was fine with her.

After dinner they sat in the parlor, listening to news reports and drinking more wine. Amanda knew where the evening would end, and she schemed and plotted, trying to invent a way to avoid it. The mere thought of Manfred's body against hers, the stench of alcohol on his breath, his rough hands raking her body, made her faint with fear and disgust.

As the hours passed she had a glimmer of hope. He seemed more interested in drinking than lovemaking. She attempted casual conversation several times, but he only nodded as he finished reading the newspaper. She sat quietly, listening to the radio as the news ended and an Italian opera came on.

He withdrew some papers from his briefcase and was soon immersed in the reports, frowning as he read them. He continued drinking, switching back to schnapps, and, after another hour she feigned a few yawns, delicately spaced to seem genuine, and then stood.

"I'm going up to bed," she said. "I can barely keep my eyes open."

He looked up from his papers, after having ignored her for the last thirty minutes. He put down his glass and smiled. "I'll join you."

She walked up the steps, praying for an escape, hoping something happened to avert what was about to occur. She went into the bathroom and washed, taking more time than normal, stalling, hoping he'd fall asleep before she was done. But when she emerged he was laying on the bed, stripped to his pants and undershirt, his red suspenders still wrapped over his shoulders.

"I've been waiting for you," he said softly. He patted the bed beside him.

She knew resistance would not only be futile, but potentially painful. And to resist violently would earn her a place beside Gerhard Faber at his execution. She had to get through it, had to somehow separate herself from what was actually happening.

She fiddled with clothing in one of her bureau drawers, stalling. Then she picked up two magazines that were on a chair by the door, and laid them on a table in the hallway. But as the minutes passed, and Manfred's eyes never left her, she realized she couldn't delay any longer.

When she sat down on the bed, Manfred roughly pushed her to the pillows. He pulled her hands over her head, holding them in place with his left hand, and moved his body on top of hers, kissing her neck while his hand moved over her body, squeezing and pawing. She lay there motionless, not resisting, but not cooperating.

"Manfred, please," she pleaded. "You're hurting me."

He continued, not even listening. The kisses turned to bites, playful at first and then rougher, bruising the skin. He pulled her nightgown down over her shoulders, exposing her breasts.

295

She resisted, gently trying to push him away. As she tried to slide out from under him, he held her tighter, squeezing her wrists more firmly, his body grinding against her.

She turned her face away, repulsed, her eyes misting. "Manfred," she said, having trouble breathing. "Please. Let me go."

He laughed, tightened his hold, squeezing, pinching, hurting her.

Just as she was about to scream, air raid sirens began to wail. Explosions were heard in the distance, coming closer. The Allies were bombing Berlin.

# CHAPTER 55

Eight-hundred RAF planes swarmed over the city, flying high in the clouds to evade anti-aircraft guns. The rumble from their engines sounded seconds before the bombs fell, leaving little warning or time to escape for those not in shelters. The targets, unlike the small, sporadic raids previously launched against the German capital, were residential areas west of the city center: Tiergarten, Charlottenburg, Schöneberg and Spandau. It was the second air raid in a week, the first had focused on industrial targets, but it was the most intense of the war. It introduced a more aggressive strategy for the Allies, a further decline in Nazi fortunes, and a disaster for the residents of Berlin.

York survived the air raid, huddled in an underground shelter, worried frantically about Amanda, and concerned for Erika and the children she cared for. He spent the night with strangers as the ground above them shook, dirt falling from the ceiling, muffled explosions announcing that a new day had dawned. They tried to make the best of it, the room dimly lit with candles that cast shadows on the concrete walls. Strangers idly chatted, some tried to sleep, others quietly prayed, but all knew that the landscape above would never again be as they left it.

They exited just after sunrise, silently filing up the shelter stairs. York mingled among them, tired, anxious, and shaken, wondering what the new day delivered. When he reached the surface he was shocked by the devastation, standing motionless with the others, their mouths agape, staring in morbid wonder.

The entire block had been destroyed. Fires raged; structures were crumbling. Some buildings were just shells, the walls standing but roofs and interiors collapsed. Others were like paper waving in the wind, still standing but so severely damaged they would fall with the slightest provocation.

He walked down the street with crying children and stunned adults, leaning on his cane. Many had nowhere to go, and they wandered aimlessly, a vacant glaze in their eyes. Buildings once called home were now piles of brick and broken timbers, shards of glass covering damaged furniture, some of which sat serenely in a house with no walls. The street was passable, but barely; debris covered most of the pavements. Smoke hung in the air, gray and black, shielding the weak rays of the sun, the acrid stench of gunpowder stinging their nostrils.

His hotel was intact, except for the collapsed roof on the side porch, but many of the windows were cracked or broken. Two large flower pots that flanked the entrance lay in pieces on the ground, dirt shadowing the sidewalk. The awning that protected the front steps still stood, torn and tattered, the frame intact.

York walked into the hotel, passed a few other stunned guests, and saw cracked plaster in the lobby, falling from the ceiling to form piles of white dust on the carpet. The striped wallpaper held the walls intact, but the damage beneath it was easily visible: bulges, depressions, small holes. He walked up the staircase, which still seemed sturdy, but noticed the windows on each succeeding elevation were cracked or broken. A light bulb in a hallway lamp had shattered, the small particles of glass lying on the maroon carpet.

He entered his room and saw that one of the panes in the window had broken, glass littering the table. He brushed the glass into a trash can and filled the hole with a towel. When he held the curtain back and looked out, studying the city of Berlin, he saw smoke spiraling to the clouds, marring the rising sun, dust hanging heavy on the autumn breeze. Although nearby buildings had sustained varying states of damage and partially blocked his view, he could still see that large sections of Charlottenburg had been destroyed or severely damaged.

He left a note on the table for Amanda, saying he was safe, noting the time, and that he would be back in a few hours. He went into the hallway and put his key in a plant that sat in an alcove beside his door. She would know to look for it there, should she come.

He went back outside. The streets were filling with response vehicles: ambulances, fire engines, and military transport trucks with troops to assist, all struggling to evade cars, buses and taxis that were stranded or trying not to be. Streets and pavements were still cluttered with those who had lost their homes, stunned and bewildered, knowing what they once considered sanctuary no longer existed.

York found a taxi parked on the side street. The driver stood outside, leaning on the side of the vehicle, his face pale, watching the horror unfold before him. When York approached, he looked at him strangely, almost as if he were living a nightmare.

"Can you take me to a few addresses around the city?" York asked. "I'm concerned for some friends."

He was an elderly man, his glasses thick. "Are you serious?"

"I am," York said. "I'm very worried and the telephone lines are down."

"How far do you want to go? Some of the roads are blocked completely."

"A few places in Charlottenburg, one in Tiergarten."

"That will take all morning."

"I have time."

The man shrugged. "It's your money."

As they moved through the streets of Berlin, York found the landscape similar to the area near his hotel. Fires raged, buildings crumbled, smoke drifted on the horizon, choking those that wandered the streets, their faces telling a story of horror and despair. The buildings had sustained varying degrees of damage, from minimal to massive. Curiously, there were entire blocks that had been spared, while others had only a few residences impacted.

They continued down the boulevard, uprooted trees and downed streetlights impeded traffic, along with debris that had spilled into the streets. Several Nazi flags had been dislodged from their perches and now lay in the dirt, no different from other rubbish borne by the bombs, a forecast of the future.

York directed the driver past Amanda's house. As he approached, he saw a crowd standing in front of the building, surveying the shattered pavement and front steps, a broken tree limb protruding from a window on the first floor. Damage seemed slight, even though across the street three successive townhouses were piles of rubble, dust still drifting from the debris. He breathed a sigh of relief, assuming she was safe.

Next he passed the home of Erika Jaeger. There was little destruction on her street, only a corner property destroyed. Its outer walls still stood, the windows blown from their frames, but the roof and any semblance of an interior lay in a heap at the building's base. Residents milled about the street, afraid and confused, but most appeared thankful that they had been spared. The war had been suddenly and viciously dropped on the doorsteps of Berlin's residents.

He directed the driver to the end of the Ku'damm, where he found the city icon, the Kaiser Wilhelm Memorial Church, in ruins, its steeple stunted, a tower destroyed. Many of the buildings around it fared worse, and York couldn't tell by what remained what had been there before.

Fires and debris forced his driver to take a torturous path, each journey taking three or four times longer than normal. The Braun residence was near their route to Kaiser's, so York asked the driver to stop there next. Most of the buildings were intact, the Chinese embassy among them, but others were in varying states of destruction, like most of the other neighborhoods.

The Braun mansion still stood, but a bomb had landed in the new garden, leaving a large crater and shredded shrubs covered with dirt and shattered stone from the borders and walkways. Every window was cracked or broken, the front steps had collapsed, the iron railing bent and twisted. As they idled past the house, closer to the garden, York could see clapboards on the side of the house were damaged and peeling away, exposing studs that supported the roof. But he suspected the women were safe, and were already searching for a new benefactor.

York directed his driver to Potzdamer Platz, hoping to pass the apartment block owned by Albert Kaiser. The first route attempted was blocked by debris, with horrific damage to adjacent buildings. They diverted a few blocks and tried an alternate, but met the same results. Two more attempts, each from the north, were also unsuccessful. Given the extent of damage, the obliterated landscape and mounds of debris, York had doubts whether Albert Kaiser or his friend Captain Klein had survived the attack.

York told the driver to return to the hotel, but asked him to pass Max's boarding house. It had survived the bombing, along with the café, but not much else on the block stood. York knew that Max was all right. He always managed to come out on top, always the winner while others lost. His life had always been charmed, fated for few challenges, unlike the rest of mankind.

When he got back to the hotel he found the key missing from the potted plant. He rapped on the door and, a second later, Amanda let him in.

She hugged him frantically, kissing his face and neck and ears.

"I was afraid something happened to you," she whispered.

He kissed her, enjoying her embrace, smelling her perfume, feeling her hair in his face.

"I left you a note."

"I know, but I've been waiting for almost an hour."

"It would take more than an air raid to keep me from you."

"I was afraid," she said. "I couldn't bear to lose you. Not after it took my whole life to find you."

He smiled, kissing her again.

"The bombing was horrible," she said. "I could have never imagined destruction like that."

It was the first time she had seen the total devastation war delivers. Her face was pale; she was still in shock. It's hard to watch buildings and belongings that have been part of your life suddenly vanish. Not to mention the injured, or the dead.

"It's only the beginning," York said, warning her of what was to come.

He told her about his drive through the city, and the areas inspected. He didn't mention knowing Kaiser or Erika, but described their streets and neighborhoods so she could reach her own conclusions.

"I suppose Erika is safe," she said, relieved. "Or at least her neighborhood suffered little damage. But I'm worried about Albert."

"Hopefully he survived," York said. "How

about Manfred? Was he home?"

"Yes, he arrived just before dinner. It's the first I've seen him in weeks. I was a wreck, trying to act normally, even though he knows I hate him. We had dinner and talked, and then he started to make advances. It was the first time he's done that since the weekend I met you."

York felt as if his heart had been ripped from his body, so severe was the hurt. He stared at the ceiling, an empty ache consuming him, dwarfing any other emotion.

Amanda smiled. "The air raid started before he got very far. I never thought I'd be so happy to hear bombs falling."

He laughed and hugged her tightly.

"I do have bad news," she said, burying her face in his neck. "Manfred said we're going to Berchtesgaden next Friday. That's ten days away. Not three weeks like I thought. Can we be ready before then?"

York had already decided, after witnessing the devastation from the air raid, that the sooner they left Berlin, the better. Regardless of what London said.

"I'll make sure we're ready," he said. "We should target next Wednesday. I just need to make some final arrangements."

"Manfred left this morning, but I'm not sure how long he'll be gone. I would give anything to never see him again."

"I understand," he said, knowing how difficult it must be. "But don't worry. The bombing will have him occupied for a while."

She sighed and released him. "Michael, I don't know what makes me feel this way, but I think he knows about us."

York's face tightened. "If you have any doubt

whatsoever, then we have to leave as soon as possible. We can't take the chance."

She looked at him somberly. "Then we had better go."

He was silent for a moment, pensive, calculating risk and reward. "You're right. We have to leave in the next few days, before he gets back."

She hugged him. "That would be so wonderful."

He pulled away, remembering a final detail. "Are you absolutely sure you have petrol?"

# CHAPTER 56

York walked to Max's boarding house, wearing an overcoat and scarf, almost oblivious to the bombed buildings that had become Berlin's landscape. He stopped frequently, leaning on his cane and turning abruptly, wary of being followed, but he didn't see the man who had trailed him during his last visit. Maybe he had been killed in the air raid.

Much of the debris had been cleared from the main roads, pushed into high piles where houses had stood, but the smaller avenues looked the same as they had after the bombs had been dropped. Residents combed through wreckage, collecting personal belongings, seeing what could be salvaged, still dazed and shaken, anxious and afraid.

York stopped to look at one residence where a piano sat on a heap of debris. It was originally on an upper elevation but had fallen through the collapsed floor. Two broken chairs and a lamp were beside it, a mattress still covered in sheets and blankets a few meters away. Ceiling joists were strewn haphazardly where they had fallen, broken plaster coating everything.

The blocks he walked didn't look the same, the levels of damage were different, but in stores and houses that were still intact, life went on. People slept and went to work and school, shopped in stores and ate in cafes. For some, it was like nothing had happened. For others, their lives had changed forever.

York walked into Max's hotel, finding little damage from the bombing. The buildings on each side were also intact, while those farther down the road were destroyed. He entered the lobby, finding it vacant, then hurried up the stairs. He noticed a framed portrait of

Bismarck on the wall. The glass was shattered; the frame was intact. It was an interesting contrast of past to present.

York went to Max's room and rapped on the door. It opened a moment later.

"York, old boy," he said, greeting him warmly. "Survived without a scratch, I see."

"And you did, also," York said, not surprised.

"Were you worried about me?"

"You're a survivor. You always have been."

Max smiled and motioned to a chair. "How does it look out there?"

York described the drive he had taken, and the condition of the neighborhoods and houses of those they were interested in: the Richters, Erika Jaeger, Kaiser, and the Brauns. They realized how fortunate they were to survive. Others weren't that lucky. But both agreed it signaled the beginning of the end for the Nazis, coupled with Allied successes after invading Italy and the Russian advances on the Eastern Front. With invasions of the continent expected in the spring, the Third Reich was starting to unravel.

"Richter's plans for the Fourth Reich are even more important now," York said. "The end will come sooner than they expected."

"Which makes the escape routes critical," Max added. "The more we learn about them, the easier it'll be to prevent Nazis from escaping."

They were silent for a moment, reflecting. Nothing was more important than stemming the flow of Party leaders to other continents, where they planned to spread their maniacal message to unsuspecting populations. The world couldn't survive a war fought on so many fronts.

"Have you learned anything else?" Max asked.

"You were right about Faber," York said.

"Amanda told me Richter said he was selling secrets to the Russians."

"I'm not surprised. He was probably working with the Americans, too. He thought he was in control, but in the end, he was being controlled. It would still be nice to get the V2 rocket plans, if you're willing to risk it. But I suppose you're focused on the escape."

"I might check the cemetery, just to see if it's under surveillance. But I want to get Amanda, Erika and the children to Switzerland. Amanda is spooked by Faber's arrest. And she's convinced Richter is on to her."

Max was quiet for a moment, looking out the window, studying the bare limbs of a tree. Then he shrugged. "Maybe he is."

"All the more reason to act quickly, although I know London won't like that."

Max didn't reply. He got up and went to the bed, reached underneath the mattress and removed a paper that was tucked in the wooden strut. He returned to the table.

"Don't worry about London," he said. "I'll clear everything with them." He opened a map of Germany, a path from Berlin to Switzerland marked in black ink. "I've taken the liberty of making some arrangements. It's time to get you out."

York studied the route identified. It used older roads, lesser traveled, but still offered a somewhat direct path. The Swiss border would be crossed just south of Gottmadingen, a small German hamlet.

"The border crossing is crucial," Max said. "On Tuesday at dawn, and not at any other time, you will leave the vehicle in Germany and walk across the border. The road is Steiner Weg; it branches off the highway in Gottmadingen. It's four or five hundred meters to the Swiss border."

"Why is the timing so critical?"

"Because there will be no patrols anywhere near the border at dawn on Tuesday. I can't guarantee that at any other time. The area may look unguarded, but it's not."

"Which leaves everything resolved except a few details," York said.

"Agreed," Max said. "You and Amanda and Erika, if she chooses to go, can use your existing identity papers. Given the remainder are children, and your strategy, which I think is absolutely ingenious, no further documentation is needed."

York had shared his plan during their last visit, but Max made no comment and didn't appear to be listening. "I'm surprised you're impressed," he said. "You didn't seem interested when I told you."

"Quite the contrary," Max said. "I think it's a marvelous plan. But I had to evaluate it, make sure you would be successful. What else is left?"

"I estimate we need seventy liters of petrol, assuming the vehicle has a full gas tank at the start."

"Can Amanda provide that?"

"She says she can. But I'll make sure the next time I see her. Manfred must have a stash somewhere. That leaves one last detail, with only a few days to solve it."

"The vehicle," Max said. "It's brilliant to use an ambulance. The red cross symbol will afford some leniency in regard to search and seizure, even during the war."

"And I think securing the rear doors, and using signs that warn we're carrying tuberculosis patients, will prevent anyone from getting curious."

"You're right," Max said. "Not a single person in Germany will investigate. At least, not anyone interested in preserving their health."

"There's a hospital right on Olivaer Platz. I was going to steal an ambulance the night we depart."

"But that leaves the whole plan to chance," Max said, rubbing his chin, thinking. "Better get the vehicle first, ensure it's the right size, and has the correct markings."

"And a full tank of gas."

"Let me see if I can help with people in my other networks. If I can't find an ambulance, maybe I can get the use of a garage. Then you can steal the vehicle earlier."

York rose to leave. "That's the last detail. I'll tell Amanda and Erika we're leaving just before dawn on Monday."

"Check out the hospital. Make sure you can get an ambulance. And go to the cemetery drop. Maybe you can get the rocket plans."

"I think everything's coming together," York said. "I'll see you Friday."

"That's assuming the air raids don't kill us first."

# CHAPTER 57

York left the boarding house and rounded the corner, abruptly bumping into the man who followed him on his last visit. "Excuse me," he said, stunned but trying to hide it. "I'm so sorry. I should watch where I'm going."

The man was almost a head shorter and, even though he was stout, he was all muscle, like a bear. He peered at York from behind round spectacles, his eyes a pale blue, memorizing every aspect of York's face. He stepped back, removed a billfold from his pocket and opened it, showing Gestapo identification.

"May I see your papers, please?" he asked.

"Yes, of course," York stammered, reaching into his coat. He removed his papers, knowing they were in order, and handed them to the Gestapo agent.

The man peered through his spectacles, studying one document after the other, feeling the texture of the paper, even smelling the ink. When he was finished, he briefly scanned them a second time. Then he gave them back to York.

"I've seen you in this neighborhood several times, walking with no apparent destination," he said. "What made me suspicious was your determination not to be followed. Why is that?"

York shrugged, feigning confusion. "I'm not sure I know what you mean. I am out walking every day," he said, motioning to his cane. "It's to strengthen my leg. I was hit by a machine gun in North Africa, serving with Rommel. I've been given a staff assignment here in Berlin while on convalescent leave."

The man stared at him icily. He really didn't care. "Maybe we need to get you back to the front, instead of wandering the streets, attracting the attention of the Gestapo. The Fuehrer needs good soldiers."

"It won't be too long, I hope," York said, faking enthusiasm. "In another month or two I should be ready."

The Gestapo agent nodded and stepped aside. "I'm watching you," he said warily. "You can be certain of that."

York tipped his hat and moved down the street. Now he had one more reason to get out of Berlin. He walked to the end of the avenue and, as he turned left at the cross street, he stole a glance behind him.

The Gestapo agent stood in the same spot, staring at him.

York walked for another block, circled it and, when he saw no sign of the Gestapo, he took the streetcar for two blocks, got off and walked around that block before summoning a taxi. He gave the driver directions to Erika Jaeger's house. Throughout the drive he continually looked behind them, but they weren't being followed.

York wondered how he had attracted the Gestapo's attention, especially so close to his hotel. It significantly increased the danger they faced. What had the man seen? What had made him so suspicious? How long had he been watching?

The escape had to occur in the next week. It was too dangerous to delay any longer. There were too many close calls: Faber's arrest, the Gestapo, Manfred Richter, Allied bombings, a different officer where he did his translations. At least now he had a definite plan, including a departure date and time. All he needed was a vehicle.

Just to be safe, he had the taxi driver let him out two blocks and one street over from Erika Jaeger's house. Then he circled the block, ensuring no one watched, and did the same in reverse, finally coming to a stop at the door to her flat.

Erika answered the door and urged him in. She gave him a quick hug.

"Michael, I'm so relieved," she said. "I was afraid you didn't survive the bombing."

"Is everyone here safe?" he asked anxiously.

"Yes," she nodded, looking tired, as all residents of Berlin did. "But it was horrifying. What does the rest of the city look like?"

He gave her an account of his travels around western Berlin. Carefully avoiding any hint that he might know Amanda or Kaiser, he described touring their neighborhoods. He mentioned the numerous risks they faced, including his recent encounter with the Gestapo, and the need to accelerate their departure.

She listened attentively, a look of relief on her face. York wasn't sure if she wanted her children safe from another air raid, or from the danger they faced on a daily basis, hiding from the most brutal regime in history. Or, more likely, she just wanted them safe, regardless of the threat.

"I have no way of protecting the children," she said when he finished. "They can't go to bomb shelters; they have to remain hidden upstairs. It's terribly dangerous. I'll be so relieved when they're out of Berlin and somewhere safe."

"This is just the beginning of the bombings," York said, with a sense of compassion. "It's going to get worse. And now that the Allies have a foothold in Italy, and the Russians are advancing on the Eastern Front, the end is coming. Maybe not in a year, or two, but it will come."

Her face paled. Most Germans hadn't considered defeat. The government had stolen enough from conquered countries to keep those in the homeland satisfied. There were few shortages, only minor rationing, and the propaganda made it seem like they were winning the war. But Allied bombings were hard to dispute. The war seemed very real when you watched your house get destroyed and your friends and neighbors die.

"Why don't you come with us?" he asked.

She was such a marvelous person. He didn't want her left to Allied bombings, or an invading army. He hated to think of what might happen to her after he was gone.

"I can't," she said, although she did seem to waver. "I have my mother to tend to."

"You can take her, too," York offered. "Please, at least consider it."

"Thank you, that's kind. But we should stay here."

He admired her, he really did. She was brave, compassionate, caring. He just hoped she realized what might happen to those that remained in Berlin.

"There's still time to change your mind," he said casually, trying not to be forceful. "I really think that you should."

She smiled weakly. "I'll speak to my mother again."

York scanned the apartment, knowing they were alone, and asked the question that had plagued him since their last meeting. "Tell me how you got the children."

Her expression changed, the pain apparent. She sighed, the past running through her mind, memories unpleasant, images horrific. "I told you how I first became aware of what was happening when the child was taken from my class."

"Yes, you did. But how did you come to hide seven children in your house, and where did Inga come from?

She was silent for a moment, never having told the story before. "When the student taken from my class died, I went to the administration office to find out what happened. The woman who tried to help me actually lived nearby, about two blocks away. I knew her. Her husband was killed near the same time as Wilhelm."

"Was she able to do anything?"

"No, not really. She only processed paperwork. But when I explained what I thought was happening, very delicately, a knowing glance passed between us."

"And then she started to help you?"

"Yes, although some time passed before she did. The first was a young boy. With the woman's help, the paperwork was lost and I took him."

"You've had him ever since?"

"Yes, and while the program existed, I was able to save six more."

"Then what happened?"

"The woman who helped me disappeared."

"What do you mean she disappeared?"

"Vanished," Erika said sadly, pain in her eyes. "With no trace. I was terrified. I left my teaching job because I thought I might be discovered. I couldn't do anything that endangered the children."

"Do you know the parents of these children?"

She shook her head. "We were only able to save orphans. There was too much risk with other children because their parents would ask for them. And I couldn't contact parents because I wouldn't know if I could trust them."

"Who was this woman?" York asked. "She risked her life to save seven orphans."

Erika nodded. "Yes, she was a good woman. I will never forget her." She paused, hesitant, not knowing whether to reveal any information, but then she continued. "She was Inga's mother."

York was overwhelmed, unable to fathom the bravery of Erika and Inga's mother. For a moment, he couldn't speak. His eyes misted, both from the sacrifices they had made and from the atrocities the Nazis had committed.

Erika saw his reaction. She was moved, but wanted no sympathy. She changed the subject. "Tell me about the escape," she said. "Maybe I can convince my mother to go."

York explained his plan to her, the ambulance used for transport, the signs for tuberculosis, and the Monday morning departure.

She listened intently, impressed with all that had been done on her behalf. "Are you sure this will work?"

He hesitated. "There's always risk. But we've tried to mitigate it by planning so carefully."

She seemed satisfied. "I'll prepare some food to take. The children will get hungry. It will be one less thing for you to worry about."

"That would be helpful, and much appreciated."

He looked at her, wondering how he could change her mind. Her eyes were dull, her face pale, she could only see yesterday. She couldn't envision a future without the Nazis, or that another man might take the place of her deceased husband. She was a wonderful woman, with a heart as big as the universe, but if she remained in Berlin, she would have no one to share it with. Somehow he had to convince her.

"Is there anything else I can do?" she asked.

He thought for a moment, still planning the final details. "How are we going to get eight children out of your apartment and into an ambulance without them being seen?"

She was quiet, reflective. "Let me think about it. I have some ideas, but I want to walk through the path the children will be taking. Can you come back on Thursday?"

# CHAPTER 58

The terror continued just after midnight when Allied planes again bombed Berlin. They flew at high altitudes, hidden by clouds, the eerie whistle of descending bombs causing fear and panic in those running frantically towards bomb shelters. The few cars and buses and taxis on the road stopped where they were, doors ajar, as the seats emptied. Within minutes, not a soul was seen.

The heavens smiled on Charlottenburg, attacked so fiercely during the previous assault. Although bombs were still dropped on already destroyed neighborhoods, they were more the exception, and the attack was centered on northern and eastern sections of the city. For those in the bomb shelters, the ground still shook, explosions still caused dirt and dust to fall from the ceiling, and the inhabitants were still anxious and afraid. But they survived an uneasy night, the raid ending just before dawn.

Amanda arrived at York's hotel room the following morning, her face a bit pallid, dark circles under her eyes. Few in Berlin had slept much during the past few days. It was more than the immediate danger that kept them awake. The future was too uncertain, minutes now precious, years almost unthinkable, too distant to consider.

She kissed him, wrapping her arms around him, clinging to him tightly but briefly. "I don't think I can endure these air raids," she said.

"Were you hurt?"

"No, I'm fine," she said as she walked to the table and sat down. "But it's so painful to watch such a beautiful city destroyed. I have friends and neighbors who are homeless. And others who are much worse."

"At least we're safe."

"I know. I shouldn't complain."

She took a deep breath and looked out the window, observing a delivery truck negotiate the turn on to the Ku'damm, steering around the remains of an uprooted tree. York watched her, reading her thoughts. They had studied the same tree from their window from summer to winter. Now it was destroyed.

"Manfred hasn't been home since the first bombing," she said. "I don't expect him until next week, just before we're supposed to go to Berchtesgaden."

York was relieved. He didn't want Manfred near Amanda. There were obvious reasons why, given his feelings for her, but she also knew too much. He was sly and manipulative and could get information without her even realizing it.

"I do have some good news for you," York said, offering hope where it was waning. "We're leaving Monday morning at dawn."

She was surprised. For a moment she could only cast him a stunned stare, not speaking. She blinked, as if she hadn't heard him correctly, and then finally reacted. "What a relief that is. Five more days and I'm free of Manfred forever." Her expression changed suddenly, sadness consuming it.

"What's wrong?" York asked. "I thought you would be happy."

"I am. But I'll miss Kurt. I won't even get to say goodbye."

York shrugged. "You can always contact him after the war. It might be sooner than you think."

She smiled. "That would be nice."

"I do have some details to work out, one of which is petrol. Can you tell me how much you have and where it is?"

"Manfred has a boat that he keeps on Wannsee Lake. When we went to Goebbels' party, he had our driver stop at the boathouse. I went in with him. While he was checking the boat, I noticed petrol stored against the wall."

"How much was there?"

"Probably a dozen ten-liter cans."

"We need seventy liters to get to Switzerland, assuming we have a full tank to start with. Are you sure they weren't empty?"

"Manfred checked to make sure they were full. He has always kept fuel there. The last time we went out was in the spring. And he hasn't used the boat since." Then she paused, looking away for a moment. "At least not with me."

York was satisfied with the petrol. He moved on to another topic. "I told you before that there are other people going with us. I can tell you about them, if you want me to. I can describe our escape plans, too. But knowing that information will be dangerous if anything happens and the authorities question you. I can wait until the day before we leave if you want."

"No, tell me now," she said with no hesitation.

He thought for a moment, summarizing the information. "We'll escape in an ambulance labeled with warning signs that claim those inside have tuberculosis. That should keep everyone away."

Her eyes widened. "I'm impressed. That's very clever."

"And now for the surprise," he said. He told her the address they would depart from on Monday morning.

She was confused. "But that's Erika's address."

"Yes, it is," he said. "And there's more. Erika is hiding seven mentally handicapped children in her apartment, with a young teenager that helps care for them. She's been sheltering them for some time."

Amanda was stunned, quiet and pensive. It took a minute for her to accept what he said, but when she thought about the last few years, and the discussions she and Erika had shared, it became clearer.

"I don't understand. I've sat with her mother many times and never heard a sound to suggest anyone was hidden in her building. But, that's why she needs money so badly," she whispered. "So she can feed the children."

"Yes, primarily," he said. "But her mother is very ill, too."

She wiped a tear from her eye. "I understand. What a fabulous person. But I can't believe she bore that burden alone. I would have gladly helped her."

"She didn't want to take any chances. So she kept it a secret and just worked harder. She has many admirable qualities."

"Being a good friend is one of them. Will she be coming, too?"

"No, she wants to stay in Berlin."

Amanda shook her head, unable to understand. "I hope she's not making a terrible mistake. Have you told her I'm going?"

"Not yet. But I will on Thursday."

"We have to convince her to go. And her mother, too. There's no future in Berlin."

"I agree," he said. "I talked to her a bit yesterday. She is reconsidering. I think it depends on her mother."

York watched her closely. She seemed different, as if she had much more on her mind than the escape. Something wasn't right. Her eyes were evading his; her breathing was a bit anxious. She looked ill, wearier than a few sleepless nights from air raids would cause. Even the hug she gave him was hesitant.

"Are you all right?" he asked quietly. "It seems like something is bothering you."

She took a deep breath, anxious. She started to speak, but paused, flustered.

He watched her, concerned. "Don't be afraid. Tell me what's wrong."

Her eyes met his, a few moments passing before she spoke. "I'm afraid that I have a secret, too."

He looked at her curiously. "Really? And what is that?"

She cast a weak smile, her eyes almost apologetic. "I'm pregnant."

# CHAPTER 59

York walked to Olivaer Platz, leaning on his cane but making good progress. He was still coping with Amanda's revelation, stunned and shocked. He was going to be a father, a distinction he didn't think he would ever have again. Amanda, who had such a difficult time getting pregnant with Richter, would now be the mother of his child. It was something they both held supreme given their childhoods, he as an orphan, her as the single child of a wealthy couple that shuffled her between boarding schools. Nothing was more important, nothing more blissful, than family.

It was the timing that was wrong. Amanda was married to Richter. The world was mired in a horrendous war. They were in the capital city of the enemy. But in a week they could be in Switzerland. And when the time was right, they'd be back in London. Someday, maybe someday soon, the war would end.

He wondered how Elizabeth would react. She was about to have a younger sibling, a sister to spoil, or a brother to mentor. He fingered the photograph in his pocket. It would be so wonderful to have her back in his life. If he got to England, he could find her. He knew it.

York circled the hospital. It specialized in digestive and metabolic diseases, but given the world at war, many German soldiers with battlefield injuries were treated there, too. There was a small parking lot near a side entrance, dedicated to service vehicles that supported the facility. Two military ambulances sat in the lot, one a large panel truck, the second smaller with room for only one or two patients. They were flanked by two cars, probably used by hospital personnel.

The larger ambulance was just what York

wanted. It was designed to hold eight patients, with two rows of upper and lower racks on each side. The rear was about five meters long and appeared closed to the cab, but as he strolled closer he could see a small opening, like a porthole, in the partition between the driver and the patients. The exterior was military gray, with white squares on the roof and side panels, the Red Cross symbol dominating the squares. The vehicle was perfect. Now he just had to steal it.

The parking area was not near the main entrance, but at a lower elevation reached by an inclined driveway. It was flanked by trees and shrubs, although most were bare now that winter approached. It was somewhat secluded, the eyes weren't drawn there when passing on the street, but it was still visible. It would work. He could steal the ambulance, maybe in the hours just before dawn.

Satisfied with his reconnaissance, York hailed a taxi and went to the cemetery, directing the driver to Trakehnerallee, not the main entrance. He asked him to wait and then exited, hobbling with his cane. He had to be careful. Faber had definitely been tortured, and he had probably revealed the drop location. Someone might be watching it, or the information had already been removed. But there was a chance, a small one, that the rocket drawings were still there.

He walked through the entrance and continued straight ahead. The drop was three lanes away, to the right. He would approach from the far side, and then come back down. He looked at the visitors, an elderly couple, a woman with a small child, an older lady, and discounted them all as potential threats. He reached the third lane and walked down it.

As he approached the drop he saw a man on a nearby bench, leafing through a newspaper. He was older, past sixty, and might be waiting for someone. Or he could be an informant. He was close to the drop, and he could see the entire lane from his location.

York had taken precautions. He had long ago scribbled the name from a nearby tomb on a piece of paper. If ever questioned when approaching the drop, he would claim to be looking for his relative, pulling the paper with the name on it out of his pocket. He decided this was an opportune time to use it.

"Excuse me," he said, approaching the man and holding the paper in his hand.

The man looked up from the newspaper, startled by the intrusion. He arched his eyebrows in a question, but did not reply.

"I'm looking for a relative's tombstone," he said, handing the man the note. "Have you noticed this name?"

The man didn't even read it. "I haven't looked at any graves. Only that one," he said, nodding towards the drop. "I can't help you." He returned to his paper.

"It's supposed to be in the third row," York said, maintaining the charade.

"Then look for it," the man said with a hint of irritation.

York nodded and continued on, pausing at each grave to read the name. His question was answered. The drop was being watched. Faber had told the Gestapo everything. One more reason to flee Berlin.

He hobbled down the lane, still studying each marker, finally finding the tomb that matched the name on the note in his hand. A quick glance showed the informant still there, but not reading the paper. He was watching.

York paused in front of the grave, made the sign of the cross, and pretended to say a brief prayer. He stayed a respectable amount of time, pasting a pained expression on his face, all for the benefit of his observer.

When he started to leave, he looked back at the informant. He was gone. The man probably didn't believe his story and had gone to get help. York had to hurry.

He made his way back to the entrance and got in his taxi, warily looking for the informant. Just as the vehicle pulled away, a black Mercedes screeched to a halt in front of the entrance, occupying the space the taxi had vacated.

York ducked down in the seat, peering through the bottom of the window. Two men in black suits exited the sedan. One was tall and thin, the second short and stocky, with round spectacles. It was the Gestapo agent who had followed him near Max's boarding house.

A few seconds later the informant came running towards them, leaving a nearby telephone booth. He yelled to the Gestapo, his motions excited and animated, and pointed at the taxi.

York urged the driver on while keeping a careful watch on the street behind them. As they started for Heerstrasse, the main boulevard, he saw the Mercedes racing towards them. Just as they turned and the Gestapo momentarily passed from view, York told the driver to quickly turn right, and then left, taking the road parallel to Heerstrasse.

They traveled two blocks more before York directed another quick right, followed by another left. He turned, looking behind them. There were several black sedans, most in the distance. He couldn't tell if the Gestapo still followed or not.

The driver was getting suspicious. He eyed York in the rear view mirror, suspecting he was in some sort of trouble. He might not know the men in the Mercedes were Gestapo, but he did know that York was acting strangely.

York saw the driver watching, his face hard and chiseled, his eyes wary. He had to do something to erase the suspicion. If he didn't, the taxi driver would summon the police.

He saw a cafe just ahead of them. He signaled the driver to stop, pretending the cafe was the reason for the diversion, and went inside. Several black sedans passed as York took his time, casually watching the traffic from the cafe window. When no vehicles stopped, he went to the counter and placed an order.

A moment later he returned to the taxi with two coffees and two kreppels. He handed one of each to the surprised driver, who expressed his thanks, no longer interested in his passenger's strange behavior.

York asked him to return to the Heerstrasse, and then back to Olivaer Platz. He would walk back to the hotel from there, just in case he hadn't satisfied the driver's curiosity. The taxi returned to the main boulevard, moving eastward towards York's hotel.

The Gestapo were gone.

# CHAPTER 60

York went to his interpreter assignment wearing his uniform and exaggerating his limp, leaning heavily on his cane. He had to be overly cautious. Berlin was starting to unravel, from Faber's arrest to Allied bombings to Manfred Richter to the Gestapo. He knew he was running out of time, and it took considerable effort to continue his daily routine, acting like everything was normal.

The building had been spared by bombings, although much of that section of Charlottenburg had not. York hobbled down the Ku'damm, turned down the side street, and was about to walk into the alley that led to the office entrance when he stopped short.

A black Mercedes, similar to what the Gestapo drove, was parked at the end of the lane. A man sat in the driver's seat, the sun visor lowered, hiding his face. York moved back a few steps and stood on the corner. He looked at his watch, pretended to wait for someone, and then eased back onto the street, hiding behind the building.

He saw another black sedan parked a block away. It was also occupied, the man in the driver's seat studying pedestrians. York waited for traffic to pass, as if he were about to cross the street, watching the man who now watched him.

The vehicles could be innocent, but he doubted it. The drivers might be chauffeurs, waiting to pick up high-ranking Party officials. Or they could be Gestapo, waiting for him.

A half dozen pedestrians came towards him, hurrying down the street. York turned quickly, sandwiched himself among them, and maintained the same pace, struggling with his cane. He made his way back to the Ku'damm, where even more people bustled by, mingling with the crowd. A block later he hailed a taxi and took it back to the hotel. He waited a few hours, continuously looking out the window and, when satisfied it was safe, he left to see Max.

York knew he had to be careful as he walked to Max's boarding house. He had seen the Gestapo during his last two visits. He had seen them at the cemetery. They knew who he was, and now they probably knew what he was. They just didn't know where he was.

He took a different route, walking down Ku'damm towards the city center a few blocks farther than he would have. It was cold and overcast, gray skies either hinting of the future or painting pictures of the past. Buildings destroyed by air raids lay in crumpled heaps of debris, their scarred rooflines marring a peaceful skyline.

After walking three or four blocks farther east, he turned to the north and started towards Max's. He walked up to Kantstrasse, feeling the winter chill, passing bare trees and empty cafes. The city was different with winter approaching. It wasn't as alive as it used to be, not teeming with people or flooded with traffic. But the bombing probably had more to do with that than the weather. People had fled the city, especially those who lost their homes.

When York reached an alley just before the main street, he ducked into it. He hid behind some rubbish cans, peering out at the street beyond. Cars and bicycles passed, an occasional truck, but nothing seemed unusual. A few pedestrians walked by, housewives returning from the market, children playing. There was no one suspicious, no Gestapo or informants.

He continued to Kantstrasse, turned towards the west for three blocks and then to the side street leading to Max's boarding house. He walked past the building, studied the ruins of a nearby home, and circled the block, walking as quickly as his injured leg permitted. After studying the immediate area, he was certain he wasn't followed.

York entered the boarding house, saw no other guests, and went to the second floor. He walked down the corridor to the far end of the hall, climbed the back stairs to the third floor and then went to Max's room. The door was opened seconds after he tapped on it, and Max led him in.

York gave a detailed description of the Gestapo agent who was so close to capturing him, as well as the informant staged at the cemetery. Although the drawings for the V2 rocket would have been valuable information, they had been taken by the Gestapo, now part of the evidence that would lead to Gerhard Faber's guilty verdict and subsequent execution.

"It's obvious the Gestapo are on to you," Max said with a frown. "They weren't sure a few days ago, when they saw you on the street, but after the cemetery and the sedans parked at the military intelligence office today, there's no doubt. Now we've got to get you out of Berlin."

"I only have a few more days," York said. "I can manage."

"You'll have to," Max said. "But I think the sooner you're gone, the better. You've become a huge risk for me, too. I have a lot at stake. I can't let you jeopardize that."

"I still don't know what happened. It must be fallout from Faber."

"It could be, but Faber never met you. So it must have something to do with the cemetery drop. You never should have kept going there. It can't be Amanda or Erika or you would all be in prison. But it doesn't

329

really matter now. You have to stay out of sight until you leave."

"I plan to."

They were quiet for a moment, reflecting. It made them both uneasy to have the Gestapo so close, especially when they weren't sure how York had been exposed.

"I didn't do as well as I wanted with the vehicle," Max said. "But I did locate an ambulance at St. Francis hospital, which is on Budapester Strasse, just off Tiergartenstrasse, a few blocks east of here. On Sunday evening it will be in the parking lot with a full tank of petrol. The keys will be in the ignition. Given those arrangements, I didn't bother looking for a garage."

"How big is the ambulance? Will it hold everyone?

"It'll be cramped. It's a short-body panel truck, probably holds four stretchers in racks. But it has the right insignias, clearly identified as a medical vehicle."

York digested the information, comparing it to what he had discovered. "I found a larger vehicle by Olivaer Platz. It's closer to the hotel, and not far from Erika Jaeger's residence. I think that will work well."

"Use one as a back- up," Max suggested. "At least you know the vehicle will be at St. Francis, should you need it. Is everything else ready? Did Amanda get the petrol?"

York told him about Richter's boathouse, where a hundred-liter supply was maintained. "I'll get the ambulance, go to Wannsee Lake and take some reserve petrol, and then travel the route you provided."

Max thought for a moment, and then looked at York. "That seems to be it. I can't think of anything else. Everything is ready."

York nodded, the details drifting through his

mind. "Erika is packing food for the trip. But I still have to make the warning signs to put on the ambulance doors."

Max smiled and extended his hand, which York shook. "Good luck, old boy. I think this will be the last time we see each other for a while."

"What are my orders when I get to Switzerland?"

"You'll go to Basel with Amanda. British Intelligence will spend some time debriefing her. You'll get further orders when you arrive. Stay in the same hotel you did last year. They will contact you. London wasn't too happy about you leaving Berlin, at least not at first. They're better now."

"What about the children?"

"There are several Swiss organizations that will help. I didn't make any arrangements, but Intelligence knows you'll have them when you cross the border."

York was pensive for a moment, trying to think of any uncovered detail. When he couldn't, he turned to Max.

"I can't thank you enough," he said, shaking his hand again.

Max smiled. "I'm sure our paths will cross again."

# CHAPTER 61

York walked to Erika Jaeger's home, constantly looking over his shoulder, trying to minimize his limp. He still never went anywhere without his cane. Not only did he need the support, he needed the weapon. Especially with the Gestapo so close.

They sat in her parlor, talking quietly while her mother rested in the bedroom.

"I know how to get the children into the ambulance," Erika said.

"Without being seen?" he asked.

"Yes, I think so. There's a garage in the alley, an old carriage house that belongs to my neighbor. I'm sure the vehicle will fit in it. We'll just have to get the children across the back lawn."

He was interested, but wary. "How do you know it isn't used for storage? Have you been inside?"

"Yes," she said, a hint of pain crossing her face. "My husband rented it for his woodworking. Some of his tools are probably still there."

"I'm sorry," he said, seeing her sorrow. "I didn't realize."

She nodded, forcing a weak smile. "So what do you think?"

He was skeptical. "What about your neighbor? Are you sure we can trust him?"

"He left for his daughter's house in the country after the first bombing. I don't think he plans to return until Christmas."

York was intrigued. The location was perfect, and it would be easy to load the children. "Who else has access to it?"

She shrugged. "I suppose everyone does. It's not locked. But I don't know who would bother. Come with me, we can see it from the window."

She led him into the kitchen, and they looked out the window to the ground below. There was an alley between the blocks, the houses on the adjacent streets backing up to it. It was filled with trees, some gardens, and a few outbuildings, including four old carriage houses spread over the length of the street. Each had access to the alley.

"Do the doors have windows?" York asked.

"No," Erika said. "They're wood panels that slide on rails. I looked yesterday."

"But there is a window on each wall that anyone could look in," he said, weighing the risks. "And a walk-in door in the rear. I suppose it will work, but only if the neighbors don't get curious."

"I can't guarantee that," she said. "But it is a good neighborhood. Most of the people mind their own business, although an ambulance will attract attention. People will wonder why it's there."

"I can get it just before we're ready to go, then everyone will be sleeping. We'll load the children and leave. Is there a back door to your apartment?"

She shook her head. "No, I have to take the children out the front door, down the walkway between houses, and then across the yard."

York frowned. He didn't like the visibility. "There's no other way?"

She was pensive, thinking of alternatives. "No, not really. I suppose it is dangerous."

He shrugged. "It's not as dangerous as having the children hidden in your attic."

"No, that's true," she agreed.

He turned to face her, gently placing his hands on her shoulders. "Will you and your mother please come? We have the room."

She hesitated. "It's too difficult for my mother. I

need to think of her, not what's best for me. Although I will miss the children terribly."

"The entire trip will take two days at most," he said. "And one day is more likely. It's only nine or ten hours of driving. She can make it if we all help her."

"We'd only be a burden, and I don't want to put everyone else at risk. I doubt if my mother can be convinced to leave Berlin anyway."

"Don't be so sure," York said. "From what I'm told, many elderly don't like Hitler or his policies, but are afraid to say so. You may be surprised."

"It's not the government that keeps her here," Erika explained. "Berlin is all she's ever known. She's too old to change her ways. And I don't want her to be uncomfortable, especially when she's so ill."

York was quiet, calculating. He wanted Erika and her mother to come. After giving the matter some thought, he tried a different tactic.

"I told you that another adult was coming," he said. "If it was someone you knew and admired, someone you trusted implicitly, could I persuade you to join us?"

She was perplexed. "I'm not sure. If it was a friend, someone I cared about, I would be much more willing. But it still depends on my mother."

Then the wall of strength she had always shown suddenly shattered. She sighed, her face pale, her eyes misting. "I'm just so frightened," she whispered.

He pulled her close, hugging her, wanting desperately to help. "We're all frightened," he said. "But this is the right thing to do."

"I hope so, for the children's sake," she said, wavering.

"Is there any way you can make your mother change her mind?"

She shrugged. "I don't know. It's dangerous and

taxing, and she knows that. She really isn't well, although I realize the trip is a short one. The stress and uncertainty would impact her the most."

"And that's your only reason for not going?"

Erika was quiet for a moment, thinking. "Yes, of course it is. My mother's welfare comes first."

York studied her face. She knew remaining in Berlin meant heartache and misery, and maybe much worse. But her mother wouldn't leave, and she wouldn't leave her mother. "Erika, you're making a horrible mistake. Berlin will only get worse."

"Who is the other person?" she asked, wavering.

York hesitated. "The more information you have, the more dangerous it is. Can you accept my word, that it's someone both you and your mother respect greatly, and then tell your mother it's really best for both of you if you leave?"

She was doubtful. "Mother will be difficult to convince. I've tried."

York was silent, wondering whether to proceed. The Gestapo was close, probably days away from finding them. Why should he expose her to more danger than she already faced?

"If you tell me who it is, I'll talk to my mother again," she said, relenting. "You can trust me."

"I know that. I would trust you with my own life."

"Then tell me."

He sighed, knowing once the words were uttered, he couldn't take them back. "It's Amanda Richter."

# CHAPTER 62

Amanda telephoned Erika late Saturday morning. It took several attempts to get through, so many telephone lines had been damaged by the bombing, but she persevered and was eventually successful. She knew once the call was connected, that someone could be listening to their conversation, so she chose her words carefully.

"Erika, do you have time for me to visit today?" Amanda asked cryptically. "I'm having a problem with one of the Mozart movements. May I bring my violin and we can work on it together."

"Of course," Erika said. "I would enjoy that. I can always use the practice."

"I'll stop by in hour or so. Should I bring lunch?"

"No, I'll prepare something, but thank you. And if you're bringing anything else, you're welcome to leave it here."

Amanda understood the offer. She could bring whatever she was taking to Switzerland and leave it at Erika's. Then she wouldn't have to worry about it on Monday.

She had already packed her canvass bag. It was stuffed with clothes, her photographic negatives, and her camera and lenses, with just enough room for her treasured violin. She had money hidden in the lining, sewn inside some of the clothing, and tucked in the compartments of the violin case. To maintain the appearance of normalcy, she had placed another violin, one of inferior quality that had been tucked in a closet, onto the stand in her music room.

She now had to get the bag from her townhouse to a taxi without anyone seeing her. Manfred wasn't home, but Hannah was, and she couldn't be trusted. Amanda decided to carry the violin case separately. That was easy to explain, since she occasionally visited other musicians. But the canvas bag, almost a meter long, would be much more difficult.

She went downstairs to see if Hannah was in her bedroom. Standing quietly by the door, she could hear a news program on the radio, but no movement. She decided to take the risk.

She got her bag and came quietly down the stairs, starting towards the front door. As she slowly crept forward, she warily watched the steps to Hannah's room.

"Will you be having lunch, Mrs. Richter?" Hannah called from the kitchen.

Amanda was startled, her eyes wide. Hannah was coming closer, towards the parlor. She put her bag behind a leather chair and walked towards the kitchen, trying to keep Hannah occupied.

"I may visit some musician friends," Amanda said, reaching the kitchen just as Hannah emerged. "I haven't decided yet."

They stood in the entrance, Amanda subconsciously blocking her path. Hannah looked at her curiously, and stepped around her.

"I have some bratwurst cooking, if you decide to stay," Hannah said as she walked into the parlor. She paused, as if thinking of something, moving to the table beside the couch. Amanda's bag was a few feet away, poorly hidden.

Amanda watched in horror, barely breathing. The bag couldn't be explained. If Hannah saw it, she would open it and tell Manfred what she found.

Hannah stopped, the bag almost in sight, but not quite. "I have some sauerbraten, too, if you prefer."

Amanda had to distract her, had to get her out of

the parlor. "I'll probably go to my friends," she said. "There's no need to prepare anything just for me."

Hannah shrugged, took another step, and grabbed the newspaper off the table. "I'll be in my room," she said, still facing Amanda. "Let me know what you decide."

Amanda nodded, fighting to keep her eyes trained on Hannah and not let them drop to the bag that was almost at her feet.

Hannah started walking towards her room. She turned and looked at Amanda curiously. "Are you all right, Mrs. Richter?"

"Yes, yes, of course," Amanda stammered, smiling weakly. "I'm just trying to decide."

Hannah smiled politely and walked to her flat.

Amanda breathed a sigh of relief, the tension temporarily eased. But she had to hurry. Hannah may be in her room, but she was also cooking. She wouldn't be there for long.

Amanda got her bag and tiptoed to the front door, keeping a wary eye on Hannah's room. When she got to the entrance, she carefully opened it, making as little noise as possible. She looked up and down the street and, when seeing no neighbors or strangers near her house, she set it outside.

She called a taxi, getting through on the third try, not caring if Hannah heard, and then went upstairs for her violin. When she came down the steps, she laid her instrument on the couch and got her coat from the closet. She peeked in the kitchen, but Hannah wasn't there. Bratwurst simmered on the stove, the aroma drifting through the room.

Amanda picked up her violin case and walked to Hannah's door. She listened for a moment, but heard nothing, not even the radio. She knocked lightly. The door opened a few seconds later.

"I did decide to spend the day with my friends," she said.

Hannah's eyes moved to the violin case and then to Amanda's face. "I'll be sure to have dinner ready. We'll have the bratwurst I was cooking for lunch, if that's all right."

"Thank you, that will be fine," Amanda called as she started for the door. "Enjoy the day."

The taxi was waiting when she went outside. Hannah's room faced away from the street, towards the adjacent townhouse, her windows against the alley. As long as she was in her room and didn't look out the parlor windows, Amanda was safe. It was a chance she had to take.

The driver placed her bag in the trunk, but Amanda carried her violin case. As the vehicle pulled away she looked back at the house. She saw no curtains move, no drapes disturbed, no face in the windows.

As they drove to Erika's house, she studied the bomb damage, the crumbling buildings, piles of rubble, and thought about all the people who had lost their homes. It was still the beginning. There would be many more.

The route was torturous. Some of the broader boulevards were still reduced in width due to rubble or fallen trees, while others were cleared completely. A few streets were closed, the damage too severe, the thoroughfare not worth the resources. Crews composed of foreign workers, older men, and young boys were still clearing debris. But as hard and tediously as they worked, there seemed to be a never-ending supply.

Charlottenburg would never be the same. Its quaint charm was marred, its liveliness subdued. Buildings Amanda had once photographed, enjoying their beauty or style or craftsmanship, were destroyed, shattered shells or crumbling heaps of wood and stone.

Trees that lined the streets, so graceful and stately only a few months before, sprouting leaves and providing a protective canopy from the sun, were barren and broken, limbs shattered, roots exposed, trunks split.

Amanda stopped to get some kreppels, ensuring she had enough for the children Erika was harboring. When she arrived at Erika's, the driver helped her get her bag to the fourth floor, while Amanda carried her violin and the donuts.

Erika opened the door of her flat as soon as Amanda knocked. She hugged her, clinging tightly, holding her, tears dripping from her eyes. They had battled their own demons, alone and protectively, not knowing they could share their problems with each other. They were mentally and physically exhausted, walking in worlds they never knew existed, but now able to see that the end was near.

"I brought my bag," Amanda said softly, implying what they mutually understood. "May I leave it here?"

"Yes, of course," Erika said. "I'll put it right here. Next to mine."

"You're going?"

"Yes, I finally convinced Mother. Although she only agreed after she found out you were coming. She's packing now."

Amanda hugged her again. "Oh, Erika, I'm so glad. I would like nothing more than to have you with me."

"I wanted to go from the beginning, but I was too afraid. And I had Mother to worry about. But when Michael said you were going, we each found the courage."

The two sat in the parlor, quietly discussing their plans with some lunch and a cup of coffee. Erika described the children she had hidden, how she had come to find them, and how difficult it had been to get food and supplies for everyone. Amanda discussed Manfred, all he had done, and who he had become.

When they finished, Erika took Amanda upstairs and into the hidden room to meet the children. It was an emotional experience. Amanda knew the sacrifices Erika had taken, quietly bearing the burden alone. Now she knew why.

She stayed a few hours more, most of it with the children, and then returned home. She came in quietly, trying to avoid Hannah, not wanting her to notice that she didn't have her violin. She closed the front door and walked stealthily across the parlor.

"Mrs. Richter," Hannah said with surprise, emerging from the kitchen. "I didn't hear you come in."

"I'm sorry," Amanda said, conscious of her empty hands. "I didn't mean to startle you. I came home a few minutes ago."

"You're timing is perfect," Hannah said, not noticing the missing violin. "Dinner is ready."

Amanda went in the dining room and sat down. Hannah served and, as Amanda was eating, she started talking.

"Mr. Richter called," she said. "He won't be home tonight. I think he said he was visiting a factory or people wounded in a factory during the bombing, something like that. But he promised he'll be home tomorrow night."

# CHAPTER 63

York sat in Erika's parlor, a solemn expression on his face. Confronted with a new crisis, he was evaluating options, searching for solutions. Obstacles kept appearing: Allied bombings, the Gestapo, and now Manfred Richter.

Amanda sat beside him, her fingers lightly caressing his arm. She was distraught but determined, her face firm, her eyes flashing fear, worried that the door opened for their escape was being slammed shut by her husband.

"I cannot be home on Sunday under any circumstances," she said. "I just can't do it. I never want to see Manfred again. And if he's home, I won't get out of the house."

York didn't want Amanda anywhere near him either, for a variety of reasons. The most obvious was emotional, but even if he applied strict logic it was a dangerous situation. Amanda knew too much; Richter was sly and cunning.

Erika sat across from them, watching closely, her face taut and strained. She seemed tired, defeated, her eyes dull with signs of surrender. She listened intently, concerned, but gave no indication of what might be bothering her.

"You're absolutely certain he'll be home?" York asked Amanda, keeping a wary eye on Erika.

"Yes, barring some unforeseen disaster," she said emphatically. "Hannah wrote down his message. He promised he would be home. Manfred doesn't promise anything."

"Is it a special occasion?" Erika asked quietly.

Amanda thought for a moment, and then shrugged. "Not that I can remember."

York didn't like seeing her upset. The stress and tension were mounting, and he could see it in the faces of both women. Amanda had been eluding Richter, afraid of the Gestapo, and promised an escape that never seemed to come. Erika had hidden eight people, wrought with worry about how to support them, secretly purchasing food, always wary of detection, knowing a slight miscalculation could bring the wrath of the Gestapo upon her household. Both women were boiling with anxious anticipation, like lava in an erupting volcano.

Erika listened sympathetically to Amanda's plight, but seemed restless and distracted, worried and weary. She was also perceptive, noticing how closely Amanda sat to York, leaning on him for support, touching him tenderly. She seemed to absorb it, not passing judgment, but probably knew there was much more between them than a path to Switzerland.

They sat quietly for a moment, considering options, before Erika spoke. "I also have a problem, but I haven't shared it. Just like Amanda, I must leave before Monday. I wasn't going to tell you; I didn't want to make matters worse. But it's best that you know."

York and Amanda exchanged nervous glances. Neither knew what Erika was facing. They wondered what could have possibly gone wrong, and why she never told them.

Erika withdrew a letter from an envelope and unfolded it. "I received this on Thursday. Words can't describe how upsetting it is. What sick society could invent such a disgusting, demented program?"

Amanda looked at her friend, dumbfounded. "What happened?"

"I am supposed to report to Gestapo headquarters on Monday at 8 a.m."

She handed the letter to York, who held it so

Amanda could read it. It contained the official letterhead of the Nazi Party, and opened with the deepest sympathy and appreciation for the loss of Erika's husband. It then discussed her duty to the Fatherland as a patriotic citizen. It closed with notification that her ancestry had been investigated, her natural characteristics classified and, consistent with program criteria, she had been chosen to participate in the production of Aryan offspring. Her first meeting with a preselected German officer, also proven genetically pure, was scheduled for Monday. The meetings would continue three times each week until she conceived.

York handed the letter back, stunned and disgusted. "Who could believe such horrors exist? You're right, Erika. I'm speechless."

She smiled weakly. "It convinced my mother to go to Switzerland."

Amanda was shocked. "Why didn't you tell us? We'll protect you. Surely you realize that. We'd never let anything happen to you."

Erika shrugged meekly. "I didn't want to trouble you. Michael was so busy planning our escape, and you have your own issues to deal with. I didn't want you distracted by my problems."

"What were you going to do?" York asked with disbelief. "You weren't going to go, were you?"

"No, of course not," she said. "I had no intention of doing that. I just hoped we would be gone before they came to arrest me."

"It wouldn't have worked," York said softly, showing compassion. "If we were delayed for any reason, they would have come for you as soon as you missed the appointment."

"Then that settles it," Amanda said, looking to York. "We can't endanger Erika by leaving Monday, and I am desperate. You have to do something."

He had already altered the plan, the hours until departure vivid in his mind, along with all that had to be done to get there. "You're right," he said. "We have to leave earlier."

The women exchanged glances and sighed with relief. "The sooner we can go, the better it will be," Amanda said.

"I agree," York said. He was quiet a moment, thinking. "How secure is Manfred's boathouse?"

Amanda was surprised by the question and, for a moment, her mind drifted to people and places from a different time. "It's off the road, fairly secluded. There's no cottage or anything like that, just the boathouse. No nearby neighbors."

"Can the ambulance fit inside?"

She shook her head. "No, it's not built like that. Only the boat fits in. There's little floor space, just a few meters in the back. The building sits over the water. You drive the boat inside. And then there is a hoist to lift it out of the water when needed."

York thought for a moment. "How far from the road is it?"

"Fifty or sixty meters," she said. "It's just a dirt road, surrounded by trees."

"If we parked the ambulance near the boathouse, would the trees hide it from the road?"

Amanda thought for a moment. "During summer they would, but not now. There are some evergreens, but most of the trees and shrubs are bare. It's dense, though."

York sighed. "We'll have to take the chance."

"When are we leaving?" Erika asked.

"We can go Sunday evening, but spend the night at the boathouse. We have to go there anyway for petrol."

"But it'll be harder to get the ambulance in the garage," Erika said. "The neighbors will still be awake."

York sighed, struggling to fit the pieces together. "You're right. And it's much more dangerous getting the vehicle from the hospital. Even if I got it tonight, we would take a chance having it in the garage."

"We can cover the windows," Erika said.

"But someone still might notice," York said.

"We have to leave early Sunday evening," Amanda said firmly. "There's no alternative for me or Erika."

The telephone rang and Erika excused herself to answer it. They could hear her in the kitchen, talking. It was a pleasant conversation, accented with light laughter. She returned to the parlor a moment later.

"You'll never guess who that was," she said.

York and Amanda looked at each other, but offered no reply.

"Albert Kaiser. He called to say that we're auditioning viola players at the Renaissance Theater on Kenessebeckstrasse at seven p.m. on Sunday."

Amanda sighed with relief. "At least we know he's safe. I was really worried about him after the bombing. I kept trying to telephone but couldn't get through."

"He said his neighborhood was severely damaged. He and his wife are staying with friends. Their telephone just started working today. I was laughing as he told me how upset his dog has been."

"How long will the auditions take?" York asked, calculating the timeline.

Erika looked at Amanda and shrugged. "I'm not sure. Maybe three hours."

Amanda nodded. "That's about right, depending

on how many people come. That's how long it took when Gerhard Faber auditioned."

"I think we can make this work," York said. "We can get everything ready to go, everyone packed and waiting, while you two are at the auditions."

"And you'll get the ambulance?" Amanda asked.

"Yes," York said. "I'll put it in the carriage house. It'll be dark, which will help. And some neighbors may be sleeping."

"Then we'll leave as soon as we get home?" Erika asked.

"Yes," York said. "Your mother and Inga can have the children waiting. We should be gone by eleven p.m."

# CHAPTER 64

St. Francis Hospital was a large brick building trimmed with marble moldings, designed to be functional but still esthetically pleasing. It dominated the block, dwarfing the buildings beside it, surrounded by mature trees with bare limbs that stretched over the adjacent boulevard. One wing of the building had been bombed, and bricks from a damaged upper elevation had collapsed on the pavement and were shoved in a heap against the wall.

York went to the hospital Saturday night, well after dark, when fewer people wandered the streets or sped by in taxis. As he approached the main entrance, he saw a nurse and two patients standing outside. They were probably soldiers, their arms in slings, one with a bandage covering the left side of his face. They seemed to be waiting for someone, and ducked in and out of the entrance, trying to stay warm.

The facilities parking lot was at the rear of the hospital, close to a row of rubbish cans on a narrow back street. There were a dozen vehicles parked there: four ambulances, three small trucks, and five sedans. The area was deserted, tucked in a distant corner with a single door that led to it. It was dimly lit by a single lamp post, surrounded by shrubs, and flanked by the hospital walls.

York watched the area for thirty minutes, then moved furtively through the bushes to the vehicles. He sprawled on the cobblestones, hidden in shadows, and removed the license plates from all four ambulances, placing them in a satchel he had brought with him. License plates were identified by vehicle use. He wanted several ambulance plates so he could switch them throughout the journey.

He left the area quickly, moving down the street and trying not to lean too heavily on his cane. As he turned the corner, he stopped and looked behind him. No one was following. No one was watching. But just as he started on his way, he noticed a face peer around a building and then duck back again. It was a man with dark clothes and a dark hat, the moonlight reflecting off his spectacles.

York hurried down the street, afraid it was the Gestapo agent who had followed him before, at Max's and at the cemetery. He caught the next tram, rode for two blocks and got off, taking a bus in the opposite direction. Six blocks later he got off and immediately boarded another tram, making sure he wasn't followed.

He made his way to Olivaer Platz, leaving the tram and then taking a bus before walking the last three blocks, shivering in the chilly night. When he reached the hospital, he sat on a bench across the street, watching closely, just as he had done at St. Francis. When convinced the passing people were visitors or staff, with some patients mingled among them, he moved to the facilities parking lot.

A smaller hospital with fewer employees, York saw only two ambulances, one with two axles that held four stretchers, the other a large three-axle truck, more appropriate for their needs. They were parked beside each other, a sedan next to them and closer to the road, partially hiding them from the street. Two other cars were parked closer to the building.

After observing for thirty minutes, and seeing no activity, York made his way to the vehicles, using the foliage that bordered the parking lot as shelter, just as he had done at St. Francis. But now his objective was much different.

He lay on the ground beside the ambulance and removed the cap to the petrol tank, which was just behind the driver's door. He stuck his finger in, could not feel petrol, and then stuck a narrow wooden branch in, using it as a dipstick and letting it touch the bottom. It was just over halfway full.

York moved to the smaller ambulance, removed a narrow rubber hose from his satchel, and inserted it in the gas tank. He stretched the tube out to the larger ambulance, and sucked on it, producing a vacuum until the bitter petrol entered his mouth. He shoved the tube in the gas tank of the larger truck.

It took almost five minutes to fill. As soon as the tank started to overflow he pulled the tube from the first vehicle and replaced the cap, letting the petrol in the tube drain to the ground. He returned the cap to the tank of the second truck, staying on the ground, hidden from view. He carefully surveyed the surrounding area and when satisfied it was safe, he walked up the ramp, staying close to the foliage, and left the hospital.

He went into the park where he used to meet Amanda, and found a bench with a view of the road. He sat down and watched the few passing pedestrians, studied the vehicles on the street, and surveyed the buildings destroyed by the bombings. Most of the park was intact, although an uprooted tree and the crater beside it gave evidence to the attack. He waited for almost thirty minutes and when sure no one had seen him, he went back to his hotel.

Sunday was cold and overcast, snow flurries swirling through the air and melting when they kissed the cobblestone streets. York met Amanda at Erika's, and found the women nervous with anticipation, fearful of the unknown. They knew they were risking their lives, a million things could go wrong, but it was something they had to do. They couldn't stay in Berlin any longer.

They practiced the escape planned for that night: how the children would be taken to the ambulance, how to load the luggage, who would serve as lookout, what to do if they were discovered. Then they made the warning signs to place on each side of the truck and at the rear doors: *Gefahr: Tuberkulose! Nicht betreten!* Danger: Tuberculosis! Do not Enter!

Hours passed slowly, the tension mounting, and when early evening arrived, it was time for the women to leave. York stood in the doorway and said his goodbyes, trying to assure them that everything would go smoothly. Amanda hugged him tightly and kissed him. She wouldn't let go, burying her head in his shoulder.

York saw Erika watching, their poorly kept secret revealed. She smiled shyly and looked away, not wanting to intrude, not wanting to judge.

At 9 p.m. York was standing at the hospital, studying the small parking lot tucked behind the grove of trees. He sighed with relief when he saw the vehicles in the same location they had been the night before. He had no way of knowing they would be there. But neither had moved, and any petrol he spilled on the ground had gone unnoticed. He watched for twenty minutes and saw no one. It was quiet.

He moved through the foliage, taking the same path he had previously. He went first to the smaller vehicle and lay on the ground, removing the license plates. Then he removed the plates on the larger vehicle, replacing them with ones he had stolen from the ambulance at St. Francis Hospital. He paused, lying motionless, and watched. He saw no activity.

He rose slowly, stayed close to the vehicle, and moved to the driver's door. It was unlocked. There were no keys in the ignition. He got ready to hot wire the engine but then paused. Maybe the keys were hidden. He lifted the floor mat and there they were, tucked just under the seat.

York closed the door as quietly as he could. He exercised the choke, pushed in the clutch, and started the vehicle. The engine grinded for a few seconds, but then caught, rumbling to life. He pushed the gearshift to first and eased out the clutch, guiding the vehicle towards the street.

# CHAPTER 65

The ambulance was idling across the cramped parking lot when the hospital door opened. A man came out, with no coat, an alarmed look on his face, and started running. He waved his arms wildly and screamed for York to stop, attracting the attention of those on the street.

A taxi blocked the exit, a passenger climbing out. York looked in the side mirror, the man almost at his door, pushed the lock down with his elbow, and gunned the engine.

An elderly couple across the street watched with alarm, stopped a passing soldier and pointed towards the ambulance. More pedestrians paused, wondering what the commotion was, as a middle-aged woman yelled for a policeman standing at the corner.

The taxi pulled away, its passenger on the pavement. York accelerated, speeding out of the parking lot, tires spinning. He turned right, looking back.

The man from the hospital was writing down the license number. The policeman approached, joined by the soldier, as the man frantically described the vehicle theft to a gathering crowd.

York drove down one block, made a right, went two more blocks and made another right, circling back towards the Ku'damm and then crossing over it. He went three more blocks and pulled into an alley, turning off the headlamps but leaving the engine running.

He got out of the ambulance, saw no one hiding in the darkness, no one watching from nearby windows. He went behind the vehicle, swapped the license plate with one he had in his satchel, and drove away. If there was any pursuit, he had eluded them.

When he reached Erika's block he drove around it twice. It was quiet. He saw a man walking his dog. Two young girls crossed the street. A teenage boy wearing his Hitler Youth uniform was approaching a nearby house. He glanced at the ambulance, studied it a moment, but then entered.

York drove down the alley and stopped in front of the carriage house. He got out and opened the doors, looking down the lane to study two parked sedans, ensuring they were empty. He watched windows of nearby buildings, some lit, others dark, and saw no one observing, at least not anyone he could see.

He backed the ambulance into the building and closed the doors. He stepped out the back entrance, into the shadows. The alley was still deserted. He waited a few minutes, but saw no activity.

It was just before 10 p.m. He went to the front door and rapped lightly. Erika's mother, whom he had met on Saturday, let him in. She was a nice woman named Millie, younger than he expected, but very sick. She had an emaciated appearance, her face drawn, with a pallid complexion and darkness around her eyes.

"Erika and Amanda haven't come home yet," she said. "I'm beginning to worry."

York checked his watch and shrugged. "They said they would be about three hours. I'll put the signs on the ambulance and carry the bags out while we wait for them."

He grabbed three bags and the signs and left, seeing no activity as he crossed to the garage. He used a flashlight to see, and put the bags at the back of the rear compartment, against the partition behind the driver's seat, conscious of Amanda's violin.

The ambulance had ample space for storage. Bags could be stowed against the partition, or in compartments with sliding access doors that ran along the roof, stuffed with blankets and medical supplies. There were two rows of cots, one knee high, the second suspended by chains at shoulder height. York spread some blankets on the floor and cots, knowing the children would be comfortable on either.

He got the signs and affixed them to the doors, leaving the Red Cross symbol clearly visible. It was a good effect. They offered an ominous warning that should keep the curious away.

When he stepped out to go back to the house, he saw the man walking his dog turn back into the alley. York ducked into the garage and watched from the window. The man came closer.

The dog stopped to sniff a shrub just across the lane, stretching the leash. The man stood patiently, waited while the dog lifted a leg and urinated, and then pulled him forward. A moment later he was beyond the carriage house, not even turning to look.

York crept through the shadows and returned to the house. Millie was waiting at the door, Erika's belongings and eight smaller bags for the children beside her. York picked up four bags and returned to the carriage house.

Carefully crossing the yard, he quickly entered the building. He stored the bags under the lower stretchers, keeping the adults' belongings near the partition where they were accessible. He put more blankets against the back, creating an area where Erika and Millie and maybe the teenage girl could sit. The children would fit on the cots.

He returned to the house, collected three more bags and stored them in the ambulance. Prior to leaving the carriage house he studied the alley, saw nothing, stepped out and looked at all the windows. It was quiet.

When he reached the house he grabbed the

remaining bags just as Erika and Amanda arrived home. Amanda hugged him and gave him a quick kiss.

"I can't wait to leave," she said, her voice shaking with fear and excitement. "I thought the audition would never end."

"It won't be long now," he said. "This is the last of the bags. Is there anything else to load?"

"I have two baskets of food in the kitchen, but I can carry them out," Erika said.

York opened a bag he had left near the door. It contained a nurse's uniform for Amanda, and his German sergeant's uniform, all part of their charade posing as a transport vehicle for seriously ill soldiers.

"Here's your uniform," he said to Amanda. "I'll get changed in the carriage house."

"We'll get the children," Erika said. "It'll only take a few minutes. We practiced yesterday."

"Bring them out as soon as they're ready," York said. "I don't think anyone saw me, but we have to get out of here as soon as we can."

He retraced the route he had just taken, paused by the building to study the alley, and then made his way into the carriage house. He stored the bags, was about to walk out the door, when he heard a noise, like someone stepping on a branch. He froze, leaned against the wall, and waited.

A few seconds later a shadow passed the window. York moved beside the open door, listening intently, hearing nothing. The shadow reappeared. It grew larger, approaching the window. York waited, barely breathing, until the face was visible in the window.

It was the teenage boy with the Hitler Youth uniform, peering into the carriage house. His face was pressed against the window, the ambulance visible in the darkness a few feet away. He turned his head in each direction, looking down the slender aisle to see if anyone was inside.

York leaned against the wall, out of sight, watching the shadow. He looked out the opened door and saw Erika and her mother with two of the children, about to cross the yard. He moved to the door and waved them back. Then another twig snapped and he ducked behind the door jamb.

Erika and Millie paused, looking quizzically towards the carriage house. They were vulnerable, standing in the open space between house and garage, easily seen.

York paused, waiting several seconds. When he heard no other noises, he returned to the doorway and motioned them towards the building, where the shadows would hide them, where the intruder couldn't see them.

Erika understood; she sensed danger. She whispered to her mother, and they quietly retreated, protecting the children. They peeked around the corner, standing still, waiting for direction.

The Hitler Youth was crouched by the window, studying what he could see in the darkness. A few tense moments passed and then he stood, uncertain, not quite satisfied. He was waiting, but he didn't know what for.

One of the children shouted and then laughed, but was quickly silenced by Erika. The Hitler Youth turned, peering towards the noise. Seconds ticked by, quiet, no sounds from the street or nearby houses. The youth's gaze returned to the garage.

York moved to the opened door. He withdrew the pistol from his pocket and leaned his cane against the door, knowing he should use the knife concealed within it, but not for a child, not if he could help it. He heard footsteps on the ground outside, coming closer, cautiously taking each step.

The shadow appeared in the doorway, looming larger. York tensed, taking the barrel of the gun in his hand. He would use the handle as a weapon. He held it over his head, waiting.

The Hitler Youth stepped into the carriage house, slowly, deliberately. He crossed the threshold and paused, listening, looking. He took another step.

York stepped from the shadows and brought the handle of his pistol down on the youth's head. He crumbled to the floor, moaning.

York waved Erika forward, and pulled the Hitler Youth to the edge of the garage. He found some rags on a shelf against the wall and tore them into strips. He pulled the boy's arms behind his back, binding them tightly, and then did the same for his ankles. With the last two rags he fashioned a blindfold, wrapping it around his head, and rolled the last one into a ball and stuffed it into his mouth.

"Who is that?" Erika hissed as she entered, watching York.

"A nosy neighbor," he replied. "Come on, we have to hurry."

Erika led her mother into the rear of the bus, where she perched on the blankets against the partition. The two children, a girl and the boy with thick glasses, went to Millie's side. They sat there, hands folded across their laps, quiet and docile. They were tired, ready for bed.

Erika returned for more children just as Amanda, now dressed in a nurse's uniform, arrived at the carriage house with two more. York briefly described the encounter with the Hitler Youth.

"Don't underestimate him," Amanda warned. "They get intense training."

"I'll watch him," York assured her. "Come on, we have to hurry."

Erika returned with two more children. The Hitler Youth remained in the corner, bound and unconscious, each of the women glancing at him warily.

"I'll get everything ready," Amanda said. She climbed in the back with Millie and started to spread the remaining blankets for the children.

The teenage girl, Inga, was waiting with the last child. Erika urged them on and then, after one last, lingering look at her apartment, she closed the door and locked it. She probably pictured her husband standing on the porch, watching the sunset or coming home after work. She wasn't just leaving Berlin, she was leaving him, even though she would always treasure the memories.

They came into the carriage house and settled everyone in the ambulance, the teenager helping. York watched Erika as she studied the garage in the darkness, as if imagining her husband working, taking slabs of wood and producing works of art. She looked at a shelf by the door and saw a slender chisel sitting on it. She picked it up, the initials W.J. carved in the handle: Wilhelm Jaeger. She smiled sadly and put the chisel in her pocket.

Amanda stepped from the rear of the vehicle. "I think we're ready," she said.

Erika nodded, and summoned the courage to climb in the ambulance. She smiled at the children, trying to seem calm, even though her heart was racing. She didn't want them to be afraid.

There was a moan from the corner. The Hitler Youth stirred, collected his wits, and started to struggle. He shouted, the noise muted by the rag, and panicked, thrashing about, struggling, trying to release himself. Turning towards the wall, he rubbed his face against the wood, trying to force the rag from his mouth.

359

York whipped him with the pistol, not hard enough to do damage but enough to knock him unconscious. When satisfied he no longer posed a threat, he walked to the rear of the ambulance, took one last glance at his passengers, and closed the doors.

Amanda climbed into the passenger's seat while York opened the carriage doors and looked up and down the alley. It was quiet. No one watched from their windows; no one walked down the lane.

"Just tell me how to get to the boathouse," York said as he climbed in the ambulance and started the vehicle.

He put the vehicle in gear and slowly pulled into the alley. When he reached the cross street, he looked in the mirror. The alley was still quiet. He turned right, driving towards Ku'damm.

"We won't look as suspicious on the main roads," he said.

Once on the Ku'damm, he saw a vehicle behind them in the distance. As he continued on, merging with light traffic typical for late evening, he saw it coming closer. It was a black Mercedes, probably the Gestapo.

# CHAPTER 66

York turned left at Konstanzer Strasse, past Olivaer Platz. The vehicle followed. He maintained a constant speed, trying not to seem suspicious. The sedan stayed the same distance behind them.

"I think we're being followed," he said to Amanda.

Two blocks later the vehicle moved beside them. A Gestapo officer leaned out of the passenger's window and motioned for York to pull over and stop.

"What are we going to do?" Amanda hissed, her eyes wide.

"There's nothing we can do," York said calmly, his plan already formed. "Just let me do the talking."

He guided the ambulance to the side of the road and came to a stop. The Gestapo pulled in behind him, headlamps still lit. York watched in the side mirror as two men exited the vehicle.

"Michael, I'm afraid," Amanda said anxiously, touching his arm.

He forced a smile he didn't feel. "Don't be. Everything will be all right."

He got out of the ambulance, leaning heavily on his cane, making sure the Gestapo saw his German uniform. He walked slowly towards the rear of the vehicle as they approached. They wore uniforms, black pants, jackets and ties with white shirts. A black and red arm band was marked by a swastika.

"Good evening, sergeant," the first man said as he walked towards York. His stern expression softened when his eyes moved to the cane.

His partner stood at the rear of the ambulance, a few meters away, reading the sign affixed to the door. He seemed concerned, almost as if he didn't want to be

361

there.

York nodded. "Good evening, sir."

"War wound?" the first officer asked, motioning to his limp.

"Yes, sir, North Africa," York said. "It was a machine gun. But I can manage the ambulance. The clutch can be painful, but I get by."

"Where are you going?" he asked as his partner came and stood beside him.

"To a country hospital," York explained. "I have to get these patients out of the city. The last thing authorities want is a tuberculosis epidemic."

The Gestapo agents exchanged nervous glances.

"It's very contagious," York continued, reading their expressions. "If not contained, it can spread everywhere. It starts with a cough, a bit of wheezing. Then they start spitting up blood. Not many survive."

A scream came from the ambulance, followed by giggling. It lasted several seconds, child-like and innocent, before subsiding to hushed whispers.

"Who are the patients?" the first officer asked, showing skepticism.

York felt his heart start to race. "All soldiers from the Eastern Front," he replied. "They're delirious from medication. Many revert to childhood memories, their behavior regressing."

"It sounds like children," the officer said sternly. "Misbehaved children."

"Actually, they're all from the same regiment. That's how contagious the disease is. One man probably caught it from some peasant, and now I have a whole ambulance full. And there are more at the hospital."

The officer was listening to York, but was focused on the ambulance. He hesitated, wondering whether to search the vehicle. He wavered, and looked back at his companion.

York was still talking. "But they're good men who did their duty for the Reich. They deserve decent care." He lowered his voice, as if not wanting anyone to hear. "At least for as long as they need it."

"I wasn't aware of any tuberculosis epidemic," the second officer said, uncertain, his voice quivering.

"And we're hoping to keep it that way," York replied. "Hopefully these are isolated cases." He withdrew two half masks from his pocket. "You had better wear these if you're going to stand near the truck. Just to be safe. Or we can move away."

The Gestapo agents quickly stepped away. One whispered to the other and nodded.

"Who is in the passenger's seat?" the first asked.

"A nurse," York replied. "The patients need constant attention. Not that their condition has shown any improvement."

Another loud outburst came from the rear of the ambulance. Shouting, followed by laughter, and then blathering, incoherent conversation.

The Gestapo officers looked at the vehicle, quizzical looks on their faces.

"Poor men," York said, slowly shaking his head. "Not much left of them I'm afraid, mind or body. Sometimes they giggle and ramble on like idiots."

"Excuse us a moment," the first man said.

The Gestapo agents moved a few feet away, whispering, their hands over their mouths. One walked towards the rear as the other watched. He took a piece of paper from his pocket and held it against the license plate. Then he got down on one knee and looked under the vehicle. He held an ear to the door, listening to the rumbling inside. And then after a brief inspection, he stood, returned to his partner, and said a few words.

"That will be all, sergeant," the lead agent said with a nod.

"Thank you, sir," York replied as the two men went back to their car.

York sighed with relief, beads of sweat on the back of his neck, and watched as the Gestapo pulled away. He put his hand over his heart, touching the photograph that was in his breast pocket, as he always did when eluding danger. It made him remember what he had to live for.

He got back in the ambulance and turned to Amanda. "They're gone," he said, lightly brushing her cheek with his fingers. "We're safe."

"What happened?" she asked hoarsely, frenzied. "I didn't know how to help you. Should I have gotten out, too?"

"No, you did fine. There was really nothing you could do. But we have to find a way to keep the children under control. Especially in situations like that. Maybe Erika has some sedatives."

"She did the best she could," Amanda said. "The children are excited. They haven't been out of Erika's apartment for years. They'll settle down. They should be asleep in a few minutes. Now, tell me what happened."

He described the exchange, emphasizing the fear in the Gestapo officers' faces as he described tuberculosis. "They didn't ask to see my papers, or to look at the patients, even though they did get very suspicious when the children acted up. But they never asked where we were going. They just wanted to get as far away from the ambulance as possible."

"Why did they stop us to begin with?"

"They must know an ambulance is missing from the hospital. This fits the description, but I changed the license plates. They had another license number written on a piece of paper, probably from the hospital employee who chased me. But when they saw a German soldier get out, they wondered if they had made a mistake. When the plates didn't match, it confirmed it."

Amanda sighed, weary and distraught. "Let's hope there's no more Gestapo."

They continued to Wannsee Lake, the traffic thinning as they exited the city proper and the night wore on. There was a sprinkling of taxis and police cars, a few more dark sedans which may or may not have been the Gestapo, and an occasional streetcar. Thirty minutes later they arrived at the edge of the city, and Amanda guided them down a road that ringed the lake, past a boat club, and into a secluded drive.

There was a long, dirt lane that led to the boathouse, hidden from the road by trees and foliage. Winter had stolen most of the leaves, except for scattered pines that bathed the landscape in green. York backed the ambulance down the road, almost to the building, but stayed close to the trees. The woods were thickest at that point, and even though the foliage was sparse, it still served to screen them from the road.

It was just after midnight. York left the vehicle and walked the entire length of the driveway, up one side and down the other. He squinted in the darkness, searching for signs that anyone was nearby, even looking for lights from any nearby cottages, but found nothing.

He walked back to the ambulance, motioning for Amanda to get out. Then he went to the rear of the vehicle and opened the back doors. The children and Millie were sleeping. Erika was awake, and she moved around the others and got out of the vehicle and joined them.

"I'm sorry about the children," Erika said.

"They're so excited, I couldn't control them. Did the Gestapo hear them?"

York looked at Amanda. "Yes, but I managed to convince them the patients were delirious."

Erika cringed. "Try to give me more warning if anything else happens. Inga and I can try to calm them."

"It doesn't matter," York said. "As long as we're safe." He glanced at the sleeping children. "One more day and they'll be out of danger. For the first time in their lives."

Erika acted as lookout while Amanda and York went to the boathouse. The entrance was on the side, away from the road, on a brick path that led to the water's edge. Amanda withdrew a key and opened the door.

They entered the building, the glow from York's flashlight illuminating the room. The walls were made of vertical wood planking, a window on each side. The front was open to the lake, the rear had carriage doors that were locked and barred. The roof was supported by six trusses, the space below an extension of the lake with a two-meter-wide walkway on each side. Against the side walls were a dozen ten-liter cans, hopefully filled with petrol. But one thing was missing.

"Where's the boat?" York asked.

She shrugged, confused. "I have no idea. It must be on the water."

"I thought Manfred was home."

"So did I," she said. "At least that's what Hannah told me. But he wasn't there when I left."

"Does he use the boat often?"

"No, he never uses it."

York went over to the petrol cans. One by one he lifted them, finding each can empty. Finally, at the end of the row, he found three that were full. They needed seventy liters. They had thirty.

"There's not enough," he said. "We'll have to find petrol somewhere else."

Amanda grabbed his arm. "That's the least of our worries."

"Why?" he asked, confused by her statement.

She pointed to the lake. "Here comes the boat."

# CHAPTER 67

"We have to get out of here," York said grimly. He watched the boat, which was still some distance away, coming towards them. "Is there someplace we can hide over night?"

Amanda nodded, still wondering what Manfred was doing out in his boat at midnight. And who was with him. Why did he tell Hannah he would be home Sunday night, the very night she intended to escape?

"There are other boathouses just like this. We can use one of them."

He looked at the petrol cans. It was too risky to take them, even an empty. If Manfred just took the boat out, he would know exactly how many cans were there, empty or full.

York looked at Amanda. She was tired, stressed and strained. And she was carrying their child. He had to protect her. He hugged her for a moment, and then kissed her on the forehead.

"Come on," he said. "Let's go."

They exited the boathouse as the lights coming in from the lake grew brighter. They quickly told Erika what had happened and she got in the rear of the ambulance. York closed the doors behind her.

As he got in the driver's seat, he stopped, perplexed. "Where's his car?" he asked Amanda.

She scanned the area before climbing in the passenger's side. "I'm not sure. But he rarely drives anyway; an armed guard takes him everywhere."

York started the engine. "Then where is the armed guard?"

They drove down the lane without headlamps, the approaching boat coming closer. York toyed with the idea of circling back to see who Manfred was with, but it wasn't worth the risk. It was probably a woman, anyway. Maybe they were spending the night on the boat, and his chauffer was getting them in the morning. Or maybe it was a clandestine meeting for Manfred's favorite mission, the Fourth Reich. What better place to have a secret rendezvous than on a boat in the middle of the lake?

York guided the vehicle back on the road, still without lights, driving south. The first kilometer passed uneventfully, the lane to the boathouse no longer visible in the mirror, and York's mind turned to a safe place to spend the night.

"Where do you suggest we stop?" he asked. "We should try to get some sleep."

"There's a boathouse a few kilometers down the road," she said. "It used to be abandoned. It's off the road, just like Manfred's. We should be safe there."

They drove a few more minutes and Amanda directed him to a lane on the right. The entrance was a bit overgrown, the shrubs untrimmed and stretching into the roadway. York guided the vehicle in reverse, moving all the way back to the building and keeping it against the trees. The area was more secluded than where they had left, a few more pine trees, the underbrush denser.

York turned off the engine. He opened the sliding port to the rear and told Erika they would be spending the night there. She snuggled under a blanket and prepared to sleep.

"I'm going to have a look around," York said, his hand caressing Amanda's arm. "Try to get some rest."

"Be careful," she said. "Should I go with you?"

"No, try to sleep. I won't be long."

He stepped out of the vehicle, quietly closing the door. The half-moon provided some light, but for

369

the most part the area was cloaked in darkness. He walked the entire length of the lane, checking how dense the foliage was, visibility from the road, and how far away the nearest neighbor was. It seemed isolated.

He went to the boathouse. The design was similar to Manfred's, the size comparable. The condition was a bit deteriorated, paint peeling off the vertical clapboards, the path to the entrance impeded by overgrown branches.

When he reached the door, he found the hasp for the lock had been pried from it. Someone had broken in, although he couldn't tell how recently. He slowly pushed the door open.

He checked around for intruders, and then turned on a flashlight. The boat slip was empty, water glistening under the light, gently lapping the sides. He shone the light along the walkways and walls. The building was deserted.

He walked down one side towards the lake. A few tools still hung on the walls, but there were no petrol cans, empty or full. Whatever had been in the boathouse was probably stolen when someone broke in. A canvass lay in a heap in one corner, some trash on the floor beside it: a milk carton, a crumbled paper bag, a sausage wrapper. On the wall above it hung a homemade fishing pole.

York walked over to the canvass and stood beside it, not moving. He then went to the door, closed it, and flicked off the flashlight. But he remained inside the boathouse. He stood there, silent, waiting and watching.

Several minutes passed with no sound except for gentle lapping of the water on the sides of the boathouse. A little light from the moon slipped into the building, bathing the far end in a muted light. He looked out on the water, peaceful and serene. Then he saw the canvass move.

He stood still, peering through the darkness, not moving a muscle. Ever so slowly the canvass was pushed away, a few centimeters at a time. He waited patiently until it moved a half meter, and he saw a head appear in the darkness.

He snapped on the flashlight. The beam illuminated the frightened face of a child, maybe eight or nine. His eyes opened wide, his jaw dropped. His face was smudged with dirt.

The boy pushed the tarp to the side, exposing a young girl about four years old. Her black hair was braided into a pony tail. She looked at York, her eyes wide, fear marking every cell of her body.

The boy grabbed her hand and yanked her up, and they started to run.

"Wait," York called. "Don't run."

They didn't listen, and continued towards the water.

"I won't hurt you," he yelled. "I'm an Englishman."

They stopped short and slowly turned, wondering whether to believe him. The German uniform proved he lied.

"Please, I can help you," he said.

They reached the end of the walkway. There was no place else to go. Water was in front of them; water was beside them. The boathouse wall stood behind them. They could jump in the water and swim, or they could surrender.

"It's all right," York said. He raised his hands, showing no weapons, proving no danger. "I won't hurt you. I promise."

They looked less afraid, but wary. They stood there, not coming towards him, unable to move away. The boy protectively shielded the little girl, not knowing what else to do.

"I have food," York said, trying to convince them. "And I can take care of you. I have other children with me, too."

They stared at him, eyes wide with fear, not knowing what to do. The girl started to cry, sobbing at first, then the tears fell faster.

York walked up to them slowly, cautiously, not wanting to scare them. When they didn't move, he knelt before them. "Are you alone?"

They both nodded.

"Where are you parents?"

The boy spoke. "Our father died in the war. Soldiers came and took my mother."

"Why didn't they take you?"

"My mother made us hide. Then the neighbors came and said we had to leave before the soldiers came back."

"And you came here."

"Yes."

"How long have you been here?"

"For two days."

York looked at their clothes. They wore pants and shirts, and had jackets on, but they weren't warm enough for winter. His eyes moved to the yellow star affixed to the jackets. He felt like a hand had grasped his heart, clenching it firmly and then ripping it out. They were Jews, probably among the last left in the city. If their father was in the army, he was German. Their mother must have been Jewish. As long as their father was alive, they had some rights. But once he died, they had none.

"What are your names?" he asked warmly, forcing a smile but appalled at their dilemma.

"Samuel and Sarah."

"Why don't you come with me, Samuel and

Sarah? I have a truck outside with blankets and food and other children you can play with. You're safe now."

He offered each his hand and they reluctantly took it, not knowing whether it was safe to trust him, but too tired and afraid to do anything else. He led them out of the boathouse and brought them to the ambulance.

Amanda was still awake, and when she saw him with the two children she hurried out of the vehicle to greet them. "Where did they come from?" she asked, surprised but sincere, worried for the children's welfare.

As York told their story, she pulled them towards her, hugging them both. "It's all right," she said. "We'll take care of you."

"Can you find our mother?" Sarah asked.

Amanda hid the tears that clouded her eyes. "Someday soon we'll find her. But for now, we have to go somewhere safe."

They woke Erika and told her what happened. She was surprised, but didn't care what dangers came with two Jewish children. She quickly left the ambulance and greeted them, calming their fears, making them feel comfortable.

After they chatted a few minutes, and the children were no longer afraid, Erika brought them into the back of the ambulance. She showed them the sleeping children, gave them some food, then wrapped them in blankets. Minutes later, they were fast asleep.

Erika and Amanda removed the yellow stars from their clothes, knowing the hatred they symbolized, disgust evident on their faces. York buried them at the edge of the foliage.

"Is their story realistic?" York asked. "I know Jewish spouses of German citizens were exempt from the laws, but I thought that ended long ago."

"It was only enforced for the privileged this year," Amanda said. "The father of these children must have been a high-ranking officer. When he was killed, they no longer had protection. Apparently their mother understood this and made sure they survived. I'm certain she didn't."

York couldn't understand a society so distorted, so sadistic. And he didn't try to. "We have to get some sleep," he said as they returned to the cab. "Tomorrow will be a long day."

"What beautiful children," she said. "But what a horrible story. I'm so glad we came here. They would have died if we didn't." She turned, looking at York. "It was good of you to rescue them. You could have left them. You have enough people to look after."

York shrugged. "I could never do that."

"I know," she said, smiling. "That's because you're such a good person. One more reason why I love you so much."

He leaned over and kissed her. Then they wrapped themselves in blankets and fell asleep.

# CHAPTER 68

The noise woke York abruptly. It was a pounding sound, like a hammer. At first he thought he was dreaming, but it continued. He opened his eyes, squinting, sunlight offending them, and sat up.

A man was knocking on the window. "What are you doing here?" he demanded.

He was older, tall and thin, anger in his eyes. His suit was hand-tailored, his gray hair meticulously combed. He was some sort of professional, maybe an attorney.

York held up a finger, asking the man to wait, hoping he wasn't a doctor. He turned to Amanda, who had stirred with a start, rubbing her eyes.

"We have a visitor," he said softly. "Don't worry. I'll take care of him."

She looked at him sleepily, her eyes wide with alarm. "Is everything all right?"

"I'm sure it will be. Wait here while I talk to him."

York opened the door and climbed out, ensuring he had his cane. He took the safety catch off the pistol. Just in case he had to use it.

The man backed away from the vehicle, still angry and annoyed, staring at York defiantly. His arms were folded across his chest.

York exaggerated his limp as he walked, knowing it created sympathy. "I'm sorry, sir. I'm bringing patients to the countryside. I pulled off the road for some rest."

The man's face softened, the glare diminishing. "You can't rest here, sergeant. This is private property. Did you break into my boathouse? The lock is damaged."

"No, sir, it wasn't me," York said, walking towards the building, trying to keep the man away from the ambulance. Even though the children were sleeping, he knew how noisy they would be if awakened. "I would never damage personal property."

A black sedan was parked in front of the boathouse, a newer model, shiny and well-maintained. It contained no passengers. The man was alone.

He led York to the door, pointing to the broken hasp. "See what I mean?"

"Yes, sir, I do. But I didn't hear anything. Maybe it happened a while ago. When was the last time you were here?"

The man ignored him and pushed the door. It opened, the hinges squeaking. He started to enter but York stopped him.

"Let me go first," York said, feigning concern. "Just in case it's not safe."

He stepped into the boathouse, followed closely by the owner. The building was partially lit, the rising sun streaming through the windows and open side that faced the lake. York used his flashlight in the darker corners.

"There's no one here," he said a minute later. "But there's some trash at the other end. Maybe it's from a vagrant, or someone fleeing the authorities."

"Thank you, I appreciate your help. I'll have the lock repaired."

"The damage is minor," York said. "I suppose it could have been worse."

"Yes, I'm sure it could have. But now I'm afraid you'll have to leave."

"Of course, sir. I understand. We'll leave right away."

"What are those signs on the ambulance? I'm not going to catch anything, am I?"

"No, sir," York assured him. "As long as you don't get too close. I'm transporting some soldiers with tuberculosis to a remote hospital. After all, we do need to take care of our servicemen. No matter how sick they are."

"Yes, of course," the man stuttered. "I just don't want to become infected."

York limped away. "I understand. Thank you, sir. We'll be on our way."

He climbed back in the ambulance and started the engine, looking back in the side mirror. The man was writing down the license plate number on a piece of paper. York turned onto the road, telling Amanda what happened.

"What should we do?"

"We'll stop and change the license plates. We have four sets with us."

"There's a public beach two or three kilometers down the road. It should be empty this time of year. There's also a bathroom there. We can all get cleaned up."

York drove to the beach and parked the ambulance by the bathroom entrance, hiding the vehicle from the road. He changed the license plates while Amanda and Erika took the children to the bathroom, including the new additions, Samuel and Sarah. Millie and the teenager followed.

Erika had brought plenty of food and they ate some breakfast, bread and cheese with ham and some juice. York looked at the back of the ambulance, now home to twelve souls.

"Can you manage with all the people in there?" he asked Erika.

"I think so. It's a bit cramped, but as long as we keep the children occupied or asleep, we can keep the discomfort to a minimum. I suppose today will be the worst."

York studied the map while both adults and children took the opportunity to stretch and move about. As Erika had said, it would be a long day.

Thirty minutes later they were back in the ambulance. York handed Amanda the map. "The route is a mix of autobahn and minor roads. We'll have a stretch of highway soon. The ride should be better."

An hour later they were on the autobahn, which was dominated by military vehicles and delivery trucks. The ambulance blended with the traffic and, after thirty minutes of troop trucks passing without seeming to notice them, York and Amanda became more comfortable.

"I am looking forward to returning to London," Amanda said as they passed one mile marker after another. "How long will we have to stay in Switzerland?"

"I'm not sure. It might be a while. But Switzerland is beautiful. I love it. We can always stay there until after the baby is born."

She smiled, subconsciously rubbing her belly. "Do you want a boy or a girl?"

"I'm happy either way," he said. He felt the photograph in his pocket and thought of Elizabeth.

Amanda touched his arm. "You're excited, aren't you?"

He smiled. "Yes, I am. I can't wait to have a family. But I am a little worried about finances."

Amanda started laughing. "Darling, surely you're joking."

He was confused. "No, I'm not. It costs money to raise a family. And I have to hire a private detective to find Elizabeth. A history professor doesn't earn that much."

"Michael, I come from Scottish royalty. I am an

only child. I inherited the family fortune, and a Scottish estate. The money is managed by Lloyds. It's safe. We can hire a dozen private detectives to find Elizabeth if you want to."

York was stunned. He never really considered wealth, or ever achieving it. A Scottish estate? He couldn't even imagine. "I'm speechless," he said softly.

"The money was never moved to Germany and the estate was never sold. It's just outside of Edinburgh, not huge, maybe a thousand acres. It comes with a caretaker. He's looked after the property since my parents passed. And well before, actually."

"I had no idea," he stammered.

"I know you didn't," she said, the grin still present. "But it makes everything a lot easier."

"Yes, it does," he said, still shocked. It would take a while to get used to the latest revelation. His life was changing in so many ways, whether he tried to control it or not.

They left the highway for a rural road early that afternoon, and found a wooded area where they pulled the ambulance into the trees. They ate lunch and let the children wander around for twenty minutes before they all piled back in the vehicle and resumed their journey

Once back on the road, York tapped on the fuel gauge indicator. "I have to get petrol somehow," he said. "We have a little more than a quarter tank. Maybe we can stop at a restaurant or store where there are other vehicles. Anywhere I can siphon petrol."

They drove thirty minutes more and rounded a bend. York braked abruptly, finding an empty German troop truck blocking most of the road. The front end on the passenger's side had hit a tree, a broken limb falling on the canopy. A staff car was in front of it, askew, as if they had collided.

Amanda hurriedly opened the port to the back.

"Keep everyone quiet," she hissed.

The children didn't cooperate. Although not as loud as the evening before, they talked and laughed, screamed lightly when a fly buzzed about the cab, and were easily distracted. The adults tried to keep them occupied.

A German soldier ran up to the truck. He looked in the cab, past York, and saw Amanda. "Nurse, we need your help," he said. "Two men have been injured."

"Follow my lead," York whispered to Amanda.

He got out of vehicle and addressed the soldier. "Don't let anyone near the ambulance. The soldiers in the back are highly contagious."

The soldier, who looked about sixteen, grew pale. "No, of course not," he said, his eyes wide. "We'll stay away. What's wrong with them?"

A shout came from the rear of the ambulance, followed by another, not as loud, and then laughter. The soldier looked at the vehicle, and then at York, a confused look on his face.

"I have masks if you have to get closer," York said sternly, ignoring both the question and the soldier's reaction to the noise the children made. "You'll need them for your own protection."

"No, there's no need for that. I won't come any closer."

Although York faced the soldier, his attention was focused on the rear of the truck. It was empty; there were no more men. But more importantly, there was a ten-liter fuel can strapped to the bumper.

"Show us the injured men," York said, softening his tone.

He and Amanda followed the soldier past the truck, eyeing the damage, a dented fender and the tree branch resting on the canopy. A German staff car coming from the other direction had collided with it.

The car's bumper and fender were smashed, the right front tire flat.

"What happened?" York asked, scanning the scene.

"A deer ran across the road. The staff car veered, and so did we. I hit the tree and the car crashed into our bumper."

Two soldiers stood in front of the truck. The driver of the staff car held a bloodied rag to his forehead. Another soldier, apparently the truck passenger, was holding his left wrist. Like the first soldier, both were much too young to be wearing uniforms. York wondered if they were making the transition from Hitler Youth to soldier, like Kurt, Amanda's step-son.

York limped towards them, leaning on his cane, Amanda just behind him. They examined each soldier quickly, assessing their injuries. The driver of the staff car had a gash on his head, right below the hairline. It was bleeding badly and needed stitches. The passenger in the truck had a broken wrist.

"Amanda, can you see if there's a first aid kit in the ambulance?" York asked.

As she returned to the vehicle, York noticed the soldiers eyeing him with awe. But he didn't know why. It wasn't until they spoke that he realized how highly they regarded a battle-scarred veteran.

"Where were you wounded, sergeant?" the soldier with the broken wrist asked.

"North Africa," York replied. "I was carrying a wounded comrade on my back, fleeing the enemy, when a machine-gun raked my leg. It's starting to get stronger, though. I'm hoping I can soon walk well enough to get back to the front."

Amanda returned with a gray box marked with a red cross. York laid it on the ground by the soldier with the head wound. He rooted through it, finding some cloth and gauze, and small strips with adhesive on each end.

"Here's some cloth," York said, handing it to Amanda. "If you wipe the blood away, I'll apply these strips. That should stop the bleeding for now."

With Amanda assisting, York managed to close the wound, which was about four centimeters long. The skin around it was swelling and turning purple.

"Where are you stationed?" York asked.

"At a camp about ten kilometers up the road," the soldier replied.

"You'll need to get back to your base. Do you have medical personnel there?"

"Yes, we do."

York looked at the flat tire on the staff car. "You should probably leave the car here for now."

He moved to the soldier with the broken wrist, searching through the first aid kit, and then frowned. "Amanda, I'm going to see if we have a splint in the ambulance. We have to stabilize this man's wrist before he can travel."

Her eyes widened, afraid to be left alone. "I can get it," she offered.

"No, it's fine. I'll only be a minute."

He left them in front of the truck and walked to the ambulance. He stopped at the rear bumper and, when convinced he couldn't be seen, he unstrapped the petrol can from the staff car. It was full. He carried it back to the ambulance, opened the rear doors, and put it in.

"Did Amanda tell you what's going on?" he asked Erika.

"Yes, when she got the first aid kit. We'll try to keep the children quiet."

"I stole this fuel can off their truck. I need a

splint or board, maybe twenty centimeters long."

Erika and the teenager rooted through the ambulance, but found nothing.

"It's all right," York said, eyeing the fallen tree branch. "I think Mother Nature can help us."

He went to the rear of the truck, stepped up on the bumper, and broke a narrow branch off the fallen limb. He then hurried to the front of the vehicle, knowing Amanda was frantic.

"Nothing in the ambulance," he called as he approached. "But this tree branch should work. We just have to keep it immobile."

He broke the branch to a more manageable length and placed it against the man's wrist and forearm. Amanda wrapped cloth around it, tying it tightly.

"This should keep it stationary until you reach camp," he said to the soldier.

"How do we get the tree limb off the canopy?" one of the soldiers asked.

"I think if you slowly drive forward it will slide off. We'll clear the road when you're gone. You can send someone back for the car."

They all climbed into the truck, squeezing into the front seat. The driver started the vehicle and eased out the clutch, idling forward, his eyes trained on the side mirror.

York stood in the rear, motioning forward with his hand as the driver gradually increased his speed. The fallen branch slipped from the canopy and crashed to the ground. With a last wave from York, and a nod from the driver, the vehicle drove away.

"We have to hurry," York said, as he and Amanda pulled the limb from the road. "I want to siphon fuel from the car. Then we need to get away before they come back."

The car's fuel gauge showed three-quarters full. York parked the ambulance adjacent to the car's petrol tank and got the rubber siphon hose. He sucked until he tasted petrol, and stuck it in the ambulance's tank. For five minutes the fuel transferred, the flow gradually slowing and then stopping.

York put both caps on and hurried back to the ambulance. He stowed the hose, started the engine, and drove down the highway.

"How do we get off this road?" he asked Amanda.

She had been studying the map, approximating their position. "They said the camp was ten kilometers away. It looks like the first crossroad is about six kilometers. Turn right, go five kilometers and turn left. If we stay on that road for about twenty kilometers, it merges back with this one, bypassing the camp."

York shifted gears, urging the vehicle forward. He doubted the Germans suspected their story. But as soon as they found the staff car with an empty fuel tank they would. He covered the six kilometers quickly, and then turned right. He drove quickly, covering another five kilometers before turning left and slowing to a normal rate.

"I'll drive until we have less than half a tank of petrol," he said. "Then we'll pull over in the woods somewhere and sleep. We'll be more than halfway. But we have to find more petrol. That's our biggest worry."

He looked in the side view mirror and saw a troop truck behind them, rapidly approaching.

# CHAPTER 69

Manfred Richter sat at a window table in a restaurant on Wannsee Lake, gazing out at the water. Only a handful of customers were scattered about the dining room, the lake less of an attraction in colder weather. But even in late November he could see a few boats in the distance, one with its sail tilted at an angle to catch the wind and propel the vessel forward. He watched it for a moment, wondering how difficult it was to captain a sailboat. He preferred motors. They were much more predictable.

Trees surrounded the lake, but much of the shoreline showed wide expanses of beach that overflowed with people in the summer, enjoying the sun and water. A few houses were visible, mostly mansions or older cottages that had existed for a century or more, peeking from the seclusion offered by the trees. A handful of boathouses similar to his could be seen along the shore, scattered haphazardly into the distance.

He returned to his sausage and sauerkraut, putting another forkful into his mouth. The food was good, even if it was off season, and he had always enjoyed the restaurant. Spread on the table before him, just beyond his plate, was a map of Germany. He looked at it closely while he ate, studying the arteries and veins that crossed it, rivers and roads, routes and rails. Then he put it away and finished his sausage and sauerkraut.

The three men he was waiting for arrived an hour later. He was still sitting at the same table, gazing at the lake, his meal replaced by a mug of beer. The men sat down, no introductions needed since they knew each other quite well, and Richter removed the map from his coat pocket and laid it on the table.

There was a distinct red line drawn across it, starting in Berlin and wandering southwestward towards Switzerland. Other lines were marked in blue, but not as heavily, signifying alternate and secondary routes. Each man in turn looked at the map, studying all that was identified, examining the natural terrain as well as the highways, knowing both the starting point and final destination.

"What do you think?" Richter asked. He only asked for opinions when he didn't want them, just to see who agreed with him.

The apparent leader of the three glanced at his watch and shrugged. "I'm not sure how we lost them."

"Or why they diverted from the route selected," said another.

"But you did lose them," Richter said. "There must be a reason why. I want to know what it is, and I want them found."

"It could be anything," the leader said with a helpless shrug. "But at this point it doesn't matter. We know where their final destination is."

"No, we don't," Richter said, his patience exhausted. "We only know the destination we gave them. But we don't know the destination they're seeking."

The three men were silent, furtively glancing at each other, never quite as insightful as their mentor. They knew how critical the mission was, and they didn't want to disappoint him, but the solution he sought escaped them.

"For all we know, they could have taken a separate route entirely," Richter said. "What if they became suspicious and changed the plan? They could be anywhere."

The third man sighed, knowing Richter could be

right, and then spoke. "Although we have no reason to believe that's the case."

The muscles of Richter's face tightened and he turned a faint red. "How do you know for certain? You don't. You don't know anything."

The three men were quiet, considering the consequences, knowing it was futile to argue. It was their leader who finally spoke. "No, you're right," he said. "They could be anywhere."

"They need to be found," Richter continued. "How do you intend to do that?"

"It should be easy enough," one of the three said. "How many ambulances are on the road?"

Richter was irritated. "More than you think. There's a war raging, remember?"

"We'll find them," the leader said. "I promise you."

Manfred eyed each in turn, his eyes showing anger, annoyed at their incompetence. "See that you do," he warned, waving a finger in their faces. "Because if you don't, the plans I had for them will instead be used for you."

# CHAPTER 70

York kept a wary eye in the mirror, watching the troop truck get closer, maintaining a constant speed. He didn't want to act suspiciously, or seem like he was trying to flee, but he didn't want to get captured either. The truck was traveling much faster than he was and, as the minutes passed, the gap between them closed.

"What's the matter?" Amanda asked, watching him closely, her eyebrows knitted with concern.

"There's a troop truck behind us. And it's moving quickly. I can't tell if they're coming after us or just on the same road."

"Is it the truck from the accident?"

"I'm not sure. But it's gaining."

They continued on the country road, approaching the merge that would take them back to their original route. But they were still ten kilometers away, and the map showed no intersections. The truck would reach them well before then.

Amanda watched the vehicle in the side mirror. "There are two men in the cab," she said. "But I can't tell if the fender is dented. It may be a different truck."

"They could still be after us. Maybe when the injured soldiers got back to camp and described what happened, someone thought it was suspicious. They could have sent the truck after us. Better tell Erika to keep everyone quiet."

Amanda opened the port and explained what was happening. The noise from the back, aimless chatter, a child singing, and Millie talking to the teenager, gradually subsided as Erika asked for silence.

York watched the mirror. The truck was close now, only a few meters behind their bumper. He eased up on the accelerator and guided the vehicle closer to the shoulder, waiting patiently for the truck to pass.

It didn't. The truck slowed to the same rate of speed, hugging the bumper of the ambulance. York sped up, just a bit.

The truck increased its speed also, keeping the same distance. They were so close he could see the driver's face. It was a man, not the boy involved in the accident. It was someone with experience, someone who may have seen combat.

York was annoyed. "I'm not sure what they're doing," he said. "They don't want to pass. They don't want to stop us. They want to stay glued to our bumper. Maybe they're waiting for us to make the first move."

He watched the driver's head turn, talking to the passenger, before moving his eyes back to the road. What were they discussing? Was it the ambulance?

They were five kilometers from the merge when they passed a narrow dirt road on the left, barely visible through the trees. Suddenly the troop truck braked, slowed considerably, and turned into the woods.

York breathed a sigh of relief. "That lane must lead to the camp."

The strain so visible on Amanda's face slowly dissipated. "This has been the longest day of my life," she said. "I've never dealt with danger before. Now it never leaves me."

"Tell Erika another fifteen minutes or so and we'll stop. I'll find a spot in the woods somewhere once we're on the other road."

Five minutes later they were back on their original route, the road little-traveled surrounded by forest. After driving for fifteen kilometers, York saw a slender dirt trail. He pulled off the road and into a grove of evergreen trees and got out of the ambulance, stretching.

The children remained well behaved, and once

again York was struck by their innocence, their absolute trust in Inga, the teenage girl that managed them, and in Erika. They seemed incapable of thinking evil thoughts; it would never occur to them that someone might treat them badly. They were content with what they had, trusting who they were with, and marveling at what most take for granted: the height of the trees, the sound of the birds, the beauty of a flower. As York watched them, eating and skipping around the forest, he realized that his life would always be a bit richer because they had walked into it.

Samuel and Sarah quickly adapted to their new family, clinging to Millie, Erika's mother. She was so frail, so thin and tired, that they felt compelled to care for her. York wondered if they had any family left. He wasn't sure what to do with them when they reached Switzerland, but he was sure someone would be willing to care for them.

York studied the map as Amanda chatted with Erika. It was another two hours to Nuremberg, which was more than halfway. The route had them take rural roads around the city, almost in a semi-circle, and then remain on country roads the rest of the journey, bypassing the last metropolitan center, Stuttgart, on their way to Switzerland. The remainder of the trip would be through forest and farm fields, safer and more secluded than the first half.

They got back in the ambulance an hour later and continued on. York watched the needle on the fuel gauge slowly move, knowing he had the ten-liter tank as reserve. They drove two more hours, until darkness slowly consumed the skies. He pulled the truck into another dirt lane, this time at the edge of the forest just before a stretch of farmland, the fields fallow for winter.

York walked to the edge of the trees and studied

the farm beyond. He could see a barn in the distance, built sturdily of stone, a long sloping roof to ease the winter snows to the ground. It was several stories high, rising in a steep triangle, the top of the pyramid stucco and timber. An outbuilding extended perpendicular to the barn, one wall open to the weather. He could see a tractor and another vehicle, maybe a small truck, parked in the lean-to. A large house sat on the other side of the barn, its roof line and chimneys visible from where he stood.

He emptied the ten-liter can into the ambulance's petrol tank and did a quick calculation. If he could get ten more liters, they would be close. But maybe not close enough. Nothing would be worse than being stranded near the Swiss border, but not near enough to get to it.

Amanda and Erika were sitting with the children in and about the ambulance, all wrapped in blankets. York finished filling the petrol tank and walked to the rear of the vehicle.

"I'm going to see what's at that farmhouse," he told them. "I should be back in about thirty minutes."

A flicker of fear crossed their faces, the thought of being alone overwhelming. He realized how traumatic the journey was for two people more accustomed to violins and concert halls.

"I won't be long," he promised.

He set off with the fuel can, working his way through the darkness and staying near the edge of the trees. It took him longer than he thought, the distance across the open field farther than he estimated, but he soon reached the edge of the lean-to. He could hear rustling in the barn, probably cows or chickens or whatever livestock the farmer had. He paused, waiting, but heard no voices. Hopefully the farmer was done for the day and was now sitting in front of a fire or radio, having enjoyed a good supper.

York slipped into the building, moving stealthily to the tractor. Its fuel tank sat high, making it easier to siphon. He slipped the rubber hose in until it touched the bottom, and then withdrew it, trying to gauge what was in the tank.

It wasn't much, definitely less than half and probably closer to a quarter. But it was a large tank. He might get ten liters. He sucked through the hose, spitting out petrol, and stuck the end in his can.

It took about five minutes and, as the level increased in his can, he pulled the rubber hose from the tractor tank, letting the remnants drain in his container. He was getting much better at siphoning, and hadn't spilled a drop. He put the lid back on the tractor's fuel tank and secured his container.

He was about to slide out from underneath the tractor when he heard a noise. It was faint at first, maybe an animal in the fields. He remained still, listening intently, watching.

He heard the noise again, louder, footsteps, someone walking. He peeked from around the tractor's tire. A pair of legs came into view, coming from the barn.

# CHAPTER 71

The children were inside the ambulance, overseen by Millie and Inga, sheltered from the cold. Amanda and Erika sat on the front bumper, anxiously waiting for York's return. Sounds of the forest kept them alert: an owl hooting, unseen creatures scrambling through fallen leaves, branches swaying in the breeze. They felt vulnerable without York, and the slightest sound produced an uneasy fear of the unknown.

"Erika, you're the strongest, most compassionate person I've ever known," Amanda said. "I can't even fathom the hardships you've faced, devoting your life to these children."

Erika sighed, her face grim, hiding exhaustion. "Thank you so much, but anyone would have done it, if faced with the same dilemma. But it hasn't been easy."

"How long have you been caring for them?"

"I started with two children, Rudolph and Gertrude, about three years ago. The rest came over the next year or two. Inga arrived last, the same time that Friedrich, the last of the children did. She's an orphan, and so are all the children." Her eyes clouded, misted by memories. "Inga came just after Wilhelm was killed."

Amanda rubbed her arm, knowing how devastated she was by her husband's death. "I would have helped you, if I had only known. Even financially, so you wouldn't have had to work so hard."

"I was afraid to tell anyone," Erika said. "Even you. I had Wilhelm in the beginning, and my mother helped before she got sick. She was working then, too, so we had more money. But it's been so difficult the last year or so. Even those times when you helped with my mother, I was afraid the children would make noise

393

and you would suspect something."

"I don't know how you did it. I know I never could."

"I took any work I could find: scrubbing floors, sewing clothes, waitressing. At times I was so tired, I could have slept for a week straight."

Amanda hugged her. "It'll be over soon."

Erika took a deep breath. "I just want the children to be safe and free. You see how excited they are to be outside. Imagine living in one room for years."

Amanda was overwhelmed by all Erika did, all she had accomplished. It seemed so incredible. "Do you know what I want to be?" she asked.

"No, tell me," Erika said.

"I want to be more like you."

Erika blushed. "Amanda, you're too kind."

"I mean it. And I want to help you."

"Thank you, but I haven't even thought about what I'll do when we get to Switzerland. I hope people there will help the children. My mother and I don't have a lot of money."

"Wherever we finally end up, whether it's Switzerland or London, I want to help you and your mother, Inga and the children, and any other children in need."

Erika showed surprise, her eyes wide. "It's very much appreciated. But I can't ask you to do that. Not that you even could."

"You don't have to ask me. Just tell me what you want or need, and I will provide it. For as many children as you have the strength to care for. And you can even hire people to help you."

"Are you serious?" Erika asked with disbelief.

Amanda smiled. "Yes, I am. I never really talked about it, but I have the family fortune tucked away in London. It's time I started to use it, especially for a good cause. It's more money than I could ever spend. So I am going to help you. And I won't take no for an answer."

Erika was stunned. "Amanda, I don't know what to say. You would really do all that for me?"

"Absolutely, and with no hesitation."

Erica was overwhelmed, her mind traveling in a dozen different directions. "There are so many children that need care. I would love nothing more than to devote my life to helping them."

Amanda smiled, touching her friends arm. "Then that's what you should do."

Erika hugged her, clinging to her tightly, her eyes tearing. They sat for a moment, each stealing a few seconds to envision a future that lived only in their dreams. After a moment had passed, Erika thought of something she had wanted to ask, but wasn't sure she should. But it seemed like the right time.

"Is there anything you want to tell me?" she asked Amanda.

"Not that I can think of," Amanda replied, pensive. "What about?"

"Michael."

Amanda smiled, and leaned closer to her friend. "Is it that noticeable?"

Erika laughed. "Yes, it is. I didn't realize at first. I thought you were just grateful he was rescuing you from Manfred. But I started to notice that you always sit next to him, you're always close, and your eyes twinkle when you're near him."

"Oh, Erika, I can't even begin to tell you how happy I am. We have so much in common I feel like I met the male version of me. He's a classical music lover, and can discuss the masters as easily as we can. He loves architecture, buildings and bridges, and he spends hours looking at my photographs. And I think he actually likes them!"

Erika laughed. "And you're both from the United Kingdom with similar backgrounds and beliefs. It's no wonder."

"I feel like I have a second chance at life," Amanda said. "Each day we've been together has been a gift from heaven. We have our whole life ahead of us."

Erika hugged her again. "If anyone deserves happiness, it's you."

Amanda was sheepish. "There's more."

Erika cast a quizzical look, seconds passing in silence, the suspense building. "Are you going to tell me what it is?"

Amanda smiled, her face lighting the darkened night. "I'm carrying Michael's child."

# CHAPTER 72

York watched the legs move towards the lean-to, unable to see the upper body. They belonged to a man, his thighs thick, pants smudged with dirt, boots sturdy. His stride was long and measured, without hesitation, even in the darkness. The man had walked the same path many times.

York pushed the petrol can as far underneath the tractor as he could. He crouched behind the rear tire, peeking around the edge.

The legs came closer, the bottom of the jacket and then the torso were visible, but the face was not. York knew the man would never suspect someone was in his shed, stealing his petrol. But he also knew if the man saw him, he wouldn't hesitate to protect his property. And if he perceived the threat to be dangerous, he would protect his life.

The man walked into the lean-to, moving through the narrow space between tractor and truck, just a few meters away. He paused for a moment, his hand rummaging through his pocket, and then continued towards the back of the building. If he moved much father, he was certain to see York.

The tire was large, over a meter high, and York squeezed closer behind it, hoping to stay hidden in the darkness, knowing the man was near. But he realized he was trapped, with no place left to go. And he didn't want to resort to force. Not with an innocent farmer, probably elderly, who was as far removed from the battlefield as any German could be.

The truck door opened. There was a slight rustling sound, faint unknown noises, and then a moment later the engine started.

York breathed a sigh of relief but stayed where

he was, crouched low against the ground, and waited. The truck remained where it was, idling.

A few seconds passed painfully, neither man nor machine moving. If the farmer started both vehicles, letting them run a few minutes to warm the engines, York would never get out. But he had his cane, and he had his pistol, and he would use them if he had to.

A moment later, the truck door closed. The vehicle was put in gear and driven out of the shed, traveling down the dirt lane. It turned at the road, moving in the opposite direction from where the ambulance was parked.

York didn't know how long the man would be gone, but he didn't want to linger. He picked up the fuel can and left, crossing the field but staying in the shadows by the forest where the moonlight couldn't cut the darkness. Twenty minutes later, after hobbling through the furrowed field, he was back at the ambulance, Amanda and Erika waiting for him.

"What took so long?" Amanda asked, alarmed. "We saw that truck cross the field and were worried sick. We were afraid something happened to you."

"Only a slight delay," he said. "I had finished filling the petrol can when the farmer came out. I hid, not knowing what to expect, but he got into his truck and drove away. I don't know where he's going this late at night, unless he's visiting a neighbor."

York's own words caused him concern. What if the farmer saw him and went to get the authorities? That didn't seem likely. But what if he returned and the ambulance was visible from the road, especially with the headlamps trained on it. He needed to check.

"I'm going to make sure we're well hidden," he told Erika and Amanda. "I'll only be gone a minute."

He went out to the road and then into the field, but the ambulance couldn't be seen, at least not in the darkness. He wasn't sure when morning came.

When he returned, Amanda and Erika were inside the vehicle putting the children to bed. York watched as they shared the available space, doubling up, evenly placed along the four two-meter cots. Blankets were placed along the aisle, and Samuel and Sarah and Inga slept there. Erika and her mother took the space against the partition.

York and Amanda returned to the cab. They talked for a few minutes but, as time passed, York noticed that Amanda's responses took longer and longer, until he heard the contented rhythm of her slumber.

He stayed awake a while longer, thinking of the future, and fingered the photograph in his pocket. What a fabulous family he would have, Amanda and the baby, with Elizabeth in his life again. It seemed almost too good to be true.

The farmer returned around 11 p.m., pulled into the lean-to, and parked the vehicle. He walked towards the house, hidden from view after the first few steps. York was confident they were safe, and soon after he drifted off to sleep.

Amanda awoke just after dawn, nudging York. He was surprised he had slept that long. But it felt good. They needed the rest for the last day of their journey.

She awakened the children and they all had some cheese and bread and juice, walked through the woods a bit, and washed at a small stream. It was a pleasant morning, even if a bit crisp, and an hour later they nudged the ambulance from its hiding place and were soon back on the country road.

As the morning passed, York realized they had seen few vehicles; the roads traveled were quiet and deserted except for an occasional truck, or sedan, or wagon. The scenery switched from forest to farm, rolling hills to gentle streams, and the bucolic views gave little evidence of a world at war. York knew that someone, either Manfred Richter or one of his staff, had planned the route well. It would provide a perfect escape for the Nazis when their imminent defeat arrived.

They stopped for lunch, pulling off the road into the trees as they had before. Amanda got her camera and took photographs of the children, and then the adults, before capturing images of owls and deer.

There was little distance left to travel, maybe a hundred and fifty kilometers. The fuel gauge registered a hair above the empty mark. York added the last ten liters of petrol, knowing it would be close. He might have to steal more fuel.

They drove the entire afternoon, making several stops since they had the time, and let the children play outside. They stopped again for dinner, a little later than they had the day before, and took a long break to let everyone rest. Their food was almost exhausted, but there was enough for breakfast. And York had plenty of money. They could buy whatever they needed. But he knew they needed it in Switzerland, especially to care for the children.

They returned to the road, the tension easing the closer they got to the Switzerland. York decided to drive to the border, or at least within sight of it, before retiring for the evening.

It was after dark when the roads no longer matched the route they had planned. York pulled the ambulance to the side of the road and studied the map with a flashlight.

"What's wrong?" Amanda asked.

"We should have reached Gottmadingen by now," he said. "It's a small village, right on the border.

We must have missed a turn."

"Can't you tell where we are by the map?"

He looked a moment more, and then studied the fuel gauge. "No," he said. "Everything looks the same."

"But we should be able to find the village."

"All I know is that we're lost, we have to be at the border before dawn, and we're almost out of petrol."

"Let me see the map," Amanda said. "It's late. And you're tired."

York stretched and yawned, glanced at his watch, and gazed out the window. There were pockets of light, the distance to them hard to judge, but he assumed they were tiny villages. One of them must be Gottmadingen. They just had to determine which one.

Amanda studied the map, trying to assess where they were. There were few landmarks she could use to gauge their location. The landscape was farmland, fallow for the winter, intersected by groves of trees. The terrain was hilly, with occasional rocky outcrops, narrow ravines sometimes beside the road, all bathed in blackness. None were remarkable enough to be noted on the map.

"Let's get out and look around," she said.

She left the vehicle, York right behind her. They turned in a full circle, unable to identify anything more than what they saw from the window. They were lost.

"It's easy to get disoriented," York said. "Especially when everything looks the same."

"Let's look from a higher elevation."

There was a small knoll on the far edge of the road. They climbed to the top and, even though it wasn't very high, they could see the lights from a hamlet a few kilometers away, what they thought was the east, which could be their destination. But there were also lights in the opposite direction, what they assumed was southwest.

"Maybe that's Gottmadingen," Amanda said, pointing east.

"But how do we know?" York asked. "I can't waste petrol driving the wrong way."

She pointed to the map with the flashlight. "I think we missed this turn, which would have taken us through town. If we go to the next crossroad and make a left, it will take us around the village and to the road across the border. A little farther, but it gets us there."

York shrugged. "Let's give it a try."

They got back in the ambulance and started the engine. York eased out the clutch and they went to the next crossroad. He turned left and followed the road about a kilometer when the engine started to cough, the vehicle jerking forward and then stopping.

They looked at each other, sharing an anxious glance, as York turned the starter. The engine came to life, sputtered, moved the vehicle a few feet, and stopped again.

A series of large haystacks sat evenly spaced by the side of the road, with acres of farmland beyond them. York started the engine again, coaxed the ambulance off the road, and forced it forward before it came to rest behind a haystack. Then the engine died.

"We're out of petrol," he said. "Keep everyone in the ambulance and I'll have a look around."

"Should I come with you?"

He shook his head. "No, it's better if you stay here. Let me see where we are."

He got out of the vehicle and opened the rear door. Everyone was sleeping. He grabbed the empty petrol can and walked to the road.

The vehicle was hidden by the haystack. He walked to the west. The rear door was visible from the road, but only if you knew to look. He went east. It was the same; the front end could be seen from the road. Since they hadn't seen a vehicle for the last two or three hours, and they were now in a very rural area of dirt lanes, he thought they would be all right for the night.

The road ran to the east and, assuming Amanda had correctly identified their location, he started walking in that direction. The lights on his left should be the town of Gottmadingen. If she was right, the border crossing was very close. They could walk to it. If she was wrong, he would have to steal more petrol.

He had gone just over a kilometer when Gottmadingen spread a bit to the south, a narrow dirt lane twisting from the tip of civilization. He walked to the road, which was unmarked, and went due south. Just ahead a fence intersected the farm fields, and a grove of trees sat on either side of the lane. Two rectangular stones protruded a half meter from the ground.

York walked up to the first stone and saw *Steiner Weg* etched in it. He had the right road. He went to the fence, where the larger stone was located. One side read, *Deutschland,* while the other side, facing Gottmadingen, was marked *Schweiz.*

York was standing in Switzerland.

# CHAPTER 73

York considered Max's instructions, which were very explicit: only cross the border at dawn. Yet he just saw a deserted crossing. They could all walk to safety, if they left immediately. Or could they? York knew what he saw, but what didn't he see?

He returned to the ambulance and found Amanda waiting anxiously.

"Did anyone come by?" he asked.

"No, I saw nothing but darkness. And I checked the back. Everyone's asleep."

He looked at his watch. It was after 11 p.m.

"What did you find out?" she asked.

"You were right," he said. "We're just southwest of Gottmadingen, a kilometer or so from the border crossing. Do you think everyone can make it if we walk? We can cut across the fields to make it shorter."

Amanda pictured those in the back of the bus. "I'm not sure about Millie. She's very sick. And there's one little girl, the one with the thick glasses, that seems to have a breathing disorder, maybe asthma."

"We can stop and rest as often as we need to," he said. "And I can carry Millie."

"Should we leave now?" Amanda asked.

York hesitated. "My contact said we had to cross the border at dawn."

"You were just there and no one stopped you."

He shrugged. "I know. But maybe I arrived at the right time. The guard may have been taking a break or getting a cup of coffee."

"Then I suppose we should get some sleep," Amanda said. "We seem safe here."

"We should still leave before dawn, while it's

dark. We'll be walking through open fields most of the way. We would be easy to see. There are fourteen of us."

"It's almost midnight now. What time should we leave?"

"Before six, if we can. We'll have a quick breakfast, grab our belongings, and start walking. Sunrise is after seven, probably near eight."

"I have an alarm clock," she said. "We just we haven't needed it until now. But I'll set it for 5:45."

York was thoughtful for a moment, undecided. "I still don't understand why it's so critical to cross the border at dawn. We haven't seen a German soldier for miles."

She studied his face, noting the concern. "If you want to go now, I can wake everyone. But there won't be anyone in Switzerland to greet us. They'll all be in bed."

He thought for a moment. Max had been so specific. It was the one detail he emphasized. And more than once. He must have had a reason.

"The children are tired," he said reluctantly. "They need their rest. And so does Millie. Let's set the alarm earlier. If we eat quickly, and can maintain some sort of progress during the walk, we'll be at the border by seven at the latest."

"All right, I put the batteries in and set the alarm for 5 a.m."

Amanda put the clock on the dashboard and they drifted off to sleep. It had been an exhausting few days, tense and stressful, wrought with danger. But knowing they were so close offered sweet dreams, especially with the prospect of freedom and all that came with it. They slept soundly.

It seemed like only minutes had passed when the alarm sounded. Amanda turned it off and returned the clock to her purse, yawning and stretching. She leaned over and kissed York on the forehead.

"Time to get up, darling," she said.

She opened the portal and called Erika, and a few minutes later they could hear the children stirring in the back of the ambulance.

York rubbed his face, willing away the weariness. He checked the pistol in his coat pocket, then climbed out, his cane in tow. Amanda followed.

They opened the back door and let the children mill about. They ate a light breakfast and then washed up with some water Erika had left. When everyone was finished, York removed all the baggage, stacking twelve bags of various sizes on the ground. Once unloaded, he made one last check of the ambulance to make sure they had everything they wanted.

"Can you pick up your bags?" he asked the children. "And then we'll go for a walk across the fields."

They started out slowly, Samuel helping Millie, while Inga and Erika managed Sarah and the others. They started walking single file but soon merged into a group. York found the hardest task was to keep the children focused. It took little to attract their attention, a butterfly or a bird, even the remnants of a corn cob.

They stopped often so Millie could rest, perching her on two of the bags, like a princess, while she regained her strength. The children did remarkably well, trying to be adults, and once again York marveled at how well-behaved they were, even if a bit noisy and distracted, a tribute to both Erika and Inga.

Even with frequent pauses they made steady progress and, in a little over an hour, the road was clearly defined in the darkness. York realized they would reach their objective early, but given his reconnaissance the evening before, he saw no issues.

The sooner they got to Switzerland, the better. He even regretted not having gone at midnight.

They passed the grove of trees on the side of the border and reached the road. York waited for all to assemble, and then he pointed to the markers that were only meters away.

"Those stones identify the border," he said. "We'll be safe once we cross it."

They moved forward, taking a few tentative steps to freedom, and then the entire road was flooded with light.

# CHAPTER 74

The blinding glare came from headlamps, two cars hidden in trees on each side of the lane. The children screamed, startled and afraid, covering their eyes. The adults were stunned, unable to grasp that triumph had been stolen by tragedy. They stood in front of the children, trying to shelter them.

Four men stepped from the shadows, two from each side. They converged on the road, standing between the refugees and the Swiss border.

"You're early, Michael," a voice called.

York was startled. He thought he recognized the voice, but he couldn't confirm it. Blinded by lights, he could only see shadowy figures.

"Max?" he asked tentatively, blinking.

Max stood on the road, an older man beside him. York had seen the man before. He had been with Max at different cafes around the city, a member in his network.

"Thank you, Mr. York," a voice boomed. "You verified my escape route. If you can get out of Germany with a bus full of imbeciles, then anyone can."

"Michael, drop your pistol to the ground," Max said sternly. "And then kick it away."

York did as ordered, his heart sinking. He was numb, unable to believe what was happening. He trusted Max with his life, and he always had. How could he have been so wrong?

Manfred Richter stepped forward, Albert Kaiser standing beside him.

"Amanda, darling, how nice to see you," Manfred said, a sly smile pasted on his face. "I was afraid my liaisons might make you betray me."

Amanda cast him a sullen stare, her face

contorted with hatred. She then glared at Kaiser, a man she loved and trusted, now knowing she never should have.

"Mr. York's purpose in Berlin was to test you," Manfred continued, looking at Amanda with contempt. "I thought you might be persuaded to cooperate, but I never dreamed you would run away with him."

"Let us walk across the border," Amanda said bitterly. "And you'll never have to see me again."

"Oh, my dear, Amanda," Richter, his arms open. "I could never do that. We love each other too much. Fortunately, I have a big heart. So we can forgive and forget."

"Not a chance," she said. "I despise you. That will never change."

Richter ignored her and turned to Erika Jaeger. "I always liked you, Erika. But I must say I'm disappointed."

Erika lunged forward, her husband's chisel in her right hand. The blade glistened in the light, sharp and defined, dangerous and deadly. She aimed for his throat, channeling her hatred into one deadly strike.

Richter raised his left hand, blocked the blow, and smacked her face. He wrenched the chisel from her hand and threw it into the brush beside the road.

She stood timidly, her hand touching her bruised cheek, and moved back towards the children, fighting tears.

"Leave her alone, Richter," York said. His warning was weak. Outgunned and outnumbered, he had no way of protecting anyone.

"No one told you to speak, Mr. York," Richter said. "So shut up."

York ignored him. Even though he suspected the truth, he didn't want to believe it. He turned towards his old friend. "Max, what's going on?"

"Oh, Michael, how can you be so stupid," Max scolded. "These are my associates." He pointed to his left. "Captain Klein, an acquaintance from the last war. You know Mr. Kaiser. And I'm sure you've heard of our leader, Manfred Richter."

York felt like a fool, stupid and betrayed. His mind wandered through the past, searching for signs, a thousand questions now unanswered.

"What about the posters?" he asked Max. "The whole city was looking for you."

"I needed to make sure you trusted me," Max said simply. "You walked past Richter and me at a café. I was certain you saw us. But I overestimated your powers of observation."

"Why do all this?" York asked, crestfallen. "Why create this charade?"

"Do you mean why did I let you and your companions get your hopes up? Or why did I bring you to Berlin at all?" He paused, enjoying the drama. "I had to know who the spy was. I knew it wasn't Kaiser. Richter and I were afraid it might be Amanda. But I knew whoever it was sold valuable information to the Allies, and we had to find them. You proved it was Faber, and you kept British Intelligence happy with nonsense, like stupid photographs of Hitler and Goebbels."

"I enjoyed it immensely," Manfred Richter added. "Sorry about the boathouse. I couldn't help toying with you, taking the boat out. But you're a resourceful man, Mr. York. You surprised me."

"You're an animal, Richter. I will hunt you down and kill you."

Richter laughed. "I doubt that."

"Michael, you're beaten," Max said. "Accept it."

Richter turned to Amanda. "Come with me,

Amanda. You, too, Erika. Get your bags, you're returning to Berlin. Mr. Kaiser has selected a new viola player and we need violinists. A concert has already been scheduled for Saturday."

Amanda lunged forward, crying, pummeling his face, clawing and scratching, her arms swinging wildly. "I hate you!" she screamed.

He took a step back, surprised, and raised his hands to defend himself. Once he fought her off, he swung his right fist, hitting her on the side of the head. She dropped to the ground.

York moved to help her, but was stopped by Max. He thrust his pistol in York's face. "Not a good idea."

Amanda staggered to her feet, disheveled, and looked towards York.

Richter watched her, sneering. "He can't help you, Amanda. We have other plans for him. Come along."

"What about my mother and the children?" Erika asked, her voice shaking, fear framing her face.

"We have no need for the sick or subhuman. It's not worth the effort to exterminate them." He motioned to Inga, the teenager. "Take them down the lane. I'm sure the Swiss will find something to do with them."

The teenager hesitated, looking at Erika, weeping.

"Go ahead," Erika said, trying to sound calm, fighting not to cry. "You'll be safe there. Go to the nearest house and ask for help." She went to her mother and hugged her, holding on tightly, knowing she might never see her again.

The children walked down the road, led by a feeble Millie and apprehensive Inga. They kept looking back, sobbing.

"Into the car," Richter said sternly. "And I mean

411

it."

Amanda and Erika stared at him defiantly, but knew resistance was futile.

York locked eyes with Amanda, showing his love and strength and devotion. He tried to imply, from the look alone, that he would never desert her. The battle wasn't over; the war wasn't won. He would come for her, save her, and they would have all in life they wanted, dreams they only imagined.

She nodded, wiping tears from her eyes, her left hand covering her womb, subconsciously protecting their child.

Kaiser led them away at gun point. They were forced in the back seat, their bags in the trunk, while Kaiser got in front. Richter spoke quietly to Max, and then got in the driver's seat. The engine started and the car pulled away, moving down the lane and into the village beyond.

York stood in the road, his bag at his feet. Max was in front of him, Klein beside him. They both held pistols aimed at his torso.

"So what am I to do with you, old boy?" Max asked quietly.

"I have a suggestion," Klein said. "Let me kill him."

Max turned to face Klein. "We should be able to find some use for him."

York took advantage of the distraction. He unlatched the safety for the pistol in the cane's handle, aimed it at Max, and fired.

The bullet hit his chest, just under the heart. His eyes grew wide, shocked and confused, staring at York and then the cane. His body twisted, contorted with pain, and collapsed.

York rotated the handle, exposing the knife, and rushed Klein, tackling him as he fired. York buried the blade under his ribcage.

Klein gasped, coughing, and then spit blood. He tried to fight, his strength waning, kicking and crawling, moving slower, weaker, until he no longer moved at all.

A loud, hissing sound came from the sedan. Klein's errant bullet had found the radiator, blowing a hole in it, coolant escaping.

York turned to Max, lying on the ground, pale, in agony. His gun was beside him, just out of reach. He clutched his torso, blood trickling between his fingers.

"Michael," Max uttered, choking. "Michael, come here."

York looked at his former friend, sprawled on the ground, dying, a pool of blood beside him.

"Don't be stupid," Max gasped. "Listen to me."

York stood over him, consumed with hatred. How many lives had been lost because Max was a double agent? How many secrets had been stolen and given to the Nazis?

"You're five steps from freedom," Max said, choking. "It's your only chance. Forget the girl and take it. Don't underestimate Richter. He would enjoy killing you."

# CHAPTER 75

Far down the road, a few hundred meters into Switzerland, York could see Millie and Inga and the children at a farmhouse, tucked away on a slight hill overlooking the road. An older couple was leading them inside, where they would be safe and warm until authorities arrived. He didn't have to worry.

York ran to the sedan, water pouring from the radiator where the errant bullet had struck, spilling onto the moss. The keys weren't in the ignition. He checked the floor, under the mat, but found nothing.

He went back to Klein, blood oozing from the knife in his torso, the stain on his jacket spreading. His face was gray, his eyes closed, his chest moving. He was dying.

York withdrew the knife, grimacing as he pulled it from Klein's body. He wiped it on the jacket, cleaning off the blood, and reassembled his cane. Then he rummaged through Klein's pockets, finding the keys.

Max was lying in the road, his face ashen, his eyes open, staring vacantly at the approaching dawn. If not already dead, he was close. York wondered if Covington Blair, wealthy socialite, was ever really Max of British Intelligence. Maybe he was always Max, the traitor. Did he betray his country during the last war, when he met Klein? Or after, when England slept and Germany awakened.

York paused at the edge of the lane, searching through the vegetation until he found Erika's chisel. He put it in his pocket, intending to return it.

He climbed in the sedan and started the engine, driving out of the trees and onto the dirt road, past Klein's body. Sixty meters down the lane the sedan jerked in protest, the coolant leaking, the engine fighting to function. He nudged it forward, to the intersection, and turned left.

The vehicle made it forty meters more before steam billowed from the radiator and the engine stalled. He started it again, the vehicle moving a few more meters. Then it died.

York got out of the car and ran back to the ambulance, hobbling on his bad leg, stumbling and falling as he moved through the furrowed field. He retrieved the fuel can and siphon and again started running, gasping for air, his leg throbbing, the cane bending under the strain he placed upon it.

When he reached the sedan, he opened the fuel tank, inserted the rubber hose, and started to siphon. After he had captured a few liters, enough to get the ambulance started, he stopped, put the cap on, and started hobbling back. He struggled with his leg, carrying the ten-liter can, his muscles aching and cramping.

Sweat dotted his forehead, dripping from his hair, even though the rising sun had done little to warm the chilly morning. It took almost fifteen minutes to get to the ambulance, gasping, his muscles burning. He poured the fuel into the tank and put the can in the back.

He jumped in the driver's seat, started the ambulance, and pulled it from behind the haystack. A wagon passed on the crossroad behind him, the back filled with hay. The driver glanced curiously in his direction, paused, but then continued. The hamlet of Gottmadingen was waking, lights visible in a soft glow, muted by an eerie mist that drifted from the melting morning's dew.

When he reached the sedan he pulled beside it, aligning the fuel tanks, and started siphoning gas. He wondered what route Richter was taking to Berlin. Would it be the same he had used to reach the border? Probably not, they had nothing to hide. He did.

He finished siphoning, climbed back in the driver's seat and started the engine. The petrol gauge showed a half tank, nowhere near enough to get to Berlin. But it was enough to get to a train station. He turned the ambulance around, planning to take the road that looped around the village. He reached the intersection, turned right, and looked in the mirror.

A German staff car, the Nazi flags on the bumpers hanging limply in a light breeze, was exiting the village, driving towards the bodies of Max and Klein. The vehicle halted just as York turned, and a soldier got out, watching the ambulance. He then moved to the bodies of Max and Klein, joined by his partner.

York knew he could never explain why an ambulance was on the Swiss border. He also knew if either Max or Klein were alive, they were telling the Gestapo what had happened. Either way, he had to hide the ambulance.

He sped down the dirt road, spotting a barn in a distant farm field, close to the village. He checked his mirror, saw no pursuit, and turned, the tires of the ambulance bouncing on the ruts of the plowed field. He knew most residents were awake, but the barn hid the farmer's house and the village that sprawled beyond it.

He parked beside the building, facing the road, engine idling, and glanced in all directions, making sure he wasn't seen. He then climbed out and peeked around the barn.

A man dressed in a plaid winter jacket had his back to him, twenty meters away. He was studying the broken handle on a stone well, a wooden bucket on the ground beside him. A moment later he picked up the bucket, water sloshing over the edge, and walked towards a chicken coop nestled in a grove of trees.

The barn door was open, suspended on a metal rail, most of the contents pushed against the walls. After the man was out of sight, York returned to the vehicle and drove into the barn, moving forward until the bumper reached the far wall. It fit, but barely.

The building was large, plows and other farm equipment stored around the perimeter; rusted from years of neglect. A loft above had hay slipping through the slots of the floor, a vertical ladder by the side wall leading to it. York searched the building, but there was nothing he could use, not even a bicycle. He grabbed his bag and left, leaning on his cane, and slid the barn door closed.

He walked through the trees, using evergreens and shrubs to hide him from both the house and road. When vegetation was sparse, he moved as quickly as he could, risking discovery, knowing there was nothing else he could do.

The village lay before him, the farmer's house sitting on the last street. York emerged from the foliage and walked down the road, away from the residence, and quickly turned a corner, avoiding the road he had traveled on.

He walked for another block, searching for a vehicle, when he passed two teenage girls carrying schoolbooks. They nodded, but looked at him strangely. He turned after they passed. They had stopped, and were watching him curiously. He was a stranger in a town where everyone knew each other. He had to get away, and quickly.

A small motorcycle turned the corner, a teenage boy sitting on it. He went in the same direction as the girls, also casting an odd glance at York. When he traveled fifty meters more he slowed and circled, looking back at York before continuing on his way.

York followed them, even though he knew they would probably contact the authorities, but he realized they were on their way to school. If he could steal the motorcycle, even though it was small, he could elude the Germans and get to a train station.

A block later he saw a framed building of alpine construction, a half dozen children walking towards it. By the time he reached the school yard it was empty; classes had started. He studied the building, wary of the windows, moving close to the wall, and found the motorcycle parked by the side door.

He crept up to the bike, crossed the starter wires, and the engine sputtered to life. After a quick look around to make sure no one was watching, he stowed his bag and cane on a rack in the back, climbed on, and drove away.

There were no people visible. Maybe they were working the fields, or repairing equipment to be ready for spring. York kept the throttle idling for the first block, so he didn't attract attention, but sped down the next block, and crossed another. When he reached the last street in town, he turned right, finding the road that bypassed the village. He gunned the engine, increasing his speed.

A gunshot startled him, echoing in the quiet morning. He looked over his shoulder, swerving as he did so. The German staff car was in close pursuit, barely sixty meters behind him. A soldier leaned out the passenger's window, his pistol pointed at York.

York opened the throttle, forcing the cycle forward as fast as it would go, but the Germans were still gaining. He knew he couldn't outrun them; he had to elude them.

A second shot was fired, the bullet ricocheting off the handlebar. York veered sharply to the left, hurdling the drainage gully beside the road, almost falling. It was hard to control the bike, the frame vibrating, tires bouncing. He continued through a farm field, the rows remaining from fall plowing, trying to stay in furrows whenever possible.

The staff car stopped where he had left the road. A soldier got out, studied the gully, and realized the sedan couldn't pass over it. He abandoned his pistol and raised a rifle, took aim, and fired.

York crunched over the handlebars, offering the smallest profile possible. He heard the shot, cringed, but felt no impact. He swerved back and forth, presenting an elusive target should another shot be fired.

As he continued across the field, the soldier got back in the car and the Germans drove down the road, turning left at a distant crossroad. They were trying to stay parallel, knowing at some point York had to return to the road. But they were too far away to try another shot.

York sped forward, but veered farther from the road. He crossed one farmer's field, and then two more, before coming to a main highway. He halted, studied the few passing vehicles, and withdrew the map he had taken from the ambulance.

He was on a major route, about one hundred kilometers from Stuttgart. The staff car would intersect the road just around the next curve. But his path across the farm fields had been far shorter. If he hurried, he could escape. And if he had enough petrol to get to Stuttgart, he could catch a train to Berlin when he got there. He opened the cap on the fuel tank and checked the level. It was almost full. He could make it.

He returned the map to his pocket, and drove the motorcycle as fast as he could. He was cold, not dressed for the wind, and his hands were frozen, more numb

419

with each kilometer traveled. Once he was sure he had lost the Germans, he stopped to get warm, finding a grove of evergreen trees along the road that hid him while he rested. But he was afraid to stop for long.

He wondered where Amanda and Erika were. They were closer to Berlin than he was, he knew that. But if they were driving, and he took the train, he might arrive before them. He started to develop a plan, how to rescue them, and what to do with Manfred Richter.

# CHAPTER 76

Two hours later York reached the outskirts of Stuttgart, a major rail center, home to Daimler and Porsche automotive factories, and several military bases. Since it was a valuable industrial production region, it was also a prime target for Allied bombers.

As York entered the southern suburbs, he saw how widespread the devastation was. He drove through residential areas heavily damaged, some blocks nothing but rubble, and industrial areas where factories were destroyed, brick shells with collapsed roofs. Still others, charred and crumbling, continued their contribution to the war effort, their smokestacks belching, their workforce producing.

The train station was located in the center of the city, a dominant building of limestone and brick, supported by pillars and marked by a large rectangular tower. It too had been severely damaged, with parts of the façade lying in piles of debris, walls toppled, windows shattered. But it still functioned, trains coming and going, carrying troops and material, travelers and weapons.

York guided the motorcycle to a street adjacent to the terminal, little more than fumes left in the fuel tank. He parked the bike beside a street light, collected his cane and bag, and hobbled into the station.

He studied arrivals and departures, finding a train that left for Berlin forty minutes later, and went to the counter and purchased a ticket. A nearby café had tables inside the terminal, and he got a cup of coffee and a kreppel, as well as a newspaper.

He sipped his coffee and ate his donut and pretended to read the newspaper, but he was really thinking about Amanda and Erika. What would Richter

421

do with them? He couldn't imagine them returning to their normal lives, dominating the concert stage, as if nothing had happened. Or would they have to? Was the grand illusion that important to the German people, Hitler's favorite musician, the Scot, Amanda Hamilton?

They might be sent to prison, or a concentration camp, where the Nazis literally worked people to death. Far more likely was a staged accidental death, followed by public mourning for the violinists of the Berlin String Quartet, the nation grieving the loss of their musical masters. That was more typical of Richter, sneaky and sinister, the deception visible for all to see, yet for no one to doubt. York got anxious, his last thought overwhelming, time far more critical.

He tapped his foot on the floor, impatient, and looked at his watch. He didn't see the two men in green police uniforms approach. They motioned for an elderly couple at a nearby table to quietly move out of the way. Then they walked up, standing just behind him, and withdrew their pistols.

"Don't move," one of the policemen said.

York froze. The voice was commanding, authoritative. He remained motionless, hands on the table, and considered the possibilities. The Gestapo would be the worst, a local policeman the least likely to determine who he really was.

He watched from the corner of his eye as a man came into view. It was a policeman, walking in front of him, the green uniform easily identifiable.

"Raise your hands," the policeman said.

"There is still a gun in your back," said a second voice behind him.

"Now stand up," the first policeman ordered.

A crowd started to gather, standing on the perimeter of the café: a few soldiers, an old man with a newspaper under his arm, a teenage girl. They watched curiously, wondering why two policemen were arresting an army sergeant.

York did as he was told. He stood, pasting a surprised look on his face, chewing the remnants of the kreppel still in his mouth.

"What is wrong?" he asked innocently.

"Step away from the table."

"May I get my cane?" York asked. He nodded towards his leg. "A war wound in North Africa."

The policeman hadn't expected that information. It didn't fit the description of the man he had been told to arrest. He didn't answer him, but exchanged a wary glance with his companion.

"Are you armed?" the policeman asked.

"Yes," York replied. "I have a pistol. Military issue."

The second policeman moved closer behind him, putting the barrel of his gun in York's back. "Put the pistol on the table."

York moved his shirt aside, exposing the holster, ensuring the man in front of him could see it. He pinched the handle between his thumb and index finger, gently lifted it, and put it on the table.

The policeman relaxed noticeably once York was disarmed. "Papers, please."

York pointed to his pocket, and slowly and deliberately withdrew his documents. He laid them on the table and raised his hands again.

The policeman reached forward and retrieved them. Once satisfied York wouldn't move, and that his partner's pistol was poking his back, he studied them carefully. He fingered the texture of the paper and examined the seal, before leafing through them. Then he laid them on the table, looked at his partner and shrugged.

The first policeman eyed the growing crowd and

shifted uncomfortably. "You're papers are in order, but we have a few questions to ask you. Please, come with us for a moment."

York looked back at the boarding area. "I have to catch a train in twenty minutes."

"We have an office just down the corridor. It won't take long."

"You resemble a wanted criminal," the other policeman explained. "We must ensure you're not him."

They took his gun and papers, searched his bag without finding anything, and nudged him through the terminal. The crowd began to dissipate, although a few stragglers with time to spare followed, wondering what had caused the excitement.

The office was only thirty meters away. York kept a wary eye on the train as they led him in and had him sit down.

"Where are you coming from?" the first policeman asked.

"Freiburg," York said, knowing his original story would be hard to verify.

"Why were you in Freiburg?"

"I have an uncle who lives there. I took advantage of my medical leave to visit him."

"Why are you going to Berlin?"

"I have a staff assignment while convalescing, although I'm hoping to return to active duty. I can manage, with the cane. There must be something I can do for the war effort."

"You were wounded in North Africa?"

"Yes, I served with Rommel. It's been over a year now. And I want to fight again."

"How long were you in Freiburg?"

York shrugged. "Five or six days." He had to be careful. They could detain him and check train records.

"So you arrived at the terminal this morning?"

"No," York replied, acting annoyed. "I arrived yesterday and visited with a friend from the army."

"What's his name?"

"Sergeant Kerr."

"What unit is Sergeant Kerr with?"

"He's with the Seventeenth Infantry Division. He's on leave from the Russian front after sustaining minor injuries." York glanced at his watch. "You are going to make me miss my train."

The policemen moved to a corner of the room, talking among themselves. They came back a moment later and handed York his papers and the gun.

"You may go," the policeman said sternly, offering no apology.

York nodded, showing his respect, and hobbled out, breathing a sigh of relief. He knew if they verified his story, they would find it was false. He just hoped they didn't have time to check. Or they didn't care to.

He made his way across the terminal and boarded the train with five minutes to spare, finding a window seat. The train was not fully booked, and there were many empty seats, so no one sat beside him. He opened his newspaper, but wasn't reading the words. He was studying the passengers, making sure none posed a threat.

The train departed on time, pulling away from Stuttgart and barreling down the tracks. York looked out the window, watching destroyed buildings pass, the urban landscape gradually changing to woods and farms.

The journey would take seven hours, and he would arrive in Berlin early that evening. He settled back in the seat, tucked his cane and bag under his legs, and wondered where Amanda and Erika were. He still hoped to get to Berlin before they did.

425

The rhythmic motion of the train, combined with his weariness, made him drift off to sleep. It was hours later when an explosion woke him. Another blast followed, louder than the first, and then another, each getting closer. Shouts and screams filled the car and he bolted upright, wondering what was happening.

He craned his head against the window and saw a group of American aircraft flying by, grayish-green bodies with the stars and stripes visible on the tail and wings. They flew low, the pilots' heads visible in the cockpit in the approaching darkness.

Another explosion sounded, rocking the train. It began to weave back and forth, unstable. Screeching metal from the brakes drowned the passengers' screams, and the car began to slow reluctantly, the line of cars to the rear pushing those in front forward.

The train came to a halt, still intact, no damage visible or sustained. The chaos gradually subsided, shouts and screams muted, transformed to frantic conversation. After a few minutes had passed, an announcement from the conductor came over the loudspeaker.

"Ladies and gentlemen, enemy planes have bombed the tracks in front of us. We will be delayed while repairs are made."

# CHAPTER 77

The conductor made another announcement a few minutes later, warning the travelers that repairs would take hours rather than minutes. The doors were opened so anyone who wanted fresh air could step out but, given the cold weather, there were few takers.

York grabbed his bag and his cane and hurried to the door. He had no idea where they were or how long he had slept. But he had to get to Berlin; he had to find Amanda.

He pushed past passengers mingling in the aisle, moving towards the door. It was getting dark, past seven p.m., close to their original arrival time, so they shouldn't have much farther to go. But he doubted repairs would be done that night. It would take time just to arrange the crew and machinery.

Once off the train, and standing on the side of the tracks, he could hear traffic. They were close to a main road, but the view was blocked by trees. He went to the front of the train, past the engine, and joined a group of observers, travelers, a few soldiers, and men from the train: the conductor, engineer, and coal handler.

The train had stopped twenty meters from a bomb crater. Although the timber and steel rail were intact, and most of the bed, the embankment was undermined, the crater leaving little support underneath the tracks. The engineer had acted quickly to stop the train and prevent a potential disaster.

York realized filling the hole would take time. But he didn't have time. Although he had no idea what happened to Amanda and Erika, he suspected they were taken to Berlin. He wanted to get there before them, but even if they had driven the entire way, and he didn't know that they had, they were already there. He had to hurry; he had to find a way to rescue them.

He stepped in the underbrush, tentatively poked through the shrubs, and started walking towards the traffic noise, moving frantically through the brush, hobbling on his cane. He picked his way through, with no path and little light, using the sounds to guide him.

After ten minutes, he came to a clearing on the edge of a highway. Cars, trucks, buses, and military vehicles were passing, scattered, the traffic not very heavy. He saw a sign on the road a few meters ahead. It read *Berlin: 57 kilometers.*

He walked quickly, running when he could, hoping for someone to take sympathy on a limping soldier with a cane, carrying a travel bag. There wasn't much else to do. There were no residences nearby; he couldn't steal a vehicle. There were no bus stops or trolleys. But he had to get to Berlin. And he had to get there quickly.

A light drizzle started to fall, bathing the street in a glistening sheen. Darkness descended across the landscape, a hazy quarter moon dimly lighting his path, accented by the glow of passing headlights. Several vehicles sped by, more intent on their destination than helping a crippled soldier.

He had walked almost thirty minutes, gasping, and just about to give up hope, when a troop truck pulled to the side of the road, the canvas on the back rippling in the light breeze. It stopped just beside him, and the driver leaned across the passenger's seat and rolled down the window.

"Do you need a lift?" the soldier asked. He was young, with blond hair and a warm smile. He seemed innocent, not yet tainted by the war.

York smiled, relieved. "That would be fabulous. I was on a train to Berlin, but the track was damaged by the bombing."

"Climb in," the soldier said. "I'm going to Berlin, too."

York got in the passenger's seat, stealing a quick glance in the back. It was empty.

"Where are the soldiers?" he asked, faking a grin. "This is a troop truck."

The driver laughed. "I'm going to pick up some patients at a Berlin hospital."

"On their way back to the front?" York asked.

"Yes, I think so," the soldier said. "Although I'm not sure where."

"I only wish I could go," York said, feigning frustration.

"I saw you limping. Where were you wounded?"

"North Africa," York said. "I'm going to Berlin to get medical clearance to return to active duty. So far I've only been permitted to drive an ambulance. But I want to fight. Like I did before."

The conversation continued. It was pleasant, focused primarily on the war but drifting to family. The soldier wasn't a fanatical Nazi. He was doing his duty, serving the Fatherland, like millions of other men. York relaxed, knowing he faced little danger, his mind drifting to his planned rescue.

The drive went quickly, the mile signs passing, Berlin getting closer. An hour later the outskirts of the city was visible. They approached a checkpoint, slowing the vehicle, but were waved forward by the sentries. Thirty minutes later, the soldier dropped York off on the Ku'damm, a few blocks from Amanda's house.

It was late, almost 10 p.m. There were few people on the streets, some soldiers with dates, a policeman, an elderly couple walking their dog. York walked quickly, making sure no one followed.

He reached Amanda's house and studied it from across the street. There were lights on; the block still had electricity even with the Allied bombings. Neighboring residences were mostly dark, a few windows lit but, for the most part, people had retired for the evening.

York walked around the block, ensuring nothing was unusual, no military or police presence. He studied the parked vehicles, the darkened windows, the bombed ruins of a nearby residence, and saw nothing suspicious. He returned to the front of Amanda's townhouse and tucked his bag under a shrub by the front steps.

He walked quietly up the steps, staying close to the shadow cast by a nearby evergreen tree, avoiding the moonlight. When he got to the entrance he tried the door, but it was locked. He removed the knife from his cane, sliding it along the keeper until he heard a clicking sound, and again twisted the handle. The door opened, and he returned the knife to the cane.

York entered the residence, tiptoeing into a vestibule, the floor covered with black and white ceramic tile. A stairway to his right, six or seven carpeted steps, led to a higher elevation, a similar stairway to the left, led lower, probably to an apartment or storage area. He started up the steps.

A floor board creaked and he stopped, listening intently. He withdrew the pistol from his holster, slowly climbing one step then the other, pausing. He could hear no voices, but the light was on in the room he approached.

When he got to the last step, it opened into the parlor. He could see a dining room beyond, and a kitchen behind it. Both rooms were dark, barely lit. As he walked into the parlor, taking each step tentatively, he saw two bags beside the entrance. They belonged to

Amanda and Erika. He stepped forward cautiously, looking into the rooms, ensuring no one was waiting.

"You are persistent, aren't you Mr. York?" came a voice from behind him, near the stairs. "Now drop the gun. Or I'll shoot you where you stand."

It was Richter, stepping from the shadows of an alcove just past the steps. York had walked right past him.

York sighed, defeated, and dropped the gun. He stood still, waiting further direction, every muscle of his body tense. He kept glancing about the house, searching for some sign of Amanda.

"Turn around," Richter said.

York turned to find Richter standing just beyond the steps, pistol in hand, a sly smile on his face. York leaned on his cane, staring at him, his hatred evident.

Richter grinned. "I was wondering if you would show up."

"Let Amanda and Erika go. You have me. I'm the one with all the information. They know nothing."

Richter sighed and shrugged. "I'm afraid you're too late, Mr. York. They're gone, destined for a concentration camp. They can play their violins for the prisoners."

York shifted his weight, ever so slowly positioning his cane. "Their bags are right there," he said, nodding towards it. "I know they're here."

"Their bags are here ready for the garbage," Richter replied. "But they are not."

York ever so slowly leaned back, tilting the cane, pointing the handle at Manfred. "I doubt you would throw their belongings away," he said, stalling for time, perfecting his aim.

Richter laughed. "But I would, minus the violins, of course, which are quite valuable. The rest has no purpose. They don't need clothes, not where

431

they're going. And no one cares about Amanda's ridiculous photographs."

York fired. The bullet caught Richter in the forehead and blew off the top of his head.

# EPILOGUE
London, England
November 26, 1946

Michael York continued turning pages of the photography book as customers milled around him, browsing, reading dust jackets, and conducting their shopping. Some stopped to look at the display, interested in the book, others purchased it, while some merely stared at it with a mild curiosity, reflecting on a time they would rather forget.

He thumbed through the pictures, coming towards the end. There were photographs of the handicapped children with Millie and Inga, and the orphans Samuel and Sarah. An entire page showed Erika Jaeger and Amanda, posing during their journey to Switzerland. And there was a photograph of Manfred Richter, at Joseph Goebbels' party, the caption describing his murder.

He thought about those two days in November of 1943, their flight for freedom, now three years past. He remembered Amanda suggesting they cross the border into Switzerland at midnight and not wait until dawn, and Max telling him to forget Amanda and escape.

Then he reflected on life, the paths we take, the choices we make. Sometimes the pain that lingers, breaking our hearts and destroying our souls, comes not from what we did, but what we didn't do, the actions we chose not to take. And then sometimes, when the world collapses around us, we find our way regardless, and somehow manage to overcome.

"Dad, are you almost ready to go?"

He smiled, caressing the hair of the teenage girl

433

beside him. "Yes, Elizabeth. Whenever you are."

A woman walked up to them, her belly swollen with child, a young boy holding her hand. She was petite, with dark hair and eyes, a smile consuming her face.

"Should we go?" asked Amanda Hamilton York. "We're meeting Erika for lunch.

Michael kissed her on the forehead. "Of course, darling."

She smiled. "Little Michael is hungry," she said, looking at the toddler.

They walked into the London street, tomorrow always brighter, yesterday starting to dim.

The End